For my mom

Part I

* * *

elilith (el·LIL·lith) *noun*

Tattoos given to the girls of Weep, around their navels, when they become women.

Archaic; from the roots eles (self) + lilithai (destiny), signifying the time when a woman takes possession of her destiny, and determines the path of her own life.

🪶 1 🪶

Like Jewels, Like Defiance

Kora and Nova had never seen a Mesarthim, but they knew all about them. Everyone did. They knew about their skin: "Blue as sapphires," said Nova, though they had never seen a sapphire, either. "Blue as icebergs," said Kora. They saw those all the time. They knew that *Mesarthim* meant "Servants," though these were no common servants. They were the soldier-wizards of the empire. They could fly, or else they could breathe fire, or read minds, or turn into shadows and back. They came and went through cuts in the sky. They could heal and shape-shift and vanish. They had war gifts and impossible strength and could tell you how you'd die. Not all of these things together, of course, but one gift each, one only, and they didn't choose them. The gifts were *in* them, as they were in everyone, waiting—like an ember for air—should one only be so lucky, so blessed, to be chosen.

As Kora and Nova's mother had been chosen on the day, sixteen years ago, that Mesarthim last came to Rieva.

The girls were only babies then, so they didn't remember the blue-skinned Servants and their gliding metal skyship, and they didn't remember their mother, either, because the Servants took her away and made her one of them, and she never came back.

She used to send them letters from Aqa, the imperial city, where, she wrote, people weren't just white or blue, but every color, and the godsmetal palace floated on air, moving from place to place. *My dears*, said the last letter, which had come eight years ago. *I'm shipping Out. I don't know when I'll return, but you will certainly be women grown by then. Take care of each other for me, and always remember, whatever anyone tells you: I would have chosen you, if they had let me choose.*

I would have chosen you.

In winter, in Rieva, they heated flat stones in the fire to tuck into their sleeping furs at night, though they cooled off fast and were hard under your ribs when you woke. Well, those five words were like heated stones that never lost their warmth or bruised your flesh, and Kora and Nova carried them everywhere. Or perhaps they *wore* them, like jewels. Like defiance. *Someone loves us*, their faces said, when they stared down Skoyë, or refused to cringe before their father. It wasn't much, letters in the place of a mother—and they only had the memory of the letters now, since Skoyë had thrown them in the fire "by accident"—but they had each other, too. Kora and Nova: companions, allies. Sisters. They were indivisible, like the lines of a couplet that would lose their meaning out of context. Their names might as well have been one name—*Koraandnova*—so seldom were they spoken separately, and when they were, they sounded incomplete, like one half of a mussel shell, cracked open and ripped in two. They were each other's person, each other's place. They didn't need magic to read each other's thoughts, only glances, and their hopes were twins, even if they were not. They stood side by side, braced together against the future. Whatever life might force on them, and however it might fail them, they knew they had each other.

And then the Mesarthim came back.

* * *

Nova was first to see. She was on the beach, and she'd just straightened up to swipe her hair out of her eyes. She had to use her forearm, since she held her gaff in one hand and flensing knife in the other. Her fingers were cramped into claws around them, and she was gore all the way to her elbows. She felt the sticking drag of half-dried blood as she drew her arm across her brow. Then something glinted in the sky, and she glanced up to see what it was.

"Kora," she said.

Kora didn't hear. Her face, blood-streaked, too, was blanched with numb endurance. Her knife worked back and forth but her eyes were blank, as though she'd stowed her mind in a nicer place, not needing it for this grisly work. An uul carcass hulked between them, half flayed. The beach was strewn with dozens more carcasses, and more hunched figures like theirs. Blood and blubber clotted the sand. Cyrs skirled, fighting for entrails, and the shallows boiled with spikefish and beaked sharks drawn to the sweet, salty reek. It was the Slaughter, the worst time of year on Rieva—for the women and girls, anyway. The men and boys relished it. They didn't wield gaffs and knives, but spears. They did the killing, and hewed off the tusks to carve into trophies, and left all the rest where it lay. Butchering was women's work, never mind that it took more muscle, and more stamina, than killing. "Our women are strong," the men boasted from up on the headland, clear of the stink and the flies. And they *were* strong—and they were weary and grim, trembling from exertion, and streaked with every vile fluid that leaks out of dead things, when the glint caught Nova's eye.

"Kora," she said again, and her sister looked up this time, and followed her gaze to the sky.

And it was as if, though Nova had seen what was there, she couldn't process it until Kora did, too. As soon as her sister's eyes fixed on it, the shock rocked through them both.

It was a skyship.

A skyship meant Mesarthim.

And Mesarthim meant...

Escape. Escape from ice and uuls and drudgery. From Skoyë's tyranny and their father's apathy, and lately—sharply—from the men. Over the past year, the village men had started pausing when they passed, looking from Kora to Nova and Nova to Kora like they were choosing a chicken for slaughter. Kora was seventeen, Nova sixteen. Their father could marry them off anytime he pleased. The only reason he hadn't yet was because Skoyë, their stepmother, was loath to lose her pair of slaves. They did most of the work, and looked after their troupe of little half brothers, too. Skoyë couldn't keep them forever, though. Girls were gifts to be given, not kept—or more like livestock to be sold, as any father of a desirable daughter on Rieva was aware. And Kora and Nova were pretty enough, with their flax-fair hair and bright brown eyes. They had delicate wrists that belied their strength, and though their figures were secret under layers of wool and uul hide, hips, at least, were hard to conceal. They had curves enough to keep sleeping furs warm, and were known to be hard workers besides. It wouldn't be long. By Deepwinter, surely, when the dark month fell, they would be wives, living with whoever made their father the best offer, and no longer with each other.

And it wasn't just that they'd be split apart, or that they had no will to be wives. The worst thing of all was the loss of the lie.

What lie?

This is not our life.

For as long as they could remember, that was what they'd told each other, with and without words. They had a way of looking at each other, a certain fixed intensity, that was as good as speaking it out loud. When things were at their worst—in the middle of the Slaughter, when it was carcass after carcass, or when Skoyë slapped them, or they ran out of food before they ran out of winter—they kept the lie burning between them. *This is not our life. Remember. We don't belong here. The Mesarthim will come back and choose us. This is not our real life.* However bad things got, they had that to keep them going. If they had been one girl instead of two it would have died out long ago, like a candle flame with just one hand to cup it. But there were two of them, and between them they kept it alive, saw it mirrored in each other and borrowed faith back and forth, never alone and never defeated.

They whispered at night of what gifts they would have. They would be powerful like their mother, they were *sure*. They were meant to be soldier-wizards, not drudge-brides or slave-daughters, and they would be whisked away to Aqa to train for battle and wear godsmetal against their skin, and when the time came they would ship Out, too—up and out through a cut in the sky, to be heroes of the empire, as blue as sapphires and glaciers, and as beautiful as stars.

But the years went by and no Mesarthim came, and the lie

stretched thin, so that when they looked to each other for the faith they kept between them, they began to find fear instead. *What if this is our life after all?*

Every year on Deepwinter's Eve, Kora and Nova climbed the ice-slick ridge trail to watch the sun's brief appearance, knowing it was the last they'd see of it for a month. Well, losing their lie felt like losing the sun—not for a month, but forever.

So the sight of that skyship...it was like the return of the light.

Nova let out a whoop. Kora laughed—with joy and deliverance and...accusation. "Today?" she demanded of the ship in the sky. The reeling, brilliant sound of her laughter rang across the beach. *"Really?"*

"You couldn't have come last week?" cried Nova, her head flung back, the same joy and deliverance alive in her voice, and the same edge of asperity. They were matted with sweat, rank with gore, and red-eyed from the sting of guts and gases, and the Mesarthim came *now*? Along the beach, among the wet-hollow husks of half-butchered beasts and the clouds of stinging flies, the other women looked up, too. Knives fell still. Awe stirred in the slaughter-numbed blankness as the ship soared nearer. It was made of godsmetal, vivid blue and mirror bright, catching the sun and searing spots into their vision.

Mesarthim skyships were shaped by the minds of their captains, and this one was in the likeness of a wasp. Its wings were knife-blade sleek, its head a tapered oval with two great orbs for eyes. Its body, insect-like, was formed of a thorax and abdomen joined in a pinch of a waist. It even had a stinger. It flew overhead, aiming for the headland, and passed out of sight behind the rock palisade that sheltered the village from wind.

Kora's and Nova's hearts were pounding. They were giddy and shaking with thrill, nerves, reverence, hope, and vindication. They swung their gaffs and knives, embedding them in the uul, both knowing, as they unclenched their fingers from the tools' well-worn hafts, that they would never return to retrieve them.

This is not our life.

"What do you two think you're doing?" Skoyë demanded as they stumbled toward the shore.

They ignored her, falling to their knees in the icy shallows to scoop water onto their heads. The sea-foam was pink, and flecks of fat and cartilage bobbed in the swaying surf, but it was cleaner than they were. They scrubbed at their skin and hair, and at each other's skin and hair, careful not to step too deep, where the sharks and spikefish thrashed.

"Get back to work, the pair of you," Skoyë scolded. "It's not time to quit."

They stared at her, incredulous. "The Mesarthim are here," said Kora, her voice warm with wonder. "We're going to be tested."

"Not until you finish that uul, you aren't."

"Finish it yourself," said Nova. "They don't need to see *you.*"

Skoyë's expression curdled. She wasn't used to them talking back, and it wasn't just the retort. She caught the edge in Nova's tone. It was scorn. Skoyë had been tested sixteen years ago, and they knew what her gift had been. Everyone on Rieva had been tested, save the babies, and only one had been Chosen: Nyoka, their mother. Nyoka had a war gift of staggering power: *literally* staggering. She could send shock waves—into the earth, into the air. She'd shaken the village when her power first woke, and caused an avalanche that obliterated the path to the boarded-up mineshafts. Skoyë's gift, technically, was a war gift, too, but of such a low magnitude as to make it a joke. She could cast a sensation of being prickled with needles—at least, she could for the brief duration of her test. Only the Chosen got to keep their gifts, and only in strict service to the empire. Everyone else had to fade back to normal: Unworthy. Powerless. Pale.

Piqued, Skoyë drew back her hand to slap Nova, but Kora caught her wrist. She didn't say anything. She just shook her head. Skoyë snatched back her hand, as stunned as she was enraged. The girls had always been able to enrage her—not through disobedience, but by this way they had of being untouchable, of being *above*, peering down at the rest of them from some lofty place they had no right to. "You think they're going to choose you, just because they chose *her?*" she demanded. Perfect Nyoka. Skoyë wanted to spit. It wasn't enough that Nyoka had been chosen, plucked from this hell-rock frozen nowhere of an island, but she lingered here, too, in her husband's heart and her daughters' fantasies, and everyone else's charitable memories. Nyoka got to escape *and* be preserved in false perfection, always and forever the pretty young mother called to greater things. Skoyë's lips curled back in a sneer. "You think you're better than the rest of us? You think *she* was?"

"*Yes,*" hissed Nova to the first question. "*Yes,*" she hissed to the second. "*And yes.*" Her teeth were bared. She wanted to bite. But Kora grabbed her hand and tugged her away, toward the trail that snaked up the rock face. They weren't the only ones headed for it. All the rest of the women and girls had started back up to the village. There were visitors. Rieva was at the bottom of the world—where a drain would be, if worlds had drains. Strangers of any kind were as rare as storm-borne butterflies, and these strangers were *Mesarthim*. No one was going to miss out, not even if it meant the uuls spoiling on the beach.

There was eager chatter, stifled laughter, a hum and buzz of thrill. None of the others had bothered to wash. Not that Kora and Nova could be called *clean*, but their hands and faces were scrubbed and ruddy, and their hair, salty-damp, was combed back with their fingers. Everyone else was smeared and greasy and dark with blood, some still clutching their hooks and their knives.

They looked like a swarm of murderesses boiling out of a hive.

They reached the village. The wasp ship was in the clearing. The men and boys were gathered around it, and the gaze they turned on their women was full of distaste and shame. "I apologize for the smell," said the village elder, Shergesh, to their esteemed visitors.

And so Kora and Nova saw Mesarthim for the first time—or the second, maybe, if they'd been babes in Nyoka's arms sixteen years ago when she stood where they were now, her life about to change.

There were four of them: three men and one woman, and they were, indeed, as blue as icebergs. If there had been any wisp of hope that Nyoka might be with them, here it died. Nyoka had been fair-haired like her daughters. This woman had tight black curls. As for the men, one was tall with a shaved head, and one had long white hair that hung in ropes to his waist. As for the last, he was ordinary, apart from the blue skin. Or...he ought to have been ordinary. His hair was brown, his face plain. He was neither tall nor short nor handsome nor ugly, but there was something about him nevertheless that wrested the eye from his comrades. His wide stance, the arrogant angle of his chin? For no clear reason, Kora and Nova were certain that he was the captain, the one who'd shaped godsmetal into a wasp and flown it here. He was the smith.

Of all Mesarthim gifts—and there were too many to count, new mutations all the time in an ever-expanding index of magics—one gift was prime. Every person born in all the world of Mesaret had a dormant ability that would wake at the touch of godsmetal—as they called the rare blue element, mesarthium. But out of millions, only a handful possessed the prime ability: to manipulate the godsmetal itself. These few were called smiths, because they could shape mesarthium as common smiths shaped common metals, though they didn't use fire, anvils, and hammers, but their minds. Mesarthium was the hardest substance known. It was perfectly impervious to cutting, heat, or acids. It couldn't even be scratched. But to the mind of a smith, it was infinitely malleable and responsive to mental command. They could mine it, mold it, awaken its astonishing properties. They could build with it, fly in it, *bond* with it, so that it was something like alive.

This was the gift that children dreamed of, playing Servants in the village, and it was the one they were whispering about now, flushed and eager, saying what their own ships would be when they got their commands: winged sharks and airborne snakes, metal raptors and demons and rays. Some named less menacing things: songbirds and dragonflies and mermaids. Aoki, one of Kora and Nova's little half brothers, declared that his would be a *butt*.

"The door will be the *hole*," he piped, pointing around at his own.

"Dear Thakra, don't let Aoki be a smith," whispered Kora, invoking the seraph Faerer to whom they prayed in their little rock church.

Nova muffled a laugh. "A butt warship *would* be terrifying," she said. "I might steal that idea if it turns out I'm a smith."

"No, you won't," said Kora. "Our ship will be an uul, in loving memory of our home."

Their laughter this time was insufficiently muffled, and caught their father's ear. He silenced them with a look. He was good at that.

They thought that should have been his gift: mirth-queller, enemy of laughter. In fact, he'd tested as elemental. He could turn things to ice, and that was fitting, too. His magnitude was low, though, like Skoyë's and everyone else's on Rieva, and really, nearly everyone's everywhere. Strong gifts were rare. It was why the Servants went out on search like this and tested people all over the world, seeking out those needles in haystacks to join the imperial ranks.

Kora and Nova knew they were needles. They *had* to be.

Their giddiness faltered, and it wasn't their father's look that quelled it, but the Servants' as they surveyed the gathering women—and smelled them. They couldn't keep their disgust from showing. One murmured to another, whose answering laugh was as harsh as a cough. Kora and Nova couldn't blame them. The smell was grotesque even if you were used to it. What must it be like to the uuluninitiated, and those who'd never had to gut or flay anything? It was painful to be part of this milling gruesome crowd and know that to the visitors they were indistinguishable from the rest. They both formed the same desperate plea in their minds. They didn't know that they thought the same thought at exactly the same moment, but neither would it have surprised them.

See us, they willed the Mesarthim. *See us.*

And as though they had spoken aloud—as though they had shouted—one of the four stopped talking midsentence and turned to look straight at them.

The sisters froze, clutching each other's knife-stiff fingers, and shrank back from the stare. It was the tall Servant with the shaved blue pate. He'd heard them. He had to be a telepath. His eyes bored into theirs, and...*poured* into theirs. They felt him there like a breeze stirring grass, riffling through and seeing, just like they'd wanted to be seen, and then he said something to the woman, who in turn said something to Shergesh.

The village elder pursed his lips, displeased. "Perhaps the boys first..." he ventured, and the woman said, "No. You have Servant blood here. We'll test them first."

So Kora and Nova were led inside the wasp ship, and the doors melted closed behind them.

❧ 2 ❧

FRESH HORRORS

Sarai had lived and breathed nightmares since she was six years old. For four thousand nights she had explored the dreamscapes of Weep, witnessing horrors and creating them. She was the Muse of Nightmares. Her hundred moth sentinels had perched on every brow. No man, woman, or child had been safe from her. She knew their shames and agonies, their griefs and fears, and she had thought... she had believed... that she knew *every* horror, and was beyond surprise.

That was before she had to kneel in the blossoms of the citadel garden and prepare her own body for cremation.

The poor broken thing. It lay in the white blooms, beautiful and rich with color—blue skin, pink silk, cinnamon hair, red blood.

For seventeen years this had been *her*. These feet had paced the citadel floors in endless restless circuits. These lips had smiled, and screamed moths at the sky, and sipped rain from chased silver cups.

All that it meant to be Sarai was anchored in the flesh and bones before her. Or it had been. Now she was ripped out of it, unskinned by death, and this body, it was...what? A thing. An artifact of her ended life. And they were going to burn it.

There would always be fresh horrors. She knew that now.

❧ 3 ❧

A RAGGED LITTLE GIRL WITH
BEETLE SHELL EYES

Last night, the citadel of the Mesarthim had almost fallen from the sky. It would have crushed the city of Weep below. If any survived the impact, they would have drowned in the floods as the underground river broke free and swamped the streets. But none of that had happened because someone had stopped it. Never mind that the citadel was hundreds of feet tall, wrought of alien metal, and formed by a god in the shape of an angel. Lazlo had caught it—Lazlo Strange, the faranji dreamer who was somehow a god himself. He'd stopped the citadel from falling, and so instead of everyone dying, only Sarai had.

Well, that wasn't quite true. The explosionist had died, too, but his death was poetic justice. Sarai's was just bad luck. She'd been standing on her terrace—right in the open palm of the giant seraph—when the citadel lurched and tilted. There'd been nothing to hold on to. She'd slid, silk on mesarthium, down the slick blue metal hand and right off the edge.

She'd fallen and she'd died, and you'd think that would be the end of terror, but it wasn't. There was still evanescence, and it was worse. The souls of the dead weren't snuffed out when the spark of life left the body. They were emptied into the air to be languidly unmade. If you'd lived a long life, if you were tired and ready, then perhaps it felt like peace. But Sarai *wasn't ready* and it had felt like dissolving—as though she were a drop of blood in water, or a hailstone on a warm red tongue. The world had tried to dissolve her, to melt her and resorb her.

And . . . something had stopped it.

That something, of course, was Minya.

The little girl was stronger than the world's whole sucking mouth. She pulled ghosts right out of its throat while it tried to swallow them whole. She'd pulled Sarai out. She'd saved her. That was Minya's godspawn gift: to catch the souls of new dead and keep them from melting away. Well, that was *half* her gift, and in the first heady moments of her salvation, Sarai gave no thought to the rest of it.

She was unraveling, alone and helpless, caught in the tide of evanescence, and then, all at once, she wasn't. She was herself again, standing in the citadel garden. The first thing she saw with her new eyes was Minya, and the first thing she did with her new arms was hug her. Forgotten, in her relief, was all the strife between them.

"Thank you," she whispered, fierce.

Minya didn't hug her back, but Sarai hardly noticed. Her relief was everything in that moment. She had almost dissolved into nothingness, but here she was, real and solid and *home*. For all that she'd dreamed of escaping this place, now it felt like a sanctuary. She looked around and everyone was here: Ruby, Sparrow, Feral, the Ellens, some of the other ghosts, and . . .

Lazlo.

Lazlo was here, magnificent and blue, with witchlight in his eyes.

Sarai was wonderstruck by the sight of him. She felt like a breath that had been inhaled into darkness, only to be exhaled again as song. She was dead, but she was music. She was saved, and she was giddy. She flew to him. He caught her, and his face was a blaze of love. There were tears on his cheeks and she kissed them away. Her smiling mouth met his.

She was a ghost and he was a god, and they kissed like they'd lost their dream and found it.

His lips brushed her shoulder, by the slim strap of her slip. In their last shared dream he'd kissed her there, as his body pressed hers into feather down and heat spread through them like light. That had been only last night. He'd kissed her dream shoulder, and now he kissed her ghost shoulder, and she bent her head to whisper in his ear.

There were words on her lips: the sweetest words of all. They had yet to speak them to each other. They'd had so little time, and she didn't want to waste another second. But the words that came out of her mouth weren't sweet, and...they weren't *hers*.

This was the other half of Minya's gift. Yes, the little girl caught souls and bound them to the world. She gave them form. She made them real. She kept them from melting away.

She also controlled them.

"We're going to play a game," Sarai heard herself say. The voice was her own, but the tone was not. It was sweet and sharp, as a knife blade dripping icing. It was Minya speaking *through* her. "I'm good at games. You'll see." Sarai tried to stop the words, but she couldn't. Her lips, her tongue, her voice, they were not under her control. "Here's how this one goes. There's only one rule. You do everything I say, or I'll let her soul go. How does that sound?"

Do everything I say.

Or I'll let her soul go.

She felt Lazlo tense. He drew back to see her face. The witchlight was gone from his eyes, replaced with dread to echo her own as their new reality sank in:

Sarai was a ghost now, in Minya's thrall, and Minya saw her advantage and seized it. Lazlo loved Sarai, and Minya held the thread of Sarai's soul in her grasp, so . . . she held Lazlo, too. "Nod if you understand," she said.

Lazlo nodded.

"No," said Sarai, and the word was harsh with her horrified dismay. She felt as though she'd snatched her voice back from Minya, but it hit her that Minya must have *let* her—that anything she did now she did because Minya either *made* her do it or *let* her. *Dear gods.* She had vowed to never again serve Minya's twisted will, and now she was slave to it.

This was the scene in the citadel garden: the quiet blooms, the row of plum trees, and the ribbons of metal Lazlo had peeled down from the walls to intercept Minya's ghosts' attack. Their weapons were captured and held fast in it, and a dozen ghosts hovered behind. Ruby, Sparrow, and Feral were still huddled by the terrace railing. Rasalas, the metal beast, stood almost still, but its great chest rose and fell, and it seemed, in other ways, too, quiescent but alive. Above them all, the great white eagle they called Wraith made circles in the sky.

And in the middle of the garden, on its bower of blooms, lay the blue and pink, the cinnamon and blood of Sarai's corpse, across which Sarai and Lazlo faced Minya.

The girl was so small in her unnatural body, still dressed in the fifteen-year tatters of her nursery clothes. Her face was round and soft, a child's face, and her big dark eyes blazed with vicious triumph.

With nothing but the burn of those eyes to contradict the rest of her—her tininess, her grubbiness—she managed to radiate power, and worse than power: a malignant zealotry that was its own law and covenant.

"Minya," Sarai entreated, her mind spinning with all that was new—her death, Lazlo's power—and all that was not—the hate and fear that ruled their lives, and the humans' lives, too. "Everything's changed," she said. "Don't you see? We're *free*."

Free. The word sang. It *flew*. She imagined it took form, like one of her moths, and spun shimmering through the air.

"Free?" Minya repeated. It didn't shimmer when she said it. It didn't fly.

"Yes," Sarai affirmed, because here was the answer to every-thing. *Lazlo* was the answer to everything. With her death and her retrieval, she'd been slow to grasp what it all meant, but she seized it now, this thread of hope. All their lives they'd been trapped in this prison in the sky, unable to escape or flee or even close the doors. They'd lived with the certainty that sooner or later the humans would come and blood would flow. Until last week, they'd been sure it would be *their* blood. Minya's army changed that. Now, instead of dying, they would kill. And what would their lives be then? They would still be trapped, but with corpses for company, and hate and fear that weren't a legacy left by their parents, but new and bright and all their own.

But it didn't have to be that way. "Lazlo can control mesarthium," she said. "It's what we've always needed. He can move the citadel." She looked to him, hoping she was right, and new sunbursts went off in her at the sight of him. She said, "We can go anywhere now."

Minya regarded her flatly before swinging her gaze to Lazlo.

He couldn't tell what the little girl was thinking. There was no question in her eyes. They were as black and blank as beetle shells, but he seized the same thread of hope as Sarai. "It's true. I can feel the magnetic fields. If I pull up the anchors, I think—" He stopped himself. This was no time for uncertainty. "I *know* that we can fly."

This was momentous. The sky beckoned in every direction. Sarai felt it. Ruby, Sparrow, and Feral did, too, and they drew nearer, still clutching one another. After all their helpless years here, all their hiding and all their dread, they could simply *leave*.

"Well, all hail the Savior of Everyone," said Minya, and her voice was as flat as her gaze. "But don't go charting a course just yet. I'm not finished with Weep."

Finished with Weep. Sarai's mouth went dry. With that bland tone, that turn of phrase, she might be talking about anything, but she wasn't. She was talking about vengeance.

She was talking about slaughter.

They had fought so much these past days, and all of Minya's ugly words clamored in her mind.

You make me sick. You're so soft.

You're pathetic. You'd let us die.

The insults, she could take, and even the accusations of betrayal. They stung, but it was the bloodlust that left her hopeless.

I'll have had enough carnage when I've paid it all back.

Minya's conviction was absolute. The humans had slain her kind. She had stood in the passage and heard the screams dwindle, baby by baby, until silence reigned. She had saved all she could, and it wasn't enough: a mere four of the thirty who were slaughtered while she listened. Everything she was, everything she did, grew out of the Carnage. Sarai would have wagered that in all of time there had never been a purer wrath than Minya's. Facing her, she wished for something she had never desired before: her mother's gift. Isagol, the goddess of despair, had manipulated emotions. If Sarai could do that, she could unwork Minya's hate. But she couldn't. What was she good for but nightmares?

"Minya, please," she said. "There's been so much pain. This is a chance for a new beginning. We aren't our parents. We don't have to be monsters." Her plea came out in a whisper. *"Don't make us monsters."*

Minya cocked her head. *"Us,* monsters? And you defend the father who tried to kill you in your cradle. The great Godslayer, butcher of babies. If that's what it means to be a hero, Sarai—" She bared her little milk teeth and snarled, *"I'd rather be a monster."*

Sarai shook her head. "I'm not defending him. This isn't about him. It's about *us,* and who we choose to be."

"You don't get to choose," snapped Minya. "You're dead. And I choose monster!"

Sarai's hope failed her then. It hadn't been strong to begin with. She knew Minya too well. Now that Sarai was a ghost, Minya could make her do what she had long refused to: kill her father, the Godslayer, Eril-Fane. And what then? Where would Minya's vengeance lead them? How exactly would she pay back the Carnage? How many had to die to satisfy her?

Sarai turned to Lazlo. "Listen to me," she told him quickly, afraid Minya would stop her voice. "You can't do what she says. You don't know what she's like." After all, it depended on *him.* Minya might choose monster, but without Lazlo's power, she was no more a threat than she had been ever been, trapped in the citadel, unable to reach her enemies. "You can stop her," she whispered.

Lazlo heard her, but her words were like symbols waiting to be deciphered. There was too much to take in. She'd *died.* He'd held her broken body. It was lying right over there. In everything he ever knew of the world, that would have been the end. But she was here, too, standing right here. She was there *and* here, and though he knew it was her ghost he held, he couldn't quite believe it. She felt so real. He smoothed his palm down her back. Fabric slipped just like silk over skin, and her flesh gave under his fingers, soft and supple and warm. "Sarai," he said. "I have you now. I won't let her let your soul go. I promise."

"Don't promise that! You mustn't help her, Lazlo. Not for me, not for anything. Promise *that*."

He blinked. Her words got through but he couldn't accept them. Sarai was the goddess he'd met in his dreams and fallen with into the stars. He'd bought her the moon, and kissed her blue throat, and held her while she wept. She'd saved his life. *She'd saved his life*, and he had failed to save hers. It was unthinkable that he should fail her again. "What are you saying?" he asked, hoarse.

Sarai heard his anguish. His voice was extraordinary. It was so rough, and suffused with emotion. It affected her like texture, like the sweet stroke of a callused palm, and she wanted to lean into it and let it stroke her forever. Instead, she forced out bitter words. The terror of her unraveling still pulsed in her, but she meant it absolutely when she said, "I would sooner evanesce than be the ruin of you and the death of Weep."

Ruin. Death. Those words were all wrong. Lazlo shook his head but he couldn't shake them free. He had *saved* Weep. He could never harm it. But neither could he lose Sarai. Was that really the choice before him? "You can't ask me not to save you."

Minya chose to speak up then. "Really, Sarai, what do you think?" Her tone suggested sympathy for Lazlo's plight—as though it were Sarai putting him in this impossible position, and not herself. "That he could just let you fade away, and have *that* on his conscience?"

"Don't talk about his conscience," cried Sarai, "when you would tear it in half without a second thought!"

Minya shrugged. "Two halves still make a whole."

"No, they don't," Sarai said bitterly. "I should know." Minya had made her what she was—the Muse of Nightmares—but years of immersion in human dreams had changed her. Hate used to be like armor, but she'd lost it, and without it, she'd found herself defenseless against the suffering of Weep. Her conscience *had* torn in half, and the rip was a wound. Two halves did not make a whole. They made two bloody, sundered halves: the part that was loyal to her godspawn family, and the part that understood the humans were victims, too.

"Poor you," said Minya. "Is it my fault you all have such frail consciences?"

"It isn't *frail* to choose peace over war."

"It's frail to run away," snarled Minya. "And I won't!"

"It's not running away. It's being free to leave—"

"We're not free!" barked Minya, cutting her off. "How can we be free if justice isn't done?" Her rage kindled. It was always there, always smoldering, and it didn't take much to set it ablaze. The thought of the murderers going unpunished, of the Godslayer walking untroubled in the sun-washed streets of Weep, it lit a hellfire in her hearts, and she couldn't fathom—would *never* fathom—why it failed to light one in Sarai's. What was missing in her that the Carnage meant nothing? She said, seething, "You're right about one thing, though. Everything *has* changed. We don't have to wait for them to come to us now." With a calculating look at the winged beast, Rasalas, she said, "We can go down to the city anytime we like."

Down to the city.

Minya, in Weep.

Lazlo and Sarai were standing close together. His hand was warm on the small of her back, and she felt the jolt that went through him. It went through her, too, at the idea of Minya in Weep. She saw how it would be: a ragged little girl with beetle shell eyes, trailing an army of ghosts. She would set them on their own kith and kin, and every life they ended would be one more soldier for her army. Who could fight such a force? The Tizerkane were strong but few, and ghosts could not be hurt or killed.

"No," choked Sarai. "Lazlo won't take you there."

"He will if he loves you."

The word, which had been so sweet on Sarai's lips just moments ago, was obscene on Minya's. "Won't you," the little girl said, turning her dark eyes on Lazlo.

How could he answer? Either choice was unthinkable. When he shook his head, he didn't mean it as a response. He was unmoored, spinning. He only shook his head to clear it, but Minya took it for an answer, and her eyes cut narrow.

She didn't know where this stranger had come from, or how he was godspawn like them, but she knew one thing for certain: She had won. He had Skathis's gift and she'd beaten him anyway. Didn't they understand that? She *had* them, and yet they stood there arguing as though this were a discussion.

It was not a discussion.

Whenever Minya won at quell—and Minya *always* won at quell—she upended the game board and sent the pieces flying, so the loser had to crawl around on hands and knees and gather them up. It was important that losers understood what they were; sometimes you had to drive the point home. How, though?

Nothing easier. The stranger held Sarai as though she were his. She wasn't his. He couldn't hold her if Minya chose to take her.

And Minya did.

She snatched her away. Oh, she didn't move a muscle. She simply compelled Sarai's substance to obey. She could have made it seem as though Sarai were moving of her own accord, but where was the lesson in that? Instead, she seized her by her wrists, her hair, her *being*. And pulled.

❧ 4 ❧

WAR WITH THE IMPOSSIBLE

Lazlo felt as though he were clinging to the edge of reason by his fingertips, and that the spinning world might at any moment shake him off and hurl him, as the blast had hurled him last night. That was surely part of it: He'd hit his head on the cobblestones. It throbbed. Dizziness came and went, and his ears still rang. They'd bled. The blood was dried on his neck, caked with the dust of the explosion, but that was the least of the blood on him. His arms and hands, his chest, they were dark with Sarai's blood, and the reality of it—what was more real than blood?—stirred a war in him between grief and disbelief.

How could he make sense of all that had happened? In the most beautiful dream of his life, he'd shared his hearts with Sarai, kissed her, flown with her, and tipped over the edge of innocence with her into something hot and sweet and perfect, only to have her ripped from him with sudden waking—

—to find the alchemist Thyon Nero at his window, cold with accusations that had led Lazlo to the extraordinary discovery of who and what he was: no war orphan of Zosma, but the half-human son of a god, blessed with the power that had been Weep's curse, just in time to save it.

But not Sarai.

He had saved everyone but her. He still couldn't draw a full breath. He would be haunted forever by the sight of her body arched backward over the gate it had landed on, blood dripping from the ends of her long hair.

But the chain of wonders and horrors hadn't ended with her death. This was not the world as Lazlo had known it, outside his books of fairy tales. This was a place where moths were magic and gods were real, and angels had burned demons on a pyre the size of a moon. Here, death was not the end. Sarai's soul was safe and bound—oh *wonder*—but a grubby little girl dangled her fate like a toy on a string, plunging them both back into horror.

And now Minya snatched her away, and the bottom fell out of Lazlo's despair, proving it an abyss, its depths unknown. He tried to hold her, but the tighter he gripped, the more she melted away. It was like trying to hold on to the reflection of the moon.

There was a word from a myth: *sathaz*. It was the desire to possess that which can never be yours. It meant senseless, hopeless yearning, the way a gutter child might dream of being king, and it came from the tale of the man who loved the moon. Lazlo used to like that story, but now he hated it. It was about making peace with the impossible, and he couldn't do that anymore. As Sarai melted right out of his arms, he knew: He could only make war with it.

War with the impossible. War with the monstrous child before him. Nothing less than *war*.

But...*how could he fight her when she held Sarai's soul?*

He clamped his jaws shut to keep unwise words from flying out of

29

his mouth. Breath hissed out between his clenched teeth. His fists clenched, too, but there was too much fury for his body to contain, and Lazlo did not yet comprehend that he was no longer just a man. The boundaries of his self had changed. He was flesh and blood, and he was bone and spirit, and he was *metal* now, too.

Rasalas *roared*. The creature that had been Skathis's, and hideous, was Lazlo's now, and majestic. Part spectral, part ravid, it was sleek and powerful, with vast mirror-metal antlers and such fine rendering that its mesarthium fur felt plush to the touch. Lazlo didn't mean the beast to roar, but it was an extension of him now, and when he clamped his own mouth shut, Rasalas's came open instead. The *sound*...When the creature had screamed down in the city, the sound had been pure anguish. This was *rage*, and the entire citadel vibrated with it.

Minya felt it rattle through her and she didn't even blink. She knew whose rage mattered here, and Lazlo knew it, too. "I don't speak beast," she said as the roar died away, "but I hope that wasn't a *no*." Her voice was calm now, even bored. "You remember the rule, I trust. There was only the one."

Do everything I say, or I'll let her soul go.

"I remember," said Lazlo.

Sarai was by Minya's side now, rigid as a board. She was suspended in the air, like she was hanging from a hook. Horror and helplessness were plain in her eyes, and he was sure the moment had come—the impossible choice between the girl he loved and an entire city. A rushing filled his ears. He raised his hands, placating. "Don't hurt her."

"Don't *make* me hurt her," Minya spat back.

A sound came from behind Lazlo. It was part gasp, part sob, and, small though it was, it spidered a crack through the atmosphere of threat. Minya cast a glance to the other three godspawn. Ruby, Sparrow, and Feral were still reeling with shocks. The citadel's lurch, Sarai's fall, and this stranger carrying her back to them dead. It was shock upon shock, and now *this*.

"What are you doing?" Sparrow asked, disbelieving. She stared at Minya with haunted eyes. "You can't . . . *use* Sarai."

"Clearly I *can*," replied Minya, and to prove it she made Sarai nod.

It was grotesque, that jerk of a nod, all while Sarai's eyes pleaded with them. It was the only weakness in Minya's gift: She couldn't keep her slaves' horror from showing in their eyes. Or perhaps she simply preferred it this way.

Another soft sob tore from Sparrow's throat. "Stop it!" she cried. She came forward, wanting to go to Sarai and grab her away from Minya—not that she *could*—but she stopped short at the corpse, which lay in her way. She might have gone around it or stepped over it, but she came to a halt and stared. She'd only seen it from across the terrace, when Lazlo laid it down. Up close, the brutal reality robbed her of breath. Ruby and Feral came up beside her, and they stared down at it, too. A whimper escaped from Ruby.

Sarai had been impaled. The wound was right in the center of her chest, an ugly ravaged hole. She had hung upside down, so the blood had run up her neck, into her hair, saturating it. At the temples and crown it was still cinnamon, but the long waves of it were wine-dark and clumped into a sticky mass.

The three of them looked from Sarai to Sarai and back again—from the body to the ghost and the ghost to the body—trying to reconcile the two. The ghost wore the same pink slip as the body, though it was without blood, and there was no wound on her. Her eyes were open; the body's were shut. Lazlo had kissed them closed when he laid it down, though it couldn't be said that it looked peaceful. Neither did, the one lifeless and discarded, the other frozen in midair, a pawn in a treacherous game.

"She's *dead*, Minya," Sparrow said, a tear tracing down each cheek. "Sarai *died*."

With a little chuff, Minya said, "I'm aware of that, thanks."

"Are you?" asked Feral. "I mean, because you called this a game." His own voice sounded thin to him now in contrast to this stranger's. Unconsciously, he deepened it, trying to match Lazlo's masculine burr. "Look at her, Minya," he said, gesturing to the body. "This isn't a game. This is death."

Minya did look, but if Feral was hoping for a reaction, he was disappointed. "You think I don't know what death is?" she asked, amusement quirking her lips.

Oh, she knew. When she was six years old, everyone she knew was murdered in cold blood, except the four babies she saved just in time. Death had made her who she was: this unnatural child who never grew up, who never forgot, and would never forgive.

"Minya," said Ruby. "Let her go."

Lazlo couldn't know how unusual it was that they were standing up to her. Only Sarai ever did that, and now, of course, she couldn't, so they did what they knew she would do, and lent their voices for hers, which had been silenced. They spoke in little surges of gathered breath, their cheeks flushed violet. It was frightening, and also freeing, like pushing open a door that one has never dared try. Lazlo waited, grateful for their intervention, and prayed Minya would listen.

"You want me to *let her go*?" she asked, a dangerous glint in her eyes.

"No—" he said quickly, reading her intent, to release Sarai's soul to evanescence. It was like a fairy tale, a wish unclearly phrased, turned against the wisher.

"You know what I mean," said Ruby, impatient. "We're family. We don't *enslave* each other."

"*You* don't because you *can't*," retorted Minya.

"I wouldn't if I could," said Ruby—rather unconvincingly, if truth be told.

"We don't use our magic on each other," said Feral. "That's your rule."

Minya had made them all promise when they were still little children. They'd put their hands to their hearts and sworn, and they had abided by it—the occasional rain cloud or burned bed notwithstanding.

Minya regarded them, gathered now around the stranger. They seemed all arrayed against her. She gave her answer slowly, as though instructing idiots in the obvious. "If I didn't use my magic on her, she would evanesce."

"So use it *for* her, not *against* her," Sparrow implored. "You can hold her soul but leave her free will, the way you do with the Ellens."

The Ellens were the two ghost women who'd raised them, and there was a problem with Sparrow's innocent statement. The women, they all now noted, *weren't* currently exhibiting "free will." If they had been, they would not have remained apart, huddled behind the metal barrier Lazlo had made when he fought off Minya's assault. They would be right here with them, tangled up in their business, clucking and bossing as was their way.

But they were not, and as this dawned on them, their shock pivoted in this new direction. "Minya," said Feral, appalled. "Tell me you aren't controlling the Ellens."

It was unthinkable. They weren't like the other ghosts in Minya's sad, dead army. They didn't despise the godspawn. They loved them, and were loved, and had died trying to protect them from the God-slayer. Theirs were the first souls Minya had ever caught, on that dire day when she'd found herself alone with four babies to raise in a blood-spattered prison. She could never have managed without them, and it was as Sparrow said, or at least it always had been: She used her magic *for* them, not against them. Yes, she held their souls on strings, like she did with all the rest, but that was just so they wouldn't evanesce. She left them their free will. Supposedly.

Minya's face tightened, a flash of guilt no sooner showing than it vanished. "I needed them. I was defending the citadel," she said with a special glare for Lazlo. "After *he* trapped my army inside."

"Well, you're not defending it now," said Feral. "Let them be."

"Fine," said Minya.

The ghost women emerged from behind the barrier, freed. Great Ellen's eyes were fierce. Sometimes, to get the children to tell her the truth, she turned her whole head into a hawk's. They could never defy that piercing gaze. She didn't transform now, but her gaze pierced nonetheless.

"My darlings, my vipers," she said, coming over. She seemed to glide, her feet not touching the floor. "Let's have an end to this bickering, shall we?" To Minya, in a voice equal parts fondness and censure, she said, "I know you're upset, but Sarai's not the enemy."

"She betrayed us."

Great Ellen clucked her tongue. "She did no such thing. She didn't do what you wanted her to. That isn't betrayal, pet. It's disagreement."

Less Ellen, who was younger and slighter than her broad, matronly cohort, added with some humor, "*You* never do what *I* want you to. Is it betrayal every time you hide from a bath?"

"That's different," muttered Minya.

To Lazlo, watching, with the awful sensation that his hearts were in a vise, the tone of the interaction was bizarre. It was so casual, so entirely not on par with Minya holding Sarai's soul prisoner. They might have been scolding a child for hugging a kitten too tight.

"We should all decide what to do," said Feral in his newly deepened voice. "Together."

Sparrow added, with a note of pleading, "Minya, this is *us*."

Us, Minya heard. The word was tiny, and it was huge, and it was *hers*. Without her, there would be no "us," just piles of bones in cradles. And yet they gathered around this man they had never seen before, and stared at her as though *she* were the stranger.

No. They were staring as though she were the enemy. It was a look Minya knew very well. For fifteen years, every soul she'd captured had looked at her just like that. A frisson of . . . *something* . . . ran through her. It was as fierce as joy but it wasn't joy. It shot through her veins like molten mesarthium and made her feel invincible.

It was hate.

It was reflex, like drawing your knife when your foe's hand twitches. It pounded through her like blood, like spirit. Her hands tingled with it. The sun seemed to brighten, and everything became simple. This was what Minya knew: Have an enemy, *be* an enemy. Hate those who hate you. Hate them better. Hate them *worse*. Be the monster they fear the most. And whenever you can, and however you can, *make them suffer*.

The feeling welled up in her so swiftly. If she'd had fangs they'd be beaded with venom and ready to bite.

But . . . bite *whom*?

Hate whom?

These were her people. Everything she'd done for the past fifteen

35

years had been for them. *This is us*, Sparrow had said. *Us us us*. But they were over there, looking at her like that, and she was no part of their *us*. She was outside it now, alone, apart. A sudden void opened up in her. Would they all betray her, as Sarai had, and . . . what would she do if they did?

"We don't have to decide the whole course of our lives right this moment," said Great Ellen. She fixed her gaze on Minya. Her eyes weren't hawk-like now, but soft and velvety brown and filled with devoted compassion.

Inside Minya, something was coiled, growing tighter and tighter the more the others faced her down. Telling her what to do could only back her into a corner, where she would, like a trapped thing, fight to the bitter end. From the start, Lazlo had raised her hackles by coming out of nowhere like an impossible vision—a Mesarthim, astride Rasalas!—and ordering her to catch Sarai's soul. As though she wouldn't have on her own! The gall of him. It burned like acid. He'd even pinned her to the ground, Rasalas's hoof hard on her chest. It ached, and she was sure a bruise was forming, but it was nothing next to her resentment. By compelling her by force to do what she'd been doing already, it was as though he'd won something, and she'd lost.

What if he'd asked instead? *Please, won't you catch Sarai's soul?* Or, better yet, trusted that she just *would*. Oh, it wouldn't have been all how-do-you-do and sitting down to tea, but would Sarai be frozen in the air right now? Perhaps not.

And though Lazlo couldn't be expected to know her, the others certainly should. But of them all, only Great Ellen understood what to do. "One thing at a time and first things first," she said. "Why don't you tell us, pet. What's first?"

36

Instead of ordering, the nurse asked. She deferred to her, and let her choose, and the coiled thing in Minya relaxed just a little. It was fear, of course, though Minya did not know it. She believed it was rage, only and always rage, but that was the costume it wore, because fear was weakness, and she had vowed to never again be weak.

She might have replied that first they would kill Eril-Fane. It was what they expected. She could see it in their wariness. But she saw something else in them, too: a budding defiance. They had tested their voices against her, and they still had the taste in their mouths. It would be stupid to push them right now, and Minya was not stupid. In life, as in quell, direct attacks meet with the greatest resistance. It's better to be oblique, lull them into lowering their defenses. So she took a step back and, with effort, grew calm.

"First," she said, "we should see to Sarai."

And with that, she let her go—her substance, not her soul. No tricks. She'd made her point.

Released from her grip, Sarai fell back to the ground. It was abrupt, and she collapsed to her knees. All those long moments she'd been held rigid, paralyzed, she'd been fighting it, probing for weakness. But there was no weakness. Minya's hold on her had been absolute, and now that she was freed, she began to shake uncontrollably.

Lazlo rushed forward to hold her, murmuring in his gravelly voice. "You're all right now," he said. "I have you. We'll save you, Sarai. We'll find a way. *We'll save you.*"

She didn't answer. She rested against him, depleted, and all she could think was: *How?*

The others—except Minya—all clustered around, stroking her arms, her hair, asking if she was all right, and casting shy looks at

Lazlo, who was, after all, the first living stranger to ever stand in their midst.

It was Sparrow, face clouded, who turned to Minya and asked, uncertain, "What did you mean by 'see to her'?"

"Oh," said Minya, screwing up her face as though the subject were regrettable. "As you were so kind to point out to me before, Sarai's *dead*." She fluttered her fingers toward the body. "We can't just leave that lying there, can we? We're going to have to burn it."

❦ 5 ❧

The Sting and the Ache

Burn it.

It shouldn't have come as a shock, but it did. The soil in the garden was too shallow for burial, and of course Minya was right: You couldn't just leave a body lying around. But they were none of them ready to face what must be done. It was all too raw, the body too real and too... *Sarai.*

"No," said Lazlo, stricken pale. He still couldn't reconcile the two of her. "We... we have her body and we have her soul. Can't we just... put them back together?"

Minya raised her eyebrows. "Put them back together?" she parroted, her tone mocking. "What, like pouring an egg back into its shell?"

Great Ellen placed a quelling hand on her shoulder and told Lazlo, with utmost gentleness, "It doesn't work like that, I'm afraid."

Sarai knew her body was beyond repair. Her hearts had been pierced, her spine shattered, but still she wished for this same miracle. "Weren't there godspawn who could heal?" she asked, thinking of all the other magical children born in the citadel and vanished from it over the years.

"Indeed there were," said the nurse. "But they'd do us no good. Death can't be healed."

"One who could bring back the dead, then," she persisted. "Weren't there any?"

"If there were, they're no help to us now, bless them wherever they may be. There's no saving your body, love. I'm sorry for it, but Minya's right."

"But to *burn* it," said Ruby in soft panic, for it was she who would have to light the fire. "It's so...permanent."

"Death *is* permanent," said Less Ellen, "while flesh very much is not." She was less a force of nature than Great Ellen, but she was a steady presence with her calming hands and sweet voice. When they were small she had sung them lullabies from Weep. Now she said, "It's best done soon. Nothing to be gained by waiting."

The Ellens should know. They had tended their own murdered bodies once upon a time, and burned them in a pyre along with all the gods and babies who'd died that same dark day.

Sparrow knelt beside the corpse. The movement was sudden, as though her knees gave out. A compulsion forced her to put her hands on the body. Her gift was what it was. She made things grow. She was Orchid Witch, not a healer, but she could sense the pulse of life in plants even at its faintest, and had coaxed forth blooms from withered stalks that to anyone else would seem dead. If there was life yet in Sarai, she thought she would at least *know*. Hesitating, she reached out, her hands trembling as they came to rest on the bloodied blue skin. She closed her eyes and listened, or did something like listen. It was no ordinary sense, and was akin to the way Minya felt for the passage of spirits in the air.

40

But Minya had sensed the flutter of Sarai's spirit and hooked it. Sparrow felt only a terrible echoing *nothing*.

She drew back her hands. They were shaking. She had never touched a dead body, and hoped she never would again. It was so inert, so...*vacant*. She wept for all that it would never do or feel, her tears following the dried salt paths left by many others since last night.

Watching her, the rest of them understood that this was final. Lazlo felt a sting behind his eyes and an ache in his hearts, and so did Sarai, even though she understood that her eyes, her hearts, weren't real, and so neither were the sting and the ache.

Ruby sobbed, turning to Feral to crush her face to his chest. He spread one big hand over the back of her head, his fingers disappearing in her wild dark hair, and bent over her to hide his face while his shoulders shook in silence.

The Ellens wept, too. Only Minya's eyes were dry.

Lazlo alone caught the moment that she glanced down at the body in the flowers and looked, for an instant, like an actual child. Her eyes weren't beetle shells then, and they weren't ablaze with triumph. They were...lost, as though she hardly knew what she was seeing. And then she felt him watching and it was over. Her gaze slashed to meet his and there was nothing in it but challenge.

"Clean this up," she told them, with a wave of her hand dismissing the corpse as naught but a mess in need of tidying. "Say good-bye. Do what you need to do. We'll discuss Weep once you've finished." She turned away. It was clear she intended to stalk off without another word, but was thwarted by the arcade, which Lazlo had earlier closed to trap her army. "You," she commanded without looking back. "Open the doors."

Lazlo did. As he had melted them closed, so did he melt them back open. It was the first time he'd done it in a state of calm, all else having happened in a blur of desperation, and he marveled at the ease of it. The mesarthium responded to his merest urging, and a small thrill ran through him.

I have power, he thought, amazed.

When the archways had been restored, he saw the ghost army waiting within, and worried that Minya would renew her attack, but she didn't. She just walked away.

He had, in his hearts, declared war on the dark child, but Lazlo was no warrior, and his hearts had no talent for hate. As he watched her go, so small and all alone, a moment of clarity shattered him. She might be savage, beyond redemption, broken beyond repair. But if they wanted to save Sarai and Weep . . . they had to save her first.

6

Every One Cried "Monster"

Minya pushed through the clot of her ghosts. She could have moved them aside to clear a path for herself, but it suited her just now to shove. "Back to your posts," she commanded, harsh, and they immediately moved off to take up their prior positions throughout the citadel.

She needn't have spoken aloud. It wasn't her words the ghosts were obeying. Her will smothered theirs. She moved them like game pieces. But it was good to speak and be obeyed. It flitted through her mind how simple it would be if everyone were dead and hers to command.

From the gallery it was only a few turns and a short passage to reach the door she sought. It wasn't properly a door, not anymore, having frozen in the act of closing at the moment of Skathis's death. It was tall—twice the height of a man—and though it must have been wide once, it was now a mere gap. She could only just squeeze through. She had to work her head from side to side. It would be easier, she thought, without ears. Everything would be. Then she wouldn't have to hear the breathless, righteous weakness of the others, their begging talk of mercy, their dissent.

Once her head was in, she wedged a shoulder into the gap. The rest should have slipped right through, but her chest was too puffed up with furious breathing. She had to forcibly exhale and thrust herself in. It hurt—especially where Rasalas's hoof had pinned her—but it was nothing under the steady seethe of her rage.

Inside, there was an antechamber, and then the walls opened up into the space that had become her sanctuary: the heart of the citadel, they had dubbed it as children.

No sooner did she enter than she let loose the scream she had been holding inside. It ripped up from the core of her, scouring her throat and filling her head with a battering gyre of sound. It felt like screaming an apocalypse, but the sound that left her lips fell flat and small in the big, strange room, no match at all to what she heard inside her head. The heart of the citadel ate sound, and when Minya screamed in here, it seemed to eat her rage, too, though she could never scream long enough to pour all of it out. Her voice would die before she ran out of rage. She could scream a hole in her throat and come unraveled, fall to pieces like moth-chewed silk, and still, from the leftover shreds of her, the little pile of tatters, would pour forth this unending scream.

Finally, coughing, she cut it off. Her throat felt like meat. Her apocalypse still boiled inside her, but it always did. It always did.

She sank down onto the narrow walkway that ran the circumference of the room. It was a mystifying space: spherical, like the inside of a ball, but vast—some hundred feet in diameter—and all smooth mesarthium. A walkway threaded all the way around it, fifty feet of empty air above, and fifty feet below. Or not quite empty. Dead center, floating on air like the citadel itself, was a smaller sphere, smooth and fixed in space, some twenty feet wide and tall.

And then there were the wasps: two of them, huge and terrible and beautiful, sculpted of mesarthium and perched on the curvature of the walls.

All below was just a great bowl of air. Minya was unaccustomed to its emptiness. All these years she'd kept her army here, building it up soul by soul. Now they were out standing guard along the passages, in the garden, and in the open palms of the great seraph's hands, from where they could spot any hint of threat that might rise up from Weep.

Only one ghost was with her now: Ari-Eil, who was the newest, save Sarai. He was the Godslayer's young cousin, very recently dead. She'd been keeping him by her as a bodyguard. She met his eyes. They were as hard as ever. How he hated her. All the ghosts did, but his hate was freshest, and it made a good whetstone upon which to sharpen her own. She had only to look at him and it sang bright in her, a defensive reaction to the human gaze. *Hate those who hate you.*

It was easy. *Natural.* What was unnatural was *not* hating them.

"What?" she snapped at him, fancying she saw a glimmer of satisfaction in his eyes. "They didn't *beat* me, if that's what you're thinking." Her voice was scream ravaged. "I let them have a break. To burn the body."

She allowed him his voice, so that he could insult her and she could punish him, but he only said flatly, "You are benevolence itself."

Her face twitched, and she spun him around to face the door. She didn't want him watching her. "Don't think your city is safe," she

45

whispered, and though she gave him the freedom to answer her, he declined to make use of it.

She sat, letting her feet down to dangle over the edge of the walkway. She was trembling. Minutes passed thickly, and she quieted into stillness, finally, and then into something else.

Minya went blank.

The others didn't realize: Minya rarely slept. She *could*, and did when it was essential, when she began to feel like a ghost herself. But sleep was a deeper submergence than she was comfortable with. She couldn't control her ghosts from that state, but only set commands they'd obey until she changed them. There was this other state, though: a kind of shallowing of her consciousness, like a river that, pouring out of a slot canyon, widens and grows slow. She could rest here, drifting, without ever having to surrender to the deeper pull of darkness.

Minya had never heard of leviathans. Lazlo could have told her how in the west, where the sea was the color of a newborn baby's eyes, people captured sea monsters when they were still young, and lashed them to great pontoons to prevent them from submerging to freedom. They would serve their whole lives as ships, some for hundreds of years, never able to dive and disappear into the deep. Her mind was like that. She *kept* it like that: captive at the surface, only very rarely sinking into the wild and unknowable deep.

She preferred these shallows, where she could react, keep control of all her tethers. Her eyes were open, vacant. She seemed an empty shell—except, that is, that she was rocking. It was ever so slight, her thin, hunched shoulders jerking back and forth. Her lips were moving, shaping the same words over and over in silence, as she lived the same memories she always did, and the same screams echoed forever.

Always and forever: the children. Each face was seared into her mind, two versions of them, side by side: alive and terrified next to dead and glassy-eyed, because *she* had failed to save them.

They were all I could carry.

Those were the words her lips formed, over and over as she rocked back and forth. A mere four she had saved, out of thirty: Sarai and Feral, Ruby and Sparrow. She hadn't chosen, just grabbed who was nearest. She'd meant to go back for the others.

But then the screaming had begun.

Her hands in her lap made loose fists, and her fingers moved constantly, smearing imagined slickness over her palms. She was remembering the sweat, and trying to hold on to Sarai's and Feral's wriggling hands. Ruby and Sparrow had been infants; she'd held them in one arm. Sarai and Feral had been toddlers. Them, she'd dragged. They hadn't wanted to come with her. She'd had to squeeze to keep hold of their little fingers. She'd hurt them and they'd cried. "Come on," she'd hissed, tugging at them. "Do you want to die, too? *Do you?*"

The Ellens' bodies had lain in their way. They'd been too small to step over them, and had to crawl, tangling in the nurses' bloody aprons, stumbling right through their ghosts. They couldn't see the ghosts, of course. Only Minya could, and she didn't want to look.

The others didn't remember. They'd been too small. The whole slick, screaming day was lost to them, and they were lucky for it. Minya could never lose it. Other thoughts might pass in front of it, obscuring it for a time, but always they cleared or moved on, and there it was, as vivid as the day it happened.

In the fifteen years since the Carnage, Minya hadn't seen another corpse. Now, in the nursery of her memory, between the Ellens' bodies, she saw Sarai's there, too. It was pink and blue and broken, cinnamon and red, and when she went to step over it, its eyes flew open. "Monster," it hissed. The word echoed.

"Monster," said Great Ellen's corpse.

"Monster," agreed Less Ellen's.

And the babies' screams morphed into words, and every one cried "Monster."

❦ 7 ❦

WRAITH

Out in the garden, Lazlo repaired the wall he'd poured down on Minya's ghosts. The weapons that were trapped in it fell free, and the mesarthium flowed upward, returning to the smooth wall of the seraph's chest, re-forming its elegant clavicles, the column of its throat.

It took but a moment. He turned back to Sarai. He marveled, to see her in the sun—her hair, spice hues in rich ripples on blue shoulders, her face, full and soft-cheeked, soft-lipped and generous, tapering like a heart to her little pointed chin. Her brow was creased with worry, her eyes heavy with reluctant resolve. "You have to go," she said, bleak.

He thought he must have misheard. "What?"

"You must see, Lazlo. You have to leave so she can't use you."

It was the last thing she wanted to tell him. He was *here*. She wanted nothing more than to tuck her face into his neck and breathe the sandalwood scent of him, but since when did she get what she wanted? There was too much at stake. She had to be brave.

"Leave?" he repeated, looking lost and confused. "I'm not going anywhere without you."

"But I *can't* leave. I'm bound to her, and it's too great a risk for you to stay. You must see that. She won't give up. She never does. I don't think she can."

Lazlo swallowed hard. The thought of leaving choked him. "I belong here," he said, feeling the truth of it all through him. With Sarai, whom he loved, and with others like himself, and with the metal, too. It had awakened a dimension of him that he had never known existed, a whole new sense, as real as sight or touch. It was part of him now. He was part of *this*. To leave would mean losing not only Sarai but a piece of himself as well.

"If you stay," said Sarai, "she'll find a way to break you."

"I won't break."

She wanted to believe him. She was weary of being brave. "Not even if she lets me evanesce," she said. "Promise me you won't bring her to Weep, no matter what."

"I promise," Lazlo said, and underneath that promise he made another to himself: that he wouldn't fail Sarai again. *No matter what.* And if the two vows were in conflict? He would find a way. He had to. "We'll get through this," he told her. "Together."

He reached for her, and she gave up all resistance.

The others watched, transfixed, as she melted against him, sweetly heavy and his to hold. Their eyes closed, and they rested their foreheads together as they breathed soft words from each other's lips. They didn't kiss, yet the moment was as intimate as any kiss, and it was clear to the others by the sure draw of his arms, and the smooth glide of her into them, that they'd done this before. *When,* though? How could Sarai have kept such a secret? A *lover,* and never a word!

"I'm sorry," said Ruby, her voice bright and intrusive. "I feel I should know this already. But...who *are* you?"

Sarai and Lazlo both turned. "Oh," said Sarai, biting her lip. "Right. This is Lazlo. Lazlo, this is Ruby, Feral, Sparrow." She gestured to them one by one. "Great Ellen, Less Ellen."

"I'm very pleased to meet you," he said, earnest, fixing his dreamer's gray eyes on each of them in turn. "I've heard so much about you all."

"Have you?" inquired Feral, skewing a look at Sarai. "Because we can't say the same."

"We've never heard of you," Ruby clarified tartly.

Sarai felt a flush of guilt, but it didn't last. With a lift of her chin, she said, "If you'd come to me yesterday when I was trapped in my room without food or water, I might have told you about him."

"Now, now," said Great Ellen, coming between them. "It's no time for sniping." To Lazlo, she offered her hand, and he took it. "It's my pleasure, young man," she said. "Welcome. Or perhaps..." She cocked her head, considering him. "Welcome *back?*"

Welcome *back?* They all stared at her, Lazlo most of all. "Do you know me?" he asked.

"I might," she answered. "Though if it is you, you've changed a bit since I saw you last. Babies all rather look the same."

"What do you mean, Ellen?" Sarai asked her. "Was Lazlo born here?"

"I couldn't say for certain." She frowned, thinking back. "But there was a baby, a boy—" And they didn't get to hear the rest, not then, because a scream split the air and they all flinched and looked up.

It sounded like a woman's voice, high and plaintive, but it was a bird. Well, it was no ordinary bird, but the great white eagle they called Wraith, for its phantom habit of vanishing in thin air. It wasn't a ghost—they knew that because if it were, Minya would have power over it, and she didn't. It had been around as long as they had, appearing now and then to draw its floating circles in the sky over the citadel, watching them from a distance. It had always been silent. But not now.

It drew lower in its circling than ever before, so that they could make out its eyes for the first time, gleaming dark like gemstones. The dagger hook of its beak opened in another scream before it luffed its huge wings to land on a slender branch of one of the plum trees at the garden's edge. The bough bobbed under its weight, a few plums detaching to fall to the city far below.

It screamed again, neck stretched forward, eyes intent. They all stood transfixed.

Lazlo's heartbeats quickened. The moment he'd first glimpsed the bird, out the library window back in Zosma, he'd felt an affinity, a *rush*—like the turn of a page and a story beginning. It was at that moment, before he ever laid eyes on the Tizerkane or the Godslayer, that his tame patience with the gray of his life had smashed and spilled him tumbling toward his future. *This* future. It hadn't begun in the courtyard, when the warriors had entered on spectralback and cast the whole library into uproar. It had begun when he glanced out the window and saw a huge white bird hovering on an updraft.

But he'd had no context for the affinity then. He hadn't known what he was. Now he did, and the sight of the bird up close stirred memories too deep to claim. He had only been a baby. How could he possibly remember... if indeed it had actually happened?

If his suspicions were right, it was this bird that had carried him to Zosma.

Why?

Wraith lifted off the bough. One last scream, and it dove, disappearing from their sight, so that they all moved to the balustrade and peered over, to watch it veer and glide down in a widening spiral until it was naught but a scrap of white against the rooftops far below.

"Well," said Sarai. "That was new."

"What do you mean?" asked Lazlo.

"It's never done anything like that before. It's never made a sound, or come so near us."

"Do you think it was trying to tell us something?" mused Sparrow.

"Like *what*?" asked Ruby, who couldn't begin to imagine.

And Lazlo couldn't, either, and yet that feeling, that affinity, made him certain there was something. Because if he was right, the bird had changed the whole course of his life. What *was* it? he wondered, and would have asked, but just then Feral pointed down, over the balustrade at the city below. "Look," he said, and they forgot Wraith for the moment.

Something was happening in Weep.

8

STREETS AS FULL AS VEINS

The bird swooped low over the city.

Its shadow flew with it in a perfect ballet, flickering over rooftops where, for the first time in fifteen years, the sun shone down. The golden domes blazed with morning light. The topography of the city had changed overnight. Where there had been four anchors— monumental blocks of mesarthium—now there were only three. Where the fourth had been was just a melted lump and a great, ragged sinkhole flanked by charred ruins.

Melted anchor, folded wings, and a new blue god in the citadel over Weep. It *meant something*, and the bird grew restless. It had been waiting for so long. It let out a final wail and vanished, taking its shadow with it.

The streets below were as full as veins, streams of people pulsing like blood, like spirit, through the city's arteries and out. Weep was bleeding its citizens into the countryside. A hundred thousand souls, and all of them wanted *out*. They were bottlenecked in the narrow lanes, pressed together like tinned fish—if tinned fish could curse, and had elbows with which to prod one another. Their panic made a low thrum. They pushed handcarts piled with possessions, grandmothers perched on top like wizened queens. Chickens flapped in cages. Children rode their parents' shoulders; babies were tied to backs, and dogs stuck close with their tails between their legs. As for the cats, they would stay put. Weep was theirs now. The citizens were fleeing the night's disaster and revelation.

Godspawn.

The word was cursed and spat a hundred thousand times, and whispered and moaned a hundred thousand more as the city's heartbeats pumped its people out the eastern gate in a roiling, frightened flow.

Mounted Tizerkane warriors rode among them, keeping the peace. An orderly evacuation would have been better, neighborhood by neighborhood, but the folk would have rioted sooner than stay at home awaiting their turn to leave. So the Tizerkane didn't try to stop them, but only to prevent them from trampling one another in their haste. The warriors were well trained, and managed to conceal their own fear, when most just wanted to fall in line and flee with the rest.

There were outsiders in the city, too—the faranji from the Godslayer's delegation—and most of them sat in carriages, stuck in the slow throb of the exodus. They rapped on ceilings with fists and canes, trying to urge their drivers to move. But the drivers just shrugged, gestured to the density of bodies—and wagons and leashed pigs and at least one four-poster bed set on wheels and drawn by a great brute of a goat—and kept their pace, ever so slowly grinding toward the gate.

Some parts of the city were quiet—notably the quarter of the melted anchor, where last night all hell had broken loose.

The fires had died away. The dust clouds had settled on the rubble of the explosion, and a young man with golden hair stood at the rim of the sinkhole. He was the alchemist, Thyon Nero, and he could hear the river moving below, and remember the roar when it had nearly burst through. His eyes traced the sunstruck rivulets of blue metal that disappeared into the ground. Somehow, Strange had shored up the cracked bedrock.

Thyon's mind was undergoing a sensation of warp, as though it were shrinking and expanding, shrinking and expanding, trying to discover its new boundaries. Sometimes the limits of understanding shift too quickly to track, and it felt like being swept out to sea by a rogue wave and having to swim back, against riptides, finally staggering ashore to a landscape made unfamiliar by cataclysm. If the kingdom of knowledge was a city, then a swath of Thyon's had been shaken to the ground, and he was standing knee-deep in rubble both in his thoughts and in reality.

What had he witnessed last night?

What was Strange?

"Oh. *You're* still here."

Thyon whipped around at the sound of the voice. He'd been absorbed in his thoughts and hadn't heard anyone approach. His expression didn't change at the sight of Calixte Dagaz—acrobat, climber, convicted jewel thief, possible assassin, and, like himself, esteemed member of the Godslayer's delegation.

"I thought you'd have fled with the others," she said, her voice light with careless scorn.

"Did you," said Thyon, flat, as though making it a question would take too much effort. "Then you're a poor judge of character."

Calixte was a slip of a young woman, narrow-hipped, flat-chested, and lithe. Her shorn hair, only now growing back from its prison shave, might have made her look like a boy, but it didn't. Her face, if not pretty in the way Thyon had been trained to judge such matters, was undeniably feminine. Her lips were full, her eyes knife-shaped and thickly lashed, and there was a delicacy to her features that was at odds, Thyon thought, with the crude way she spoke, and the too-loud laugh she'd no doubt honed among circus folk, striving to be heard over the bellows and guffaws of sword swallowers and fire breathers. "I'm an excellent judge of character," she said. "Which is why I made friends with Lazlo, and not you."

The barb struck but didn't hurt. Thyon didn't care what Calixte thought of him. "You say that as though I was an option."

He meant, of course, that he—son of a duke, godson to a queen, and the most celebrated alchemist of the age—was above befriending a circus waif sprung from prison out of pity, but she turned his words against him. "No. You don't have friends. I noticed that straightaway. It would have been wasted effort. Still, I've been known to exert valiant efforts when someone's worth it."

He gave her a wan smile. "If I'm not worth your efforts, why are you bothering me now?"

It was a fair question. She skewed her mouth to one side. "Because I have no one else to bother?"

"What about your girlfriend? Has she tired of you already?" Thyon might not have involved himself in the lives of the others—if that was what friendship was, being involved in the mess that was other people's lives—but it hadn't escaped his notice that Calixte had paired off with one of the warriors. The other delegates had gossiped about them like washerwomen, following them with hot eyes even as they called them unnatural and worse.

No one from Weep, Thyon had noted, had seemed in any way troubled by the pairing.

"It's impossible to tire of me," Calixte stated as simple fact. "Tzara's busy." She waved a hand toward the chaos to the south. The noise was only a low rumble here, in this abandoned quarter. "Preventing stampedes and such." She spoke blithely, but worry lurked in the corners of her mouth and eyes—for Tzara, charged with keeping the peace; for Weep, whose worst fears stirred in the hated metal angel; and for Lazlo, who'd gone up there and hadn't come back.

"Why stay, if you have no one to play with?" Thyon asked, still matching his tone to her scorn. He was irritated. This banter was beneath him; *she* was beneath him. In truth, he'd had little experience consorting with common people. He was baffled by their casualness, and stymied by their disrespect. Back home, someone like Calixte wouldn't dare address him, let alone *insult* him. "You could still catch the carriages. I'm sure Tod would be happy to make space for you."

Calixte mock-smiled her eyes to squints. She had not been well received by her fellow delegates, and her countryman Ebliz Tod was the worst of the lot. "Oh, he must be long gone by now," she said. "He probably ran out of here first thing, using the heads of the populace as stepping-stones."

In spite of himself, Thyon smiled. He could just picture it.

"I'm not going anywhere," Calixte added with quiet intensity. She joined Thyon at the edge of the sinkhole and peered into it as intently as he had been. "I want to know what happened last night."

"Which part? Nearly being crushed to death, or the metal coming alive, or—"

"*Lazlo turned blue.*"

Thyon had been about to say that, though he would have called him Strange, not Lazlo. But the way Calixte said it—intense, confused, and fascinated—brushed away the veil of casual banter. There was nothing casual here.

"That he did," said Thyon.

They'd both seen it happen. They'd watched him run to the sinking anchor and brace it with his bare hands, as though with the strength of his body he could keep it from capsizing. And, impossibly, he *had*—though not, they both gathered, with the strength of his body. It was some other strength they couldn't begin to fathom. They fell into a momentary silence, their mutual disdain muted in the presence of this mystery.

"How?" she wanted to know.

There were worlds in that word. Thyon had no doubt that both metal and gods had come from some other world, but he was an alchemist, not a mystic, and he only knew one thing for certain. "It was the metal," he told her. "It's a reaction to touching the metal."

She squinted at him. "But I've touched it plenty, and I'm not blue."

"No. Me either. It's just him. It's something about him."

"But what does that mean? That he's one of them? One of the gods who made that thing?"

Strange, a god? Through all his musing, Thyon had not allowed those words to scrape against each other. "That's absurd," he said tightly.

Calixte agreed, though for a different reason. Thyon objected to the notion that Lazlo could be divine, powerful. She objected on the grounds that the Mesarthim were evil. "No one's less evil than Lazlo. And the girl, she didn't look evil, either, poor thing."

The girl. Thyon was assailed anew by the brew of feelings that had churned in him at the sight of Lazlo Strange cradling a girl to his chest. He'd hardly known how to interpret the image. It was so unexpected as to be incomprehensible. Strange with a girl. The details—that she was *blue*, that she was *dead*—had filtered in slowly, and he'd still been processing them after Strange carried her away. Into the air. On a statue brought to life. Indeed, he was still processing them now.

Strange had known a girl—a goddess, no less—and she had died, and he was grieving.

Thyon Nero was late awakening to the understanding that other people are living lives, too. He knew it, of course, intellectually, but it had never much impressed him. They had always been minor players in a drama about *him*, their stories mere subplots woven around his own, and it floored him to experience a sudden shift—as though a script had been shuffled and he'd been handed the wrong pages. *He* was the minor player now, standing in the settled dust, while Strange flew metal beasts and held dead goddesses in his arms.

Setting aside, for a moment, the question of *how* he had known a goddess, there was the more pertinent issue of: "Evil or not, how was she up there? Eril-Fane told us the citadel was empty."

The Godslayer had assured the delegation that the gods were dead, the citadel empty, and they weren't in any danger.

Calixte pursed her lips and looked up at the great hovering thing. "Apparently he was wrong."

❊ ❊ ❊

Eril-Fane and Azareen were positioned halfway between the amphitheater and the eastern gate, where a bottleneck of merging streets made a nasty tangle. They were mounted on their spectrals, side by side on a small bridge that arced over the city's main thoroughfare. Below them, their people passed in graceless turmoil, too many at once, frustration and dread turning them volatile. Their presence, they hoped, would calm the boil to a simmer.

The newly revealed sun glared down on them. It felt like being watched.

"Why is it still here?" Azareen asked, flinging a hand upward, to where the citadel still hovered. "He said he could move it, so why hasn't he? Why isn't it *gone*, and the godspawn with it?"

"I don't know," said Eril-Fane. "Perhaps it isn't so easily done. He may have to learn how to master it." There was also the matter of grieving, he thought but didn't say.

"He mastered it quickly enough last night. You saw the wings. Rasalas. If he can do that, he can move the citadel. Unless he has other plans."

"What other plans?"

"We need to be ready, in case of attack."

"Lazlo won't attack," said Eril-Fane, uneasy. "As for the others, if they could, why didn't they before?"

"You can't just assume we're safe."

"I assume nothing. We'll make ready as best we can, though I don't know how we could ever be ready for that." To fight an army of their own dearly departed? It was the stuff of nightmares.

"And there could be more out there besides," said Azareen, gesturing to the Cusp and beyond. They knew now that there were godspawn in the citadel, but Lazlo's transformation bespoke a new and unsettling possibility: that there were more out in the world, too, living in far-off countries, their flesh un-blue, their heritage a secret, perhaps even to them.

"There could be," Eril-Fane agreed.

"They can pass as human," said Azareen. "They can hide in plain sight, like he did."

"He wasn't hiding," Eril-Fane replied. "He said he didn't know."

"And you believe him?"

He hesitated, then nodded. In the young faranji, Eril-Fane's starved and stunted paternal feelings had found a place to fix. He was more than fond of the young man. He felt protective of him, and in spite of everything, he couldn't help trusting him.

"You think it's a coincidence that he studied Weep?" asked Azareen. "That he learned our language, our legends?" Now that she knew what he was, Lazlo's fascination took on a sinister character.

"Not a coincidence, no," said Eril-Fane. "I think there was something that called to him, something he didn't understand."

"How did he end up there, though, all the way in Zosma? Is he . . . one of ours?"

Eril-Fane turned to look at her—his wife, who'd been gotten with godspawn like so many other daughters of Weep. When she said "ours," she was asking if some woman of the city had given birth to Lazlo up in the sterile room in the citadel the gods had used for that purpose.

"Let's hope," said Eril-Fane. "Because if not, then there could be more Mesarthim out there, maybe another citadel floating over another city, somewhere on Zeru." It was a big world, much of it unmapped. In what distant places might bad gods reign? But Eril-Fane had a sense that Lazlo was tied to Weep, that all of it hinged on this city, this citadel, these gods and godspawn.

For fifteen years, the people of Weep had lived with the certainty that the monsters were dead, and Eril-Fane had lived with the burden of it: his the hands that had slain them, gods and their children alike—and *his* child, too, or so he'd believed. He had committed a crime as heinous as the gods' own, and though he'd never tried to forgive himself, he had lived with it by telling himself there had been no choice, that it had been necessary to ensure that Weep would never again be forced to its knees, or its belly, or its back.

Now he was tracing the implications of this new discovery—that the metal activated Mesarthim power—and even that small, sickly faith was eroding. What if it *hadn't* been necessary to kill them? "When they're away from the metal," he ventured, reluctant to speak his suspicion aloud, "does their power just...wear off?"

Azareen tried to read his face, as she'd been trying to do all these years. He had been the plaything of the goddess of despair. Isagol had mangled his emotions, poisoned his faculties for love and trust until they were so tangled with hate and shame that he hardly knew one from the other. She understood his meaning, though, and felt a stab of the remorse she knew he was inflicting on himself. That was Azareen's burden: to feel all the pain of Eril-Fane's torment, and be unable to help him. "Even if it does," she said warily, "you couldn't have known."

"I should have waited. Babes in cradles, what was the rush? They couldn't hurt us. I should have tried to understand."

"Someone else would have done it if you hadn't," she said, "and it would have been worse."

Eril-Fane knew it was true, but it hardly helped to hear that the rest of his people would have been more barbaric than he had been. "They were babies. I could have protected them instead of—"

"You protected *us*," said Azareen fiercely.

"I didn't, though." His voice had dropped low. The look he

gave her was one she knew well—it was helplessness, guilt. He was remembering her cries in the citadel, and her belly swelled with a baby that wasn't his, that wasn't human. "I didn't protect *you*."

"And *I* didn't protect *you*," she said. "No one protected anyone. How could we? They were gods! And yet you freed us. *All of us*, my love. The whole city." She pointed to a little girl in the flow of people beneath them. She was riding on her father's shoulders, red-cheeked and wide-eyed, her hair sticking out in black sprouts of pigtails. "Because of you, that child will never be a slave. Her family will never answer Skathis's knock and see her borne away on Rasalas."

She could have gone on reassuring him that he was a hero, but she knew he didn't want it. It had never helped, and he probably didn't even hear it. He was still looking at the little girl in the crowd, but there was a haunted vagueness to his gaze, and Azareen knew he was seeing someone else—his own daughter, whose broken blue body Lazlo had lifted off an iron gate in the earliest hours of dawn.

Eril-Fane had fallen to his knees at the sight of her, and he'd done something that Azareen hadn't seen him do since Isagol had her way with him, body and mind. He'd wept. She was still trying to decide if it was a good thing or bad. For years he couldn't cry, and now he could. Did that mean the broken pathways of his emotions were healing?

Just in time to mourn the death of his daughter.

It was Azareen's turn to do something she hadn't done in years. She reached for her husband's hand, slipping her fingers into his, feeling his calluses, his scars, the warmth of him, the realness. They'd had only five days and nights as husband and wife, nearly two decades ago now, but she remembered the feel of these hands—

these—on her body, learning everything about her, or at least as much as a young husband could learn in five days and nights. After the liberation, he wouldn't touch her or let her touch him. Now Azareen's hearts seemed to pause in their rhythm, waiting to see what he would do.

For a moment, he only fell still. She watched him look down at their hands—at hers inside his much bigger one, both of them scarred and callused, a far cry from the young hands that had known each other so well. She saw him swallow, and close his eyes, and then gently, gently fold his fingers over hers.

And when her hearts resumed beating, she imagined she could feel a spill of light into the veins that carried her spirit.

＊ ＊ ＊

The Godslayer's mother, Suheyla, stood in her garden courtyard and lifted her face to feel the sun. She closed her eyes when she did it, though, so she wouldn't have to see the citadel.

She couldn't believe the sweet young man who'd been living in her home was up there right now, that he was one of them. She hadn't witnessed the transformation. She'd missed everything—an old woman can't go running through the streets!—so it had the feel of a tall tale to her. She just couldn't picture Lazlo blue. What did it mean? What would happen now? She couldn't feel the shape of it, but it was clear that everything would change. It was hard to think of tomorrow, though, when grief spat like grease in the pit of her belly.

Yesterday she'd discovered she had a grandchild, living—a grandchild who was half monster, yes, but the blood of her blood nonetheless. She hadn't sorted out how to feel about it until the girl was dead. Now she knew: She wanted her. And it was too late.

She busied herself with her usual routine, like any other day, as though the streets weren't choked with people flooding out of the city like fleas deserting a corpse.

Weep wasn't a corpse, and Suheyla wasn't a flea. All her old fears persisted, but she just couldn't add Lazlo to them, blue skin or not. Of all the possibilities laid out like a feast of uncertainty and doom, there was simply no scenario in which Lazlo Strange hurt Weep, or anybody in it.

She surveyed her sad garden, so long starved of sun. She might make something of it now, she thought. Oh, she'd need to go out into the countryside for cuttings, and that wasn't happening today. But she could make it ready. She could do that.

Suheyla rolled up her sleeves, and got to work.

*　*　*

"What's that?" Calixte asked.

Thyon turned to her, expecting her to be looking up at the citadel, but she wasn't. She was pointing down into the sinkhole.

"What?" he asked, squinting where she pointed.

The sinking of the anchor had sheared right through the crust of earth beneath the city, exposing layers of stone and sediment, like an excavation. The Godslayer had told them that the gods had set the anchors down with precision, crushing the buildings beneath them, "which happened to include," as he had said, "the university and library, the Tizerkane garrison, and the royal palace."

Which had this been? It was impossible to tell from the layers of rubble ground down by the anchor's weight. But what Calixte was pointing at was *beneath* those layers, where, if you looked, you could make out the remnants of foundations, and the suggestion of deeper subterranean levels. Was it possible they hadn't all caved in?

"There," she said. "You can just see the corner of it. It looks like..."

Thyon saw. He finished her sentence with her. In unison, they said, "A door."

9

A DEAD GOD'S CLOSET

They didn't simply burn the body and have done with it. "You need to honor this good vessel," Great Ellen told Sarai, "the same as you would with a loved one you'd lost."

It would be a strange sort of funeral, with Sarai's own ghost attending, but it had been a strange sort of life, so why should death be any different? Great Ellen took charge, as was her way. She sent Less Ellen to the kitchens for water, soap, a soft cloth. "Scissors, too," she called after her before turning to Ruby and Sparrow. "You two, fetch a clean slip from Sarai's dressing room."

"What color would you like, Sarai?" asked Sparrow, and the question, so seemingly ordinary, was surreal, because the slip wasn't for *her*, but her body.

It was only a week since Sarai had chided Ruby for burning up her own slip after Feral drenched her with a rain shower. "We won't live long enough to run out of dresses," Ruby had said then, and her nonchalance had shocked Sarai. But now that prophecy was fulfilled, for her at least, and it struck her that she was through with her dressing room and all her dead mother's things. Or she would be, after this. One last time her body needed to be dressed.

"White," she said. She would be burned in white.

The girls went off to fetch the slip and Great Ellen turned to the boys. "Feral," she said, "won't you please show our guest where he can get himself cleaned up?"

Lazlo objected. He wanted to stay with Sarai, but was made to understand in no uncertain terms that it wouldn't be decent, not while they washed the body, on top of which he was filthy himself. So he acquiesced, parting from Sarai with difficulty, and followed Feral inside.

It was his first sight of the citadel's interior, and the first thing he noticed was the living wall of orchids that Sparrow had grown to soften the effect of so much metal. It couldn't be disguised, though. Everything was metal here—walls, floors, ceilings, fixtures, furniture. So much metal, all mesarthium, and all of it seemed to be holding its breath, waiting for him to awaken it. He didn't know what to do with the feeling. It was overwhelming. It felt like *claiming*—the metal claiming him, or he it? Of course this whole vast otherworldly citadel didn't *belong to him*, but . . . he couldn't shake the feeling that it was somehow *his*, eager to yield itself up to him.

Ghosts stood at attention against the wall: some old men, a girl. They were stiff, facing forward, and didn't—couldn't—turn their heads to watch the young men walk in. Their eyes rolled to the side, though, showing too much white. The sight was disturbing. Lazlo saw Feral glance at them and look quickly away.

"This is the gallery," said Feral, leading Lazlo through the big room with its long mesarthium table. "Kitchen's through here. We bathe in the rain room." He stopped in the doorway and looked Lazlo up and down. "I don't suppose you have a change of clothes."

Lazlo held his arms out to his sides to show that, of course, he carried nothing.

It wasn't the first time. When Lazlo Strange changed his life, he went with only the clothes on his back. This was the third time—or, he supposed, the fourth, if you counted his journey as a baby, though he couldn't take credit for that one. The next had been at thirteen, when he stowed away at the Great Library, and then again when he rode out through the gates with Eril-Fane. Lazlo's chances came without warning, and when they did, he didn't dither, and he didn't stop to pack.

"We'll find you something," said Feral, who was torn between wariness and awe of him.

He led Lazlo deeper into the citadel, giving him a rudimentary tour. "That way to the sinister arm," he said, pointing left. Lazlo knew that *sinister* meant "left" in the language of heraldry, but something in Feral's tone made him think the word applied in more ways than that, even before he added gruffly, "We don't go there."

He led the way to the dexter arm instead. It was a long corridor, sleek and tubelike. It curved to the right; Lazlo couldn't see to the end. He realized that he was inside the seraph's right arm.

They passed a door with a curtain strung across it. A pair of ghosts stood guard outside it. "Minya's chambers," said Feral. "They were Skathis's, so they're the biggest."

Along the corridor were several more doors. Feral named them all as they went by. "Sparrow's room. It was Korako's before. Ruby's was Letha's. Here's mine. It was Vanth's. My father." He said the word without feeling. At each door there were guards, and he continued to look past them. "And here's Ikirok's. No one uses it, so I guess it's yours."

His? Lazlo hadn't thought as far as having a room here, of *living* here. His mind flashed to Sarai. He wanted to be where she was. As though Feral read the thought, he pointed ahead. "Sarai's is next. The last one." There was a kind of furtive curiosity in the younger man's manner. He clearly wanted to ask a question, and finally he came out with it. "How do you know her?" he blurted. "How does she know you? When...*how* could you have possibly met?"

"In dreams," Lazlo told him. "I didn't know she was real until the silk sleigh, when she saved us."

"That was you." Feral hadn't realized. He hadn't gotten a good look that day, and of course, Lazlo had still been human. Shame flashed through him. Sarai had tried to persuade him to summon clouds so that the craft couldn't reach the citadel, but he'd been too afraid to defy Minya. If it had been left up to him, Lazlo would be dead.

And if Lazlo was dead, he realized with a queasy lurch in his gut, they'd *all* have died last night. He swallowed down the sickening feeling. "But I didn't think people could see her," he said.

It was true. Normally, when Sarai entered a dream, she was an invisible presence there. For years she'd felt like a phantom. And then Lazlo. His first sight of her was emblazoned on his memory: a beautiful blue girl with wild red-brown hair and a slash of black paint from temple to temple, her blue eyes vivid as she stared at him with unmasked intrigue.

"I can see her," he said. See her, touch her, hold her. Last night: the feel of her beneath him, her body full against him. She'd clasped his head with both hands, twining her fingers through his hair as he kissed a path down her throat. How real it had been—as real as anything that ever happened when he was awake.

"I wonder why," said Feral. "Maybe it's because you're not human."

"Can *you* see her?" Lazlo asked.

Feral shrugged. "Don't know. She's never come into my dreams. Any of ours. Minya forbade it."

"And you obey her."

Feral let out a short laugh. "Always," he said. "Do you blame us?"

"Not at all," said Lazlo. "She's terrifying."

Feral pushed aside the curtain in Ikirok's doorway and motioned Lazlo to precede him. He did, thinking how the curtains—linen bedsheets rigged in place—were incongruous with the sleek design of the citadel. "There aren't doors?" he asked.

"There were. The metal responded to touch, apparently. The Ellens say the doors could recognize those authorized to enter. But it all froze when Skathis died, and it's been like this ever since." He cocked his head to one side. "Maybe you could make them work again."

Lazlo ran a hand down the edge of the doorframe. It was smooth, cool, and . . . waiting. He could feel the scheme of energies that governed it as surely as he could feel the metal itself, and he knew that he could make the doors work, that he could make the citadel fly, that he could bring this whole immense seraph to "life" as easily as he had awakened Rasalas.

"I could try," he said, because to put his confidence into words felt arrogant.

"Well, later," said Feral. He showed Lazlo to the dressing room. "Basically, if your thing is wearing twenty pounds of stiff jeweled brocade with fox skulls for epaulets and knife-tipped boots, today's your lucky day."

"Um," said Lazlo, getting his first sight of a god's wardrobe. "Not really."

"In that case, there are underclothes."

As the girls wore slips, so did Feral wear linen undershirts and cut-to-the-knee breeches. His were Vanth's, and he showed Lazlo where to find Ikirok's. The cloth was simple and very fine. "There are pajamas, too," Feral said, holding up a silk sleeve in deep, shining crimson stitched with silver thread and seed pearls. "They're a bit much." He dropped the sleeve. "Have a look. There's sure to be something that works."

Lazlo had never imagined a day he'd be rummaging through a dead god's closet, but then, it was far from the strangest thing to happen to him today. He didn't fuss. He just pulled out a set of linen underclothes like Feral's and held them up to himself.

"A bit short, maybe," said Feral with a critical eye. "Skathis's would probably fit you better." Matter-of-factly, he added, "I suppose you're his son."

Lazlo almost dropped the clothes. *"What?"*

"Well, you have his gift, so that's my guess. You could claim his things if you wanted. It's not like Minya needs them. Gods, she hasn't changed her clothes...*ever.* But today's not really the day to go knocking on her door. So to speak. Since, you know, there are no doors."

"I'll make do," said Lazlo.

"I wouldn't expect any sisterly affection from her, but I suppose you've already gathered that."

Again, Lazlo was stunned. *"Sisterly . . . ?"*

Feral raised his eyebrows. "She's Skathis's daughter. So if you're his son..." He shrugged.

Lazlo stared. Could it be true? Was Minya his *sister*? The idea floored him almost more than his transformation, and he didn't properly hear the next several things Feral said to him. He had been a very small boy when he'd given up hope of ever having family, the monks having spared no effort in impressing on the boys how utterly alone they were in the world. Lazlo had channeled all his yearning into an equally impossible dream: going to the Unseen City and finding out what happened there. Well, here he was. So much for impossible. Had he found family, too?

"Bring those," said Feral, gesturing to the clothes. "I'll show you where the bath is."

They met Ruby and Sparrow in the corridor, coming from Sarai's room with her white slip in hand, and they all walked back together. A shyness overtook them in Lazlo's presence. Even Ruby was subdued. A couple of times she almost blurted out questions, but stopped each time, and Feral and Sparrow were surprised to see her blushing.

For his part, Lazlo would have welcomed an opening. These three were Sarai's family, even if not by blood, and he wanted them to like him. But he had scarcely more practice at conversing with strangers than they did, and couldn't think where to begin.

In the gallery, Sparrow parted from them to carry the slip to Sarai, while Ruby went with Feral and Lazlo to help prepare the bath. It was awkward for Lazlo, being catered to—until, that is, he watched Feral hold up his hands and summon a cloud out of nothingness, right above the big copper drum that served them as a tub. The air grew dense, carrying with it a thick jungle scent, and for a span of minutes the only sound was rain pelting metal.

Lazlo smiled at the wonder of it. "I've never seen a trick like that before."

"Well, it's nothing like your gift," said Feral, humble. "It's only rain."

And here, Ruby should have jumped in to disagree. It's tacky to sing one's own praises; your friends ought to do it for you. Your lover absolutely should, but Ruby was clueless, her attention all on Lazlo, so Feral was forced to add, "Though of course we'd have all died ages ago if we didn't have water."

"Water's important," agreed Lazlo.

"So's fire," said Ruby, not to be outdone. She held out her hands, and both kindled into fireballs in an instant. It was a flashier show than she usually put on when heating bathwater. Instead of pressing her hands against the side of the tub, which would have done perfectly well, she plunged them into the water itself, sending up great jets of steam where fire met water, and swiftly bringing it to a boil.

"Are you trying to cook him?" asked Feral, producing another cloud. There was no jungle scent to this one. It filled the room with a clean, cold tang, dosed the hot water with a flurry of snow, and brought it down to a reasonable temperature.

Ruby, her lips pressed thin, summoned a spark to her fingertips and flicked it, unseen, at Feral's rear end. He managed to stifle his yelp, and favored her with a glare.

"This is amazing," said Lazlo, marveling. "Thank you both."

"It's not much," said Feral, one hand to the back of his neck. "This used to be a meat locker. It isn't very fine. There are baths in the rooms, but they don't work anymore...."

"This is excellent," Lazlo assured him. "Until I came to Weep I never had a proper bath in my life. In winter, when I was a boy, we had to chip the ice off the bucket before we could wash." He gave Ruby a smile. "You'd have been very welcome there. Well," he reconsidered, "except that the monks would have thought you were a demon."

75

"Maybe I *am*," she said, locating her sauciness, her eyes glimmering with flame.

"Anyway," said Feral, a touch more loudly than necessary. "The soap's just there. We'll leave you to it."

They went out. Feral drew the curtain behind them, and Lazlo considered it. He wondered if it would be rude to close the door. He decided it would be, since they'd lived all their lives without doors, and it would give the impression that he didn't trust them to give him privacy.

In fact, it was a near thing. Feral and Ruby had reached the gallery when Ruby said, "I'll be back in a minute. I just have to go to the kitchen."

Feral raised an inquisitive eyebrow. "Oh? What for?"

She was evasive. "I want to tell Less Ellen something."

"I'll come with you," he said.

"No need to trouble yourself."

"It's no trouble."

"Well, it's trouble to me," she declared, beginning to scowl. "It's private."

"Funny you should use that word, 'private,'" said Feral, who knew perfectly what she was about. "It's almost as though you know what it means."

She rolled her eyes. "Fine," she said, giving up the mission. "I was just going to peep a little."

"Ruby. Peeping's not okay. Surely you know that."

He sounded so condescending. She shrugged. "I've peeped on *you* often enough, and you never minded."

"You've *what*?" Feral demanded. "How could I mind if I didn't know?"

76

"It didn't hurt you, did it?"

He covered his face with his hands. "Ruby," he groaned, censorious, though secretly a little pleased. He'd have been jealous if she'd tried to spy on Lazlo and not ever on him.

"I suppose you've never peeped on *me?*" she asked.

"Of course I haven't. *I* respect the curtains."

"Or you just don't care," she said, and there was a note of hurt in her voice.

Though he'd grown up in a nest of girls, Feral still didn't understand them. *"What?"*

Ruby was remembering what Sparrow had said to her last night, before the citadel's lurch had tipped them into chaos and grief. To her own assertion that if Sparrow had been the one to go to him, she'd have had Feral instead, Sparrow had replied, "If that's true, then I really don't want him. I only want someone who wants only me." Well, Ruby did, too. In fact, she wanted someone who would look at her the way Lazlo looked at Sarai, and not some passive manboy who'd go along because you literally put yourself in his hands.

"If I'd respected your curtain," she told him now, "we'd never have done anything. *I* came to *you*, I'm sure you remember. I climbed into your lap. I *made* you kiss me. It's obvious you don't care, and that's fine." She lifted her chin. "It was just something to do in case we died, and look, we're still alive." She gave him a brittle smile. "You don't have to worry anymore. I'll leave you alone now."

Feral had no idea where this was coming from. It was true that she'd initiated everything, but that didn't mean he wanted it to stop. "Are you angry that I never spied on you naked?" he asked, incredulous.

"I'm not angry," Ruby replied. "I'm just through with this. At least

77

it was good practice, for when I meet someone who gives a damn." And she tossed her wild dark hair so that he had to dodge it or be hit in the face, and then she walked away.

"Fine," Feral said to her back, but his head was spinning and he hardly knew what had just happened. One thing he was almost certain of, though, was that he wasn't happy at all.

❧ 10 ❧

GHOSTS DON'T BURN

Sarai dipped the sponge in the basin of water Less Ellen had prepared. It smelled of rosemary and nectar, like the soap she'd used all her life. She held the sponge in trembling hands and looked down at herself.

No. She squeezed her eyes shut. That wasn't her *self*. It was her body. *She* was herself. *She* remained. She opened her eyes again. Her mind reeled. She was there and she was here, undead and unalive, kneeling beside herself in the flowers.

How can you kneel beside yourself? How can you wash your own corpse?

The same way you do anything, she told herself firmly. You just do. She'd been washing her body all her life. She could do it this one last time.

"Let me help you," said Sparrow, her voice raw as a wound.

"It's all right," said Sarai. "I'm all right."

Great Ellen had cut the slip away with scissors, and the body lay naked now, its familiar terrain made strange by this new perspective.

The jut of hip bones, the pink areolae, the divot of the navel all seemed to belong to some other girl. Reaching out, Sarai squeezed the sponge and let a trickle of water run down her dead chest. And then, gently, as though afraid of causing pain, she began to wash the blood away.

When she had finished, the water in the basin was muddy red and she was, too, from holding her own dead head in her lap to rinse the blood from its hair. She looked down at the wet, stained silk clinging to her legs, and grappled with the knowledge that it was all illusion. The slip wasn't wet. The slip wasn't *there*, and neither was the body beneath it. Everything about her was illusion now. She looked and felt exactly as she had before, but none of it was real, and none of it was fixed. She knew that this ghostflesh copy was an unconscious projection—her mind's re-creation of her accustomed self—and that she didn't have to stay this way.

Ghosts weren't bound by the same rules as the living. They could shape themselves however they liked. Less Ellen, who in life had lost an eye, in her ghostself restored it. Great Ellen was ever-changing, a master of the medium. She might wear singing birds as hats, or sprout an extra arm when need arose, or turn her head into a hawk's.

As children, enchanted by their nurses' transformations, Sarai and the others had liked to say what they would do if they were ghosts. It hadn't been morbid, just fun, like the most amazing game of dress-up ever. You could have ravid fangs or a scorpion's tail, or turn yourself miniature, like a songbird. You could be striped or feathered or made of glass, translucent as a window. You could even be invisible. It had seemed a grand game back then.

Now that it came to it, though, Sarai just wanted to be herself.

She brushed her fingers over the sodden, discolored silk of her lap, willing it clean and dry. And, just like that, it was.

"Well done," said Great Ellen. "It takes most of us a deal of time to figure out how to do that. The trick is to believe it, and that's quite a hurdle for most."

Not for Sarai. "It's like in dreams," she said.

"You have an advantage there."

But in dreams, Sarai had control over everything, not just the fabric of her self. Cleaning blood out of silk was nothing. She could turn day to night and up to down. "In dreams," she said with longing, "I could bring myself back to life."

"Would that you could," said Great Ellen, reaching out to stroke her hair. "My poor, lovely girl. It'll be all right. You'll see. It isn't *life*, but it has its merits."

"Such as being a slave to Minya?" Sarai asked bitterly.

The nurse let out a sigh. "I hope not."

"There *is* no hope. You know how she is."

"I do indeed, but I'm not giving up on her and neither should you. Come, now. Let's get your body dressed."

The girls had fetched the white slip; they'd chosen a halter style to cover the wound. It took all of them to put it on, maneuvering stiff limbs, lifting and arranging. They lay the body with its arms at its sides, orchids tucked all around it, and fanned out the cinnamon hair to dry in the sun before studding its ripples with blooms. It was easier to look at now that the evidence of its violent end was disguised, but it didn't lessen the ache of loss.

Sarai was glad when Lazlo returned. He was dressed, like Feral, in clothing of the citadel, his dark hair clean on his shoulders, shining damp in the sunlight. She drank in again the sight of him blue, and could almost imagine they were back in a dream, alive and full of wonder, holding hands after the mahalath transformed them.

"Are you all right?" he asked, such sweetness and sorrow in his dreamer's gray eyes that she felt his sorrow absorb some of her own. She nodded and was able to smile, a small gladness alive even inside her loss. He pressed a kiss to her brow, and the warmth of his lips flowed into her, giving her strength—which she needed for what came next.

The fire.

Ruby didn't want to do it. She didn't want to touch the body. She didn't want to burn it. Her eyes were pools of fire; when she wept, the tears hissed into steam. She was shaking. Sparrow steadied her, but with what she had to do, no one would be able to stay near her.

"Should we wait for Minya?" she asked—anything to buy time— and they all looked to the arcade, their breath catching, as though the mention of the little girl might summon her. But the arcade was empty.

"No," said Sarai, who couldn't forget how it had felt to hang in the air, powerless over her self. She'd been at odds with Minya for years, but they'd gone beyond "at odds" now, and every minute the little girl stayed away was another minute of doom forestalled.

"I'll help you," she told Ruby, and they knelt down together. She placed her hands atop Ruby's where they lay on the body's smooth skin. And she kept them there, even when Ruby kindled. They called her Bonfire. This was why. The flame burst into being; it blazed hot and white. It started in her hands but leapt like a living thing, engulfing the corpse in seconds. The heat was intense. The others had to back away, but Sarai stayed with Ruby to share the burden of this terrible task. She felt heat, but no pain. Ghosts don't burn, but corpses do. It was over in under a minute.

The flames rushed back to Ruby's hands. She absorbed them, and they all saw: there was no body now beneath her palms, no orchids, no cinnamon hair. The bower was untouched, though; the white blossoms all remained. They were anadne, Letha's sacred flower, from which, before all this chaos, Sarai's lull had been brewed to keep her safe from dreams. Their pale petals were tinged pink from bloody bathwater, but they lived, while where the body had lain there was naught but absence, like a gap in the world where something precious had been and now was lost. Even the scent of singed flesh was weak, the immolation having been so hot and fast, and the breeze was already sweeping it away.

Sarai sobbed. Lazlo stepped up behind her and wrapped his arms around her, holding her against him. She twisted so she was facing him and wept against his chest. Everyone clustered close. No eyes were dry.

"There, now, love," said Great Ellen. "You're all right. You're still with us, and that's what matters."

At least the dissonance of two Sarais had resolved. There was only one now. Her body was gone. Only her ghost remained.

* * *

The Ellens shepherded them to the table. They weren't hungry, but they were indisputably empty. It had been many hours since they ate or slept, and in their numbness, they let themselves be led.

They cast wary glances at the head of the table, but Minya still did not appear.

It wasn't a proper meal. With the events of the night and morning, the Ellens hadn't prepared one. There was only a loaf and a pot of jam, representing their two inexhaustible resources: kimril and plums. The others took slices and spread them with jam, but when the tray came to Sarai, she just looked at it. She could no longer consume food, but she was still prey to the habitual sensations of life, and a feeling like hunger stirred in her. Before she had time to feel sorry for herself, Great Ellen came up behind her.

"Watch," she said, reaching for the bread. She cut a slice, and picked it up—or seemed to, anyway. It came away in her hand, and yet remained where it lay. She had conjured a phantom slice, upon which she proceeded to spoon phantom jam before lifting it to her mouth and taking a dainty bite. If you weren't watching closely, you wouldn't even notice the real food had stayed on the plate.

Sarai did as Great Ellen did, and took a bite of phantom bread. It tasted just as it always had, and she knew she was eating her memory of it. She watched Lazlo's face as he took a bite of the real thing, encountering kimril for the first time—the nutrient-rich tuber that was their staple—and laughed a little as his expression registered the startling absence of taste.

"Lazlo," she said with grave formality, "meet kimril."

"This..." said Lazlo, striving to keep his voice neutral, "is what you live on?"

"Not anymore," said Sarai, a wry twist to her lips. "You're welcome to my portion."

"I'm not very hungry," he demurred, and the rest of them laughed, enjoying this acknowledgment of their private torment.

"Wait'll you try it in soup," Ruby said. "It's purgatory in a spoon."

"It's the salt," lamented Great Ellen. "We've herbs, and that helps, but with salt running low, there just isn't a lot you can do to help kimril."

"I think we might manage to procure some salt," ventured Lazlo.

Ruby pounced on the notion. "And sugar!" she said. "Or, better yet, *cake*. The bakeries must be empty now, cakes going stale in the cases." They had all witnessed the exodus from Weep. "Go and get them." She was deadly serious. "Get them *all*."

"I didn't mean right now," said Lazlo, laughing a little.

"Why not?"

"Ruby, really," said Sarai. "Now's hardly the time for raiding bakeries."

"It's fine for you to say. You could turn *that* into cake if you wanted." She indicated the phantom bread Sarai held in her hand.

Sarai looked at it. "You make a good point," she said, and transformed it. In an instant it was cake, and Ruby gasped at the sight. It was three layers tall, white as snow, with a froth of cream filling and the palest pink icing piped into flowers. Sparrow and Feral gasped, too. It seemed so real, as though they ought to be able to reach out and take it, but they knew better, and just stared—or, in Ruby's case, glared. "*I* deserve cake," she sniffed. "After what I just had to do."

"It's true," said Sarai. "You do." Though she felt that the ravid's share of pity was hers in this situation. "All things considered, I'd rather have real bread than imaginary cake." She took a bite. They all watched hungrily, as though they could taste it by witnessing her expression.

"How is it?" Sparrow asked, yearning in her voice.

Sarai shrugged and vanished it, feeling a little wicked. "Nothing special, just sweet." She looked to Lazlo with a secret smile. "Like eating cake in dreams."

He smiled back, and they all could see that there were memories shimmering between them. "What dreams?" asked Feral.

"What *cake*?" demanded Ruby.

But Sarai had no will for storytelling. She wished, rather, to spend whatever time she had left, if not *living*, then at least doing and being and feeling. Never before had time seemed so like currency, each moment a coin that could be well- or ill-spent, or even, if one wasn't careful, wasted and lost. She looked to Minya's chair at the head of the table. Even empty, it seemed to reign over them. Ominously, the quell board was there, all set up and ready for a game. *I'm good at games*, she heard in her mind. She wanted to dash the board to the floor.

If only it could be that easy to put an end to all of Minya's games.

"You must be tired," she said to Lazlo, rising from her chair. "I know I am."

"Tired?" asked Ruby. "Can ghosts sleep?"

Feral shook his head at her, his expression sour. "How can you have lived your whole life with ghosts and never wondered that before?"

"I've wondered. I've just never asked."

"Ghosts can do everything the living can do," Sparrow told her, looking to the Ellens for confirmation. "As long as they believe it."

"And," Sarai added, "as long as Minya lets us."

But she wasn't thinking of sleep in any case. As she took Lazlo's hand and led him from the gallery, sleep was the last thing on her mind.

11

CANNIBALS AND VIRGINS

"We should come back with some rope," said Thyon, eyeing the crumbling edges of the sinkhole.

"While you do that," said Calixte, "I'll just go down and open the door."

"It isn't—" *Safe*, he was going to say, but there wasn't much point. Calixte had already jumped into the hole.

Thyon let out a hard breath and watched her, seeming weightless as she passed between handholds or simply leapt, landing on narrow ledges with virtually no sound of impact. In a matter of seconds she was down in the pit, crossing it in little skips, like a child crossing a stream on stepping-stones. Except the stepping-stones were veins of mesarthium gleaming amid chunks of broken rock and shifting piles of earth, beneath which an underground river raged.

Thyon held his breath, watching her, half expecting the ground to give way and suck her into the dark. But it didn't, and then she was scaling the far side of the sinkhole, if possible even faster than she'd descended. She paused, only yards below the door, to look over her shoulder at him and call up, "Well?"

Well indeed. What to do? Go for rope, knowing she'd open the door while he was gone and have the discovery to herself? Or follow her and take the risk of plunging into the Uzumark to be swept away flailing and drown in the dark?

Neither choice appealed.

"If you're afraid," called Calixte, "I can just tell you what I find!"

Gritting his teeth, Thyon paced the edge, looking for a place to go over. Calixte had made it look easy. It wasn't. Where she'd leapt, he skidded, kicking off a minor avalanche, only to slide into his own dirt plume and choke on the laden air. He reached out to catch himself on a protruding rock, but it came away in his hand and he pitched off balance, only saving himself from tumbling headlong into the pit by sprawling out like a starfish. Lying there hugging the dirt, his mouth full of grit, he seethed with resentment for the bounding girl who'd lured him into danger, as though his life were worth no more than hers, to be thrown away on senseless risk.

"Get up," she called. "I'll wait for you. Go slow. We aren't all so blessed to be descended from spiders."

Spiders?

Thyon picked himself up—sort of. He kept on hugging the slope and made his way down like that, getting dirtier with every step. Crossing the pit, he found leaping unnecessary. He set his feet on a seam of mesarthium and followed it, windmilling his arms for balance. Calixte's leaping had been showmanship, he concluded, or else the sheer joy of motion. Reaching the slope below her, he looked up and saw that she had, indeed, waited.

She was pretending to have fallen asleep.

Peeved, he picked up a pebble and threw it at her. He missed, but she heard it plink against the ledge of rock and cracked open an eye midsnore. "You'll regret that, faranji," she said with equanimity.

"Faranji? You're a faranji, too."

"Not like you." She picked herself up from her pretend-slumber slump and dusted the dirt from her behind. "I mean, there are faranji, and there are *faranji*." On the second *faranji*, she grimaced and raised her eyebrows, indicating a specially pernicious breed of outsider, in which category, clearly, she placed him. She helpfully pointed out a foothold to him while saying, "There's the kind of guest who's honored to be invited, and the kind who believes he's bestowing honor by accepting."

He stepped on the foothold and reached for a rock she indicated next. "The kind who expresses interest in the culture and language," she went on. "And the kind who disdains it as barbaric, and insists on an entire camel to carry foodstuffs from their own land, as though they might perish on native fare."

"That wasn't me," argued Thyon. It was Ebliz Tod who'd done that. So all right, he'd brought *some* rations, but they were in case of emergency, and hardly a whole camel's worth. He'd had a lot of gear, transporting a working alchemical laboratory. Any extra camels were well justified. "And I've never called anything barbaric," he said. That charge he could cleanly dispute.

Calixte shrugged. "Thoughts count, too, Nero. If you think you've concealed yours, you're mistaken."

His impulse was to angrily dismiss everything she'd said, but could he? The truth was, he *had* been sensible of bestowing upon Weep the honor of his presence, and why not? Any city in the world would be grateful to host him. As to their language, that brought up more complicated feelings. Back in Zosma, he'd learned enough from Strange's books to make a fair greeting and impress Eril-Fane...that is, until Strange had gone and opened his mouth and outshone him. It only made sense. It was Strange's life work. Of course he spoke better than Thyon could after such brief study. Had Thyon thought he *wouldn't* speak up?

He *had* thought that. He'd thought Strange would meekly subside while Thyon stole his work and his dream, and he'd been wrong.

Instead, Strange left with the Godslayer and his warriors, and when Thyon next saw him, several months later, he'd practically become one of them, riding a spectral, wearing clothes like theirs, and speaking their language fluently. After that, Thyon had told himself it was beneath him. He wasn't about to suffer in comparison to a foundling librarian. He was the golden godson. If they wanted to address him, *they* should do the work, not he. And so he hadn't learned any more of their language than he could help.

He found the next handhold himself and hoisted himself higher. "You're the good kind of faranji, I suppose."

"Oh yes," she said. "Very good. I even *taste* good, or so I'm told."

He was focused on not falling to his death, and so he missed the mischief in her voice. "Taste," he scoffed. "I suppose they're cannibals. Who's calling them barbarians now?"

Calixte laughed with delighted disbelief, and it was only then, too late, that Thyon took her meaning. Oh gods. *Taste*. He flung back his head to look up at her, nearly losing his balance in the process. She laughed harder at the shock on his face. "Cannibals!" she repeated. "That's good. I'm going to start calling Tzara that. *My sweet cannibal*. Can I tell you a secret?" She whispered the rest, wide-eyed and zestful: "I'm a cannibal, too."

Thyon flushed with mortification. "I'll thank you to keep your private matters to yourself."

"You're blushing like a maiden," said Calixte. "Honestly, you're as innocent as Lazlo. Who'd have thought it?"

"It's not innocence, it's propriety—"

"If your next sentence starts with 'a lady would never,' you can choke on it, Nero. *I'm no lady.*"

The wicked relish with which she disavowed the word robbed Thyon of any easy insult, so he put his energy into swinging himself up to the little lip of earth on which she stood. Now he was level with her and could hardly avoid her merry eyes, though he tried his best, and blushed anew.

"*Are* you a maiden?" Calixte asked. "You can tell me."

A *maiden*? He kept right on climbing. Did she mean a virgin? Was she really asking him that? It defied belief. The doorway was nearly within reach now, and she was still busy mocking him.

"It's nothing to be ashamed of," she told his back. "Plenty of fine gentlemen wait until marriage."

"And you've been acquainted with 'plenty of fine gentlemen,' have you?"

"Well, no," Calixte admitted. And then, as though a new thought had occurred to her, she asked with a note of piquant curiosity, "Have *you*?"

Her innuendo struck him, and it stunned him. In Zosma, such a suggestion could only end in a duel. Thyon flashed hot and cold. He wore his dueling blade at his side as always, but one did not fight women. He had to struggle to remind himself it wasn't an insult here, much less a matter of honor, especially considering the source. He shot her a warning look and kept climbing, reaching the door ahead of her.

It was blocked by several large rocks. "We should have brought tools," he said.

"Tools," scoffed Calixte. "Tools are for people with nothing better to do than think things through and make sensible plans."

Thyon raised his eyebrows. "And...what sort of people are *we* at the moment?"

"The foolish sort who do things like this." She folded herself up like a piece of paper and slipped into the narrow gap between one large rock and the slope. Thyon couldn't understand how a body could *do* that. It hardly seemed decent to watch. Somehow her knees were *behind her shoulders*. Her back was flat to the slope, her feet to the rock, pushing. She bit her lip white with the strain, and the rock creaked, shifted, and plunged over the edge.

Thyon shot out a hand to make sure she didn't plunge with it.

"Thank you, good sir," she said, dropping quite an elegant curtsy on the narrow foothold they shared.

He snatched back his hand and wiped it off on the side of his dirty trousers.

The rest of the rocks were smaller, but still Thyon's hands were bleeding by the time they'd cleared them away. The door they uncovered was stout, wooden, and, like everything else in Weep, carved. It depicted a single great tree, roots to branches, and each leaf was a lidded eye that seemed to watch them, lazy and judgmental.

It would have been frustrating to find the door locked after all that, but the knob turned in Thyon's hand, and between the two of them, they were able to grind it open on rusted hinges—

—to reveal a corridor, its ceiling inlaid with glavestone that lit it up like morning. Dust hung in the air, and the smell was...well, it was *stale*, much staler than any air Thyon had breathed before, and in it were undertones of long-ago death, trapped bodies, old bones, but there was leather, too, and crumbling paper and dust. Thyon knew this smell. For all that he was a duke's son, born in a castle,

92

with a palace of his own gifted him by the queen, he was a scholar, too, and he *lived* this smell. It was unmistakable. Universal.

It was *books*.

He gave a laugh that spun the dust in front of his face and sent ripples through the heavy air. "It's the library," he said, and his very first thought was that Strange would give a limb to get to wander in this place. "It's the ancient library of Weep."

12

WITCHLIGHT AND RUE

Sarai held her curtain for Lazlo, and drew it closed behind him. There were ghosts in the corridor, and more out on her terrace. She drew that curtain, too, then paused. She looked at the doorways, then at Lazlo, and, blushing, asked, "Can you close them?"

Her voice was low, warm, and silken, and Lazlo blushed, too. This was real. It wasn't a dream, some filament spun between them across space. It was him facing her, his real hand clasping her ghostflesh one. They wouldn't be wrenched apart by sunrise, or the sad demise of a fragile moth, or an alchemist pelting stones. They were here, awake, together.

They *could* be wrenched apart by Minya, though, at literally any moment, and their hearts felt ragged, frayed by desperation and the thoughtless drub of time.

Lazlo shut the doors.

If it had been a dream, the room could have melted away, transforming into some other scene, without metal walls and ghosts at the doors. Sarai would have loved to re-create last night's dream and slip right back where she had been: to the bed with its feather down, and Lazlo's weight on top of her, a revelation of sensation. His mouth would be on her shoulder, the strap of her slip eased aside.

But to will it was one thing. To *do* it was another. Their dream-smith skills wouldn't serve them now, and for the moment they only stood there, their gazes mingling witchlight and rue.

Lazlo swallowed. "So this is your room," he said, and tore his eyes from her to look around. He noticed at once its central feature: the huge bed, bigger than his whole room at the Great Library. It was raised on a dais and curtained like a stage, and his eyes grew wide at the sight of it.

"My mother's," Sarai said quickly. "I don't sleep there."

"No?"

"No. I have a smaller bed back by the dressing room."

Talking about beds wasn't helping. It made their desire too transparent. While Sarai might have silently led Lazlo there, now that it was spoken aloud, it seemed far too bold. They both grew bashful, as though all that had passed between them in dreams remained there, and these bodies with their awkward arms would have to learn it all over again.

"It's actually beautiful," said Lazlo, still looking around the room. The ceiling was soaring and fan-vaulted, the walls much more ornate than anything he'd seen in the citadel so far. They reminded him of the carvings down in Weep, though these, of course, were wrought of mesarthium, not stone. "Skathis did all this?" he asked, reaching out to trace a songbird with his finger. It was one of hundreds, and stunning in its perfection, perching among vines and lilies equally lifelike, as though they were the real thing dipped in metal, gilded in molten mesarthium.

Sarai nodded, reaching out to stroke the eye ridge of a life-size spectral in bas-relief. Its antlers projected from the wall; she had used them as a hook to hang her robe. "It makes him harder to imagine. Shouldn't all his creations have been as hideous as Rasalas was?"

Nothing in the room was hideous. It was a luxurious temple wrought of water-smooth metal. Lazlo skimmed his fingertips over a sparrow and freed it. Buoying it on the same magnetic field as the citadel itself, he shook its little wings and gave it flight.

From Sarai's lips came a soft sound of wonder. Lazlo loved it, and wanted to hear it again, so he quickened more birds and they came and flew in a ring around her. Her laugh was music. She held out her free hand, the one not still clasped in his, and one of the birds alighted on her palm.

"I wish I could make it sing for you," said Lazlo, but that was beyond his power.

A new bird appeared beside it, coalescing out of nowhere. For an instant it startled Lazlo, but then he realized Sarai had made it. Like herself, it was illusion, and flawless: a phantom sparrow, brown and faun, with a little black beak the size and shape of a rose thorn. It did sing. The notes were sweet as summer rain, and it was Lazlo's turn for wonder. These two birds, side by side, represented their new selves, god and ghost, and their new abilities, too. Both had their limitations: Sarai's sparrow could sing but not fly. Lazlo's could fly but not sing.

With a flick of her wrist, she sent them airborne. Hers vanished at once, unable to exist apart from the illusion of her self. Lazlo flew his, and the rest of the flock, to find new perches and fall still.

"How does it work?" he asked her, intrigued. "This transformation business. Are there limits?"

"Only of imagination, I think. Tell me." She waved a hand over herself. "What should I change?"

"*Nothing.*" He breathed a laugh. The idea was so absurd. "You're perfect as you are."

Sarai blushed and looked down. They were drifting across the room, unconsciously—or maybe not—in the direction of the nook behind the dressing room, where Sarai's little bed was tucked out of sight. "Oh, I don't know," she said. "What about wings? Or even just clothes that never belonged to the goddess of despair."

"I have to admit," said Lazlo with a furtive glance down at her pink slip. "I'm rather fond of these clothes."

His voice was warm. Sarai's cheeks warmed, too. "These *under-clothes*, you mean?"

"Is that what they are?" He feigned innocence. "I didn't realize."

Sarai snorted. She touched his sleeve. "I see you also shunned the outerwear of the gods."

"I can change if you like. There's a doublet I'm almost certain is made all of beetle wings."

"That's all right," said Sarai. "Some other time."

"Some formal occasion."

"Yes."

They'd passed the door to the dressing room, into the nook. The bed was there, neatly made and narrow, barely more than a cot.

"There is one thing," Sarai said, her voice going shy.

Lazlo saw her trace a ring around her navel, over the silk of her slip. "Oh?" he asked. The word barely emerged. He swallowed, and drew his eyes back up to hers.

"Do you know about eliliths?" she asked.

"The tattoos?" He knew that girls of Weep received them on their bellies when their bleeding began. He'd never seen one, only the renderings of them engraved on the female Tizerkane's armor.

"I always wanted one," confessed Sarai. "I would see girls who'd gotten theirs, through my moths, I mean, down in the city. They'd lie in their beds and trace the patterns with their fingers, and in their dreams, I could tell that they'd changed, like they'd crossed some boundary and would never be the same. Dreams have auras. I could feel what they were feeling, and the eiliths made them feel... powerful."

She hadn't understood that power when she was a girl. She was beginning to now. Fertility, sexuality, strength, the ability to create and nurture *life*: These were the powers of a woman, and the ink honored them, connecting them with all their foremothers going back hundreds of years. But it was about more than fertility. Sarai sensed it. It was a ripening, yes, but not just for the purpose of bearing children, or being a wife. It represented a claiming of one's self—stepping forth from childhood and all the ways we're shaped by others, to choose and make a new shape, all on one's own.

And she'd wondered: What shape would *she* choose, if she were free to do so?

She'd seen many designs over the years: apple blossoms and daisy chains, seraph wings and runes that spelled out ancient blessings. Since Eril-Fane freed Weep from the gods, the most popular design had been a serpent swallowing its tail: a symbol of destruction and rebirth.

"What would yours be?" Lazlo asked her.

"I don't know." Holding his gaze, she put a hand to his chest and lightly pushed. The bed was just behind him. He couldn't step back and so had no choice but to sit, which was as she'd intended. The mattress was low. He was eye level now with her ribs and had to look up at her face. Like telling a secret, she said, "I had one the night the mahalath changed us."

The mist that made gods and monsters. It had rendered him blue

98

and her brown—the human become god, and the goddess human, so the interlacing blue and brown of their fingers had reversed. And part of Sarai's humanity had been an elilith.

"You did?" Lazlo asked. "What of?"

"I don't know. I knew it was there, but not what it was." When the mahalath came, she had let a deep part of her mind choose her transformation. It had chosen her tattoo as well. "I couldn't very well *look*." She mimed picking up the hem of her slip as though to lift it and peek under.

"I assure you I wouldn't have minded."

They both laughed, but the air was charged with a new intensity. Sarai was still tracing a slow circle round her navel, her gaze never leaving him, and he saw her smile melt into something else. Her teeth caught her lower lip—that delectable lower lip, so plump it was creased down the center, like a ripe apricot—and scraped it in a gentle bite.

"Is it there now?" he asked. Her finger kept tracing its circle, hypnotic. He could hardly hear his own voice.

Sarai nodded, and the moment held them fast. All either of them could think of was Sarai's skin under her slip. Lazlo's palms grew hot. His face did, too. A second ago, she'd mimed lifting her slip, but she made no move to do it. She took a half step toward him. She was already so near. Her hips were canted slightly forward, and he knew what she wanted him to do. He asked with his eyes, hardly daring to breathe.

She answered by coming even closer.

So he reached for her. His hands were heavy and light and tingling. He cupped them around the backs of her knees, under the hem of her slip. Her skin was hot velvet and trembling, and it shivered with gooseflesh as he slowly, oh so slowly, trailed his hands up the backs of her thighs.

The slip, pooling over his wrists, rose inch by tremulous inch.

He was hardly breathing. This was all new territory: his hands, her legs. And then... the curves of flesh above them, the lacy edges of her smallclothes, the swell of her hips.

Sarai's hearts were a pair of butterflies, fluttering in a dance. Lazlo's palms glided over her hips and still they slid higher, gathering the silk up around her waist to reveal what was secret beneath: the smallclothes, sweet and brief, and, above them, only flesh. The curve of her belly, the dip of her navel...

He had never seen a woman's navel and was transfixed by the sight: blue deepening to purple in the tiny, perfect whirl, and scribed around it: her elilith.

Real tattoos were done in ink made from pine bark, bronze, and gall. They looked black when they were new but faded to umber as the years went by. Sarai's were neither black nor umber, but gleaming silver, which suited them just right. Here were no apple blossoms or runes, no snake swallowing its tail.

"It's perfect," said Lazlo, rough-voiced and low.

It was the moon: a slender crescent shaped to the soft curve of her, with a scattering of stars to close the arc and form a perfect oval on her belly.

"The moon," Sarai whispered, loving it. "Like the one you bought for me."

Once in a dream they'd gone shopping for a moon. "And the stars we gathered," he said. They'd strung them all on a bracelet, which appeared on her wrist now as though fished from the dream—a charm bracelet of real celestial bodies, tiny and luminous, hooked to a fine silver chain.

Sarai had long been nocturnal. The moon was her sun. Every night it set her free, to send her mind and senses winging down to Weep.

100

Would it still? Tonight at darkfall, would she feel her moths burgeon? Or had death put an end to her gift? She didn't know. There was no precedent. But she hoped, *oh*, she hoped it wasn't gone. She touched a fingertip to her belly, and when she took it away, a tiny silver moth had joined the stars on her blue skin. It was a wish, that she might still be . . . *who?*

Not the Muse of Nightmares. Those days were over. But she prayed that dreams were not lost to her, nor she to them.

"Do you remember," she asked in a whisper, "the sun in a jar put away with the fireflies?"

They had lived for night and dreaded sunrise, for it would wrench them apart. But it was daylight now, and they were together. "I remember," Lazlo managed, raw. His hands were heavy on her skin, gliding over the flare of her hips to encircle her waist. His fingertips met in back. In front, his thumbs traced the moon's silver edges, the sprinkling of stars and the lone moth among them. They filled his sight. The blue of her skin, the silver stars and moon. She was the sky. Heavy, bewitched, he leaned forward and brushed his lips over a star.

Sarai shivered at the touch. The stars were on her skin, but they were inside her, too, filling her up with light. Where Lazlo's lips brushed her belly, a shimmer lit up there and she trembled.

Through half-closed eyes, Lazlo saw and marveled. He kissed another star. Light pulsed beneath her skin. It looked like glavelight beneath blue silk.

It *felt* like feathers and shivers and shooting-star trails of pleasure that transcended flesh. Sarai wove her fingers through Lazlo's hair. He stroked his thumbs down her belly, painting traceries of light. The silver ink shone bright, and wherever he touched, her skin gleamed pearlescent, lit up from within.

To come to Weep, he had crossed a sea, and he had seen, from the deck of a leviathan ship, the water glowing white-blue. It was bioluminescence, and when he'd trailed his hand in the water, it had come alive to his touch, rippling with radiance and even clinging to his fingers like a glaze of poured moonlight. And now Sarai's body was sea and sky and radiance, and even her veins glimmered in glowing rivers as though her hearts were pumping light.

Around them in the air: light flashed on metal. The mesarthium songbirds had come alive again, and were flying, soaring, glorious. He hadn't meant to do it, as he hadn't meant for Rasalas, out in the garden, to toss its head and paw at the ground, restlessly alive. And the wasps in the heart of the citadel: their wings, so long frozen, flicked and folded. And the seraph itself—the whole massive, floating angel—shivered along with him, so that all through the passages, in the garden, the kitchens, the heart of the citadel, all felt it, and stopped what they were doing.

Not Lazlo, though, or Sarai. They felt only themselves, each other. He tilted his head to gaze up at her, and she felt a surge of overwhelming love for his face with its rough edges, his nose shaped by falling stories, and his gray eyes ablaze with witchlight. She wanted more of everything, more of life and freedom and years and *him*. She wanted *all* of him. An almost unbearable tenderness threatened to crush her under its weight, and...she wanted it to. She wanted to laugh and sob and be crushed by tenderness. She wanted to *move*, delirious, forgetting what was real and what was looming, and find some way to hook herself to this world, this moment, and never leave. She wanted to taste and feel and *ache*, and she wanted to weep, too, for all she'd lost and would yet lose.

She reached for Lazlo's hand and lifted it to her hearts. They were brilliant now beneath her skin, so that his fingers, resting there, were limned in their throbbing glow.

The strap of her slip had fallen aside, the same one as last night. She held his hand in both of hers, and, pressing it full against her, drew it down over her breast, pushing the slip out of its way.

Lazlo's vision narrowed as though the sight of her like this was too much to take in all at once. Her hearts pulsed like twin suns and her mouth was decadent with want. Her breast was in his palm, heavy with its velvet heat, and its tip was the same rosy hue as her tongue.

As he had never seen a woman's navel, he had never seen this, either.

He lifted his face like a man spellbound and took it between his lips. The softness he found there obliterated him. He didn't close his eyes. She was sky and night and everything, suns and novas and the surface of the sea. Dimly he noted the absence of the bunched-up silk from around her waist. The slip was gone. She'd vanished it, and was standing against him unveiled. His body shook, and hers did, too, as he traced around her nipple with his softly parted lips.

She made a kitten sound that undid him, then her knees gave way and she was poured against him, all softness and honey and heat. He gathered her into his lap, there on the edge of her bed. She tried to will his shirt away, too, to have nothing more between them. But it stayed right where it was and she laughed at herself, because this wasn't a dream. She had to pull it off over his head. He raised his arms to let her, and then it was gone and she took his face in her hands, his perfect, imperfect face.

The birds were alive all around them. Lazlo's hands were alive on her body. Her soul *felt* alive more than ever before. Sarai could almost forget that she wasn't.

And when she leaned in to kiss him, she gave no thought to caution. How could she? The world was forgotten. His lips were warm and ardent. They parted against hers and moved with them like language, sweet and soft and slow. She loved his lips. She loved his tongue. She loved his chest against her own. His ribs rose and fell with unsteady breath. Their gazes fused, heavy-lidded, his eyes fringed in rivercat lashes. When she took his lip between her teeth, she only meant to tease it. She bit down lightly. It was tender as a plum. She stroked it with the tip of her tongue. And then:

An intrusion in her mind, quick and cold as a stab. Her will was snatched. It happened so fast. Her teeth sank *deep* into Lazlo's lip.

It didn't taste like plum.

❧ 13 ❧

TEETH

Minya surfaced from the shallow place. Her eyes, which had gone blank, sharpened into focus and immediately cut narrow. She had several hundred souls in her power. She held their tethers with her mind, which she'd always pictured as a fist clenching a tangle of gossamer threads. Each gossamer sang with its own vibration, like the string of a musical instrument. It wasn't music, but that came closest to describing it. The tethers resonated *feeling*.

Hate.

Fear.

Despair.

Those were the feelings Minya's ghosts gave off. She could tamp them down but they were always there—a beehive thrum of hate-fear-despair to match the way they looked at her when she fished their souls from the air.

The note that dragged her from the shallow place was none of these, and she knew it at once for Sarai's. There was no tamping this one down. It overwhelmed her with a symphony of feelings quite different from what she knew. There were pleasure and desire, hot and sweet, and *tenderness*, ineffable and aching. And through it all, threading them together like jewels on a golden string: *love*. It rattled her.

Minya looked like a child but she wasn't a child, and she understood very well what was happening—or at least what would happen if she let it. Spite hissed through her. Prudishness didn't enter into it. Feral and Ruby had been in heat for days, and she hadn't cared except to mock them. This was different. Sarai and Lazlo were pieces on the game board, and there was everything at stake. If they wanted their pleasure, their honey heat and little sounds, they could earn it with obedience.

So Minya sent her will racing down Sarai's tether like a fuse, to seize control of her languid, licking mouth, latch her teeth onto Lazlo's lip, and *bite*.

* * *

His cry was muffled against Sarai's mouth. In the burst of pain, he jerked, and his forehead cracked against hers. Her teeth clung a second longer, nearly meeting in the middle, while his blood filled her mouth and she screamed inside her head, unable to let go.

There was a moment when she thought that Minya would make her clench and *tear*, like a dog ripping meat off a bone.

Then Minya released her, and she released Lazlo and leapt out of his lap. Blood bubbled from the wound, running down his chin—and it was also running down *hers*, *his* blood running down *her* chin. Her mouth was filled with the taste of it, and her mind with the feeling: the powerlessness, and the *crunch and burst* of her teeth cutting into the dense tissue of his lip. She couldn't form words, but only heard herself uttering a horrified, "*Oh, oh,*" over and over as her hands reached toward him and fluttered, afraid to touch him lest she hurt him again, and sure also that he wouldn't *want* to be touched, not by her, not anymore.

He was holding his hand to his mouth. Blood drizzled all down his wrist. When he looked up, his eyes were wide with shock and glazed with pain. But he blinked and cleared them, and saw Sarai's distress.

"It's all right. I'm all right," he assured her.

"You're not all right. I *bit* you!"

"It's not your fault—"

"How does that matter? It was my *teeth*." She wiped her mouth with the back of her hand. It came away red and she shuddered.

"It's nothing," he said, touching his lip, though he flinched and rendered the claim unconvincing. "Even if you'd bitten it off, I'd still want to kiss you."

"Don't joke," she said, shaken. "What if I had?"

"You didn't." He reached for her, but she stepped back, appalled now to realize that she'd been insufficiently afraid, and put him in danger just by being near him. She was a tool now, a weapon, and, with the taste of blood in her mouth, she had an awful new apprehension of how Minya could wield her. Was there anything she wouldn't make her do? Any line she wouldn't cross? The thought made Sarai sick and light-headed—and ashamed, too, that she wasn't strong enough to resist her.

"Come here," coaxed Lazlo. "If she wants to use you to hurt me, she will, whether you happen to be kissing me or not. And I'd rather you're kissing me, if I have any say in the matter."

"You're in no state for kissing now."

It was true. His lip throbbed and stung. He could feel it swelling.

But he didn't want it to be over. She was too far away, standing out of reach, naked and blue and so beautiful it hurt. His hands were still full of the feel of her. He wanted her back in his arms. "I'm not afraid of you," he said.

"*I'm* afraid of me."

She knew their reprieve was ended, that Minya had restarted the "game," so she whispered, urgent, "Lazlo, remember your promise, *no matter what.*" And just in time, because no sooner were those words out of her mouth than others followed in a wholly different tone. They were dulcet and insincere, and she could do nothing to stop them. "If you're done rubbing your passion all over each other, come out to the gallery for a chat."

* * *

Minya picked herself up off the ledge where her little legs had been dangling. Sarai's tether felt like all the rest now, heavy with helpless despair. The tenderness was gone, and good riddance. It had felt like being cracked open, hearts served up on a platter. Why anyone would want that, *seek* that, she would never know.

She stretched and rolled her head side to side, savoring her small win. She'd thought to wait till their defenses were down. This was perfect. Leave them sloppy with want, unfulfilled, aching with desire and devotion. What wouldn't they do for each other now? It was time to play this game to its end, and have her way at last.

🌿 14 🌿

PIECES ON A GAME BOARD

"She wouldn't really let Sarai's soul go, would she?" Ruby wondered, fretful and distracted. She was with Sparrow in the garden. Sparrow was working, or trying to. Ruby was just fidgeting. They could feel time ticking by. The seconds seemed to pile up and teeter. Sooner or later they would spill, and this fraught waiting would come to an end—with havoc, and screaming, and loss.

It was a little like being on tea break from the end of the world. What was Minya doing? How much longer did they have?

They spoke in hushed voices so the ghosts couldn't hear them. "I would never have thought so before," said Sparrow. "But now I'm not so sure."

"Something's gone wrong with her." Ruby was bleak. "She wasn't always this bad. Was she?"

Sparrow shook her head. She sat back on her heels. Her fingers were dark with soil, her hair neatly braided. She was sixteen, and Ruby would be soon. They were half sisters by Ikirok, god of revelry. Their temperaments were so different: Ruby was bold and easily bored. She no sooner thought a thing than said it, or wanted a thing than she tried to get it. Sparrow was quieter. She watched and wished and kept her hopes to herself, but, however sweet her nature, she was not soft. Just the other day, she'd shocked Sarai and Ruby by suggesting that Ruby could give Minya "a nice warm hug"—by which she'd meant that she could burn her alive.

She hadn't *wanted* it, of course, but she'd seen the darkness in Minya and worried what it would come to. And now here they were, on the brink of war. "I wonder," she said, "if it's the ghosts that have made her so dark. We thought it was bad for us, when she'd catch a soul now and then—the ones we knew about—and we'd feel *obscene* because of how they looked at us. You can't help but see yourself through their eyes."

"I can," Ruby claimed. "I know I'm beautiful."

But Sparrow knew this was only bravado and that Ruby hated it, too. She even tried to win the ghosts over sometimes, to show them they weren't like their parents, not that it did any good. "And all that time, we had no idea how *many* ghosts—hundreds of them, with all their hate, and Minya's been steeping in it."

"It's her own fault. What was she thinking?"

"She was thinking about keeping us safe," said Sparrow. That much was obvious. "Keeping us alive."

Ruby huffed a half laugh. "It sounds like you're on her side."

"Don't be simple," said Sparrow. It was so easy to call sides, and so unhelpful. "We're all on the same side. Even her. You can be on the same side and have different ideas."

"So what do we *do*?" asked Ruby.

What *could* they do? At a loss, Sparrow shook her head. She sank her fingers back into the soil and felt the soft throb of life it conducted through the branching roots it embraced. This was the bed of flowers where they'd cremated Sarai. Ruby's pyre had burned hot and fast. It had eaten only the body and the orchids they'd adorned it with. The living bower upon which it had lain was astonishingly unscorched. It was only crushed down a little in the shape of a body, and Sparrow had been coaxing the stalks upright, wanting to erase the image of what they'd done here.

She fingered a flower. It was little and white—insubstantial, yet it pulsed with life. It struck her as such a mysterious force that flowed in one direction only, and, once gone, could never return. She plucked the flower. The force did not immediately snuff out. It waned. The bloom took a few seconds to die.

She was thinking of life and death, but another thought tiptoed between them. It was guileful and sly. It waited to be noticed. Sparrow noticed, and dropped the flower. She looked up at Ruby. An idea lit her eyes. A question creased her brow. She asked it.

Ruby stared. And then she smiled.

And then she answered.

* * *

Feral slouched through the sinister arm, dragging two mattresses behind him. He'd fetched them from the rooms they never liked to go in—the little rooms that were like cells with nothing in them but beds. The mattresses were just pallets, really, not at all like the thick, comfortable bedding in the chambers of the gods. That was why he'd taken two, but they would still be a poor substitute.

He thought Ruby should have them, and he should have hers. She'd burned his, after all. At the time he hadn't minded. He'd thought...Well, he was a fool. He'd thought he'd just sleep in her room from now on, as though there was something between them.

It wasn't stupid to have thought it. What they'd been doing together wasn't nothing. It might have begun that way, but...he liked it. A *lot*. And, much to his surprise, he liked *her*. Even if she was utterly unreasonable. To get mad that he'd never spied on her naked!

All right, he might once or twice have passed by the rain room when one or another of the girls was bathing, but he'd never peeped through the curtain.

Unless there was a gap in it already, and even then he hadn't slowed down too much, or gotten more than a glimpse.

Anyway, he hadn't gone out of his way, and that was what upset her.

What did she want, anyway?

Not *me*, he answered himself glumly. "We're not children anymore and we have lips," she'd said when she came to his room to seduce him. "Isn't that reason enough?" It wasn't *him* she cared for. He just happened to have lips, not to mention the significant anatomical feature that set him apart in this small tribe of girls. She'd been using him, and he'd been fine with it, but now he wasn't, and not only because he had to scrounge up new bedding.

He came to the end of the passage, where the seraph's left arm joined its shoulder and a broad hall abutted the gallery that ran the length of the chest. Halfway across he had to stumble to a stop, because a steady stream of ghosts was passing by. They were coming from the opposite direction. He never liked to look at them straight on—he disliked seeing the hate in their eyes, and the misery that was there, too—but he still could pick out this one from that one, and he recognized the guards from the dexter arm. They were all marching into the gallery.

He got a bad feeling, and then Minya appeared, and his feeling got worse. "What's going on?" he asked her.

"Come see," she replied in her icing-sugar voice. "I promise it won't be boring."

* * *

Out in the garden, Ruby and Sparrow saw the ghosts and shared a stark look. They had the same bad feeling as Feral, and went warily to the arches.

Feral abandoned his mattresses and followed the procession of ghosts.

Minya paced to the table and climbed into her chair. She arranged herself, crossing her ankles, and took some care with the folds of her torn and grubby shift. What a sight she was: an urchin with the bearing of a queen.

No, not a queen. A goddess. The wrathful kind.

She lined up her troops in formation. There were too many of them to fit in the room, so she overlapped them. It fought the eye to look at them: seeming solid but for the way they disappeared into one another like partially shuffled cards. Last, she parted them down the center and made an aisle from the door straight to her, so that when Sarai and Lazlo came round the corner, that's what they saw: Minya sitting in state at the end of a gauntlet of slave souls.

"There you are," she said. "Are you ready?"

They just looked at her, bleak, and knew that no words existed that could shift her from her course.

She cocked her head when they failed to answer. "Wraith got your tongues?" she asked. She wrinkled her nose at Lazlo. "Or maybe Sarai got yours."

He was a sight, his lip swollen, blood dried down to his chin. The others' eyes widened. "That little maniac," uttered Ruby.

Lazlo answered calmly, "My tongue is intact. I should thank you. I suppose it could have been worse."

"That's a good rule to live by. It can always be worse. But cheer up. If you're good and do what I tell you"—she spoke in singsong, dangling her words like a bribe—"I'll let you two alone later, to do as you like behind your closed door."

If they were "good"? Let them alone...? As though they would return from slaughter eager for pleasure? Sarai felt ill. Did Minya really understand so little? Had her hate devoured everything else? She let out a hard breath. "That's your bargain? Help you *kill*, and you'll let us *kiss*?"

"Oh no," said Minya. "That's just me being nice. There is no bargain, silly. Have I not made that quite clear?"

But of course she had. *Do everything I say, or I'll let her soul go.* It wasn't a bargain, but a threat.

"Come here," she said. "Why are you lurking in the doorway?" She stood up on her chair and stepped onto the table to stroll its length, hands clasped behind her back, her gaze never leaving them.

Sarai and Lazlo advanced between the phalanxes of ghosts. Ruby and Sparrow came through the arches, and Feral from the door, and all three went to stand with them, so that Minya again felt splintered from the "us" that was rightly hers. Here they were, at last, on the verge of avenging the deaths of their kindred. They should have been lining up behind her, taking up knives of their own accord. Instead they stood there like that: pallid and weak,

114

soft, pitiful things incapable of avenging anyone. She wanted to slap them awake.

No more preamble. No more waiting. She fixed on Lazlo and said, "It's time. You know what's at stake." Her gaze shifted to Sarai and back. "No need to yammer on."

And so they came to the moment, like a dark hole between them, from which there was no escape. A jolt of horror shot through Lazlo. "Wait." He was shaking. His blood and spirit were racing, and his thoughts went around in a loop, like the white bird circling, only faster. In tales, when heroes battled monsters, they always won by slaying, but that wasn't an option for him. He couldn't kill anyone, and even if he could—if he were that kind of hero—it wouldn't help. If he slew this monster, he'd lose Sarai, too. Killing could not solve this problem. "Can't we talk—"

"No." The word punched through the air like a fist. "*Take. Me. To Weep. Right. NOW!*" Minya finished on a roar, her face going red.

Sarai clenched Lazlo's hand. She could feel him trembling, and squeezed, wanting to give him strength, and take it, too. In that moment, she didn't know what scared her more: that he would keep his promise or break it. *Oh gods.* She didn't have it in her to hope for her own evanescence.

Nobody noticed when Sparrow nudged Ruby, and shot a sharp glance toward the door. Or when Ruby, with a half step, then a full step, then a duck, slipped between the ranks of ghosts and sidled out of the room.

Lazlo just stood there, reeling, flooded with the bitter choice between Sarai and Weep. But...he had already made it, when she had made him promise. *No matter what.* Helplessness vied with rebellion. His two vows clashed like swords. He was supposed to save her anyway.

How could he save her anyway?

"I can't," he choked out.

A wild disbelief flared in the little girl. Her eyes flashed back and forth between Lazlo and Sarai. How was it possible they still dared to defy her? She had thought it a certainty that they wouldn't put at risk all that tenderness and aching. What mad notion of honor was this?

Pieces on a game board, she told herself, grim, and it wasn't she who spoke next, but Sarai.

"Lazlo," she whispered, soft, at his side. "I've changed my mind. Don't let me go."

He turned to her sharply, expecting her eyes, like all the other ghosts' eyes, to give lie to her words. But they didn't. They weren't wide, showing whites, and rolling with helplessness. They were soft and hesitant, ashamed and sweet and full of fear, as though it pained her to be weak and plead for her own soul. "Sarai?" he queried, uncertain.

"No!" she screamed, but only in her head, where it was so loud to her own senses that it seemed impossible he couldn't hear it. Those weren't her words. That wasn't her plea. But her face—her *eyes*—betrayed none of the panic they sparked in her. Ghosts' eyes always told the truth, didn't they? That was what they'd always believed, that Minya's power had that limit, at least, but Sarai could tell by the intensity with which Lazlo was searching hers, and by his confusion, that they didn't. "I'm afraid," she whispered, and clutched his hand tighter, and none of it was *her*. "It's so cold out there, Lazlo. I'm so afraid."

He warred with himself right before her. She saw every nuance cross his face. He was caught between what he knew to be true and the flawless, insidious lie Minya was putting on like a show. "Just do what she wants," Sarai pleaded. "For me."

116

And he knew. And he felt sick. *No matter what*, Sarai had said. He remembered how brave she'd been, and he turned to Minya, shaking. "Stop it," he said, his bloody, swollen lip curling with fury. "She would *never* ask that." He knew it was true. Sarai would never choose her uncertain ghost future over untold human lives.

A cry of anguish escaped from Sarai. Her pleading became more insistent—and all the more unconvincing for it, as though it was only to torment him now that he hadn't taken the bait. "Don't you love me?" she asked. "Won't you save me?"

The words tore through her and she despised them, because a part of her *wanted* to say them, to beg and be saved, no matter what the cost. She was held in the world by such a fine thread. The void hovered—the ether, the tide of unmaking—and she was terrified.

Her words sank claws into Lazlo's hearts, whether they came from Sarai or not. Tears burst from his eyes, thick and full, plashing drops onto his cheekbones, his lashes dark and clumped. The midday light glazed his eyes and they shone like rising suns. He took a step toward Minya, searching her face for some hint of kinship or humanity.

But he found none.

"So that's it?" Minya asked him, both astonished and disgusted. "You would destroy *her* to save *them*?" She had the uneasy sensation of losing her grip, of rope reeling out of her hands. It wasn't supposed to go like this. They were supposed to do as she said.

Lazlo shook his head. It was all so wrong. "No," he said. "I would destroy no one."

Minya's teeth were gritted. Her eyes were slits. "That isn't one of your choices. It's simple: Choose Sarai and the killers die. Choose the killers and lose Sarai."

In her childish voice, it sounded like a nursery song, and Lazlo knew that, whatever happened and however long he lived, he would never be able to cleanse it from his mind. It was maddening, this black and white choice: One must die for the other to live. But... how could it not seem so to her? Whoever Minya might have been without the Carnage, Lazlo would never know. She'd been forged that day when the Godslayer slew babies so humans could live. He'd killed them against a future threat, because of what they were. It was he who'd set the rules of the game that Minya was still playing. Was it fair to change them now that she finally had the advantage?

Bleakly he glimpsed the world as she must see it, made simple by righteousness and fury. Could he ask her to be better than those whose hate had forged her? He knew what she would say to that, but still he had to try. "It can all end right here. You just have to let it. We're not murderers." He held Sarai and spoke to Minya. "And neither are you."

The words were out, and he thought he saw her flinch as though they struck her. She seemed to shrink and then catch herself and thrust back her shoulders, her expression turning even darker. "Don't presume to know what I am. Let's be perfectly clear. Are you refusing me? I won't ask you again."

"I...I..."

But he couldn't say it. Promise or not, Lazlo could not speak the words that would seal Sarai's fate. He turned to her. Her eyes were so wide, blue like skies, her honey-red lashes beaded with tears. She was innocent, and Minya was right: There were those in Weep, Eril-Fane included, who were guilty. Why should Sarai pay for their lives with her soul?

She whispered, "I love you," and he was lost. No one had ever said those words to him, not once in all his life. He wasn't even conscious of summoning Rasalas, but then the creature was beside him, come in from the garden, its huge metal wings at the ready. Minya mounted from the tabletop, triumphant, and sat astride her father's beast, ready to fly down to Weep.

Many a choice is made in this way: by pretending it makes itself.

And many a fate is decided by those who cannot decide.

She'll find a way to break you, Sarai had warned Lazlo. Now she saw that Minya had, and so many feelings tore through her: despair, *relief*, self-loathing. Still possessed by Minya's will, she could do nothing, say nothing, but the worst part of all was that something insidious within her relished her own helplessness, because it freed her from having to fight.

The last thing she wanted to do was fight for her own oblivion.

She tried to tell herself it would be all right. The city had emptied. The citizens were safe, and the Tizerkane could take care of themselves.

But these were all lies, and they festered inside her: her hearts, her whole self felt corrupt, like a plum gone soft with rot. It would ruin Lazlo to do this. It would break Weep, and ruin him, and she would wish for oblivion then, which Minya would not grant. Sarai would still be her puppet, with bloody teeth and ineluctable strings, after everything else was gone.

Lazlo said, "I love you, too," and it was so wrong that he should say it now, with Minya's will crammed in Sarai's soul, and murder to be done. He bent down and softly brushed the unbitten side of his mouth over hers, and rested his face, cheek to cheek, against hers. His jaw was rough, his skin too warm. He shuddered lightly against her. Sarai breathed his sandalwood smell, and remembered her first discovery of him, through her moths in the Godslayer's house. She'd thought him a brute at first glance. The idea amazed her now. There had been so many moments of wonder, but her mind leapt somewhere quite different: to the last minutes of her own life. It was just before the blast ripped the city—deep night and silent, all the streets empty. Lazlo had been walking through Weep. Sarai had been with him by way of a moth perched on his wrist, and she'd had no inkling of all that was about to occur.

It was a funny thing to think of. At first, she didn't know why she had. But then...she thought maybe she did, and a strange kind of shiver ran through her.

She had never been able to enter the minds of those who were awake. As a girl, testing her powers, she had tried and learned: The conscious mind was closed to her. And so it had been that night as well. Her moth had ridden on Lazlo's wrist as he paced through the silent city, and she'd been shut out of his mind, with no idea what he was thinking.

But...she'd sensed what he was *feeling*. With her moth perched on his skin, she had felt as though she were pressed against the closed door of his consciousness. Emotion had radiated through it, as clear and strong as music through a wall. And now, her face against his, she felt again the music of emotion. It was discordant and miserable, uncertain, desperate, and jagged.

Sarai couldn't speak, beyond Minya's false words, but her thoughts and feelings were her own. She pressed her cheek even harder against Lazlo's, felt the burn of his stubbled jaw. And then she poured out her own jagged music. At least, she hoped she did.

It was a howling wind in her mind, a storm of knives, a blood-soaked hurricane of the word *NO!*

He tensed against her. Had he felt it? Was it real? He drew back and searched her eyes. She wanted to pull him against her again.

She had no power over her eyes. Minya possessed more subtlety than they'd known. All he could see was what she put there. He squinted in consternation. Then his gaze seemed to clear—to clear and darken. He turned to Minya and said, in a voice like the chew of gravel, "I can't take you to Weep. I made a promise."

And Minya was . . . displeased.

❧ 15 ❧

Tea Break from the End of the World

As soon as she was out of the gallery, Ruby raced up the dexter arm to her room, hurtling through her doorway without pausing to part the curtain, so that it tangled round her and ripped right off its rigging. Still in motion, she thrashed it away and disappeared into her dressing room, which had once belonged to Letha, goddess of oblivion. She was in there less than five seconds, then raced out and up the corridor to slip again amongst the ghosts crowding the gallery.

This time she made her way to the kitchen door, where the Ellens stood, hands covering their mouths, eyes wet and wide with dread.

"What's happening?" she asked in an overloud whisper, which carried in the sudden hush that followed Lazlo's words. "I made a promise," he told Minya, who radiated fury.

"Then break it," she hissed through her teeth.

And Lazlo didn't say anything. He just held Sarai close and, anguished, shook his head.

Ruby met eyes with Sparrow across the room. Her sister was pale and frantic, and gave her a *hurry up* gesture. Ruby turned to Less Ellen and said...

It was *ridiculous*. She knew how it sounded—as though she were unhinged from reality. "Ellens," she said, "might we have some tea?"

They stared at her, their dread momentarily overwhelmed by surprise. "*Tea?*" repeated Great Ellen.

Ruby licked her lips and tried her best to be the picture of clueless nonchalance. "What?" she said, defensive. "Am I not allowed to be thirsty?" Her hearts hammered. There was sweat in the small of her back. "Tea's never a bad idea. You've said so yourself often enough."

"Well, you've just disproved the adage," said Great Ellen, while Less Ellen gasped out, "*Oh!*"

It wasn't to do with tea, that gasp. One glance, and Ruby saw: Sarai was gone. Lazlo was left holding air.

Too late, she thought, wild. *Too late*. But she still had to try. What else could she do? "I'll make it myself," she told the Ellens, and shoved between them through the door.

* * *

Sarai was anchored, and then she wasn't. She had substance, and then she didn't. The fragile filament that connected her soul to the world all at once fell slack.

To Lazlo, it was sathaz all over again: His arms were empty, curved around nothing. Where Sarai had been, so sweet and smooth, he now held nothing but air. He reached out as though he could find her, but she wasn't invisible. She was gone. "No!" A gasp, a terrible echo of the word that had torn through his thoughts. He spun toward Minya, wild-eyed.

"I hope you said your good-byes!" she screamed. Her voice was shrill, her face empurpled. If any could have felt her music then, "jagged" wouldn't have begun to cover it. This was all Lazlo's fault, as she saw it. He was making her do it, and she wanted him punished.

"Bring her back!" he gasped out.

"*You* bring her back! You know what you have to do!"

Lazlo didn't hear the pleading in her voice. The horrific *NO!* was still carving its hurricane path through his mind, driving out all else. Where had it come from? The others were screaming, crying, and Sarai wasn't there.

She just wasn't there.

Minya was still astride Rasalas. She scrambled to a stand, feeling the metal shift beneath her. She tried to leap back to the table, but the beast twisted, and a clawed metal paw flashed up and grabbed her out of the air. It tossed her to the floor. Lazlo loomed above her. He seized her with his own hands, clenching her rags in his fists. He lifted her up in front of him, her toes dangling, and looked her right in the eyes.

All around them, her army shifted. You could see her will flow into them, rippling them like wind over grass. Row after row, the ghosts raised up their knives, their meat hooks and mallets, gleaming-edged and fresh-sharpened. Even the Ellens held weapons. Their eyes went wide with horror as their own hands lifted, cocked back, released.

Knives flew. Someone screamed.

Lazlo didn't shift his gaze from Minya, whom he still held off the floor. Mesarthium responded, whiplash-fast. For every flung weapon, a ripple of metal disengaged from the walls to intercept it. It looked like magnetism. It looked like magic. All around the room there was a *shink shink shink* as silver metal met blue and clattered to the floor.

One blade hit the wall. Instead of bouncing off, it embedded there and stayed. All the others, too: The floor drew them down till only their handles protruded. It happened in seconds. Minya's ghosts were disarmed—of ordinary weapons, anyway. At once, their fingernails and teeth lengthened and sharpened into claws and fangs.

Lazlo didn't see. His eyes were locked on Minya's. "Listen to me," he said, savage. He wouldn't have known his own voice. "There's something you've failed to consider. *Sarai is the only thing keeping you safe.* Gods help you, if you let her soul go. There will be nothing to stop me from ending you."

The space after his words was heavy with gasped breaths and a low, steady rumble up Rasalas's throat. Minya and Lazlo stared at each other: rage against rage, will against will.

Minya, in some deep place, was grasping at the chance that Lazlo's threat offered. It was true, what he said. She might hold Sarai's soul in the balance, but she also held her own, because the minute she made good on her threat, she would lose her only leverage—and lose Sarai, too.

Here was a reason to back down, and her hearts cried out to take it, but... she couldn't. Minya's will was a blade forged by the screams of two dozen dying children—forged by screams and tempered in blood, like a red-hot sword plunged hissing into water. *Back* was not a direction she was able to go. If she conceded now, she would have nothing, and be no one. If they didn't believe that she would do it— that she would end Sarai—what reason would they have to ever listen to her again? She would lose not just this game, but every one that came after. Lazlo had to concede. She just couldn't. She bared her little teeth in a grimace. He'd told her himself that he wasn't a killer. She'd just have to trust him on that. "Do your worst, *brother*," she snarled, and saw in an instant that he already had.

This *was* Lazlo's worst. He could hold her up like a doll, her rags bunched in his fists, but he couldn't hurt her. His eyes lost their rage, the muscles around them going slack with surprise, which quickly turned to distress. He could hide nothing. His eyes revealed all. He didn't have it in him to hurt anyone.

The thought of Ruza flashed through his mind—his Tizerkane friend who'd despaired of ever making him a warrior. Well, he'd be disgusted now to see this little girl shrug and push at his hands until he dropped her to her feet.

"There's only one way to save her," she said, stepping back onto her chair and up onto the table so her eyes were level with his.

Lazlo felt like he was drowning. Minya saw right through him. Where was Sarai? Could she still be saved? *Please*, he thought. It felt like prayer, but who was there to pray to? The seraphim might have been real, once upon a time, but that didn't mean they were listening.

In that moment, Lazlo felt sure: In all the great and star-bedecked universe, nothing at all was listening.

And then, in the blank, gasping gnaw of his panic, he caught sight of the Ellens in the doorway. The two weren't stoic like the rest of the ghosts, frozen stiff but for wild, rolling eyes. Their hands were clasped as though pleading; their faces wore all the desperation he felt. As he made eye contact with Great Ellen, she actually said, "*Please*."

A small, sharp thought pricked him like a thorn: Was it possible... could it be that some part of Minya *wanted* him to stop her? How, though?

She won't give up, Sarai had said earlier. *She never does. I don't think she can.*

126

Minya couldn't give up. It was how she was made, and the Carnage had made her. Giving up meant dying. It meant small bodies in red puddles.

He was grasping at straws. His thoughts leapt around. He felt as though his soul were straining away from his body, trying to get to Sarai, to hold her in the ether so she wouldn't be alone. But he couldn't reach her. Only Minya could, if he could find a way to let her.

"I'll bring him here," he blurted. "Eril-Fane. I'll bring him here."

Minya's look grew sharp. She said nothing, waiting for him to go on.

Lazlo licked his lips. She was listening. *She wants to be persuaded.* He didn't know if it was true, but if it wasn't, there was no hope. "I'll bring him to you." He said it to buy time, to get Sarai out of danger and think of another way. It didn't mean he would really do it. But maybe he would, if there was no other way. He was sick with it. Was he *this* kind of hero, who would sacrifice one soul for another?

"Do it," said Minya.

A wave of her hand, and Sarai's shape was returned to the air. What started as a silhouette slowly filled in to reveal her, eyes rolled back to whites, lips parted in a silent scream. For minutes she had wavered on the edge of unmaking, and felt the cold all through her. Now she collapsed. Lazlo rushed to her. They all did, save Minya. She stood right where she was, a tiny, dirty goddess, and no one noticed the way her hands moved, fingers rubbing over her palms as though they were slick with sweat and little hands kept slipping from her grasp.

As though she might lose everything, all that she had left.

And then Ruby was there with a tray. It clattered as she carried it. Cups sloshed when she set it down on the table. Her voice was neutral, the desperation so slight that only Sparrow perceived it. She asked, "Would anyone like tea?"

Tea.

It was absurd. What was it she had thought out in the garden earlier? That waiting for Minya's wrath to descend was like a tea break from the end of the world? Well, here was literal tea. No one else could have gotten away with so totally tone-deaf a gesture, but Ruby was always blurting things out, heedless of what was going on around her. Still, Feral stared at her as though she'd grown another head. Lazlo didn't even hear. He was holding a shivering Sarai, and murmuring to her, "I've got you."

As for Minya, she saw the proffered cup from the corner of her eye. She took it without question. Her thoughts had come unstrung. She was at the edge of unmaking, where she'd almost sent Sarai. *They were all I could carry* ran through her mind, no matter how fierce she looked. "Bring me the Godslayer," she said, to drown out the words in her head.

Lazlo's jaw clenched. He faced Minya.

She held up her teacup in a toast. "To revenge," she said in a voice like glass, and then she tipped up her cup and drank.

Ruby watched her. Sparrow watched her. Both girls held their breath. They couldn't be sure. It was all hope and *what if*, but one didn't inhabit the chamber of the goddess of oblivion without, at least once, sampling the potion in the little green glass bottle she'd kept on her bedside table.

Minya took a deep chug. She was thirsty. The tea wasn't hot. The tea wasn't *tea*. Their tea never was. They'd run out of leaves years ago. They drank brewed herbs and called it tea, but this wasn't even that. It was just water at room temperature with a sour aftertaste.

She looked at Ruby, critical but unsuspicious, and said, "That's the worst tea I've ever had."

And then her eyes lost focus. Her knees lost strength. She staggered, looked bewildered, dropped her teacup with a smash.

And then she fell.

Time seemed to slow as Minya, monster and savior, sister and tormentor, lost consciousness and collapsed on the long mesarthium table.

Part II

* * *

astral (AS·truhl)

adjective: Of, or relating to, or coming from, the stars.

noun: A rare category of Mesarthim gift; one whose soul or consciousness can leave the body and travel independently of it.

❧ 16 ❧

OF THE STARS

The punishment for unauthorized contact with godsmetal was death. Everyone knew that. The village children, sidling closer to the wasp ship, knew it. They would never dream of touching it, but were only daring one another nearer, at least to touch its shadow, bold now that the Servants had disappeared inside with Kora and Nova.

Some in the village thought it right that Nyoka's girls should be tested first. Others grumbled. The men who'd been eyeing them of late—including old Shergesh, though the sisters did not know it—burned with the injustice of it, that outsiders could come down from the sky and carry off their girls. It would be a tremendous honor, of course, if another Rievan were made Servant, but better it be a young man. There were too many of them in the village, beginning to sniff after wives of their own, and the older men wouldn't have minded a culling of that herd. The loss of one girl, though, let alone two, would be deeply felt. Life on Rieva was hard, especially for the women. Wives were often in need of replenishing.

The gathered crowd kept avid eyes on the ship, even as they milled about, gossiping. They knew that testing took time, and so it came as a surprise when, after only a few minutes, the door on the wasp's thorax opened.

Skoyë, watching through slit eyes, felt a surge of triumph that her stepdaughters should be rejected so swiftly. It could only be rejection. A strong gift would take time to gauge. But the girls did not emerge. It was the Servant with the ropes of white hair. Stiff-armed, he was holding out two uul-hide anoraks, his face curdled with revulsion. He pitched them out like garbage, then followed them with fur chamets and breeches, balled-up woolen longskins, and, finally, the girls' hide boots.

The door closed again and the villagers were left eyeing the pile. What were Kora and Nova wearing, if their clothes were all lying there?

"There's a woman in there with them," said their father, Zyak, lest the specter of indecency bring their bride prices down.

Shergesh spat and crossed his arms. Zyak's price was uncomfortable; he smelled an opportunity. "And that matters how? They're from Aqa. You've heard the stories."

The stories of depravity, yes. The fishing boats brought them, and they were as salt to the islanders' bland fare: Rievan gossip could not compare to what went on—allegedly—in the capital.

"They're good girls," said Zyak, and Kora and Nova would have been surprised to hear him say so, at least until he followed it up with, "They have all their teeth and toes. You should be so lucky, old man."

And the old man in question harrumphed but said no more. He had to be careful, he knew. Zyak was proud, and not above taking some other man's offer, though it be lower, simply to spite him.

"Anyway," said Zyak. "If the Mesarthim want them, it's as well for me. *They* don't haggle." He should know. He had bought a new sledge and oven with what they paid him for his wife, and two skins of spirit besides.

* * *

"Names," said the female Servant, Solvay, who hailed from a desert continent as desolate in its own way as Rieva. She had been found on a search much like this one, and plucked from the middle of nowhere.

Kora and Nova stood mute, covering themselves with their arms. They were wearing only their smallclothes and socks, the rest all stripped away. The reek of uul was less easy to be rid of; it was an *entity* in the enclosed space of the ship, and disgust showed on all the Servants' faces. Nova answered first. "Novali," she said, and paused. Her full name was Novali Zyak-vasa, or Novali Zyak-*daughter*. Upon marriage, a Rievan girl would exchange -*vasa* for -*ikai*, wife, and take her husband's name. Nova wanted none of it. "Nyoka-vasa," she said instead. She wished to be nothing more than her mother's daughter, especially today.

Solvay wrote it down and looked at Kora.

"Korako . . . Nyoka-vasa," said Kora with a sideward glance at her sister. She liked the feeling of the small act of defiance that would keep her father's name from being written down and made permanent on an imperial document.

"Nyoka," said Solvay. "That was your mother's name, who was a Servant?"

The girls nodded. "Do you know her?" Nova blurted. Solvay shook her head, and Nova swallowed her disappointment. She and

135

Kora were trying to act calm, but their hearts were racing. They were more dazzled, even, than the children outside, prancing around in the wasp ship's shadow. No one had dreamed of this moment more than they, and no one else truly believed, as they did, that it was their destiny come at last to retrieve them. With their eyes they traced the thin bands of godsmetal the Mesarthim wore at their brows—the Servants' diadem, as it was called. It was what kept them in contact with the godsmetal that activated their gifts, and simple though it was, it was the most potent symbol of power in the world of Mesaret. All their lives, Kora and Nova had dreamed of wearing them themselves.

The smith, they noted, wore vambraces instead, covering his forearms and etched in intricate designs. It seemed a profligate quantity of godsmetal, and showed his importance. Smiths accrued godsmetal by imperial reward—for service, and victory in battle. With each success, their ships grew larger. The bigger the ship, the more glorious the captain. The wasp ship was small, which would suggest the smith was either not glorious, or simply young and at the beginning of his career.

"And what was your mother's gift?" asked the tall, shaved-pate telepath, whose name was Ren.

"Shock waves," answered Nova.

"Magnitude sixteen," added Kora, proud, and the girls were gratified to see the Servants' eyes widen. They were impressed. How could they not be? How many of *them* were sixteens? The scale of magnitude went to twenty, but gifts of a strength eighteen and above had been recorded only a handful of times in history. In practical reality, sixteen was about as good as it got. Moreover, magnitude was heritable, which meant...

"This should be interesting," said the white-haired Mesarthim, Antal, still trying to wipe the stench of their clothing off his hands. The girls were curious about his hair—so much of it, and so white. He didn't seem old, but then, Mesarthim didn't age. Longevity, perhaps even immortality, was a side effect of the godsmetal, so it was impossible to tell.

"Let's see what you can do," Solvay said to the girls, and then she turned to the smith.

He had not yet spoken, but only leaned against the wall, watching. His posture was lazy but his eyes were sharp. He alone of the four showed an interest in what was no longer hidden by the sisters' stinking clothes. As Kora and Nova stood there, abashed, his gaze took a leisurely journey over their bare white legs and shoulders, their thinly veiled young breasts and bellies, as if their smallclothes and crossed arms hid nothing from him.

"Skathis?" prompted Solvay when he didn't respond but only continued his brazen perusal. He turned to her, eyebrows cinching together, as though unaware that they were all waiting for him. "Shall we begin?" she prompted, and there was something brittle about her tone, something cautious.

"By all means." He turned back to the sisters. "Let's see how you look *blue*."

And those words, which heralded the girls' lifelong dream, were dirtied by Skathis's mouth, which seemed to leave a film on them, making Kora and Nova all the more anxious to hide themselves from his gaze.

He tossed something to Kora. It was an easy underhand lob, and gave her time to start in surprise and reach for it. It was as small as a packed snowball—the icy kind that hurt—and she registered that it was godsmetal just before she caught it. She thought it would be hard, but it hit her hand like jelly and burst, splashing up her arm and clinging, so that it seemed to have caught *her*, and not she it.

There was nothing haphazard in the way it pooled and flowed over her skin. It didn't drip, but spread out smoothly, thinning itself like leaf and gilding her—not gold, but blue—from the tips of her fingers, up her wrist, and over her forearm, so that she seemed to be wearing a glove made of mirror. She stared at it in wonder, turning her hand over, flexing her fingers, her wrist. The metal moved with her like a second skin.

And then she felt it: a low hum, a vibration.

At first, it was only her hand and forearm where the metal touched her, but it spread. All thoughts of modesty were forgotten as the thrum moved up her arm, even beyond the shining glove. As she watched, her skin began to change color. It grayed, like storm clouds or uul meat, flushing upward from the edge of the glove, rising toward her shoulder, carrying the thrum and the gray with it. She felt the buzz in her lips, in her teeth.

Nova saw the change come over her sister, her skin darkening to gray, then finally to Mesarthim blue. It was perfect. She'd imagined it so many times: the pair of them blue and free and empowered, and far away from here. And now it was happening. Tears pricked her eyes. It was finally happening.

They had always believed, deep in their hearts, that their gifts would be strong like their mother's. As to what they would be, it was hard to decide what to hope for: elemental, empath, telepath, shape-shifter, seer, healer, weather-witch, warrior? They changed their minds all the time. Nova, especially, had always been gift-greedy, never able to settle on one. Smith, of course, was the emperor of gifts (and the emperor himself was, of course, a smith), but Kora and

Nova knew how rare it was, and had never gotten their hopes up. Lately, with the village men eyeing them like livestock, invisibility had begun to seem appealing to Kora.

"I'd rather inflict blindness," Nova had asserted. "Why should *we* have to disappear just because men are animals?"

And now the moment of discovery was upon them. The suspense was almost unbearable. What would they be, once their gifts awoke? In what capacity would they serve the empire?

The hum surged through Kora. Once it had covered the whole surface of her body, it seemed to sink deeper, through her skin to the core of her, to penetrate her heart, the backs of her eyes, the insides of her knees, the pit of her belly.

Then in her mind: a presence. It gave her a start, but it was not unfamiliar. A short while ago, outside, she and Nova had spoken a plea in their thoughts—*see us*—and the telepath, Ren, had come into their minds, and he came again now into Kora's.

Don't think, he counseled from inside her mind. *Don't wonder. Just feel.*

I feel . . . a humming in my skin, she thought experimentally, wondering if he would hear her.

He did. *That's the physical threshold. Go deeper. Our gifts are buried within us.*

She tried to do as he said. She closed her eyes and imagined she was opening other eyes that would look inward instead of out.

Nova watched, marveling at the silky azure of her sister's eyelids, a shade darker than the rest of her skin. She was beautiful like this, majestic even in her dingy smallclothes. The godsmetal glove lent her an elegance that even homespun couldn't ruin, and her hair, which against her white skin was mild and pretty, became, set against blue, a drama of contrast. Even her pale brows and lashes stood out in a new and striking way. Nova wondered what was happening inside her sister. She wanted to be in Kora's mind with her, sharing this experience as they had shared all their dreams for all their lives. What was she *feeling*?

At first, nothing. Kora was trying to look within herself, but she didn't know what she was supposed to see, so there was nothing but the imperfect darkness of her eyelids, washed with wavering red where light glowed through.

Don't see, said Ren. *Feel. What* feels *different?*

Maybe he guided her. Maybe she did it on her own, but Kora began to become aware of the discrete entity that was *herself*, apart from environment, expectations, and the watchful eyes of these important strangers. Apart even from her sister. It was like being suspended inside herself, hearing the blood moving in her veins, feeling the throb of the heart that pushed it, and her limbs, and her breath, and her mind. She envisioned herself turning blue to her bones, the mesarthium seeping into her, and not infusing her with magic, but waking the magic that was already there.

She felt a pressure in her chest. As soon as she did, the telepath did, too.

There, he said. *There it is.*

What is it? she asked.

Bring it forth, he said. *Let it come.*

The pressure intensified, and she felt something in her chest begin to give way. It unnerved her. It felt as though some essential part of her was about to spill out of her body—as though her rib cage were going to swing open and...let something out. There was no pain. It was like discovering that, all along, her body had been made to do this, that her chest was hinged like a gate and she had simply never noticed.

Nova saw her sister's head tip back. Her eyes were still closed. Her hands flew to her chest and clawed at her undershirt, dragging at it so hard that it ripped right down the center to reveal the vale between her breasts, shadowed indigo and heaving with breath. "Kora!" she cried, and tried to go to her but found she couldn't move her feet. Looking down, she saw they'd sunk into the floor, the godsmetal trapping them in place. She nearly fell. Then the telepath spoke into her mind: *Do not interrupt her metamorphosis.*

She stopped struggling and watched, helpless and then awestruck as Kora's gift emerged.

Quite literally, it emerged.

Kora's chest felt as though it had swung open, but it had not. It was intact. The blue channel of skin visible through the rent in her undershirt became, all at once, clouded. A milky vapor extruded from it, taking shape before her like smoke poured into an invisible mold. It was big, and growing fast. Very quickly it dwarfed her. Nova's breathing matched exactly the rise and fall of her sister's chest. She looked to the Servants, frantic, to take reassurance from their expressions that this was normal and expected, but she saw only astonishment. Whatever was happening to Kora, it was anything but normal.

It was a ghostly thing in the air, and it had wings, great, sweeping wings. Nova's first wild thought was that it was a seraph, one of the six angelic Faerers who had cut the portals between the worlds. But as it took its final shape and turned from ghost to solid, she realized it was not an angel, but a bird.

The creature that spilled out of Kora took the form of an immense white eagle.

Kora's head was still thrown back, and her arms had opened at her sides, in unconscious mimicry of the bird's outstretched wings.

She herself did not see what had emerged from her. Her eyes were closed—a fact that should have rendered her blind, but didn't. She beheld the Servants, their shocked faces, and she saw Nova, mouth agape.

"An astral," said Solvay, her voice suffused with awe. "I don't believe it. An astral *here*, in this forsaken place."

"I've never even known one," said white-haired Antal, quite forgiving the stench of uul.

"And a powerful one," said Ren. "Just look at that manifestation."

Kora, seeing only what *it* saw, didn't know what they were talking about. She opened her real eyes, and was hit by a dizzying doubling of her vision, to be seeing through two sets of eyes at once. Dizzy or not, she perceived what had coalesced before her.

It was magnificent, as white as starlight on snow. Its face was fierce and beautiful, hook-beaked and black-eyed. It could be mistaken for a flesh creature—almost. But it floated with unnatural lightness, hardly needing to beat its wings, and the edges of its feathers had a melting aura that belied its seeming solidity.

"Does it have mass?" asked Solvay.

"Touch it and find out," drawled Skathis, making no move to do so.

It was Nova who did. They didn't stop her this time. Her feet remained trapped in the floor, but the eagle's size had brought its wing within her reach. She touched it, running her fingers over its long feathers. If she had ever felt silk, or even known of its existence, then she might have been able to describe such softness. But she hadn't. The closest she could come was the slippery smoothness of clean hair.

The Mesarthim talked amongst themselves, and Kora and Nova

142

heard terms like "range" and "sensory connection," not grasping what they meant. "Magnitude" they understood, though.

"Undoubtedly extremely high," Antal said, and both sisters flushed with pride, Nova's in no way less than her sister's, though it was not her own gift in question.

There was talk of further testing, but it was vague, with Ren, Solvay, and Antal glancing to Skathis, apparently waiting for him to weigh in. He remained fixed on Kora and the bird, a hard glitter to his gaze, and at length he said, "The emperor will be pleased."

And that decided the matter.

Ren helped Kora bring the bird back into herself, which seemed impossible at first. Wherever it had come from, it was real now, and massive, like something birthed that could not be put back. But she found that it could. As it had poured out of her chest, so did it pour back in, her doubled vision resolving, and the dizziness with it, so that she felt almost normal again—though it was hard to imagine ever feeling truly "normal" after this. "What does 'astral' mean?" she asked, breathless. "I've never heard of it before."

"I'm not surprised," said Solvay. "It's an extremely rare gift, my dear."

"Don't go swelling her head," said Skathis. "She'll get the idea she's special."

"She *is* special," said Solvay.

"Literally, 'astral' means 'of the stars,'" Antal explained. "Because the first astral claimed he could voyage through the stars without ever leaving his home. It means that your senses, your consciousness, perhaps even your *soul* can take form outside your body and travel, leaving your physical self behind and returning to it."

"And ... I'll be able to see what it sees, wherever it goes?"

"It's not an 'it,'" Antal answered. "It's *you*, Korako. That eagle is you, as much as your flesh and blood is you." He smiled, a glad sort of smile shared by Ren and Solvay, which made them vastly less intimidating. "And yes, you will be able to travel in astral form."

The atmosphere in the wasp ship was so different from when the girls had first been brought in. The Servants had been stiff, with the aggrieved composure of those carrying out a tedious task made worse by a truly vile stench. All that had transformed into something almost giddy. It was evident that Kora was a discovery of great value, and it seemed most certain now that she was chosen. She would not be left behind here, bereft of the godsmetal that had brought out her gift. She would keep her blue skin forever, and her mystical eagle, too. She was what she had always believed herself to be: powerful.

"I've never heard of so large a manifestation," said Solvay. "There's an astral in the Azorasp whose projection is a finch." She laughed. "Korako's could swallow it whole."

Korako. Hearing her sister's name—her full name, no less—spoken aloud and not twinned with her own, gave Nova a flutter of nerves, as though some process had begun that would split them from one double person into two singular ones. No. She pushed away the thought. It would be as they had always planned: the pair of them as soldier-wizards, serving the empire together, together always.

The mesarthium released her feet, and Nova flung herself forward, wrapping Kora in her arms. "I knew it," she whispered. "You're magnificent."

But the girls' joy and vindication could be only half formed until Nova's worth was proven as well.

The godsmetal glove began to peel away from Kora's hand. She watched the metal turn liquid once more, and pool back toward her wrist, gathering itself together. She felt a lurch of loss. She didn't want to revert to her old self, unmagical and un-blue.

And she didn't have to. Skathis didn't take the godsmetal away, but formed it into a thin, curved band lying across her palm. A diadem. Both girls' breath caught in their throats. How they'd dreamed of this moment, and even played at it with seaweed or bits of twine.

"Put it on," Skathis instructed, and Kora raised it to her brow to fit it in place. But the smith said, "No. On your throat."

Kora paused, confused. "What?"

"Like a collar," Skathis said.

Solvay's jaw tightened. She looked down at the papers in front of her and pretended to straighten them, saying nothing.

Kora, uncertain, did as she was told. As soon as it touched her neck, the godsmetal curved around it, encircling it completely, and though it was not too tight, it made her uneasy there. This was certainly not how she'd dreamed it. She ran her fingers over the thing and gave what she hoped was a brave and grateful smile.

Skathis turned to Nova. "Catch," he said, and lobbed another small godsmetal ball.

❦ 17 ❦

NICE DREAMS NOW AND THEN

Minya was out cold.

"Oh gods," said Ruby with a hysterical laugh. "I was afraid she wouldn't drink it." She pulled out a chair and dropped into it while the others gaped—all but Sparrow, who let out a shaky sigh.

"Well done," she told her sister, picking her way through shards of shattered teacup to reach Minya's limp form. The little girl was sprawled across the table, eyes closed, mouth open, one arm flopped over the side. She looked very small. Delicately, Sparrow lifted the flopped arm and tucked it onto the table.

"What just happened?" Feral asked, his eyes darting from girl to girl. "What did you do?"

Ruby lifted her chin. "Something," she said with great dignity. "You might have heard of it. It's the opposite of nothing."

He looked at her blankly. What was *that* supposed to mean? "Would you care to elaborate?"

"I drugged Minya." When she heard her own words, Ruby's eyes went wide. She repeated, with wonder, "*I drugged Minya*," and then, warming to her subject, "I saved us, that's all. Weep too. Maybe the whole world. You're welcome." As an afterthought, she admitted in a substantially lower voice, "It was Sparrow's idea."

"But you did it," said Sparrow, who felt no need to claim credit.

Sarai came up between them. She didn't have to worry about the broken porcelain on the floor, but just floated an inch or two above it. She looked at Minya's little face. With her eyes closed, and her mouth relaxed from the tight line or smirk it was usually fixed in, you could see how pretty she was, and how very young. She didn't look at all like a tyrant intent on starting a war. And now . . . for the moment, at least . . . she wasn't. She was just a little girl asleep on a table. "Thank you," breathed Sarai, reaching for Sparrow and Ruby. They were all shaking in the stillness, trying to adjust to the sudden lack of threat.

"Yes," said Lazlo, breathless. "Thank you." He was still reeling under the full horror of his predicament. He didn't know what he would have done, or whom he would have sacrificed. He prayed that he would *never* know, and never again be in such a position.

"I can't believe you two did this." Sarai laughed. It wasn't much of a laugh. It was weak and amazed and, above all, relieved. She had thought she had come to her end out there, where it was so cold, and souls melted like darkness at dawn. "It was the bottle?" she asked. "The green one?"

"It was," said Ruby. "And to whoever might have called me an idiot for tasting it, I am accepting apologies. Not granting pardons, mind you. Just accepting apologies." She didn't look at Feral, so she didn't see his scowl, but she imagined it, and, in fact, the one in her mind perfectly matched the one on his face.

"Tasting what?" asked Lazlo. "What bottle?"

Ruby held up a finger at him. "Hold that thought, please," she said, adding in a stage whisper, "I'm waiting for an apology."

"Fine," drawled Feral. "I take back what I said *when we were children*. You weren't an idiot for tasting Letha's potion. You were a *lucky* idiot."

Ruby's eyes flashed to him. "You'd know all about being a lucky idiot. But you've run out of luck. Now you're just an idiot."

And so Sarai inferred that whatever had begun between Feral and Ruby had ended. She didn't know if she should be sorry about it; it seemed rather a terrible idea, the two of them paired up. She told Lazlo, "Ruby's room used to be Letha's, and there was a green glass bottle she'd kept on her bed table. When we were little, Ruby tasted it. She thought it might be sweet, but it wasn't."

"I only touched my tongue to the rim of the bottle, like this," said Ruby, demonstrating.

"And she passed out for two days," added Sparrow.

"And woke up feeling perfectly fine," concluded Ruby. "Having understood, even as a child"—and this next bit was directed at Feral—"that Letha would hardly have kept *poison* on her bed table."

"She could have," argued Feral. "For all you knew, she murdered her lovers when she was through with them."

"What a fine idea."

"Stop it, you two," Sarai said mildly. The point was: The green glass bottle had held a sleeping draught. Looking at Minya laid out there, so vulnerable, she realized something. "I don't think I've ever seen her asleep."

Nor had the others. They had assumed she must sleep, but none of them could recall ever seeing her do it.

It was then that Sarai noted a peculiar absence from the discussion and craned her head to look for the Ellens. They ought to have been right here, tongues clucking with praises and scolds, but . . . they were still in the kitchen doorway, and they weren't moving.

They weren't moving *at all*.

Sarai said, "Ellens?" and the others turned to look. For the moment, they forgot Minya and went over to the nurses. "Ellen?" coaxed Sarai, reaching for Great Ellen's shoulder. There was no response, and…it wasn't just that she was frozen. Great Ellen was *blank*. Less Ellen was, too. There was no expression at all on their faces, and worse: no awareness in their eyes. Sarai waved her hand in front of them. Nothing. She made a quick glance round at the rest of the ghosts, and they all looked as they always did: Their bodies were rigid, but their eyes were free and they watched everything, fully conscious inside their puppet forms. But not the Ellens.

It didn't make any sense.

The nearest they could figure—this was Feral's theory; he was always good for a theory, if not for a decision—was that when Minya fell asleep, her ghosts went on in whatever state she'd left them, until such a time as they received new orders. If they were frozen, they remained so. On guard duty, the same, though that they could not prove, since all the ghosts had been gathered here in anticipation of invading Weep. As for Sarai, she'd just been given back her free will, so she retained it.

So why hadn't the Ellens?

"Maybe Minya froze them," said Sparrow, "to stop them from interfering with her?"

But Ruby had talked to them just the moment before, when she pushed back through the doorway with her tea tray. "They were normal," she said. "They were crying." Indeed, tear streaks were visible on their cheeks. "Great Ellen caught my elbow," she said. "She made the cups slosh. I hissed at her to let go." She frowned. "I wasn't very pleasant."

And even if Minya had frozen them, as they all knew she had

earlier in the garden, that couldn't explain this vacant state. It was as though the two ghost women were...*empty*.

Unsettled though they were, they had to leave them like that and turn their attention back to Minya and the very large question of what to do about her. "We can't keep her drugged forever," said Feral.

"Well, we *could*," Ruby argued, looking around at them. "I mean, it kind of solves all our problems. Sarai's free, no one's making us *kill* anyone, and it's not like we're hurting her. She's just asleep. Sarai can give her nice dreams now and then, and we can do what we like from now on."

"It's hardly a permanent solution," said Sparrow.

"Maybe not *forever*," said Ruby, "but I'm in no hurry for her to wake up."

None of them were, but it was still unsettling to think of keeping her drugged. And she wasn't the only one affected.

"What about them?" Lazlo asked, meaning the slave ghosts packed into the gallery.

Ruby grimaced as she considered them. "We could move them, I guess." Her eyes lit up. "You can make mesarthium servants to do it, so we don't even have to touch them."

He regarded her, quizzical. "I meant..." he began, at a loss, and looked to Sarai for help.

"He meant," she said with a note of censure, "that they'll be slaves, and stay trapped, as long as Minya's unconscious."

"At least no one's making them kill their own families," said Ruby. "They're fine."

Feral exhaled and said to Lazlo, "You can't expect her to have normal feelings. It's just how she is."

A look suspiciously like hurt—a normal feeling if ever there was one—flashed across Ruby's face. Sparrow spoke up before she could. "Or," she told Feral wearily, "you're just spectacularly bad at noticing feelings." She knew as much from her own experience, when she'd fancied herself in love with him. Before he or anyone else could answer, she moved back to the topic at hand. "We can't keep these ghosts prisoner forever. For now, we have to, while we think what to do. But we won't move them." She spoke with quiet authority. "It wouldn't do to shuffle them out of sight just so their suffering doesn't trouble us. We can't forget about them. They're *people*."

Sarai said, "She's right. I could never keep all these souls enslaved just for my own freedom."

"Their freedom isn't in your hands," said Lazlo, wanting to alleviate the burden of her guilt. "It's in Minya's, and you know if she were to wake, the last thing she would do is set them free."

"I know," Sarai said, feeling helpless. "There's got to be something we haven't thought of. A way of reaching her."

Her current profound relief notwithstanding, and no matter what her feelings for Minya in the worst or best of times, Sarai couldn't bear the thought of keeping her asleep forever like some cursed girl in a fairy tale. But what was the alternative? The helplessness was consuming. Every attempt she'd made to reason with her, or to appeal to her, had failed. If there was some way to reach Minya, she had no idea what it was.

But…

A small cluster of words circled back to her from the flow of conversation. They were Ruby's, and had been spoken carelessly: *Sarai can give her nice dreams now and then.*

Sarai didn't give nice dreams. She was the Muse of Nightmares. Minya had made her so. From the moment her gift awakened—the moment Minya had made her stop stifling it—the little girl had

151

taken charge, and determined how she used it and who she became. Minya had created her, and . . . the Carnage had created Minya.

Who might they have been, both of them, if they'd grown up in other times? In what service might Minya have used her gift, and in what manner Sarai? The one controlled souls, the other dreams. What *power*, between the two of them.

Sarai had wished, that morning, for her mother's gift, that she might unwork Minya's hate. Well, she couldn't. Her gift was dreams. Not specifically nightmares—that was Minya's doing. Sarai's gift was *dreams*. How might she use it, if she were making herself from scratch?

If, indeed, she even still *had* it, now that she was dead.

She took a steadying breath and looked from Lazlo to Sparrow to Feral to Ruby before turning to Minya. Her little face was relaxed in sleep, eyelashes dusky on her cheeks.

What was going on in her mind? What did Minya dream of? Sarai didn't know. She'd never looked. Minya had forbidden it when they were still little children. All of a sudden it was very clear: She had to find out. She had to go in, and talk to her there. If she *could*, if she still had her gift.

She said to the others, "Let's move her to her bed and make her comfortable." She took a deep breath. "At nightfall, if my moths come, I'm going into her dreams."

18

GRAY

Nightfall was still some hours away, and those hours had to be spent. Having determined a course of action, Sarai was antsy and uncertain, a pendulum swinging between fear and dread: the one, that her gift wouldn't manifest, the other that it *would*. What was she more afraid of? Violating Minya's innermost sanctuary, or being unable to, and having to dredge up yet another wild hope?

They settled Minya in her bed. Any of them might have carried her—she weighed nothing at all—but Lazlo was the one to pick her up, and the whole time he held her, he kept thinking with amazement, *This is my sister.*

Her rooms, which had been Skathis's, weren't like the other chambers. All those consisted of a bedroom, bath, dressing room, and sitting room. But here was a proper palace, occupying the whole of the seraph's right shoulder. There was a fountain—dry now—with mesarthium lily pads you could cross like stepping-stones. A sunken seating area was filled with velvet cushions, and great columns in the form of seraphim stood in a circle, their raised wings supporting a high, elegant dome. A sweeping staircase led to a mezzanine. From there, a long hall, lined on one side by filigree windows like enormous panels of metal lace, led to a grand bedroom, with, at its center, a bed that made even Isagol's seem modest. Lazlo laid Minya down on it. She looked, in its waves of blue silk, like a matchstick bobbing in an ocean.

"We should keep watch," said Sparrow, "in case she stirs."

They all agreed. Sparrow took the first watch, and pulled up a chair by the bedside, with the green glass bottle close at hand in case she needed to dispense a drop between Minya's lips.

"Is she saying something?" asked Ruby, bending close.

They all looked. Indeed, her lips seemed to be moving, though she made no sound. And if there were words in the movements, they couldn't make them out. It gave them a chill, though, to wonder what conversation she might be having in her dreams.

They were hungry. None of them had partaken with particular relish of the morning loaf. So they went to the kitchen, having to squeeze, unnerved, between the blank, frozen Ellens, and there they began to discover the extent of their helplessness.

The loaf was but a crust, and they didn't know how to make another. Bread might as well have been alchemy, for all that they knew what to do. There were always plums and kimril, though, so they boiled some tubers and mashed them, and stirred in plum jam for flavor, and then they carried the whole pot to Minya's room with an extra spoon for Sparrow. They ate it feeling a little proud of themselves, and idiotic for feeling proud, all reaching out with their spoons, jousting in the bowl like children. The clink of metal mingled with laughs and huffs of mock outrage as someone stole a bite or parried a thrust, or even despooned an opponent.

And in the course of things, in the kitchen and then by Minya's bedside, they grew comfortable with the stranger who, impossibly, was kin. They wanted to know how Sarai had met him, and what sort of dreams she'd given him. "I didn't," she confessed, her cheeks warming. "I liked them just how they were. I snuck into them like a stowaway."

She described "Dreamer's Weep"—the city as Lazlo imagined it: the children in their feather cloaks, the grannies riding saddled cats, the wingsmiths in the marketplace, even the centaur and his lady, all of whom she liked to think of as real people living out their days. By the end of it—and she didn't tell everything, not by a long shot—they all wanted it to be real, so they could go there, too, and live there, and say good morning to all those folk and creatures.

And they wanted to know about Lazlo, of course. They peppered him with questions, and he did his best to describe what his life had been like before Eril-Fane rode into it.

"Are you telling me it was your job to read books?" Feral asked with as much or more yearning than Ruby had earlier shown for cake.

"Not to *read* them, unfortunately," answered Lazlo. "That was for the scholars. I read in my spare moments, and by staying up too late."

All of which sounded like paradise to Feral. "How many books are there?" he asked hungrily.

"Too many to count. Thousands on every subject. History, astronomy, alchemy—"

"Thousands of books on every subject?" repeated Feral, looking dazed and skeptical.

"Poor Feral can't picture it," Sarai said gently. "He's only ever seen one book, and he can't read it."

"I can *read*," said Feral, defensive. Great Ellen had taught them all. Since there was no paper in the citadel, she'd used a tray of crushed herbs and a stick, so that without even realizing it, they all associated reading with the scent of mint and thyme. "I just can't read *that*."

Lazlo's interest was piqued. Feral fetched the book in question: the only one they had. It was like no book Lazlo had seen. It wasn't paper and board, but all mesarthium, cover and pages. Feral opened it and turned its thin metal sheets. The alphabet was angular and somehow menacing. It made Lazlo imagine that the corresponding language must be harsh to hear. "May I?" he asked before reaching out to touch it.

It hummed against his fingers, seeming to whisper to his skin, just like the anchors, the citadel, and Rasalas. It had its own scheme of energies, small but dense, and he knew at first touch that there was more to it than met the eye. With a brush of his fingers, he awakened the page, and the markings engraved on it changed.

"What did you do?" Feral demanded, reaching protectively for the book.

Lazlo let it go, but tried to explain. "There's more here than you can see. Look." He reached back out and, with a fingertip, woke the page again, the runelike engravings melting away and giving rise to all new ones. "Every sheet remembers volumes of information."

"What kind of information?"

But Lazlo couldn't say. He had, on his own, decoded the language of Weep, but it had taken him years, and he'd had trade manifests to use to build a key. The thought of translating the gods' language was daunting. When he drew his fingers away again, the page fell still on a diagram.

"What's that?" asked Sarai, bending her head toward it.

The sheet was divided into narrow vertical columns, each one labeled in the inscrutable writing. "It looks like a row of books on a shelf," said Lazlo, because the runes ran sideways, like titles printed on spines.

"They look more like plates on the drying rack to me," said Sarai, because, unlike the spines of books, each one tapered, dislike, to a point at the top and bottom.

On a hunch, Lazlo touched the page and set it scrolling, the metal coming to life, the marks rolling over its surface in waves. They all watched, transfixed. Whatever the vertical shapes represented, they went on and on. There were dozens of them, each one labeled in the angular letters of the Mesarthim.

More mystified by it than ever, Feral explained that the book had been found here, in Skathis's chambers. "I've always thought there must be answers in it. Where the Mesarthim came from, and why."

"And what they did with the others," Sparrow added softly.

Whatever mystery the diagram represented, it faded away at the mention of this one:

In the citadel, they'd lived their whole lives with the question of the others—not the two dozen godspawn slain in the Carnage, but the ones who'd vanished before. *Thousands* of them, there had to have been, over two centuries of Mesarthim rule.

"The other children," said Lazlo, looking around at their solemn faces.

"You know about them?" asked Feral.

He did. He thought of Suheyla, and all the other women who'd birthed babies in the citadel and had their memories eaten by Letha before they were returned home. Over the past days, as Weep had revealed its dark history to him, this question had emerged: Why had the gods bred themselves on humans? *Bred themselves on.* His jaw clenched and he banished the pallid term, even from his mind. Why had the gods *raped* humans and forced them to bear—or father—

their "godspawn"? Lazlo was certain that the rapes themselves weren't the point but the means—that the *children* were the point. It was too systematic to be otherwise. There was even a nursery.

So the question was: *Why?* And: *What did they do with them? What did they do with all those children?* "You've no idea what it was all about?" he asked.

"We only know that they were taken away as soon as their gifts manifested," explained Sarai. "Korako took them. The goddess of secrets."

"Korako," Lazlo repeated. "But you don't know where she took them?"

They shook their heads.

"Could you be one of them?" asked Sparrow, fixing on Lazlo.

"I think Great Ellen thinks you are," said Sarai, remembering. But they couldn't ask the nurse now which baby boy she'd meant.

Lazlo told them about his fragile wisp of memory: wings against the sky, and the feeling of weightlessness. "The white bird," he said. "I think she took me to Zosma."

"Wraith?" said Sarai, surprised. "Why?"

Why had the great white eagle carried him away from here and abandoned him in war-torn Zosma, if indeed she had? He had no idea. "Could she have taken all of them? All of *us*? Could that be the answer somehow? Did Wraith carry all the babies out into the world?"

"They weren't babies, though," said Sarai. "Most gifts manifest at four or five, if not later, and that's when they were taken."

That made a difference. Could Wraith have carried children that age? Even if she could, children would remember it, surely, in a way babies wouldn't. And if it were true, and the world was full of men and women who'd been born in a floating metal angel and carried from it by a huge white eagle that could vanish in thin air . . . wouldn't there be stories?

"I don't know." Lazlo sighed, rubbing his face. He was feeling his fatigue. They all were. "What *is* she?" he asked. "The bird. Do you know? Did she belong to the gods? Was she some kind of pet, or messenger?"

"*She?*" repeated Feral. They had never thought to assign the bird a gender. "You keeping calling Wraith *she*."

"Eril-Fane did," Lazlo told them. "As though he knew her."

"Maybe he knows something we don't," said Ruby.

"I'm sure he knows a lot that we don't," said Feral.

Sarai agreed. "He lived here for three years. He learned enough about the gods to kill them. He must have found out their weaknesses, and who knows what else."

"We could talk to him," Lazlo ventured.

Talk to her father? *Meet* her father? A thrill of anxious excitement raced through Sarai, but the anxiety quickly swallowed the excitement so that what was left simply felt like fear. Would he even *want* to meet her? Unconsciously, she glanced at Minya. The two were so tangled in her mind, all blood and vengeance and strife.

But what she saw on the bed pushed all thought of Eril-Fane from her mind. She gasped and pointed, and the others spun to look, stricken, sure to find Minya awake behind them and smiling her malevolent smile. But she wasn't awake, or smiling.

She was simply *gray*.

* * *

"Is she dying?" cried Ruby. "Have I killed her?" Because Minya *looked* like she was dying, and what else could it be but the potion? She was the color of ashes, of stone, and only Lazlo knew what it meant. He didn't hesitate, but scooped her into his arms and laid her right down on the floor.

"What are you doing?" Feral demanded.

"It's okay," Lazlo said. "She'll be all right. Look." He took her little hands in his, one at a time, and opened her curled fingers to press her palms to the floor. He held them like that, palms flat against the metal. Her legs were touching it, too, and it wasn't long before it was obvious: Her blue was coming back.

Sarai took a deep breath. Minya's death also meant her own, and she'd braced for it for a terrible second. Minya had looked so ill, but she was fine now, bluer every second, and still sleeping peacefully. "What happened?" she asked Lazlo.

"She wasn't touching mesarthium," he said. He shook his head. "Stupid. I should have thought of it. But it happened *fast*." He marveled. "I'd never have thought it would be that fast."

"What?" demanded Ruby. "That *what* would be that fast?"

"Her fading," he said, looking at his own hands. They were fully blue now, of course, but he remembered how, down in the city when he'd still been human, his hands had turned gray when he touched mesarthium. It had taken days for the tinge to wear off, but Minya hadn't been lying here for much more than an hour. "It was a lot slower for me."

"Fading?" asked Sparrow.

He stopped and looked around at them, realizing something. They were all barefoot, in constant contact with the metal. He said, "You know how it works, don't you? How it's the mesarthium that makes you blue, and gives you your power, too?"

In fact, they didn't know. The metal had always been there, and they had always been blue. They hadn't guessed the one was a con-

160

sequence of the other, and the notion was at once obvious and stag-gering. How had they never realized? Lazlo explained it as well as he was able, from what he knew of himself: As a baby, he had been gray. "Gray as rain," a monk had said, thinking he was dying. But the color had faded long ago, and he hadn't thought anything of it until last night, when he pressed his hands to the anchor and turned first gray, then blue.

"Do you mean to say," Sparrow asked intently, "that if we were to stop touching it, we would become *human*?"

Ruby straightened up. "We could be human?" she asked. "We could live as humans? In the world?"

"I suppose you could, if that's what you wanted."

Sarai asked softly, "*Would* you want that?"

No one answered. It was too big a question. They'd all daydreamed about it, Sarai too. They'd looked at their reflections and pictured themselves brown, wearing human clothes, doing human things. Above all, they'd imagined meeting new people who didn't look at them the way the ghosts did, with loathing that pierced their souls.

"You'd lose your gifts," Lazlo pointed out.

"But they'd come back if we touched mesarthium again? Yours did," said Sparrow.

"I guess so."

It was a lot to take in. They made Minya a new bed on the floor, with a pillow under her head and a folded blanket under her body, leaving her legs and hands in contact with mesarthium. After some discussion, they made a kind of gruel by watering down the mashed kimril, and Sarai spooned dribbles of it between Minya's lips while Lazlo held her semi-upright. The realities of caring for someone unconscious began to sink in, and it was all the clearer to Sarai that this was a short-term solution.

Ruby took the next watch, and held the green bottle between her knees, her eyes fixed on Minya's for any flutter of lashes that might signal her waking. The others left them there. The sun was edging toward the horizon, and Sarai still didn't know if she'd rather it speed up or stop.

She couldn't shake the feeling that Minya was waiting for her, even in her dreams, perhaps perched in a too-big chair just like the one at the head of the table, with a quell board set up and a smile on her face, the game already in play.

❦ 19 ❦

First Ghost Nightfall

Sarai led Lazlo out onto her terrace to watch the sun set behind the Cusp. With the ghost guards all inside, they had it to themselves: the whole open palm of the seraph.

"That's where I fell." Sarai pointed. She'd slid from the pad of the thumb, down the scoop of the palm, and right off the edge near the fifth finger. Lazlo's jaw clenched as he looked around. He'd almost landed here in the silk sleigh. His first sight of Sarai—his *only* sight, he realized, of her both alive and real—had been here when she'd screamed from her doorway "*Go!*" and saved his life, and Eril-Fane's, Azareen's, and Soulzeren's, too. Right in this spot, she'd both saved their lives and lost her own.

"There should be a railing," he said.

Of course, *now* that seemed like a good idea. "I never felt unsafe here," Sarai said. "I didn't know the citadel would *tip*."

She went to the edge to look out. It wasn't an edge, per se. It curved up at the sides to form a low, sloping wall. Enough to keep one from walking off the side, but not enough to catch a person if it were to tip. And though Lazlo was determined that that wouldn't happen again, still the sight of Sarai standing there raised the hairs on his arms. He willed a railing to sprout up before her.

"Silly," she said, running a palm over it. "I can't fall now. Haven't you realized? I can fly."

With that, she sprouted wings from her shoulders, like the ones from their wingsmith dream. Fox wings, they'd been, of all things, covered in soft orange fur. Those had been on a harness. These grew right from her shoulders. Why not? She spread them wide and fanned them down, and lifted into the air. She couldn't go far. She couldn't fly *away*. Minya's tether held her here, but it was still a thrill. It felt as though she were really flying.

Lazlo reached up and caught her by the waist, and drew her down into his arms, and as fine as it was to fly, it was better to land like this—to moor against him and make herself fast. She settled in, arms around his neck, closed her eyes, and softly kissed him. She kissed the side she hadn't bitten, and she was careful. She only brushed her lips against his, softly parted, playing. Lightly, she licked with the tip of her tongue. His met hers, just as lightly.

She told him what he'd told her a few nights before, when they'd had their first awed inkling of what a kiss could be. "You have ruined my tongue for all other tastes," she whispered, and felt his mouth smile against hers. There was sound in their breathing, the softest of sighs. Their bodies remembered the heat from before, his lips closing warm on the tip of her breast, and their chests, skin to skin, so brief before the bite.

And the heat leapt alive—a fire licked by winds. Licked and sucked, deep and sweet. They kissed—not lightly, no, not now.

Lazlo winced. There was blood. They'd reopened the bite. He made no move to stop. He held Sarai close, and kissed her. Her feet were off the ground. Her fingers were in his hair. They were tangled in each other on the seraph's open palm. Under her slip, her elilith pulsed silver. It wanted Lazlo's lips, his hands, his skin, his fire, as she wanted his weight, rocking with her, his heat, filling her. He wanted to trace her tattoo's shining lines and taste it, and feel it, and make it glow, and make her purr. Neither of them knew anything at all. But their bodies knew what bodies know, and wanted what bodies want.

They wanted, but they parted, with wildfires in them and blood on their tongues. "I want..." Sarai murmured.

"Me too," Lazlo breathed.

They gazed at each other, awed that fires could kindle that fast, and frustrated that they couldn't *let* them kindle. Sarai had only meant to kiss him, and now she wanted to climb him, consume him. She felt like a creature, fanged and hungry, and...she liked it. She let out a shaky laugh and loosened her hold on him, sliding down so her feet once again met the ground.

The friction made him close his eyes and take a steadying breath.

"Your lip," said Sarai with a grimace of apology. "It'll never heal at this rate."

"I like this rate," said Lazlo, his voice at its roughest—as it was, Sarai was learning, in moments of grief or desire. "I can always get another lip," he said, "but I'll never get this moment back."

Sarai cocked her head. "There's nothing at all wrong with that statement."

"No, nothing. It's perfectly true."

"Lips probably grow on vines somewhere."

"It's a big world. Chances are good."

Sarai smiled and felt like a silly girl, in the best possible way. "I like *this* lip, though. I'm appointing myself its protector. No kissing until further notice."

Lazlo's eyes narrowed. "That's the worst idea you've ever had."

"Think of it as a challenge. You can't *kiss*, but you can *be* kissed. I should make that clear. Just not on the mouth."

"Where, then?" he asked, intrigued.

She considered the matter. "Your eyebrow, for example. Probably only there. Not your neck," she said, a glimmer in her eye. "Or that place right behind your ear." She brushed it with her fingertips, sending a shiver through him. "And absolutely not *here*." She traced a slow line down the center of his chest, felt his muscles tense through the linen, and wanted to lift his shirt and kiss his skin right then and there.

Lazlo seized her hand and pressed it to his hearts, which were slamming against the wall of his chest. He gazed at her, all astonishment and simmer. How his dreamer's eyes shone. Sarai could see herself in them, and the setting sun, too: a bit of blue in each iris, some cinnamon and pink, and twin swaths of glowing orange glazed over gray. "Sarai," he said, and his voice was even rougher than in grief or desire. It sounded broken and put back together with half its pieces missing. It sounded ravaged and sweet and perfect. "I love you," he said, and Sarai melted.

It had been wrong, earlier, in the gallery, with Minya and ghosts and promises and threats, but here and now, it was right. It was perfectly right, and proved Sarai a poor protector of Lazlo's lip after all. She kissed him. She gave the words back to him, murmuring, and kept them, too. You could do that: Give them back and keep them. "I love you" is generous that way.

And when the sun touched the Cusp and sank away behind it, they stood at the railing Lazlo had made and watched light diffuse through the demonglass—the thousands of giant skeletons melted and fused to make a mountain—and a drumbeat of nerves kicked off inside Sarai.

How strange that this was her first ghost nightfall. She hadn't even been dead a full day. Would her moths burgeon, or had she lost them, too?

It was time to find out.

* * *

From the beginning, Sarai's gift had manifested as the need to scream. Her throat and soul demanded it every nightfall. If she tried to resist, the pressure would build until she couldn't abide it. This thing that was in her, it had to come out. It was who she was.

Or it had been.

Darkness settled slowly and Sarai waited for the feeling, the burgeoning of moths within her. But she felt nothing—no fullness, no scream. She put her hand to her throat as though she should feel the thrum of them in her, waiting to take shape where her breath met air.

There was nothing. No thrum, and, of course, no breath. She looked at Lazlo, stricken.

"What is it?" he asked.

"I can't feel them." Sparks of panic lit through her. "I think they're gone."

He ran his hands down her arms and back up, so he was holding her shoulders. "It might just be different now," he said. "It might *feel* different."

"I don't feel anything."

"How does it usually work?" he asked. He wasn't panicking, but

167

his hearts were in his throat. Sarai's gift had brought her to him—into his mind and his life—and he loved being in dreams with her. It was better than any story he'd ever read. It was like being inside a story and writing it all around you, and not alone but with someone who just happened to be as magical and beautiful as a fairy tale made real.

"I scream," said Sarai. "And they fly out."

"Do you want to try screaming?"

"But I scream because I can feel them, and I need to, to let them out. But there's nothing."

"You could still try," he said with such sweet hopefulness that she almost felt hopeful, too.

So she did. She'd never liked anyone to see her do it. She'd been ashamed. She'd known it must be revolting, to see a hundred moths fly out of someone's mouth, but she didn't worry that Lazlo would think so. She didn't even turn away, but stepped back, in case it worked, so that moths wouldn't fly right in his face. And then she took a deep breath, closed her eyes, imagined them, summoned them, and...screamed.

Lazlo watched, intent. He saw her lips open, and her fine white teeth part, and he saw her rosy tongue, which just a moment ago he'd savored with his own, and he saw...He took a small, sharp breath.

He saw a moth. It was twilight dark, purple black, and its wings brushed her lips as it emerged. They were plush, like velvet nap. He saw antennae like tiny plumes. He started to smile, relief swelling in his chest, but some cautious part of him paused.

And then the smile faded. The relief died. Because the moth... vanished.

No sooner did it leave her lips than it simply ceased to be.

There was another behind it. It met the same fate. Another, another. The same. They came pouring out, and all of them vanished the instant they left her lips. Lazlo remembered the birds they'd made that morning in her room: his, mesarthium, hers, illusion. When she'd sent them airborne, his had flown, but hers had vanished just like this.

Her ghostself might be infinitely transmutable, but it had this limitation: Her illusion had to be part of her, contiguous.

Sarai's eyes were closed. She couldn't see what was happening. Lazlo reached for her. "Sarai," he said softly. "That's enough."

She blinked her eyes open, closed her mouth, and looked around. The air was empty. Where were they? "I . . . I felt them . . ." she said.

"They disappeared," he told her, sorrowful. "As soon as they left your lips."

"Oh." A bleakness opened up in Sarai. For a moment, she'd been so glad. She'd known, though, hadn't she? If her moths had been winging around, she'd have been able to see through their eyes, smell what they smelled, feel the breeze. But she hadn't seen or felt or smelled anything, and she felt like she'd lost a part of herself. She leaned into Lazlo's chest. "That's that, then," she said. "I'm useless."

"Of course you're not."

"What good am I? I don't know how to *do* anything. If I don't have my gift, I can't help."

He smoothed her hair. "You're valuable no matter what you can *do*. And you aren't useless, as it happens." She couldn't see it, but his lip tugged into something like a smile—stinging his reopened wound—and he added in a tone of exaggerated consolation, "Who else could protect my lip from kissing?"

169

She drew back and looked up at him, eyebrows raised. "I think we both know I'm a failure at that job."

Sympathetically, he agreed. "You are terrible at it. But I don't care. There's no one else I want not protecting my lip. The job is yours forever."

"*Forever?* I hope it heals, though."

"Look who's already trying to shirk. Do you want this job or don't you?"

She was laughing now and could hardly believe it. How had he made her laugh, when she'd been flooded with self-pity?

"But listen," he said, growing serious again, not willing to give up on her gift just yet. "What would happen if you...I don't know, caught one of your moths on your finger, and kept contact with it, so it wouldn't vanish."

"I don't know."

"Care to try?"

She was skeptical, but she said, "Why not?" And she did it, eyes open. She willed a moth to burgeon, and as it emerged, she caught it on her fingertip, and held it out before her. They both looked at it. Sarai wondered: Was it even really one of her moths—a magical conduit to the minds and dreams of others—or was it just another shred of illusion, like the songbird from earlier, without any power at all? How could she know, unless she placed it on a sleeper's brow? "I suppose I'll have to try it on Minya," she said, though she was reluctant to go in—not just into Minya's mind, but even into the citadel. She liked being here alone with Lazlo.

He liked it, too. "You could try it on me first," he said.

"But you're awake."

"I could fix that." He strove for lightness, but Sarai could see what it meant to him—what it had meant to him from the first—to open his mind for her, and be her place of safety. *Oh, sweet.* There was nowhere she would rather go than Dreamer's Weep with Lazlo Strange.

"All right," she said. Her voice was soft. His smile was sweet. They went inside, past Isagol's bed, to the nook in the back, and he lay down. Sarai sat beside him, on the edge of the bed. It would have been so easy to fall back into their wildfire ways. But she only kissed him once, moth-soft, on the safe side of his swollen mouth, and stroked his hair while he fell asleep.

And as she felt him relax by degrees, and saw his breathing slow and deepen, she was overcome by a feeling so powerful she thought surely her ghost couldn't contain it. It wanted to spill out of her in waves of music and silver light. It *would*, if she'd let it, she thought. Literal music, actual light. But she didn't want to wake him, so she kept it inside and felt that the whole of her being was just a fragile skin wrapped around tenderness and aching love, and the kind of surprise you feel when...oh, for example, when you wake up after *dying*, and get another chance. And when she was sure he was asleep, she did as he'd suggested. She willed forth another moth, and, lifting it carefully from her lips, reached it out toward Lazlo's brow.

She meant to put her fingers down and maneuver the moth so it was touching them both, to make a bridge for their minds to cross. And...she already knew it wasn't going to work, even as she reached, because this moth, too, was a mute thing like the ones out on the terrace, not a sentinel for her senses the way it should have been. So a sob was already rising in her throat when her fingers came to rest on his skin.

It was hot. She felt that first, but only for an instant because then...she wasn't there.

She wasn't in the nook, sitting by Lazlo's side, and his brow wasn't under her hand.

She was...she was in the marketplace of Dreamer's Weep, encircled by amphitheater walls and colored tents and hawkers' cries, while, overhead, children in feather cloaks raced over wires strung taut between domes of hammered gold. And Lazlo was standing before her.

20

PLENTY OF FEELINGS

In her surprise, Sarai jerked her hand back, and the moth, perched on her finger, dislodged and vanished as Lazlo awakened and sat up. "It worked," he said, sleepy. He was grinning broadly. "Sarai, you did it."

She was looking at her fingers. The sob was still stuck in her throat. She swallowed it, bewildered. *Had* it worked? *How?* "The moth never touched you," she said. She was sure.

But Lazlo knew he'd seen her, if only for an instant. "Then how...?"

"*I* touched *you*," she said. She was still studying her fingers. She curled them against her palm and looked up to meet his eyes. "I wonder..." she said, and trailed off.

Everything had changed. She'd lost her physical body. The rules were different in this state. Was it outlandish to think her gift might have different rules now, too? What if her moths were gone? What if...she didn't need them? If there was no more bridge, but only *her*?

"Lazlo," she said, her thoughts spinning. "Earlier, in the gallery when I couldn't speak, and you pressed your cheek against mine... did you feel anything?"

He flushed with shame. He knew the moment she meant. "You were right when you said she'd break me," he told her, horrified by how close he'd come. "I was ready to do whatever she wanted."

"But you didn't." She was intense. "*Why* didn't you?"

He searched for an answer. "All of a sudden... I couldn't." His gaze sharpened as he understood. "It was you."

"What was me? What did you feel?"

"I felt... *no*," he said. How else to put it? He could still feel the way it had carved through his mind, pushing everything out of its way. "All of a sudden, it was all there was." His eyes were on hers, searching for confirmation that it had come from her. "The word *no*. It was everything. It stopped me."

She nodded. He *had* felt it. She'd done something like it in the moment before the blast shook the city, sank the anchor, tipped the citadel, and killed her. She'd seen the explosionist light the fuse, watched the flame race toward the charge, and known Lazlo was walking right toward it. Her moth had been perched on his wrist, and through it she'd assailed him with a fry of feeling that stopped him in his tracks. She'd done it through her moth that time. But today, in the gallery, she'd done it skin to skin. And she had, by touching Lazlo, just now slipped into his dream.

Her gift wasn't gone. It had *changed*, as had she. She'd lost her sentinels. She couldn't fly out into the night anymore and spy on sleepers and creep into their minds. But she could touch someone and slip inside their dreams. "It works directly now," she said. "Skin to skin." At those words, both she and Lazlo flushed, imagining how it would be.

And as much as she wanted to test it with him right now—all of him and all of her, in this bed, dozing and waking, blurring back and forth between dream and real, taking what was best from each and loving every second of it—Sarai knew now wasn't the time. Urgency pricked her. Down the corridor, a little girl was asleep on the floor, locked in unguessable dreams, while a ghost army stood frozen and a city stood empty, and all their fates teetered on such ephemeral things as a green glass bottle tucked between the knees of a flighty fifteen-year-old girl who'd fallen asleep on watch.

* * *

Sarai took the bottle before waking Ruby. She didn't want her to startle and send it smashing to the floor. And she did startle, and did what anyone does when caught sleeping on watch: She denied it. "I *am* awake," she said, instantly argumentative, though no one had suggested otherwise ... unless waking someone up automatically constitutes an accusation of sleep.

"Why don't you go to bed," said Sarai.

Bleary-eyed, Ruby peered at her. "You're talking," she said, because for most of her life, Sarai had been mute after dark. "Your gift." Even mostly asleep, she knew what this meant. If Sarai still had her voice, then her moths had not come. The two were mutually exclusive.

"It might be different now," Sarai said, still hesitant to speak with certainty. "You go on. I'll tell you how it goes."

Ruby let herself be ushered off to bed, and Sarai sank down on the floor next to Minya, her back against the bed. Lazlo took the chair and the green glass bottle. Minya lay between them.

"Look at her," said Sarai, and maybe it was just the leftover music and silver light that had filled her, but the sight of the little girl pierced her, and it felt something like tenderness. "Can you believe so much depends on this tiny little thing?"

175

"Why has she never grown up?" Lazlo asked.

Sarai shook her head. "Stubbornness?" A smile played at the corners of her mouth. "If anyone could dig in and refuse to grow, it's her." The smile faded. "But I think it's more than that. I think she *can't*." She asked it like a question, as though Lazlo might have an answer. "Is there anything like it in any of your stories?"

It wasn't strange to Lazlo that she would ask that. It seemed to him that fairy tales were full of coded answers. "There is one story," he said, more to amuse her than anything, "about a princess who decreed that it would remain her birthday until she got the present she wanted. Everyone fussed over her, how they always did, and months passed, and then years, and gifts were brought and rejected, and all the while she stayed just the same."

"What happened?"

"It's not helpful, if that's what you're hoping. Her parents grew old and died, and nobody cared anymore what she wanted for her birthday, so they put the princess in a cave and left her there and forgot her, and years later, some travelers, seeking refuge from the rain, found an old woman living in the cave, and it was her. She'd grown up."

"How?"

"All she'd wanted for her birthday was a little peace and quiet."

Sarai shook her head. "You're right. It isn't helpful."

"I know. But it's the right answer for somebody's problem, somewhere in the world."

"And does some stranger out there have the answer to ours? Can we meet them at a crossroads and swap?"

"Do you think," Lazlo asked, "that the answer is in there?" He nodded to Minya. Her mind, he meant, knowing in a way that few people do that a mind is a *place*—a landscape, a wilderness, a city,

176

a world. And that Sarai could *go* there. It filled him with awe and extraordinary pride.

"I don't know," she said. "But I know *she's* there, and I have to talk to her. I have to change her mind."

She spoke bravely, but he could see she was afraid. "I wish I could go with you."

"I wish you could, too."

"Can I do anything? Get you anything? You see, I'm the one who's useless."

"Just *be* here," said Sarai.

"Always."

She knew he would be, no matter what. And with that, fingers trembling, Sarai reached for Minya's hand, and plunged into her mind.

* * *

Feral did not like his new mattresses. In all fairness, it wasn't entirely the mattresses' fault. They could have been perfectly comfortable and he would still have tossed and turned on them, grumbling about the blistering irrationality of Ruby.

Ruby.

Angry he'd never spied on her naked?! And what was all that about "nothing" being the opposite of "something"? Anyway, it wasn't, if you wanted to be accurate. The opposite of "nothing" was "everything." And Sparrow! What had she meant by him being bad—*spectacularly* bad—at noticing feelings? He was not. You didn't grow up with four girls without noticing *plenty of feelings.* And embarrassing him in front of Lazlo, that was what really annoyed him. He hoped at least that Lazlo saw how foolish it all was. Sarai wasn't like that. Lazlo was lucky. Well, Sarai *was* dead, so maybe not *lucky* lucky.

But you'd never know she was a ghost—that was the thing. Unless Minya started in, but Minya was sleeping now, and so Feral assumed Sarai and Lazlo weren't. Maybe they were getting *lucky* lucky right at this very moment. Feral grimaced and performed a dramatic flop from his right shoulder over onto his left, only to give an unmanly gasp and skitter backward at the sight of a figure beside his bed.

Ruby.

"What do *you* want?" he asked surly.

"What do you *think* I want? Scoot over."

And poor Feral still didn't know. She slid under his sheet (he'd had to drum one up, pillows too; it was scratchy, they were lumpy; he disliked them) and she turned her back and lay still, waiting.

For what?

Did she want...*that? Now?* He considered his options and snaked out a hand in hesitant reconnaissance.

Ruby made that sound like disgusted gargling that you make in the back of your throat when someone's totally hopeless (so, *no,* apparently she didn't want *that*) and, grabbing his hand, she pulled it hard so that his whole body came up against hers in...oh. A cuddle. The spoon kind. She tucked his hand under her breasts, and that was all. She fell asleep. He didn't, not for a long time. The warmth of the back of her and all its curves was pressed against him as he lay awake wondering: *Bless Thakra, by all that's holy—and very, very unholy—what does this* mean?

21

From a Long Line of Indignant Nostrils

Books.

Corridors lined with books.

Thyon and Calixte had indeed uncovered the remains of the ancient library of Weep...or, rather, of the ancient library of whatever the city had been called before the goddess of oblivion *ate its name* and left "Weep" in its place in a spectacular act of deathbed vengeance.

There were cave-ins blocking some of the passages, and skeletons that could only be librarians trapped when the anchor came down. "Wisdom keepers." Thyon remembered that that was what they'd been called. Once upon a time, there would have been some manner of grand edifice above, but it had been pulverized. These were the stacks, the underground levels, and they didn't extend very deep, because the city was built over a network of branching waterways. Still, there were a lot of books. When they'd gotten the door open, Thyon had wandered in a daze, trailing his fingers over dusty spines and wondering what lost knowledge was here.

That was hours ago. The world had turned away from the sun. Day had darkened to night. The last of the noise of the exodus had faded along the eastward road, and a weird silence had taken over the city. The moon drifted overhead, peering down into the sinkhole as though curious what they were up to with their ropes and baskets, their midnight labors.

Thyon's neck was sore. He went to rub it, and no sooner touched it than he winced. The sweat from his neck got into the open blisters on his palm and stung like the devil. Sweat and blisters! If his father could see him now, toiling like a common laborer, he would burst half the blood vessels in his face from pure outrage. It was almost enough to make Thyon smile. But there was nothing common about this labor. He blew on his palm. It helped a little.

At his side, the Tizerkane warrior Ruza was giving him a considering look, but he averted his gaze as soon as Thyon turned, and pretended he hadn't been watching him.

"Are you two done standing around up there?" called Calixte—in Common Tongue for Thyon's benefit. She was down in the sinkhole with Tzara, the pair of them framed in the unearthed doorway.

"Just getting started," Ruza called back, though in his own language. "Do I need to apply for an idleness permit? Are you granting those tonight?"

Calixte pitched a rock at him. It was a solid throw, and would have connected with his head had his hand not shot out and caught it. "Ow," he said, resentful, shaking out the hand. "You could just say, 'Permit denied.'"

"Permit denied," she said. "Keep hauling."

Thyon only understood a smattering of words, but detected dry humor in their tones and expressions. It was beginning to grate on him, not being able to understand them. It was like handing someone the ability to mock you right to your face while you just stood there like a fool. Maybe he should have made an effort. Might he not have learned and not let them know it, so at least he could tell what they were saying about him? If Strange and Calixte had managed to learn, then certainly he could have, too.

Of course, they both had something he didn't: friends to teach them. Calixte had Tzara, more than a friend. And as for Strange, he had practically become one of them, working right alongside them, not just keeping accounts as the Godslayer's secretary, but hammering stakes and scrubbing out pots, and even learning to throw a spear, all while trading jests in their thrilling, musical language.

Most of the jests had come from this warrior, Ruza, the youngest of the Tizerkane. "Pull," he said to Thyon now, a single curt syllable in Common Tongue, with none of his sly tone or merriment.

Thyon bristled. He did not take orders. His jaw muscles clenched. His palms stung, his shoulders ached, and he was *tired*. He felt like a frayed rope that could snap at any moment, but then, he'd felt like that for years and he hadn't snapped yet. The few remaining fibers holding him together were apparently made of strong stuff. And besides, he reasoned, Ruza's Common Tongue was rudimentary; perhaps niceties were lost on him. So he bent at the warrior's side, took hold of his share of rope, clenched his teeth around the pain that immediately screamed from his raw palms, and did as he was bid. Hand over hand, he pulled.

And up from the sinkhole, on the pulley line they'd rigged from the doorway, another basket loaded with books rose slowly into sight.

"Why are books so heavy?" groaned Ruza as it reached the top, and they swung it onto solid ground.

Thyon's mind produced explanations that had to do with the density of paper, but he offered up only a grunt. He had a new appreciation himself for the weight of books. He was accustomed to a small army of librarians carting them around for him. Truth be told, he was accustomed to servants doing everything for him. In his neck, a nerve pinched. He rolled his head from side to side, grimaced, and bent to examine the contents of the basket.

What a treasure trove he and Calixte had uncovered. At least, the books looked like treasure. He had no way to judge their contents.

Alongside Ruza, he started lifting them out of the basket and stacking them in crates in the cart they'd backed up to the sinkhole. There was a donkey in harness, drowsily waiting to make the return journey to the Merchants' Guildhall. For hours they'd been trudging back and forth, stacking the books in the halls, in the dining room, anywhere there was space, just to get them away from here, lest the sinkhole give way and spill what remained of the city's lost knowledge into the roiling Uzumark. Thyon and Calixte had gone to Eril-Fane as soon as they realized what they'd discovered. They'd found him looking haggard and sorrowful, and their news had brought him a tired smile.

The Tizerkane had been involved in defensive preparations, but he had lent them Ruza and Tzara to aid in their salvage efforts. Thyon had hardly expected to work all night long, but no one had suggested stopping, so he couldn't, either, without having to imagine the meaning of the words they'd call him under their breath. They'd eaten bread and cheese a while ago, and drunk gulps from a bottle of something potent that had burned the edges off his fatigue— and perhaps the surface layer off his throat as well, not that he was complaining.

Thyon had thought that, as a scholar, *he* should be down in the library, selecting which books to save, but it had been pointed out—correctly, if not politely—that he couldn't *read* them, and was thus useless, except as a pair of arms to haul them.

Demoted to laborer. Imagine.

At least he could examine them as he unloaded them. Carefully he lifted out a tome. It was a marvel: soft white leather leafed liberally in gold. There was a moon etched on the spine. He couldn't help himself. "What does this say?" he asked Ruza, holding it out for him to see.

The warrior took it. He was shorter than Thyon and more heavily made—thick-shouldered, with big, square hands that made the alchemist's look fragile—like the porcelain hands in jewelers' shops that were used for displaying rings. "This?" Ruza squinted, tracing the gold letters with a broad fingertip, and, Thyon noted, leaving a smudge. He gritted his teeth and refrained from snatching the volume back. "It says," the warrior told him, "'Greatest Mysteries of Alchemy Revealed.'"

Thyon's hearts gave a lurch. "Really?" he asked. The alchemists of Weep had been paragons of the ancient world, and all their secrets were lost.

He could learn the language. He could read all these books. A great hunger and excitement filled him. He could stay here to study. He didn't have to go home.

Zosma. The thought of his city, of his empty pink palace, even of his laboratory, they conjured no feeling of "home." He didn't miss any of it, and not any person, either. The realization made him feel adrift, like one of the ulola flowers borne on a gust of wind.

It also made him feel the smallest bit...free.

"Mm." Ruza nodded. "But oh, what's this? Down here it says—" And, pointing at the subtitle that Thyon could see was only three words long, purported to read out, "'A practical handbook for making the rich richer and granting eternal life to greedy monarchs so that they can rule poorly forever'?" With confusion painted on his face, he looked up at Thyon, and asked, pretending to be an imbecile, "Is *that* what alchemy does?"

Thyon's excitement curdled. He bent back to the basket to hide the flush that spread up his neck. He hated being mocked. It brought up his father's voice, so elegant and vicious. "If you don't know how to read," he retorted stiffly, "just say so."

"Funny," said Ruza, unperturbed. "Seems like you're the one who can't read. Oh. Look." He picked up another book. "This one's called 'Manners for Faranji: How Not to Act Like a Supercilious *Gulik* to Your Barbarian Hosts.' Did they not have this one back in your library?"

Thyon didn't know what *gulik* meant, and supposed it was better that way. As for *supercilious*, he had to revise his notion that Ruza's Common Tongue was rudimentary. Perhaps his language lessons with Strange had gone both ways. Which meant, of course, that all his curt commands were every bit as rude as they sounded.

If Strange were here, he would have made some clever retort, and their eyes would have laughed as they strove to look serious. But Strange wasn't here, and Ruza's eyes weren't laughing. Thyon took the book without comment and added it to the crate.

With every book he unloaded, he gazed at the cover and the inscrutable title, and felt locked out of it by his own ignorance. Nothing would have induced him to ask for Ruza's help again, but one book was too extraordinary to simply stack into a crate. Lifting it out of the basket, he felt something like reverence. Its cover wasn't leather or board but cloisonné—an intricate picture of inlaid enamel and what could only be lys and precious stones. By the way it had been worn smooth in places, he guessed that it was very old, and had been much handled in its time. As for the image depicted in a hundred vivid colors, it was a battle: a battle between giants and angels.

Seraphim, he thought. And *ijji*, the monstrous race they were supposed to have slain and piled in the pyre the size of a moon. He'd scoffed at the story when Strange told it, the night before they reached Weep. But there was no more scoffing after climbing the Cusp, which was, beyond doubt, the very pyre.

Opening the book, Thyon saw there were engravings inside, depicting more monsters and angels. It might all have spilled straight from Strange's story.

"Are we taking a reading break?" asked Ruza. "Or should I say, a *looking at the pictures* break?"

Thyon closed the book and turned away.

"Don't you want to know what it says?" asked Ruza.

"No," said Thyon. He went to put the book with the rest, at the last moment sliding it instead into a gap between crates, so that he could find it later. He wasn't done with it.

They got the cart loaded again, and Calixte and Tzara climbed back out of the pit. Calixte wasn't bounding now, and even Tzara looked weary. Thyon felt hot and dirty. Too tired to think straight, he rolled his sleeves up to his elbows.

"What happened to *you*?" asked Calixte, staring at his forearms.

Hastily he rolled his sleeves back down. "Nothing."

"That's nothing?" she said, eyebrows raised. "It looks like you've been training ravid kittens how to hunt."

But that was not what it looked like. The marks on Thyon's arms were scars, too regular to make sense. They might have been measured with a ruler, they were so precise, each two inches long, and spaced a quarter inch apart. Several were fresh and raw, though not altogether new: Puckers of old scar tissue were split with red lines, as though new cuts had been made on the healed sites of older ones.

"Did you do that to yourself?" asked Ruza, confused.

"It's an alchemical experiment," Thyon lied, his voice tight. He thought of the secret only Lazlo Strange knew—how he drew his own spirit with a syringe, and used it to make azoth. And there were some bruises and little scabbed needle pricks from that, but these were something else. Not even Strange knew this secret. "You wouldn't understand."

"No, I know," said Ruza, "because I'm just a stupid barbarian."

"That's not why. Only an alchemist could understand." Also a lie. Thyon was certain that this wouldn't make sense to anyone.

Ruza snorted. "But I *am* a stupid barbarian?"

"Did I say so?"

"You say it with your face."

"That's just his face," said Calixte in a pretense of defending him. "He can't help having indignant nostrils. Can you, Nero? You probably come from a long line of indignant nostrils. Aristocrats are issued them at birth, along with haughty eyes and judgmental cheeks."

"Judgmental cheeks?" repeated Ruza. "Can *cheeks* be judgmental?"

"His manage."

To Thyon's surprise, Tzara took his side. "Leave him alone. He's here, isn't he? He could have fled like the others." She gave Ruza a shove. "You're just jealous he's so much better-looking than you."

"I am *not*," the warrior protested. "And he is not. Look at him! He's not even a real person."

186

"What?" asked Thyon, honestly baffled. "What's *that* supposed to mean?"

But Ruza didn't answer him. He only gestured at him, telling the women, "He looks like somebody *made* him, and delivered him in a velvet-lined box. He probably plucks his eyebrows. I don't know how you could possibly find that attractive."

"Us?" asked Calixte, laughing. "He's hardly *my* type."

"Too pretty for me," said Tzara, bracing herself for the exaggerated punch Calixte landed on her hip.

"Are you saying *I'm* not pretty?" she demanded with mock umbrage.

"Not *that* pretty, thank the gods. I'd be afraid to touch you."

Thyon was speechless. He was well aware of his own perfection—and his eyebrows were natural, *thank you very much*—but had never heard it discussed so openly, or, of all things, as though it were a *fault*. A small tingling of relief mingled with his indignation, though, because they'd forgotten about the cuts on his arms.

"Exactly," said Ruza. "He's like a new linen napkin that you're afraid to wipe your mouth on."

The women both laughed at the absurdity of the comparison. Thyon's brow crinkled. A *napkin?* "I'll thank you to keep your mouth away from me," he said, causing the women to laugh even harder.

"You don't have to worry about that," said Ruza, looking positively repelled.

But Tzara shut him down, saying with a sly edge, "I think you protest too much, my friend."

Whatever she meant by it, Ruza's cheeks flamed, and he looked anywhere but at Thyon. Busying himself with the donkey, he asked, sounding sour, "Are we going to deliver this load or not?" He climbed into the driver's seat. "I don't know about the rest of you, but I could use some sleep."

Finally, thought Thyon, who wasn't sure he could have managed another cartload without a break.

"Me too," said Tzara. "But we'll have to check in at the garrison."

"Not me," gloated Calixte. "I have no master. I sleep when I like. Wait—"

The cart had started to pull away. She darted forward and plucked something out. "A book didn't make it in the crates. Oh, this one. It's gorgeous."

It was the one Thyon had set aside. He started to speak, but stopped. What could he say? Words came unbidden into his mind, and he wanted to scour them out.

I thought Strange would like to see it.

Since when did he care what Strange would like? That *wasn't* why he'd set it aside.

"Is it about the seraphim?" Calixte wondered.

Tzara looked over her shoulder, and Thyon witnessed the instant her face changed, all her weariness vanishing. "Merciful seraphim," she said in awe. "It's the Thakranaxet."

"What?" Ruza jumped down from the driver's seat, and then the three of them were shoulder to shoulder, peering at the book with avid eyes. Thyon, opposite, felt a pinch of envy and, preposterously, *loss*, as though the book had been his discovery, and was being taken away from him.

As *he* had taken away Strange's books back in Zosma? No. Of course that had been much worse. A pang of shame twisted his gut at the thought of those scruffy, handmade books, labors of love brimming with years of the librarian's hard-earned knowledge. They were still back in his pink marble palace, stacked up where he'd left them. It occurred to him now that he might have brought them, and returned them to Strange on the journey. He did have one book that Strange would know. It was *Miracles for Breakfast*, the volume of tales Strange had brought to his door when they were sixteen. What would he think if he knew Thyon had read it so often he knew it practically by heart?

"What's the Thakranaxet?" he asked, stumbling over the name.

"It's the testament of Thakra," Tzara said. "She was leader of the seraphim who came to Zeru."

Even after what he'd seen, it still startled Thyon to hear the seraphim spoken of so matter-of-factly, as real historical beings. In Zosma, there was lore of the seraphim, but it was very old and had been churned under by the One God like weeds by a plow. No names survived there that Thyon had ever heard, and certainly no one knew it was *fact*.

"It's our holy book," Tzara said. "All copies were lost or destroyed when the Mesarthim came."

They went on murmuring, turning pages, but Thyon looked up at the citadel. *When the Mesarthim came*, Tzara had said, and it struck him what an extraordinary coincidence it was that both seraphim and Mesarthim had come . . . *here*. Thousands of years apart, two different races of otherworldly beings, and both came right here, and not anywhere else in all the wide world of Zeru. It was *too* extraordinary to be a coincidence, really, especially considering that the Mesarthim citadel took the form of a seraph.

Thyon's gaze glided over the contours of the great metal angel, and he wondered what it all meant. They were pieces of a story, Mesarthim and seraphim, but how did they fit together?

And what place did Lazlo Strange have in it?

"You know who'd love this book?" asked Calixte, flipping pages.

Thyon gritted his teeth, knowing exactly who and still telling himself that wasn't why he'd put it aside. What did *he* care what the dreamer would love, or who got to give it to him?

Nothing at all. Not a bit. It was none of his concern.

The golden godson, all blisters and aches, trudged stiffly ahead of the donkey.

✤ 22 ✤

Do You Want to Die, Too?

Sarai opened her eyes in Minya's dream, and realized she was holding her breath, braced for a clash that didn't come. She exhaled slowly and looked around, taking stock of her surroundings.

She knew the citadel nursery, but she knew it bare. After what happened there, Minya had ordered everything burned. Nowadays, it was an austere place—a kind of awful memorial, with nothing left but the rows of mesarthium cribs and cots, all shining blue, abstracted by the absence of bedding and babies.

This was the same nursery, but it took a beat to realize it. Sarai was standing in it, and there *was* bedding and babies—and children and tidy piles of folded diapers, and white blankets worn soft with many washings, and nippled bottles all lined up on a shelf. The babies were in the cribs, lying down, limbs waving, or standing at the bars like tiny prisoners. Some bigger children were playing on woven mats laid out on the floor. They had a few toys: blocks, a doll. Not much. One girl walked up to a crib and lifted one of the babies out and held it on her hip like a little mother.

The girl was Minya. Though in size and shape she hadn't changed, she was vastly different in presentation: She was clean, for one thing, and her hair was long, not chopped off with a knife. It was dark and shining and fell in waves down her back, and her little nursery smock was white, with nary a rip or stain. She was singing to the baby. It was her same icing-sugar voice, but it sounded different, fuller and more sincere.

It didn't surprise Sarai to find herself here. The nursery was bound to loom large in the landscape of Minya's mind. The calm of the scene did surprise her a little. She'd been braced for something ugly—a confrontation, blame. She had thought Minya might be waiting for her at the border of the dream, the way Lazlo did, except unsmiling. But that was foolish. How could Minya know she would come? Sarai didn't even know if Minya would be able to see her, and even if she could, she couldn't expect her to be lucid and present in the way Lazlo was.

He *was* Strange the dreamer, after all. He wasn't your ordinary dreamer, prey to all the vagaries of the unconscious. He moved through his mind with the assuredness of an explorer and the grace of a poet. Most dreams don't make sense, and most dreamers aren't even aware they're dreaming. Was Minya?

Sarai stood where she was, waiting to see if the little girl would notice her. She didn't, not yet. She was focused on the baby. She carried it to a table and laid it on a blanket. Sarai supposed she must be changing its diaper. She let her eyes wander, wondering if she might find herself here—her baby self. She should be easy to spot, the only one with Isagol's red-brown hair.

As she looked around, she noticed an anomaly. Whenever she tried to look at the door—the only one that led out into the corridor—there was a sort of...disruption in her vision, as though her eyes were skipping over something. She found herself blinking, trying to focus, but it was as though an area of the dreamscape was blurred out, like breath-fogged glass. She several times thought she glimpsed figures—grown-up-size figures—out of the corner of her eye, but when she turned, there was no one there.

She wondered where the Ellens were. She couldn't spot herself, either.

Minya walked back to the cribs, plucked out another baby, and settled it on her hip. She did the little bounce and sway that Sarai had seen humans do to calm their babies when they woke in the night. The baby regarded her placidly. The crib she'd taken the first one from was still empty, and Sarai glanced over at the table where Minya had been changing its diaper. It wasn't there, either.

A little shiver of unease ran down her spine.

She drifted closer, and the words of Minya's song lined themselves up and slipped into her mind, each word crystalline with the sweetness of her unearthly little voice. Sarai noticed the nursery had gone quiet. The children on the floor mats had stopped playing and were watching her. The babies, too, and she thought: If they could all see her—they who were just phantasms created by Minya's mind—then Minya must be aware of her, too.

She caught another hint of movement out of the corner of her eye, and long shadows marched past where there was no one to cast them, and Minya's song went like this:

> Poor little godspawn,
> Wrap her in a blanket,
> Don't let her peek out,
> Better keep her quiet.
> Can't you hear the monsters coming?

Hide, little doomed one,
If you can't pretend you're dead,
You'll be really dead instead!

And Sarai saw that Minya wasn't changing the baby. She was wrapping it up in a blanket, just like the song said. It was a sort of game. Her voice was playful, her face open and smiling. On "don't let her peek out," she booped the infant softly on her tiny nose and then drew the blanket across her face. It was like "now you see me," except she didn't uncover the baby's face again. On "better keep her quiet," her voice fell to a whisper, and it all became strange. She wrapped the baby up *completely*—head, arms, legs, all tucked in and covered, wrapped and swaddled into a tidy bundle, and then . . . she pushed it through a crack in the wall.

Sarai's hand went to her mouth. What was Minya doing to the babies?

When she went back to the cribs for another one, Sarai darted to the crack in the wall—that was definitely a dream addition, and didn't exist in the real nursery—and peered inside it. There she saw more bundles, baby-size and bigger.

None of them were moving.

She dropped to her knees and reached in, pulled out the nearest one and opened it. Her hands shook as she tried to be gentle but also not touch it too much because she didn't know what she'd find inside, and then it was open and it was a baby and it was alive and also utterly *still*.

It was the most unnatural thing she'd ever seen.

The baby lay unmoving, curled as small as it could make itself, peering up at her with a wariness too old for its glossy infant eyes. As though it had been told to keep still, and understood, and was

194

obeying. Sarai reached for another bundle, and another, unwinding babies like so many cocoons. All were alive, motionless and silent as little dolls. And then she opened the bundle that was *her*, small Sarai with cinnamon curls, and a sob escaped her lips.

With that sound, the singing stopped. The nursery went deathly quiet. Turning on her knees, Sarai came face-to-face with Minya. The little girl thrummed with a dark fervor, eyes big and glazed, breath fast and shallow, skin seeming to crackle with a barely contained energy. In a baleful singsong that sent chills down Sarai's spine, she said, "*You shouldn't be in here*," and Sarai didn't know if she meant in the nursery or in the dream, but the words, the tone, seemed to slide into a dance with the unmoored shadows and the thrum, and it was all getting faster and louder, and the shadows were closing in, and a terrible dread stirred in her.

She'd been inside countless nightmares, her own and others', and this could hardly even be considered a nightmare. To describe it, it would seem odd more than scary. The babies were alive. They were just wrapped up. But dreams have auras, a pervasive feeling that seeps through the skin, and the aura of this one was *horror*.

"Minya," said Sarai. "Do you know me?"

But Minya didn't answer. She was looking past her at the unwrapped cocoons and the little living dolls all scattered and lying still. "What have you done?" she cried, growing frantic. "They'll get them now!"

And Sarai didn't have to ask who "they" were. She'd seen the Carnage play out dozens of times in Eril-Fane's dreams, and in the dreams of those who'd been with him and helped him on that bloody day. She knew the awful, gruesome truth of it. But she'd never been *here*, in the nursery, waiting for it to start.

Except, of course, she *had* been. She'd been two years old.

Were they coming? Was this that day? The dread thickened around her. The shadows wove closer, like figures dancing in a circle, and all the children and babies started to cry—even the silent unwrapped dolls and all the ones still wrapped. The parcels started to writhe and wails poured out of the crack in the wall.

Minya was beside herself, darting from child to child, fussing and grabbing at them, yanking them to their feet, trying to pick up babies off the floor. They were starting to crawl away from her, coming unwrapped, no longer frozen, and her face was wild with distress. The task was overwhelming. There were nearly *thirty* of them, and no one to help her.

Again, Sarai wondered: Where were the Ellens?

"It's your fault!" Minya flung at Sarai, darting terrified glances at the open door. "You ruined it! I can't carry them all."

"We'll save them," Sarai said. The panic was infecting her, and the helplessness, too. This dream aura was an oppressive force. "We'll get them all out. I'll help you."

"Do you *promise?*" Minya asked, her eyes so big, so full of pleading.

Sarai hesitated. The words were on her lips and they tasted like a lie, but she didn't know what else to do and so she said them. She promised.

Minya's face changed. "*You're lying!*" she shrieked, as though she knew very well how this day came out. "It's always the same! *They always die!*"

The children were crying and scattering, trying to hide behind cribs and under cots, and the babies were wailing and bleating and Sarai knew it was true: They were long dead and she couldn't save a one of them. Despair overwhelmed her—or nearly.

She reminded herself who she was, *what* she was, and that she was not helpless here. She could change the dream. *They always die!*

196

Minya had just said. Did she live this, then, over and over? Was she always, always trying to save them, and always, always failing? Sarai couldn't bring the dead back to life, and she couldn't go back in time, but couldn't she let Minya win this, at least once?

She took over the dream. It was what she did, easy as breathing. She closed the nursery door, the one Minya kept glancing at. She closed it so no one could get in. And then she opened another door, out through the other side where no door had ever been. It led to the sky, and an airship was docked, a version of the silk sleigh, but bigger, with patchwork pontoons, and tassels and pom-pom garlands draped over the rails, and instead of a motor, it had a flock of geese in harness, all formed up in a V and ready to pull them away to safety. They had only to take the children and load them onto it, and Sarai could help with that, too. She could just *will* them there. They didn't need to be herded and chased. She told Minya, "We can escape," and pointed to the doorway.

But Minya flinched at the sight, and when Sarai looked back, she saw men in it, in the doorway she'd just made, and one of the men was her father, and he had a knife in his hand.

She willed him gone, but as soon as she did he appeared in the other door, open again as though she'd never closed it. And again, and again, and he came back every time. No sooner would she change the dream than it overcame her change. It was like trying to divert a river using only her bare hands. And always the Godslayer was there, grim-faced, with his knife, and his mission.

"It won't work," said Minya, her face slick with tears. "Do you think I haven't tried *everything*?"

And Sarai knew that the pushback, the dream's intransigence, was *Minya's* pushback, her own intransigence, born of a trauma so profound that she could not dream herself out of it, or even let Sarai do it for her. She was trapped here with the babies she had been unable to save.

"Come out!" She was crying, trying to pull a little boy out from under a cot. "Come with me! We have to go." But he was terrified and scrambled away, and she managed, finally, to get a different little boy who Sarai thought must be Feral, and to hoist two swaddled babies in her arm: Ruby and Sparrow. They were crying. Sarai wondered at Minya being able to hold them. She was so small herself. And she had really done it, and carried them all the way down the corridor to the heart of the citadel, where she'd pushed them through another crack and kept them safe. How had she had the strength? And then Minya stunned Sarai. She grabbed *her* hand, and started to drag her with them. "*Hush*," she said to the babies, harsh. Sarai's hand and Feral's were crushed together in a grip impossibly strong. Minya's fingers were slippery; she had to grab so tight to keep hold of them. It *hurt*. Sarai tried to pull away, but Minya whirled on her and demanded, in a savage snarl of a voice, "Do you want to die, too? Do you?"

And that was the moment it all became real. Those words were a pry bar slipped into a crack, and twisted to break it all open. Sarai had heard them before, fifteen years ago, right here in this spot. Blinding terror seized her. She felt now what she had then. The words hit her like a threat. Minya dragged her, and Feral, too. Their little feet tangled together. They wanted to stay in the only place they knew. Something bad was outside the door. But Minya wouldn't let go.

To reach the door and any hope of escape, they had to scramble over an obstacle sprawled across the floor. Here was the anomaly, the breath-fogged glass, the skip in the dream. Sarai hadn't been able to see what was here, but now she did. It was the Ellens, and she felt the

198

give of their soft bodies as she clambered over them. They were slippery and her hands got red, and Minya's hand was all red, too. *That's why it was so slick.* She'd thought it was sweat, but it was blood.

And finally it was just too much. Sarai snatched her hand back. She snatched it back in the dream and also in the room where she sat by Minya's sleeping self. She did what Minya could not: She escaped from the nightmare. Lazlo was waiting, his arms already around her, his breath and voice soft on her ear. "It's all right," he murmured. "It's just a dream. I've got you. It's all right."

But it wasn't just a dream, and nothing was all right. It was a memory, and Minya was still in it, trapped, as she had been all these years.

23

MINYA'S RED HAND

It took Sarai a while to stop shaking, and she wasn't ready to talk about it yet, so instead she sent Lazlo to the rain room for some water and a cloth, and then she very gently washed Minya's face and neck, her shoulders and arms, much the way she had washed her own body only hours earlier. She even held Minya's head in her lap, the way she had held her own. And she smoothed back her hair, and fed tiny spoonfuls of water between her lips, into which she had diluted another drop of Letha's sleeping draught—because, as much as she hated to keep Minya trapped in that room and in that day, she couldn't let her out to rule over her and threaten Weep. She had to leave her there, for now.

She had to find some way to help her.

The sun rose, and she woke Sparrow to take over the watch. "How did it go?" Sparrow asked, but Sarai just shook her head and said, "Later."

She went back up the dexter arm, with Lazlo, to her room. He closed the door behind them, and asked, "What can I do?" It devastated him to see her so shaken and not be able to do anything.

"You can sleep," she said.

"I want to *help* you."

"So help me." She drew him back toward the tucked-away nook. "You need rest, and I need your dreams. Sleep, and I'll meet you there."

He could do that. He wanted nothing more. It didn't matter that the sun was up. Sarai's gift had shaken off those limits. Her moths had been nocturnal, but they were gone, and she suspected she would miss them, but not right now. This was better: skin to skin. So much better. She vanished her slip and her smallclothes and lay down on the bed.

Lazlo stood there and looked at her. There was a roaring in his ears. Her hair was fanned out in sunset spirals. Her skin was cobalt, her moon and stars silver. Her lips and nipples were rose. His mind danced over the colors of her because it could hardly fathom the whole. Her beauty annihilated him. How could she be for him? Her need called out to him—to *him* and him alone. Almost, his own skin felt magnetized to hers, like a force pulling him off balance. He stripped off his shirt and pushed down his breeches, and this was something new, to kick them off and stand naked before her, and climb onto the bed and lay down with her, and feel her curve against him, finding out how they best fit together. He was careful with her. This wasn't a time for wildfires. She wanted his dreams and he wanted to draw her into such safety and splendor as only he could make for her, not in the world, but out of it, in *their* world. He closed his eyes and lay on his back as she tucked herself against his side and curled her leg through his own, resting her cheek on his hearts. She felt their tempo radiate through her. He let the feel of her skin ripple over his like music, and it was lucky that he was very tired, because she felt *so good*.

After a time—a surreal velvet-silk-silver-sky time of soft exhalations and the startling tickle of eyelashes and the smallest movements setting off explosions of sensation—they settled into stillness and sank into sleep, where they met again in the little room down in Weep where Sarai had first found Lazlo sleeping: a stranger with a broken nose. Her moths had perched here, and the two of them had defeated Skathis at this window. This was where they'd landed when they fell out of the stars. Lazlo knew Sarai felt safe here. She'd chosen it herself on the last night of her life.

"Where would you like to go?" he asked. He knew there was so much she wanted to see, both real things and imagined. Dragons and airships, leviathans and oceans. She'd never seen the sea.

"Here's good," said Sarai, stepping toward him. "Right here. Here's perfect."

His lip wasn't wounded in the dream. She didn't have to be careful, and she wasn't. *Careful* was not what she was.

* * *

Later, she told him about Minya's dream. They were in a tea stall in the marketplace of Dreamer's Weep, with hanging rugs for walls, and a fantastical samovar in the shape of an elephant with opals for eyes and carved demonglass tusks. The tea was fragrant, the flavor dark. The glavestones were dark, too—rare carmine stones that cast a deep red glow. They sat together in one chair. It was more like a nest than a chair, formed of two enormous, split agate eggs, one for the seat, the other for the back. Their crystal formations sparkled in the ruby light, and they were filled up with fleeces and cushions. Sarai's feet were in Lazlo's lap. His fingers played over her anklebones, traced her arches, trailed up her calves to the warm bends of her knees.

They were both dressed in the fashion of Weep. They'd helped each other, in the little bedroom, once they were ready to go out. They'd dreamed these costumes right onto each other's bodies, imagining this shirt or that tunic, this dress, no that one, again and again stripping back to start over, because there was always some detail yet to perfect. At least, that was the excuse. But they did settle on clothes eventually, and they looked well in them and admired each other, and made formal bows and curtsies. Their arm cuffs were matching silver with blue stones, and Sarai wore a fine silver chain at her hairline, with a jewel suspended from it. It was blue, too, and winked in the light, but it was nothing next to her eyes.

Outside the tent, the city was alive with folk and creatures. They could see them through a gap in the rugs, but in here it was quiet.

"I've never encountered resistance like that," she was telling him. "Trying to alter Minya's dream. Whatever I did just melted away and it came surging back with a vengeance. It was terrible." She could talk about it now, here, with Lazlo's knuckle tracing circles round her ankle, and a teacup warm in her hand. "And that's her mind. She *lives* there. It's no wonder she can't hear me talk about mercy without wanting to gouge out my eyes. It's like it *just* happened. Like it's *still* happening, over and over, all the time."

"What do you want to do?" Lazlo asked.

"I want to get her out of there."

Her answer was immediate and heartfelt, as though she *could*. As though she could extract Minya from the prison of her own mind. "But that's impossible."

"Impossible?" Lazlo gave a soft laugh and shake of his head. "There must be things that *are* impossible. But I don't believe we've gotten there yet. Look at us. We've barely begun. Sarai, we're *magic*." He said this with all the wonder of a lifelong dreamer who's found out he's half god. "You don't know yet what you're capable of, but I'm willing to bet it's extraordinary."

She felt warm and new, here with him, and his belief in her buoyed her spirits. She felt a little guilty, too, to be drinking tea in the city while music drifted past. They could even have cake if they wanted it, but that seemed *too* unfair to the others, who were stuck in the sky with kimril and plums. Sarai supposed she could go into their dreams, and bring them all here one by one. They'd like that, she didn't doubt, but what they needed was a real life, not a dream one, a city that would accept them, and food that would fill their bellies as well as their minds.

They'd have to get supplies. She made a mental note. But mostly she was thinking about the dream. The carefully wrapped babies, Minya's sweet voice—even if the song was sinister—and the way she'd held them on her hip like a little mother, while the Ellens were nowhere to be seen.

Well, no. That wasn't right. The Ellens were dead on the floor.

The horror of it was still in Sarai's throat. She already knew how they'd died, of course. Minya had told them lots of times how they'd tried to stop the Godslayer and been cut down at the threshold. She'd even seen them in Eril-Fane's dreams. He'd stepped over their bodies, as she had had to climb. She shuddered at the memory of their inert flesh, slippery with fresh blood, and of Minya's red hand, and how it had crushed hers.

Minya's red, slippery hand.

Lazlo, watching Sarai, saw her brow twitch into a furrow. "What is it?" he asked.

"It doesn't make sense."

"What doesn't?"

"The timing," she said. She cradled her hand like a wounded bird.

The bones ached from Minya's terrible grip, and she could still feel the slick slide of little fingers and blood.

Do you want to die, too?

Too. What did it mean, that Minya had said "too"? She must have meant the Ellens: *Do you want to die like them?*

But... it didn't line up. The Godslayer hadn't gotten there yet, or else how could they have escaped?

She explained it to Lazlo. "It's the bodies I don't understand. How could we have climbed over them? We had to have gotten out before the Ellens were killed. If we'd still been there when Eril-Fane came, we would have died with all the rest."

"It doesn't mean it really happened like that," he said. "Dreams aren't truth. Memory is malleable. She was only a little girl. It's probably just all out of sequence."

Sarai wanted to think that was what it was, but Minya's question had brought her back to that room, in that moment: "Do you want to die, too?" She couldn't remember anything else: just the terror and those words, like a splinter in her mind with a haze of pain around them. It had happened. She was sure.

Puzzle pieces were moving around. There were the dead nurses, their poor dear Ellens, and the question that had sounded like a threat. And there was the place in the nursery Sarai couldn't see— the breath-fogged glass, the skip—as though the dream was keeping a secret, maybe even from the dreamer. And there was the matter of Minya's red hand.

And...

It came to Sarai that she had never, in all the dreams of the Carnage, actually *seen* Eril-Fane kill the nurses. She had only seen him step over them. Her mind had filled in the rest, based on Minya's tellings. But Minya couldn't have seen it. She had to have been gone by then, shoving the four babies she'd managed to save through the crack into the heart of the citadel.

What had really happened that day? The puzzle pieces did present one possible answer, but it was incomprehensible.

"They loved us," said Sarai, as though to ward off a terrible truth that was trying to make itself known. "We loved them." But the words felt hollow somehow. The Ellens she loved were ghosts. She had no memory of them alive.

And now those ghosts, for reasons unclear, were blank as empty shells, standing in the kitchen doorway with nothing at all in their eyes.

Sarai knew she had to go back there, to the nursery in the dream. She had hoped to reach Minya, to talk to her, and . . . what? Change her mind? Talk her down? Fundamentally alter her psyche with a minimum of fuss? But the Minya she'd found was in no state for talk, and the dream had the force of a river in flood, and Sarai had not been prepared. *Could* she prepare? She had told Lazlo that she wanted to get Minya out of there—out of the nursery, out of *that day*—but was it possible?

Or would she find, no matter what she tried, that some people cannot be saved?

❧ 24 ❧

BLUE STEW

For the first time in his life, no one made Thyon Nero breakfast.

Well, technically yesterday had been the first time, but he hadn't noticed, since he had been out in the chaos of the city along with everyone else. But this morning it was quiet, and he woke hungry. He'd slept in the Merchants' Guildhall, in the opulent rooms provided for him, which he had been shunning in favor of a workshop above a defunct crematorium. He had wanted his privacy but now it was *too* private. He didn't care for the idea of no one knowing where he was. What if he woke up in the morning to find that those few who remained in the city had gone, without even thinking to tell him?

So he had slept at the guildhall, where Calixte was, too, and where they had piled the books in the passages. The Tizerkane garrison was close by. He could see the watchtower out his window and know whether it was manned. And the kitchen, he thought, would most likely be stocked, even if there was no one in it to cook and wash up after.

He dressed, stiff and sore, all aching shoulders and raw hands, and wandered toward the dining room, assuming the kitchen was probably somewhere in its vicinity. It was. It was big and full of copper pots, and the pantry shelves were lined with bins labeled with words he couldn't read in an alphabet he hadn't learned. He lifted lids, sniffed things, and had, though he did not know it, an experience similar to the godspawn in the citadel, who had also been discovering that food requires esoteric knowledge. He did not equate it with alchemy, though, since alchemy was *less* mysterious to him than flour, leavening, and the like. The kitchen was obscure to him in the way that women were obscure, and that wasn't because women worked in the kitchen. Those weren't the women he meant. Those were servants, and as such, had hardly occupied his thoughts as *people*, let alone *females*. Kitchens and women were both subjects that simply did not intrigue him.

Oh, individual women could be interesting, though this was something of a new notion. Calixte and Tzara, he had to admit, were not boring, and neither was Soulzeren, the mechanist who'd built firearms for warlords in the Thanagost badlands. But they *did things*, like men. The women he knew in Zosma did not. They wouldn't be permitted to even if they wished, he admitted to himself, though he'd hardly ever considered whether they might. Now that he had met Calixte, Tzara, and Soulzeren, not to mention the intimidating Azareen, he did begin to wonder if any of the hothouse flowers who were paraded before him in Zosma might be as bored with their lot as he was with them.

There was an expectation that he be enchanted with them for their form alone, and for the cultivated coquetry that was like a play they were acting in, all the time. Every civilized person knew the lines and gestures, and made a life out of parroting them about. Those who were counted charming and clever were the ones who were best at making them seem fresh as they patched evenings together out of the same dances and conversations that they'd done and had a thousand times before.

Thyon had played his part. He knew the lines and dances, but inside he had been screaming. He wondered if perhaps he wasn't the only one. If, behind their lacquered faces, some of those Zosma girls might have felt stifled, too, and secretly longed to steal emeralds and build airships and fight gods in a shadowed city.

Well, when he went home, he would doubtless be made to marry one of them, and then, he supposed, he could ask her.

He let out a laugh. It dropped like a stone. He pushed away the thought that was more distant and more unimaginable than librarians turning out to be gods. Discovering where the fruit was stored, he piled some on a plate and kept scrounging. There had to be cheese. There was. He piled that on, too. Then—*glory*—he found slabs of bacon in a cold box, and stood there wondering if he could figure out how to fry some.

He answered himself as though affronted. "I am the greatest alchemist of the age. I distilled azoth. I can transmute lead into gold. I *think* I can light a stove."

"What's that, Nero?"

Calixte and Tzara had come in. He gave a start, and flushed, wondering if they'd heard him talking to himself like a fool starved for flattery. "Are you arguing with that bacon?" Calixte asked. "I hope you're winning, because I'm starving."

With a wicked grin, Tzara added, "*Cannibalism* doesn't really fill you up, you see."

Ruza ate in the garrison mess, and he was halfway through his bowl of thick kesh porridge before he realized what it was that was putting him off about it. Berries tinted the porridge blue, and brought to mind "blue stew."

When had it been, the day before yesterday? It felt like a year ago at least. It was the last time he saw Lazlo before the explosion. They'd argued. He and some of the others—Shimzen, Tzara—had been joking about taking the explosionist up to the citadel to blow the godspawn into "blue stew." It had seemed funny then. What exactly had he said? He struggled to remember. That the godspawn were monsters, more like threaves than people? That if Lazlo knew them he'd be happy to blow them up himself?

Ruza's porridge churned in his stomach. He let his spoon drop into the dregs.

Lazlo was his friend. Lazlo was godspawn.

These two statements could not both be true, because one could not be friends with godspawn. Lazlo *was* godspawn. There was no denying it. Therefore, he was not Ruza's friend.

It was supposed to be that simple, but Ruza was finding his mind unable to perform the simplification—as though there were two columns, a Lazlo in each, and he was tasked to erase one of them.

In his lessons—and as Ruza was only eighteen, these were not a distant memory—he had always pressed down too hard with his pencil, committing himself to his first guess, never learning to write lightly in case he was in error. Was it carelessness or confidence? Opinions differed, but did it matter? He could never fully erase his dark pencil lines, and he had never turned his back on a friend.

Hell. He finished his porridge. It was only porridge, and Ruza had yet to meet a philosophical dilemma that could spoil his appetite. He washed up his bowl and stacked it, then headed toward the stables for the donkey and cart. It was book-salvage duty again today with the ridiculous alchemist and his ridiculous face.

Ruza ducked into the barracks for a quick glance in his shaving mirror, though he couldn't—or *wouldn't*—have said why. He knew what he looked like. Was he hoping to discover an improvement? The mirror was small, the light dim, and the four square inches of face looked as they had last time he'd checked. He tossed the mirror onto his bunk—apparently with excessive force, because it skidded into the wall and cracked. Perfect.

He did one more thing before heading on to the stable. He hit up the first aid box for a packet of bandages. He hadn't known a grown man could *have* hands soft enough to blister and rip after a few hours hauling rope. The alchemist hadn't complained, though, and he hadn't quit. That was something, anyway. No reason he should keep getting blood all over the rope.

* * *

Both Eril-Fane and Azareen had remained at the garrison overnight. They would hardly go home at a time like this, with the soldiers all on edge, waiting for something to happen. So far, nothing had. The citadel hadn't moved, or made any further transformation. They could only guess at what was going on up there.

Azareen slept for a time before dawn, and went to the Temple of Thakra at first light to make hasty ablutions. Returning, she sought out Eril-Fane. He wasn't in the mess or barracks, the practice yard or the command center. She asked the watch captain, and when she heard where he was, her already ramrod soldier's spine stiffened. She didn't say a word, but turned on her boot heel and went straight there, the walk giving her anger and hurt time to fuse into something cold.

"Eril-Fane," she said, coming into the pavilion.

He was in one of the silk sleighs. He appeared to be studying its workings, and looked up when she spoke. "Azareen," he returned in a far too measured voice. He had been expecting, and dreading, her arrival. Well, perhaps *dread* was too strong a word, but he knew full well what she would have to say about this idea.

"Going somewhere?" she asked, icy.

"Of course not. Do you think I wouldn't tell you?"

"But you're considering it."

"I'm considering all options."

"Well, you can eliminate this one. The advantage is all theirs. We could carry, what, four fighters in that thing, to attack a force of gods and ghosts on their own terrain?"

"I don't want to attack them, Azareen. I want to talk to them."

"You think they'll talk to *you*?"

She instantly regretted her tone, which conjured the specter of the man who had entered a nursery with a knife. She might as well have called him a murderer and been done with it. "I'm sorry," she said, closing her eyes. "I didn't mean—"

"Please don't ever apologize to me," he said in barely more than a whisper. Eril-Fane lived under such a burden of guilt that apologies overwhelmed him with shame. The guilt for what he'd done in the citadel was a constant acid burn in his gut. The guilt for what he could *not* do was different, more stab than burn. Every time he looked at Azareen, he had to face the knowledge that his inability to...*get over*...what had been done to him—and what he had done—had robbed her of the life she deserved. To hear the word *sorry* from her lips...it made him want to die. Everyone else had managed to pick up the tatters and mend them into wearable lives. Why couldn't he?

Of course, no one else had been the special project of the goddess of despair, but he granted himself no leniency on that account, or any other.

"I was just looking it over," he told her, climbing out of the craft. "I don't think I could fly it anyway. But if we don't hear something today, from Lazlo, or." He ended the sentence, having no way to finish it. Or *who*? His daughter? She was dead. Some other child who'd survived his massacre? The acid roiled within him. "We'll have to consider calling on Soulzeren and asking for her help. We can't go on without contact. The not knowing will eat us alive." He sighed and rubbed his jaw. "We have to resolve this, Azareen. How long can they stay at Enet-Sarra?"

That was the place downriver where their people had gone when they fled the city. For years, there'd been talk of building a new city there, and starting again, free of the seraph's shadow. But you couldn't just move thousands of people overnight to set up camps in fields, with no services, no sanitation. There would be sickness, unrest. They had to get their people home. They had to make it safe for them.

"Shall I send for her?" asked Azareen, not contrite, but subdued. "Soulzeren."

"Yes. Please. If she'll come." He thought she would. Soulzeren was not the type to shrink from being useful in a time of need. "I'm going to the temple. Do you want to come?"

"I've already been," she told him.

"I'll see you later, then." He gave her a tired smile, and turned to walk away, and she wondered, as she watched his back—so broad, so impossibly strong—if he would ever turn back to her, *truly* turn back to her, and walk toward her again.

❦ 25 ❦

Isagol's Broken Toy

Azareen fell in love with Eril-Fane when she was thirteen years old.

Her elilith ceremony had been the week before; her tattoos—a circle of apple blossoms—were still tender when the artist, Guldan, came to see how they were healing. It was the first time she was alone with the old woman. During the ceremony, all the women of her family had been gathered around them; now it was just the two of them, and Guldan unsettled her with her piercing appraisal, seeming to examine more than her tattoos.

"Let me see your hands," she said, and Azareen held them out, unsure. She wasn't proud of her hands, rough as they were from her work mending nets, and scarred here and there from the slip of a knife. But Guldan ran her fingers over them and nodded with quiet approval. "You're a strong girl," she said. "Are you also a brave one?"

The question sent a chill down Azareen's spine. There were secrets in it; she could feel them. She said she hoped she was, and the old woman gave her the instructions that would change her life.

Azareen didn't tell her parents; the fewer people who knew, the better. Two nights later, she slipped alone to a quiet channel of the underground Uzumark, spoke a password to a silent boatman, and was ferried to a cavern she had never known existed. It was hidden in the maze of waterways beneath the city, where the roar of rapids disguised the sound of what went on there. Azareen, hearts pounding with foreboding and the thrill of secrecy, came round a corner and beheld a sight she had never witnessed in her life: swordplay.

Weapons were forbidden in the city. But here was the hidden training ground of the Tizerkane, legendary warriors who had been eradicated by the Mesarthim—or *almost* eradicated. That night, Azareen learned that their arts had been kept alive and passed down through the generations. They weren't an army, but they were keepers: of skills and history, and of *hope*, that the city could one day be freed.

Azareen beheld some dozen men and women sparring. She would learn, in time, that there were more, though she wasn't to know who they were. They were careful never to gather all together. If any were caught, there would always be some left alive to recruit and begin again. It was glorious, what she saw by glavelight: a dance of grace and power, swords flashing—the traditional Tizerkane hreshteks—their clash muted by the river's roar. She had never known to want this. She'd had no idea it existed. But from the moment she first beheld the gleam and spin of blades, she knew she was meant for this.

She stood watching, mesmerized and a little shy, until someone spotted her and came over. He was the only other youth, a year older than her but already as powerful as a man. He was a blacksmith's apprentice, and though he wasn't from her district, Azareen had seen him in the marketplace. You couldn't help but see him, if he was anywhere nearby. It wasn't only that he was handsome. That seemed almost incidental. There was a warmth and energy about him, as though he were twice as alive as the next person, a fire burning in him and furnace doors thrown open so you could feel the flames. He radiated an extraordinary vitality. He held his eyes wide and saw everything, really *saw*, and seemed to love it, all of it, life and the world. Even though it was grim, it was precious, too, and fascinating, and when he looked at you ... at least, when he looked at Azareen that night and after, she felt precious and fascinating, too, and more alive than she had been before.

His name was Eril-Fane, and Guldan had chosen *her* to be his training partner. Azareen would often wonder what the old woman had seen in her to offer her this chance. It made her want to be worthy—of the sacred legacy of the Tizerkane, of being alive, and of *him*, whom she loved from the moment he grinned at her, handed her a sword, and said, blushing, "I hoped it would be you."

After that, her days were a fog, and real life was lived at night in a secret cavern with a sword in her hand, blade-dancing with a boy who burned with beautiful fire. A year passed, then two, then three, and he was no longer a boy. His face broadened; his body, too. His blacksmith's arms grew massive. And always his eyes were open wide, and he loved the world and was fearless, but he blushed when he saw her, and smiled like a boy who would never grow up completely.

On Azareen's sixteenth birthday, there was a dance in the Fishermen's Pavilion. It wasn't *for* her birthday; that was chance. She didn't tell Eril-Fane, but he knew and brought a present—a bracelet he'd made himself, of hammered steel with a demonglass sunburst. When he clasped it for her, his fingers lingered on her wrist, and when they danced, his big, sure hands trembled on her waist.

And when the dance was broken up by Skathis arriving on Rasalas to carry off a girl called Mazal, they stood frozen, powerless and furious, and wept.

That night he walked her home by a towpath underground, and they spoke with the fervor of untested warriors of overthrowing the gods. He went down on his knees before her, and, trembling, kissed her hands. She touched his face with unreality and ease: She'd dreamed of this so much that nothing was more natural, but there were details she hadn't known to imagine: how rough his jaw, how hot his brow, how soft—*how soft*—his lips. She brushed her fingers over them, dazed, half dreaming, dizzy. Time skipped, and then it wasn't her fingers but her lips on his lips, all the better to feel their softness, because her fingers were callused but her lips felt everything, and he was everything she wanted to feel.

Something in them was awakened that night. To see a girl borne off by Skathis when they had just been dancing, and to know, even if they could not bear to think of it, what she must be enduring...It was a harsh awakening, and they drowned it with each other, with their lips and hands and hunger. Mazal was hardly older than Azareen. Few girls in the city escaped the gods' attentions. Almost all were destined to take that ride up to the citadel and spend a year they would not remember. It was only a matter of time, they knew, and so time took on new meaning.

Azareen scarcely remembered the days that had followed, but the nights...oh, *the nights*. In the river cavern, they sparred with new wildness, so that the others training around them would find themselves stopping to watch. It was a deadly, passionate dance, and they were perfectly matched, her speed a counterpoint to his strength. No one else in the city could have bested them. After sparring, he would walk her home, only they wouldn't get there till close to sunup. They knew all the shadowed places where they could be alone, to kiss and touch and press and breathe and drown and live and burn.

A few months later, they wed. As Eril-Fane had made her a bracelet, he made her ring, too. On his small apprentice stipend, he rented rooms above a bakery—in Windfall, where the gods' plums rained down. They made a sickly sweet reminder, always in the air. Even if you never looked up, you couldn't escape knowing the citadel was there. But the rooms were cheap, and they were young and poor. He carried her up the steps. Azareen was tall and strong, but he lifted her like silk and air. He kicked the door shut behind them and took her straight to the bed. They'd waited. Of course they'd waited, but every night it had been harder. They were match and striker, each to the other. They touched and were set afire.

Two days earlier, with his hot mouth on her neck, she had closed her eyes and told him, "I don't want to be a maiden when he takes me."

"I won't *let* him take you," Eril-Fane had said, his arms tightening around her, his whole body going taut.

But they knew what happened to those who tried to thwart Skathis's plunder: fathers' throats ripped open by Rasalas, husbands carried skyward and dropped. They knew not to interfere; the women would be returned, and none wanted their men to die. Still, when it came to it, some men just couldn't bear it, and Azareen worried what Eril-Fane might do. The risk was not only to them. To show any fighting skill would give away their training and betray the Tizerkane, who were not prepared to mount a defense, much less a full-scale revolt. And anyway, it would be for nothing. Whenever Skathis came among them, he wore a second skin of ultrafine mesarthium under his clothes. He could not be hurt. Azareen tried to make Eril-Fane swear not to die for her, but he would not take that oath.

As for her not remaining a maiden, though, there they quite agreed. They said their vows and he carried her home, skipping their own party in favor of their bed. They were young and burning, and they lived under a terrible shadow. There wasn't a moment to lose.

For five days and five nights, they strung minutes like beads—each one a jewel, shining and precious.

On the sixth day, Skathis came. Rasalas's landing shook the street. Azareen and Eril-Fane were walking home from the market, holding hands and smiling their lovers' secret smiles. To the god of beasts, they were irresistible: beautiful, smooth, and sweet. They were like dessert for a monster like him. Eril-Fane pushed Azareen behind him. Terror rose in her. Rasalas leapt. The beast was an atrocity: a winged thing, all misshapen, skull bared by rotting flesh—metal skull, metal flesh, and its eyes just empty sockets aglow with infernal light. It flew at them, plowing into Eril-Fane. The momentum sent Azareen sprawling, so she was lying on her back on the cracked lapis stones when Rasalas's great claws closed around her husband's shoulders.

And lifted him.

She watched him grow smaller as he was borne away struggling. It happened so fast. *She* was the one left behind. She had never prepared herself for that. Sometimes men were taken, but not with the certainty of women, and she could only lie there, gasping, until someone came to help her up, to take her home to her family.

Really, it felt as though she had lain there gasping for the next two years and more. They were such a blur of longing and aching, and when Skathis finally did take her, she was *glad*—to put an end to the waiting, to find out what had become of her husband, if he was even still alive.

He was. But he was no longer her husband, not then or ever after. He was Isagol's broken toy. He could not touch or love her. He couldn't even weep. She never could stop loving him, though in the worst of times she'd tried. Thakra knows, she'd tried.

And here they were now: no longer the same smooth, young creatures they'd been. Eighteen years had gone by since the day Skathis took him, and it felt like an entire lost lifetime. Now, in these past few days, he had both wept and held her hand, and she had sensed, for the first time, a shift taking place within him. She had begun to feel the first fragile unfurling of something she thought might be healing. But was she only seeing what she wanted so desperately to see? As she watched him go, and wondered, a shadow drew a circle around him. She looked up, startled, and saw the white eagle circling. An unaccountable chill gripped her. Azareen was not one for omens, and had no good reason to fear the bird. But for a single, potent moment it felt as though fate had drawn an arrow, pointed it right at her husband, and declared him the next to die.

🏵 26 🏵

DIZZY LITTLE GODSPAWN

Sarai was as ready as she was going to get. Sitting on the floor beside Minya, preparing to reenter her mind, she couldn't help thinking of all the nights she'd sent out her moths to invade humans' dreams and unleash horrors on them. She recalled how Minya would come to her room at sunup and ask, eager, "Did you make anyone cry? Did you make anyone scream?"

For years, the answer had been *yes*. Sarai knew better than anyone: It's easy to make people cry. Grief, humiliation, anger—there are countless avenues to tears. It's easy to make them scream, too. There are so many things to fear.

But how do you *stop* someone from crying? How do you lead them out of fear?

Can hate be reversed?

Can revenge be defused?

How much more daunting these tasks were. Sarai was overwhelmed. "Trust yourself," Lazlo told her. "She may be strong, but so are you. I've seen what you can do in dreams."

She raised her eyebrows. She couldn't help it. "Yes, you have." She bit her lip in a bashful smile. "But I don't think *that* will help me now."

Lazlo grinned, cheeks warming. "Not *that*. Though I'd love to do that again later. I meant the time you defeated Skathis. You didn't think you could do it then, either."

"That was different. He was my own nightmare. Minya's real."

"And you're not trying to defeat Minya. Remember that. You're trying to help her defeat *her* nightmare."

When he put it like that, it sounded less impossible. And those were the words she went armed with when she reached for Minya's hand and traveled, by touch, into the landscape of her mind.

She found herself standing in the nursery, and was unsurprised. After the last time, she had a feeling that this was Minya's cage. Again there were babies in the cribs and children playing on mats on the floor. There was no skip or blur by the door this time, but neither were the Ellens to be seen. This seemed wrong. Whenever Sarai had imagined what it was like in here before the Carnage, she had pictured it how it was in the citadel after, only in this smaller space and with more godspawn. Her childhood memories were full of the ghost women—their good sense and good cheer, their scoldings and teachings, their jokes and stories, their singing voices and their ever-changing manifestations. Great Ellen's hawk face compelling them to tell the truth with its unblinking avian stare. Or Less Ellen helping Sparrow come up with whimsical names for her orchid hybrids, things like "Dolorous Wolf Maid" and "Frolicking Cricket in Lace Pantaloons."

So she had to wonder at their being absent from Minya's memory or imagining.

She saw Minya, looking as she had last time: clean and long-haired in a tidy smock. The pall of dread was absent, or at least greatly reduced. When Sarai closed her eyes and felt for the dream's aura, there was a low, steady thrum of fear, like blood moving under skin, and she had the impression it was a constant here, as much as the air, the metal, the babies, and that it had been Minya's reality.

Last time, Minya had been the biggest of the children, but now there was another girl her size. She was dark-haired as nearly all of them were, and half dark-eyed as well. Her left eye, though, was green as a sage leaf—a startling pop of color in an otherwise plain face.

They were playing together. They'd taken one of the blankets and turned it into a hammock. Each girl was holding an end, and they were swinging the little ones in it, one or two at a time. There were squeals, bright eyes. Minya and the other girl kept time with a chant. It was familiar—a sort of bright twin to the chant Sarai had heard last time:

> *Dizzy little godspawn,*
> *Swing them in a blanket,*
> *Don't let them fly out,*
> *Whizzing like a comet.*

And more in that vein, all innocent fun until Sarai began to notice that the low, steady blood-thrum of fear was bubbling to the surface. The girls were raising their voices so as not to be drowned out by it, and speeding their game to keep pace with it, the words coming faster and louder, smiles turning to grimaces as their eyes went flat and grim with the knowledge of what was coming.

Sarai thought she knew what it was, but when the figure appeared in the doorway, it wasn't the Godslayer, or any other man or human.

It was Korako, the goddess of secrets.

Sarai knew what Korako looked like primarily from witnessing her murder in Eril-Fane's dreams. He had slain her with the rest of the Mesarthim: a punch with a knife, right to the heart. Her eyes had lost life in an instant. She was fair-haired and brown-eyed, and Sarai knew her up close: her dying face, pale brows arced high in surprised contrast against the azure of her skin. It was practically her only vision of her. She had none at all from Weep. Alone of the Mesarthim, Korako had never gone into the city. The only ones who knew what she looked like were those who'd been in the citadel when Eril-Fane slew the gods, because only they had returned home with their memories intact.

The goddess of secrets had been a mystery. None ever knew what her gift even was. She hadn't sown torment, like Isagol, tangling emotions for the fun of it, or eaten memories like Letha, who sometimes went door to door for them, like a caroler on Midwinter's Eve. Vanth and Ikirok had made their powers known, and Skathis was Skathis: god of beasts, king of horrors, daughter-stealer, city-crusher, monster of monsters, madman.

But Korako was a phantom. There were no horrors to pin to her, save this one, and there was no one left to tell of it but Minya. Here it was, playing out: the goddess of secrets come to the nursery.

She was the one who tested them. She sensed when the children's gifts stirred and coaxed them forth. And then she led them away with her and they never came back.

She stood in the doorway now, and dread pounded like drums. Sarai understood that Minya's unconscious was layering in some retrospective knowledge. The girls in the room didn't know the goddess was there. She watched them for a moment, and her face was a mask. She spoke, or did she? Her lips didn't move, but her voice was soft and clear. She said, with a questioning lilt, "Kiska?"

And the little girl who was Minya's playmate turned, unthinking, toward her. In the next instant, she froze, and just like that she was caught. Her name was Kiska, and her gift had come. For weeks, she'd kept it hidden, but all was undone just like that when reflex betrayed her. Korako had only *thought* her name, but Kiska had heard her. She was a telepath. Korako had suspected and now she knew.

She said—was she sorry?—"Come with me, now."

Hundreds of times she'd done this before. Hundreds she expected to do it again. She little imagined, did she, that *this* was the very last time? That little Kiska with her one green eye was the last child she'd take from the nursery. Eril-Fane would rise up only three weeks later, and kill the gods and the children, too. But Kiska would be gone by then. Today was her farewell. She shrank with fear, and showed no defiance.

Minya did. Sharply, she said, "*No.*"

Sarai, a spectator, saw what Korako must have seen: a small, ferocious, *burning* girl with a presence ten times her size. "You can't have her!" She was shrill, afraid but also furious. You could see her father in her—if, that is, the god of beasts would have used his power to protect children. "*GO. AWAY!*"

Korako didn't argue.

It occurred to Sarai, watching, how easy she might have made it all. Whatever was in store for the children, why had she not simply *lied?* Why not pretend she was taking them to a lovely new life, with homes and grazing spectrals and the feel of grass beneath bare feet—with *mothers,* even. They'd have gone with her, willing, and been eager for their turn. But she didn't say a word. She seemed almost to steel herself. Her spine got a little stiffer, her face a little blanker, and she didn't meet Minya's eyes.

Sarai saw something she'd never noticed before: There was a mesarthium collar around Korako's neck. A *collar*, like an animal might wear. She searched her small cache of memories of the goddess. Had she really worn such a thing? Sarai tried to remember her death from Eril-Fane's dreams. Had it been there? She couldn't be sure.

Then, in the doorway, Korako made a gesture—a signal to someone—and...

...the skip reappeared. The anomaly, the blur. It reasserted itself in that instant. Again, Sarai had the impression that something was being obscured. She tried to look and saw only shadows. There was an *ache* in the aura, like pressing on a bruise. Was it Korako's doing? Was she hiding something? But that didn't make any sense.

This was Minya's dream. If it was keeping a secret, it was *her* secret, and *her* mind keeping it.

Could it be the answer to where the children were taken, too painful for her to remember? The mind could do that. Sarai had seen it. If something was simply unbearable, it put up a wall around it, or buried it in a tomb. She had seen horrors hidden in a biscuit tin and planted under a seedling so the roots would grow around it and hold it fast. The mind is good at hiding things, but there's something it cannot do: It can't erase. It can only *conceal*, and concealed things are not gone. They rot. They fester, they leak poisons. They ache and stink. They hiss like serpents in tall grass.

Sarai thought that Minya must be hiding something with that blur. She needed to know what it was. She gathered her power around her. She was the Muse of Nightmares. Dreams did her bidding. They could not hide things from her.

She bent all her will on the place to force it into the light. The resistance seemed to wail and thrash. It was strong, but she was stronger. It felt like ripping something open—a rib cage or a coffin. And then it was done. The blur was vanquished, and...

...the Ellens appeared.

Sarai thought she must have been wrong. Why should Minya conceal *the Ellens*? They weren't dead on the floor like the last time. This wasn't the Carnage. What was there to hide?

Her next feeling was relief. She had felt the nurses' absence so keenly. The nursery was like a half-painted picture without them in it. She thought they would comfort the girls, because that was what the Ellens did.

Or...that was what *her* Ellens did. *These* Ellens...

Sarai saw their faces, and she almost did not know them. Oh, their faces were their faces. They were shaped the same, anyway. Less Ellen wore an eye patch, but Sarai already knew that she had. Isagol had plucked out her eye. In her ghostself she restored it. It wasn't the eye patch that was the problem, though, but her good eye—or at least, the revulsion in it. She was looking at Minya and Kiska the way humans look at godspawn, as though they were obscene. And Great Ellen...

Sarai felt stricken, robbed, punched in the hearts, and laughed at all at once. Her sweet Great Ellen had round red cheeks that they called happiness cheeks, and they were still round and red, but happiness had nothing whatsoever to do with this woman. Her eyes were as cold as eel flesh in snowmelt. Her lips were puckered like a badly sewn buttonhole. And her aura was pure molten menace.

She went for Minya. Less Ellen seized Kiska and muscled her toward the door, where Korako was waiting. The whole time, the little girl was looking back over her shoulder, helpless dread on her face. Minya fought, kicking and spitting. She let out such a scream. It was the one that lived inside her—the apocalypse thing, throat-scouring, head-filling roar of endless rage. It whipped out of her like an animating spirit breaking free of the skin that contained it. In the dream, as it could not in truth, her wrath took the shape of a demon. It coalesced, red of skin, fire-eyed and huge. It dwarfed the nurses. It filled the room. What teeth it had, what a howl. Sarai was pummeled by its fury. She staggered, stunned, but also *glad*, because surely Minya was taking control. She would seize the dream, and her friend as well. She would save Kiska and *win*, and have at least a moment of peace, even if it wasn't real.

But the demon only howled with anguish as Kiska was dragged away.

And then Great Ellen drew back her arm and backhanded Minya to the floor. The howl cut off with an abruptness that Sarai could compare to just one thing: the moment her body, after its long, quiet fall, hit the gate, was impaled, became dead. The rage storm ended. The wrath demon vanished. And Minya lay like an unloved doll splayed out on the floor.

❦ 27 ❦

THE LIVING AND THE GHOSTS

Years ago, Minya had made them all swear not to use their gifts on one another. It had seemed a little unnecessary. Of course it was important that Ruby not use hers, but the rest of them? Sparrow's and Feral's gifts weren't dangerous, and Minya's wouldn't even work on the living. Still, they'd all sworn so solemnly, so completely under Minya's spell—and not grudgingly under it, but happy to be there. They'd adored her, their sharp-tongued, dark-eyed deliverer. But now it struck Sarai that it was *her* Minya had looked at while they all said their oaths. It was her gift Minya had feared. But all these years she had kept her promise, allowing Minya to keep her secrets. If even once she had defied her, might she have understood?

Now she flinched out of the dream, stunned and pale. Lazlo was there. He was holding her other hand, and he'd felt the emotion flooding through her, the same way he'd felt her screamed *NO!* His hearts were pounding. He didn't know what was happening. It felt like being locked out of a room while someone you love was trapped inside with unknowable terrors. "Are you all right?" he asked. "What happened?"

At first she couldn't even find words. She stared at Minya, lying on her pillows, and knew that on just the other side of a barrier only she could cross, Minya was lying on a cold metal floor with no pillows and no one to help her.

No one was *ever* going to help her. Everything she would do, she would do alone and with blood on her hands. Sarai swallowed the bile that wanted to rise up her throat. "Get the others," she told Lazlo. "Please. Tell Sparrow..." She swallowed again, fighting not to retch. It helped to remember it wasn't real—not the bile or her throat, anyway. Her horror absolutely was. "Tell Sparrow to bring the lull."

* * *

Out in the garden, Sparrow knelt beside a cluster of flowers. They were torch ginger, perfect red. She'd always thought they looked like little fireworks exploding.

In Weep, every year on the anniversary of the Carnage, they set off fireworks. There were, apparently, all manner of festivities, but the fireworks were the only ones that they could see from up here. And though the godspawn knew what was being celebrated, it was hard not to want to watch the fire blossoms lighting up the night.

The humans didn't call it the Carnage, but the Liberation. Sarai had brought back that fact from her visits to Weep. Through her moths she'd witnessed many things, and carried back stories for the rest of them, much like a girl who'd attended a ball and smuggled sweets home for her younger sisters.

And now she'd smuggled back more than stories, and more even than sweets. She'd brought a *man*.

Sparrow liked Lazlo very much. Based on him, she thought she would trust Sarai to go fishing for more humans and bring them back, too.

It was a dizzying idea—strangers, here—but less terrifying than the thought of going down to Weep. Sparrow longed to leave the citadel, but the city itself terrified her. When she was younger, she'd daydreamed about her unknown human mother, and of going down to live with her, certain that, given a chance, her mother would love her back. Great Ellen had been gentle with her, saying how they needed her here, while Minya had been more blunt. "They'd bash your head in with a shovel and throw you out like garbage," was how she'd put it, and Sparrow knew it was true.

She couldn't help wondering: What if she weren't blue? Would it make a difference to her unknown mother if she were human, with brown skin and no magic?

But she wasn't a starry-eyed child anymore. She knew there was not now and never would be a place for her in Weep, or a mother waiting to claim her. Now when she thought of leaving the citadel, it was forests and meadows she dreamed of. Plants wouldn't reject her. She was wild to go find some ferns, but the thought of people, crowds, cobbled streets, wrong turns, dead ends, staring eyes, gasps of shock . . .

It was just too much.

She reached out to the torch ginger and picked a flower. As she had yesterday with the anadne blossom, she held it while its life expired, feeling it ebb to a reedy pulse. There was something she'd been wondering.

The five of them hadn't had anyone to show them how to use their gifts. It was all just intuition, and who knew what they might have missed. Sparrow had never known, for example, that her gift could work in reverse. But when Sarai died, it had. Her sorrow had leeched life out of the soil, and wilted plants around her. It was an unpleasant discovery. She didn't want to be able to do that. She was Orchid Witch. She made things *grow*. Mostly plants, but not only. She had made Sarai's hair grow longer, glossier. She had also made her own eyelashes longer in a burst of foolish vanity whose intended target, Feral the Oblivious, had certainly not noticed, not that it mattered now.

Sparrow wondered if there wasn't anything more that she could do. She waited until the torch ginger flower was nearly empty of the fizz of life. Then she carefully touched its severed stem back to the stalk she'd plucked it from, lavished it with magic, and watched to see if anything would happen.

And maybe something did, or maybe something didn't, but then Lazlo was in the arcade, calling out to her to come, and that put an end to the experiment, for the time being at least.

* * *

Lull was the drink Great Ellen had brewed to keep Sarai from dreaming. She'd taken it for years at bedtime, to block the nightmares that would turn against her the minute she fell asleep. Under the influence of lull, there were no dreams of any kind, but only a calm gray nothing.

Now Sarai faced a dilemma.

"If we give her lull," Sparrow pointed out, "you won't be able to get into her dreams."

This was true. There would *be* no dreams to get into. Sarai wouldn't be able to talk to Minya, or see into her memories, either. She would be closing the only door that gave them any hope of reaching her—at least for a time. But to *not* give it to her seemed unconscionably cruel. "We're keeping her asleep," said Sarai, "which means we're keeping her locked in a loop of nightmares. We can't let her wake up. It's too dangerous. But at least this way she can have some peace." Though she knew that lull's gray "peace" was a far cry from anything like healing.

They wanted to know about the nightmares. They could see that Sarai was badly shaken. She hardly knew what to tell them. In the minutes that Lazlo had been gone to get them, the implications had unspooled around her, and where they led...

Trying to understand it, to *believe* it, it was like trying to touch a hot stove. She kept flinching back just short of it. "There are things that...may not be what they seem," she said.

"*What* things?" asked Feral. "Just tell us, Sarai."

"It has to do with the Ellens."

"You mean why they're like that?" Ruby waved a hand back in the direction of the gallery, where the nurses stood blank-eyed in the kitchen doorway.

Sarai nodded. "That's part of it, I think." This was only a surmise. How could she know? What *did* she know, really? "I saw some things in Minya's dreams. And dreams aren't reality, of course, but there's something there that's real, that's shaping it all. The Ellens...when they were alive, I..."

It was so hard to say it out loud. It felt like cruelty to force her suspicions on them. Even if it were true, she thought, did they really need to know? Wouldn't it be kinder to let them keep the lie?

No. They weren't children for her to shelter, and she needed them. They had to try to figure this out together.

She let it out in a rush. "I don't think they loved us." Already, she was thinking of two distinct sets of Ellens: the living and the ghosts, as though they weren't the same people. "And I don't think they tried to protect us. I think it's all a lie."

234

The others stared at her, nearly as blank in their incomprehension as the Ellens themselves were blank in…whatever state they were stuck in.

Sarai told what she'd seen. She laid out each piece of the puzzle, not trying to make them into a picture, but just laying them out. She hoped, truth be told, that someone would form them into a different picture and disprove her dark suspicions. But the pieces seemed to assemble themselves:

There was the revulsion in the Ellens' eyes. Sarai couldn't unsee it, or the backhand, either. And there was the red hand—Minya's red, slippery hand—and climbing over the bodies, and the timing of it all, and Minya's words, "Do you want to die, too?"

There was the matter of the blur where Minya's own mind was hiding the Ellens from her. Why would it do that?

But for Sarai, the most compelling puzzle piece was the Ellens themselves, frozen in the kitchen doorway as they had been from the exact moment Minya lost consciousness. The more she thought about them, the more they seemed like…discarded costumes hanging in a dressing room.

"Let me get this straight," said Feral. "You're saying that the Ellens aren't…" He couldn't finish. "What *are* you saying?" He sounded angry, and Sarai understood. It felt like losing someone—two someones—whom they loved and who loved them. Worse than that, it felt like losing the belief that they could *be* loved.

"That maybe they hated us like all the other humans did," Sarai said. "And that maybe they weren't kind and caring, and didn't try to save us. That maybe it wasn't Eril-Fane who killed them. I think…I think *Minya* did." It was the only thing that made sense: the chronology, the red hand.

It also made no sense at all.

"If they didn't love us when they were alive," asked Ruby, fighting the conclusion, "why would they *after* they died?"

"They wouldn't," Sarai said. It was so stark, so simple.

There was one more puzzle piece, after all, and it was the one that completed the picture. "We always thought that Minya couldn't master her slaves' eyes," she said. "That her possession was imperfect." Turning to Lazlo, she asked, "Yesterday, when I...when I begged you to save me, when I said I'd changed my mind...could you tell it wasn't really me?"

Slowly, he shook his head, and that was it: proof of nothing except that it was possible.

It was possible that the Ellens weren't really the Ellens. That the ghost women who had raised five godspawn, who made them laugh and cared for them, and taught them and fed them and soothed their hurts, who settled their squabbles and sang them to sleep, were really nothing but puppets.

Which would mean, if it were true, that they were *Minya.*

And that maybe, just maybe, the ragged little girl with the beetle shell eyes, malefic, hate-ravaged, and bent on vengeance, was only a *piece* of who she was.

A little, broken piece.

Part III

* * *

kåzheyul (kah·ZHAY·ul) *noun*

The helpless feeling that one cannot escape one's fate.

Archaic; contraction of ka (eyes) + zhe (god) + yul (back), meaning "gods' eyes on your back."

28

BURIED GIFTS

The villagers kept a vigil around the wasp ship, waiting for the door to open again, but it did not. Night was falling. Kora and Nova had been inside for four hours, which was…too long. Their father was tense, sensing a slow diminution of their value the longer they were sequestered with strange men and without their clothes. Skoyë was tense, because if her stepdaughters' gifts had been weak, they would never have been kept so long, and she loathed the prospect of their gloating faces, should they turn out to be chosen. Shergesh was tense; he already viewed the girls as his, even if he could only have one of them. Many others were anxious, too, awaiting theirs or their children's turns to vie for the only chance they would ever have at glory and a different life.

Inside the ship, the atmosphere was even more fraught.

It was Nova who now wore a godsmetal glove. She had felt the hum overcome her, and sink into her core. She was Servant-blue, like in her dreams, but that was as far as it went. Ren the telepath had gone into her mind, as he had gone into Kora's. He had coached and coaxed her.

Don't think, just feel.

Go deeper.

Our gifts are buried within us.

But if anything was buried in Nova, she had found no hint of it, and was on the verge of panic. Was it possible she had no gift at all? She had never heard of that. Weak gifts abounded, but *no* gift? Never.

"It's all right," Solvay, the lone woman on the crew, had assured her early on, when Ren's initial probing had failed to turn up any bright spot of difference, as it had with the burgeoning in Kora's chest. "Some gifts take more time to reveal themselves than others. It's an art more than a science, but we're trained at it. We'll find it."

She'd been so kind, but that was several hours ago, and even she looked dubious now. They had performed every test they had, including the simplest of all: A smith's gift was never coy. You had only to touch the metal to know. A smith would leave fingerprints, even as a baby. Nova had not. And though she thought she'd immured herself to the hope of it, still it was a blow. They had tried out water, fire, earth, to test for elemental magic. They had even administered little shocks intended to stimulate different nerve paths. It hadn't hurt *very* much, but Nova was exhausted now. The Servants were speaking amongst themselves, and she and Kora could hear every word. "It's unusual but not unheard of," Antal of the white hair was saying. "I've heard of gifts that took weeks to manifest."

"We don't have weeks," Ren reminded him. "Unless you'd like to stay here and enjoy the fascinating smells."

"We could always bring her," suggested Solvay, "and let them test her at the training house in Aqa."

"And if she's useless, what then? Are *you* going to bring her back here?"

Solvay glanced at Nova. "I imagine..." she said hesitantly, "she'd prefer not to return. She could find work in Aqa if it came to it. Why not? We've space aboard, and too few prospects to fill it."

Antal gave a deep sigh. "It is not our job to transport girls away from their dreary lives, Solvay."

"It *is* our job to find the strong, of whom there are fewer all the time. And with a mother and a sister like hers, what are the chances that she's weak?"

They all paused, glancing to Skathis, who had yet to express an opinion. Through everything, he had simply watched, his gaze *crawling* over Nova—like the flies on the beach, she thought, inwardly cringing. They seemed to be waiting for him to weigh in. They also seemed...on edge.

"Skathis?" Ren prompted, and Nova couldn't breathe, so afraid he'd say just to leave her, that she wasn't worth the trouble. She was holding Kora's hand with her own ungloved one, and she clenched it hard.

The smith straightened up from his slouch against the wall. "There's another option you haven't mentioned."

"No," said Solvay at once.

Skathis raised his eyebrows. "Pardon me?"

She looked conflicted to be arguing with her superior officer. "It's against protocol."

"This is my ship. *I* set the protocol."

"You do not set imperial protocol," persisted Solvay, breathless and flushed. "You are subject to it like everyone else."

"I am not like everyone else," said Skathis in a voice like the smoldering of embers.

A brief silence fell before Antal, clearing his throat, suggested, "Why don't we try again in the morning before we consider...other options."

"I think the girl would like to find her gift *now*." Skathis turned to Nova. "Wouldn't you."

It wasn't a question, and Nova didn't know how to respond. She was desperate to find her gift, but why did the others look so troubled? "I don't..." she began. "What...?"

"Good," said Skathis, "it's settled," though she had agreed to nothing.

"Wait." Kora stepped in front of her sister. "What are you going to do to her?"

"To *her*?" asked Skathis with a smile. "Nothing at all."

And the first hint Nova had of what he intended was when her sister's hands flew to the godsmetal collar around her neck.

Kora gave a gasp. She felt it constricting and tried to fit her fingers under it to stop it—as if she *could*, as if the godsmetal were not impervious to everything but the smith's will. It was beginning to bite in. Her gasp shallowed, turning into a choke as her windpipe flattened under the collar's pressure. She didn't even have time to draw a last breath before it closed her throat and cut off all air. A tortured sound dragged out of her. Her eyes went wide with panic.

"No!" Nova cried, lunging to her sister, to claw at the necklace, too. It was futile. She already knew she wasn't a smith. She spun toward Skathis. He was watching them with unnerving unconcern. "Let her go!" Nova cried. "You'll kill her!"

"I hope not," said Skathis. "Astrals really are very rare. It'll be a shame if she dies. It's up to you to save her life. Do you have power, or don't you? *Show me*."

Nova rushed at him. She wasn't thinking. To try to strike a Servant of the empire—a smith, no less! It was grounds for immediate execution. She didn't reach him anyway. He took a neat step back, and the floor beneath her feet warped and turned liquid, drawing her down all the way to her knees before turning solid again and trapping her. She struggled, looking wildly between Kora's face—gasping mouth and panicked eyes—and Skathis's placid one. The other three Mesarthim stood rigid, such expressions on their faces that it was clear in an instant that they feared their captain, and were powerless to stop him.

Only he could end this, and Nova saw plainly—from all their faces—that he would not, that he would take it to its bitter end, even if it cost Kora's life.

It was up to Nova, then. If there was a gift in her, she had to find it. She had given up looking. Now, frantic, she tried again to...to *feel*, as Ren had instructed, but all she could feel was her pounding heart. Kora was on the floor now, her struggles growing feebler. Nova saw that she was dying. She stopped plundering through herself, pawing for a gift as she might paw at beach sand in hopes of finding a shell. This wasn't about *hope* anymore. It was about desperation—

—which was just what Skathis was after. In a matter of life or death, the body and mind will flood with chemicals and trigger even the most stubborn gifts. This was his method, cruel, violent, effective. It was like blowing up a door when you couldn't find the key. It worked, in its way.

Rage pulsed up from Nova's core like the shock wave of a blast, ripping through her fear, her worry, even through her conscious thought, so that she stopped feeling for her gift, stopped wondering what it was, and just...*became* it.

A lot of things happened at once.

Kora took a drag of breath.

Nova climbed out of the floor that had trapped her, as easily as though it were water.

Shock registered in Skathis's eyes in the split second before the

243

godsmetal under his feet lurched like a yanked rug and sent him flying. His head hit with a crack. The other Mesarthim stared, agog, at Skathis on the floor, Kora breathing, Nova free.

"She's a smith after all," breathed Solvay.

But Ren went where the others couldn't, into Nova's mind, and when he felt what was there, he said, horrorstruck, "*No, she isn't.*"

And then he wasn't in her mind anymore. He was thrust out of it and she was *in his*, flensing it like an uul hide with her inarticulate roar of rage. His hands flew to his temples, his face contorting at the assault of her voice, her wrath, her *power*. It invaded his mind, which felt, suddenly, fragile as glass that would shatter if the onslaught did not cease. He dropped to his knees, still holding his temples. His face was a rictus of pain.

Nova's hands were fists at her sides. Her stance was wide, head dropped, chin almost to her chest, and she was peering up through slitted eyes, her breath hissing out through bared teeth. Words hissed out, too.

"*Leave. My sister. ALONE!*"

Kora was on her knees now, the collar in her hands—in two pieces, as though it had snapped in half.

Skathis rose, unsteady, his eyes bleary. There was blood on the floor and on the back of his head. He fixed on Nova, struggling to focus. A snarl of incredulous anger turned his plain face terrible.

He had brought this out of her. This method seldom failed. As Solvay had said, it was against protocol, because *it was dangerous.* But Skathis had never feared it, because he had never met anyone more powerful than he.

Until now.

He lifted his hands to conduct the mesarthium, to retaliate, to *end* her.

And *nothing happened*. It was like reaching for a sword and finding an empty sheath. Skathis's gift was gone.

"She's not a smith," he said, his voice thick with loathing, outrage, *fear*. "She's a pirate."

A *pirate*. The word penetrated Nova's red haze, but it didn't make any sense. Pirates were murdering thieves of the seas. She was not that. She was only trying to save Kora. She looked to her sister, who was out of danger, but she couldn't calm down. Power was rampaging through her, new and loud, unleashed and huge, screaming through every vein, every nerve. She didn't know even what power it was. It was just spilling out of her, grabbing whatever it could.

If astral was a rare gift, pirate was rarer still.

But where astral was a welcome gift, pirate was anything but.

It was the term for those whose gift was to steal gifts. It had seldom ever arisen, and was a kind of Mesarthim bogeyman story that sent chills down Servants' spines. Imagine a person who could reach out with their mind, snatch away your gift, and use it themselves. Such was Nova, and her magnitude was shattering.

In his outrage, Skathis was hideous, his countenance mad-dog vicious. He took a step toward her and she acted on instinct. Godsmetal surged up around him with neither elegance nor control. It reached his neck. It formed a collar.

The collar tightened.

"Stop her!" Skathis choked.

And the others tried. Well, Ren could not. The telepath was still holding his head with both hands as though it might burst apart. His face had gone violet. His eyes were squeezed shut. The chaos of Nova's mind *amplified* in his.

Solvay and Antal both tried to subdue her. Antal's gift was control of kinetic energy. He could take it away, depriving subjects of mobility, or amplify it, to make them faster, stronger. He tried to immobilize Nova. Solvay was a soporif, able to put people to sleep at will. Both were chosen for this duty for their ability to stop a subject whose gift went wild, and keep them from doing harm. But when they sharpened their minds toward Nova, they found their gifts snatched away and redoubled on them—freezing Antal in place and sending Solvay instantly slumping to the floor.

She was only asleep, but Nova, seeing her fall, thought she'd killed her, and cried out. Whatever was happening, she couldn't control it. The Servants could neither help her nor stop her, and the more her panic grew, the more her power did, too.

Outside in the village, the people of Rieva drew back from the wasp ship as it began to buck, wings scissoring—deadly godsmetal blades lashing out, skinning the roofs right off the nearest houses and swatting two children off their feet to land in a tangled heap. There were screams of horror. Villagers fled. The wasp lurched, crushed a house, and foundered halfway through the village before finally slowing and falling still.

Inside, Kora held Nova in her arms, saying over and over in her ear, "I've got you, I've got you, it's all right, my Nova, calm down, my darling, my sister," until the familiar and soothing sound of her voice began to cut through the whirlwind in Nova's mind. It was like a rope thrown into a churning sea. Nova grabbed it, and it saved her from drowning. The whirlwind, the sea, they began to abate—enough that the Servants' gifts, which she hardly knew she'd snatched, began to flow back to them in dribbles of power until, having just enough of his own back, Skathis was able to act.

Merciless, he drew a mass of metal from the wall behind the girls. It shaped into a club. They never saw it coming. It hit the side of Nova's head with a terrible resonant *thud*. Her eyes went wide, then

246

dim. She slumped in Kora's arms, and the last of her stolen power flowed back to its rightful owners.

Ren was able to lift his head and open his eyes again. They were a gruesome sight, the whites full red from burst blood vessels. Solvay stirred on the floor and groaned, and Antal was released from his paralysis. Skathis wrenched the collar from his neck and hurled it aside. He stripped the godsmetal glove from Nova's hand. He did not shape it into a diadem or collar, but only repossessed it.

Kora was crying, cradling Nova. They were a pathetic sight in their torn and dingy smallclothes, faces wet—Kora's fearful, Nova's slack.

Solvay rose to her feet, shaking her head to clear it. Antal helped Ren up to his. "That was...unexpected," the telepath said weakly.

"*That* is why there are protocols," said Solvay.

Skathis didn't even look at them. His eyes remained fixed on the girls. Dread possessed Kora. She wondered how she could ever have found his plain face benign. Something dark and wild burned in him. She had never been so afraid.

"What are you going to do with us?" she managed to ask in a shadow of a voice.

The other Servants shrank inwardly. They knew the answer. Of course Skathis would kill this girl who had made him as helpless as a mortal.

But he did not lash out unthinking. If Skathis's wrath had been purely volatile, he might have been less deadly. Instead, he was calculating. Of course he wanted to kill the girl, but he understood that if he did, he would render Kora useless—a leftover piece of something broken, and no good to him at all. He wanted her power. He was young and rising in the imperial ranks. His ship was small, only corvette class, which meant being assigned to duties like this one,

247

recruiting in backwaters. If he hoped to one day command a battle-ship, he had to win the godsmetal to grow it, which meant outsmart-ing and outmaneuvering all the other smiths in the fleet. It was a treacherous game, played with cunning and without mercy, and a spy would greatly help his cause.

What finer spy than an astral, he mused, particularly one bound to him by obligation. It was decided. He would make it clear to her later: that her sister's life depended on her own obedience. Now he wanted only to be away from this wretched place.

"You are no longer an *us*," he told Kora.

The bottom of the ship melted open to make a hole under Nova, whose limp form sagged right through it. Kora cried out and tried to hold on to her, but the mesarthium was against her, locking her in place as it dragged Nova down. She fell a good four feet to land hard on the ground below, her inert limbs splayed wide. The metal pooled back like a turned tide and Nova was gone.

"*No!*" Kora screamed, scrabbling futilely at the floor.

"You're mine now," said Skathis. "Your only 'us' is with *me*."

They did not stay to test the rest of the hopefuls of Rieva. They did not take their leave of the village elder, Shergesh. The wasp simply launched, bending its metal legs, flicking its wings that had caused so much damage to the village, and casting itself skyward, taking Kora with it, and leaving Nova, unconscious in the dirt.

* * *

Nova awakened slowly.

Her eyes ached. Her head ached. Her mouth was dust-dry. She couldn't swallow. She was in her house—her father and Skoyë's house—lying on her pallet on the floor. It was daytime, the house empty, and this was a wrongness. She and Kora were always up at first light—when there *was* light—their pallets rolled and stowed. For a moment, blinking, aching, parched, unwell, she forgot...everything. Even from here she could smell the ripe stench of uul husks rotting on the beach. The Slaughter. In her memory: the beach, a flash of blue in the sky.

A skyship.

A jolt went through her. She tried to say Kora's name. It came out a croak, and Kora did not come. She tried again, louder. Still a croak, and still no Kora.

Nova sat up—and she nearly collapsed when it seemed the contents of her head did not sit up with her. She swayed forward, palms spread out over the rush mats to keep her from tipping over. When the room stopped spinning, she peeled her aching eyes open and found herself staring at her hands.

Which were not blue.

It was only when she saw them as they were—pale as they had ever been—that she was hit by a powerful memory of staring at them *blue*, the one shining in its godsmetal glove, the other her own skin. She blinked at them through the haze of her vision, and tried to understand what was real. It seemed a dream, images coming in flashes. Kora's eagle. The flung godsmetal ball. The buzz in her skin. And...what happened after. It was hazy. It would always be hazy. The flashes sorted themselves into a picture, and a terrible sick dread welled up in her.

Where was Kora?

Footsteps, child-quick, and then Aoki, her half brother, ran inside, saw her sitting up, spun, and ran back out. He was shouting, "Ma! She's awake!"

And so Skoyë's silhouette filled the doorway. Her hands were on her hips. There was triumph in the pose. "Still alive?" she asked, disappointed.

"Where's Kora?" Nova croaked.

"Oh, don't you remember?" Make no mistake: Skoyë delighted in reminding her. "They took her." She came forward, and Nova could see her homely face, fierce with vindication. "*You* they threw out like garbage." She loomed. "What happened inside that ship, Novali?"

Kora was gone. Nova could think of nothing beyond that. She felt the truth of it. Kora's absence was a pulsing void that nothing could ever fill. "When?"

"Three days ago," said her stepmother. "They're long gone. She'll be in Aqa by now. Maybe she's found your mother, and they're together without you. Maybe they'll have a house and live together," she went on cruelly, but Nova didn't hear. It was as though a patch of reality had been torn out, leaving a hole that swallowed all sound, all thought.

Kora was gone, and she was still here.

Unchosen.

"Now, get up," said Skoyë. "You're in luck. The Slaughter's not over. Get down to the beach. The uuls won't butcher themselves."

29

WARP

Sarai did give Minya the lull, a small dose with plum syrup to cut the bitterness, in case she could taste it in her sleep. She touched the little girl's hand and, full of dread, reentered both dream and nursery, to wait beside her prone form as the gray descended and erased all pain, guilt, and fear—and everything else, too. It was better, Sarai knew from her own experience: Sometimes nothing was better than something. It all depended on the something.

She left Minya's mind, but not her side. She sat with her and took the next watch. She told Lazlo he didn't have to stay.

"Well, that's a relief," he said. "I was wondering when I'd get a break from the woman I love, who is the first and only person I've *ever* loved, and who I would happily sit beside under literally any circumstances forever."

Sarai fought a little smile, but not very hard. And Lazlo would have stayed sitting beside her on the floor, his shoulder the perfect height to rest her head against, but Feral spoke up then. "Actually, do you think you could see about making the doors work now?" He studiously avoided looking at Ruby as he made the request, and Sarai couldn't tell if his motive was to keep her out, or to give them privacy. She wondered if he even knew.

"Go on," she told Lazlo when he looked to her, and he kissed her on top of the head and went out with the others, leaving her on her own with Minya.

She watched the little sleeping girl—so much threat all put on hold by a few drops from a green glass bottle—and wondered what was hidden in the labyrinth of her memories. Could it be true, her dark surmise: that the Ellens had been puppets all along? It didn't seem possible. But neither could Sarai retreat into her old, comfortable belief in their love, not after what she'd seen in the dream.

She knew she wasn't finished with the nursery or the Carnage, and that she would have to go back there, and *keep* going back until she found a way to make a difference—to help Minya, and create a chance for a future, for all of them. But she couldn't do it right now. She needed a rest from nightmares and she wanted to give Minya one, too. Maybe the lull would let her mind calm itself, and break the terrible loop. She didn't know, but she was so grateful that the urgency was gone. They had time now. At least they had that.

* * *

Ever since he got here, Lazlo had felt the mesarthium holding its breath, waiting to claim and be claimed. There had been so much else going on—heavenly, hellish, and in-between—that he hadn't been able to focus on it, but now he was eager to give himself over to it.

They went to the dexter arm—himself, Feral, Ruby, and Sparrow—and Feral repeated what he'd told Lazlo before: that the doors used to respond to touch.

Lazlo put his hands to the wall. The sense of connection was instantaneous, and profound. The citadel was more than an enormous statue. It was a network of systems put in place by a god, all fallen dormant since his death. For Lazlo, they woke.

Energies rippled and stretched.

They absorbed him, even as he absorbed them. Nothing outwardly changed, but something crucial did: the metal, its signature, its *being*, all of it was translated. What had been Skathis's now became his. Earlier, Lazlo had told himself that this whole vast, otherworldly citadel could not possibly belong to him, but it *did*, and it went even deeper and stranger than that: It wasn't merely his. It was *him*, a part of him now in a way that felt almost as though it were alive.

He let his perception flow outward. The energies felt like ornate musical staves, weaving in and out of each other, dense with information and commands. There was a whole language at work, but it was nothing that could ever be explained or taught. Lazlo knew what it was like to learn languages. It was work. This wasn't. It simply gave itself to his mind, making sense to him in a wordless way that could only be described as magic.

Feral was right, he found. The doors could be keyed to fingerprints, so they would open only at the touch of those authorized to enter.

He keyed Feral's door to him, and there was a fraught moment of silence where they might have gone on to the next door, but neither Ruby nor Feral moved. Finally Ruby cleared her throat, and Feral asked Lazlo sheepishly, "Can you make it so she can open it, too?"

He did. And he keyed Ruby's door to the pair of them as well, and had a premonition that he would many times be asked to change them back and then back again.

Sparrow's door was keyed to her alone, but she didn't close it. She was used to her curtain, she said, and asked, "What about the other doors? Not the open ones to be closed, but the closed ones to open?"

It was an excellent question. Because mesarthium doors didn't shut so much as melt closed and become wall, it wasn't apparent where they even were, much less what lay behind them. What was the citadel hiding? A thrill went through all of them. Those of them who'd grown up here had spent hours of their childhood imagining the rest of the citadel, tormenting themselves with the notion that wonderful things were just out of their reach: libraries and racing tracks and menageries; bigger, better kitchens stocked with all sorts of delights; playrooms filled with whole other sets of trapped godspawn leading parallel lives. Basically, anything they wished they had, they would imagine existing on the other side of a wall. It had been maddening, and an integral part of their mental landscapes, these places that were closed to them, and yet, for all that they were unreachable, never so unreachable as the city. They couldn't very well dream of Weep, where they would be killed on sight. It had given their minds a place to go, even though they could not.

And now the prospect of finding out what was there raised the hairs on their arms. As for Lazlo, it was all new but no less thrilling. With his hand to the wall, he sent out his will, bidding hidden doors to open.

"There," he said as a seam appeared on an expanse of wall just up the passage. They rushed to it, breath held as it split, became a door, and revealed—

"Linens," said Ruby, disappointed. It was only a closet.

"Oh good," said Feral, helping himself to a set of silk sheets to replace his, which had been burned. "What?" he asked, flat, turning around to find them watching him with amusement. "You try sleeping on scratchy sheets."

Lazlo smiled and shook his head. He'd hardly known any sheets but scratchy ones. For all that this was a prison, it was a luxurious one.

"Let's look for some *real* treasure," said Ruby. She was on her toes, springing up the corridor. "There must be pantries in the kitchen. There might be sugar!"

They followed her, and found that she was right: a pantry door had opened on a wall beside the bank of stoves. Ruby led and the others followed, but they thumped into one another when she halted on the threshold. "What is it?" asked Sparrow. "Why did you—? *Oh.*" Peering around her, she saw why Ruby had stopped, and so did Lazlo and Feral, who could see over the girls' heads.

There were skeletons in the pantry—some cooks or scullery maids who'd been trapped when Skathis died.

"Poor souls," said Sparrow.

"They better not have eaten all the sugar," said Ruby, and plunged on in to see what she could find.

"Savage," said Feral, and followed her.

Sparrow hesitated, and followed, too, though not to scavenge for sugar. She found a large empty basket and began to gather up the bones and stack them neatly inside.

Lazlo helped her, shuddering at the skeletons' fate. "I wonder how long they lasted."

"Too long, I imagine. Trapped in a storeroom." Sparrow shook her head. "It must have felt like luck at first, until no one came to free them."

Lazlo knew what she meant. Trapped anywhere else, they'd have died within days. But here they'd had enough raw goods to keep themselves alive far past hope of rescue. It must have been a torment. He wondered how many others had been trapped when the doors stopped working. It made him worry. "Maybe I shouldn't have reactivated the doors," he said. "If something were to happen to me..." He gave Sparrow a comical squint. "Is *that* why you left yours open?"

She set a skull in the basket and let out a laugh. "Nothing so gloomy. I'm just used to it open. Though now that you mention it, maybe I'll leave it." She returned his squint and added a grimace. It was all jest, but then her gaze fixed on his swollen lip. Something seemed to occur to her, but she dismissed it and went back to the bones, only to look up a second later, pensive. "That must hurt," she said.

Lazlo, brushing the dust of the dead off his hands, said, "I can't complain."

"Well, you could. It's to your credit that you don't. Believe me, I know complainers." At that moment, as if on cue, a moan of wild lament reached them from deeper in the storeroom. It was Ruby, who had apparently found the sugar barrel empty. "Case in point," said Sparrow. "Could I try something?"

She indicated his lip. Lazlo gave an uncertain shrug. She told him to close his eyes. He did, and he felt a light touch on his mouth. He was aware of the small throb in the wound, like a miniature heartbeat, and then a tingling. And then he was aware only of noise as Ruby emerged, literally incandescent with disappointment, the ends of her hair flickering flame as she cursed the skeletons as greedy.

"Ruby." Feral tried reasoning with her. "They literally died of starvation."

Sparrow had drawn her hand away from Lazlo's cut, and the touch was forgotten in the ensuing argument. Lazlo, thinking perhaps it was best to explore the doorways one by one, reached back out with his mind to countermand his previous action.

Throughout the citadel, many doors had opened. Mostly they led down, into the torso. In Minya's domain, off the atrium with its dome upheld by angel wings, a staircase was exposed, spiraling gracefully up through the column of the seraph's neck into its head, with whatever secrets might lie therein.

And in the heart of the citadel, on the strange metal orb that floated dead center in the big, empty chamber, a seam appeared there, too. It ran vertically from zenith to nadir. Smoothly, soundlessly, the orb split and opened, and inside it there was...

...nothing.

The floating orb, twenty feet in diameter, was hollow, and it was empty. But...there was something wrong with the emptiness, though no one was there to notice. A nearly imperceptible *warp* wavered in its center. There was nothing there, but the nothing *moved*, like a pennant rippling in a breeze.

Throughout the citadel, the open doors reversed and began to melt back shut, all closing up again with no one to witness them. Except—

In the heart of the citadel, a cry poured itself into the quiet. The chamber had its way of eating sound, and what would, elsewhere, have been a banshee shriek, fell muffled, like a woman's far-off wail. It was Wraith, the white bird, materialized out of nowhere. It dove toward the floating orb just as it was closing and slipped between the metal edges to hit the nothing head on, and...disappear.

Wraith was an unnatural thing, and much given to vanishing. But this was different. The bird didn't fade or melt into the air. It hit the ripple of warp and the air parted around it, gaping open like a slash in fabric. There was a glimpse of sky, and...it was not Weep's sky.

And then the edges of the air fell back into place. The orb closed. All was quiet.

The bird was gone.

30

LIKE EATING CAKE IN DREAMS

The sun set. A bland dinner was prepared and eaten. Sarai saw to Minya, fed her and cleaned her, left Feral watching over her, and went to her room.

Lazlo had gone ahead, and her steps up the long dexter corridor were much quicker and lighter than they usually were. In fact, her feet barely touched the floor. All these years, after sundown, when the others went to bed, she had gone back to her room—not to sleep, but to send out her moths and visit nightmares on the people of Weep. And though she'd passed through hundreds of minds every night, she'd always felt so alone. Not now.

At the door, she paused. Her insides fluttered, from knowing Lazlo was here and the whole night was ahead of them.

This morning, with the pink of sunrise slanting through the window, she'd vanished her clothes and lain down on the bed, and Lazlo had lain down with her. They'd slept, skin to skin, and met in a dream, and there, too, they'd lain skin to skin.

Being a ghost had a lot in common with being in a dream. Neither were "real," in the strict sense of the word. Dreams drew on memory, experience. As Sarai had discovered with Lazlo, from their efforts at conjuring cake, you couldn't taste what you didn't already know.

It was the same with her ghostflesh. Sarai knew that all sensation now was her mind's best guess based on what she'd experienced before, and she'd experienced almost nothing. Lazlo had never touched her real skin, except to carry her dead body, and she'd only kissed him in dreams. So when his lips brushed her nipple, or his fingertips traced round her navel, she could only imagine the feeling. It felt real. It felt *wonderful*, but she couldn't help thinking it was like eating cake in dreams, which is to say: a pale phantom of the true and exquisite vastness of pleasure that is the privilege of the living.

Not that she'd appreciated that privilege while she was alive. She'd never had the chance, and now she never would. It was a sad thought, but there was a saving grace: In dreams, sensation could be *shared*, just like emotions and the flavor of cake. As long as it was known to one dreamer, it could be imparted to the other through the medium of the dream, so that when Sarai brushed her lips over Lazlo's nipple, or traced her fingertips round his navel, she could feel what he was feeling, and share in the exquisite vastness by proxy.

That was what she was thinking, flushed, warm, and eager, when she stepped into her room . . . to find it transformed.

She halted in the doorway and stared around in astonishment. It had always been beautiful, but it had been just a room, and tainted by the fact that Skathis had made it for Isagol—one monster's gift to another.

Whatever it had been, it was no longer "just a room." It was a fairyland. It was a forest glade. It was *alive*.

There were trees, tall and slender, vine-draped and swaying. You couldn't see the walls beyond them. A row of stepping-stones led between them and out of sight. Bewitched, Sarai stepped over the threshold. Just as she placed her foot on the first stone, a mesarthium snake glided over her toes. With a little gasp, she watched it vanish, sinuous, into the undergrowth. The details! Its little forked tongue. Tangles of ivy cascaded through ferns, and mushrooms no bigger than the end of her thumb grew on the mossy bark of the trees. She spotted a fox, a beetle. Both had wings, and darted out of sight.

It was, all of it, blue metal. But it was night, and everything looks blue at night. Sarai let her mind relax into the fantasy of it, and followed the stepping-stone path. It was like a fairy tale, and she might have been the maiden about to meet some mystical creature—a wish-granting crone or an enormous wise cat—and have her whole life transformed.

She came to a clearing, and it was not a crone or cat she met but Lazlo, leaning against a tree, trying to look casual with a rather large iguana perched on his shoulder. "Oh, good evening," he said. "Are you lost, miss? Can I help you?"

Sarai bit her lip to repress a smile, and tried to look demure. "I think I *am* lost," she said, playing along. She looked around. It was so changed. The ceiling was high, no longer fan-vaulted but drooping with a lacework of leaves and blooms. Moths browsed among drooping bellflowers, and fireflies flitted by, their bellies lit by chips of glavestone. "Can you tell me... I believe there was *a bed* somewhere around here?"

"A bed, you say?" Lazlo struck a pondering pose. "Can you describe it?"

"Well, yes. It was big and horrible."

"I know just the one." He wrinkled his excellent crooked nose. "It belonged to the witch."

"Yes, exactly."

"It's gone." Confidingly, he said, "There's a new one, though, made especially for the goddess of dreams."

The goddess of dreams. The words filtered sweetly into Sarai's mind, and she imagined a girl with cinnamon hair facing another in the mirror, the one the muse of nightmares, the other the goddess of dreams. Which was real, and which was reflection? "Indeed," she said. "And do you expect her to pass this way?"

"I hope so." Lazlo took his first step toward her. The iguana's tail curled over his shoulder. "I made that path just to lure her here."

"Do you mean to tell me, good sir, that you're lurking in the woods in hopes of taking a goddess to bed?"

"I admit I am. I hope she doesn't mind."

"I promise you she doesn't."

The goddess of dreams, she thought, if there were such a person, would wear gossamer and moonlight. No sooner did she think it than she *was* it. Her skin let off a subtle glow. Her dress floated like evaporating mist, and a corona of stars and fireflies perched on her red-brown hair. "Show me this bed," she said, her voice low and liquid, and Lazlo took her by the hand and led her through the trees.

The iguana was not invited.

❧ 31 ❧

A MAN WHO LOVES YOU ENOUGH TO COME BACK TO YOU EVEN WHEN YOU'RE A BITING GHOST

The next morning it was decided that Lazlo would go down to the city to talk to Eril-Fane.

He mounted Rasalas in the garden, and couldn't help but remember the day at the library when he'd mounted a spectral and ridden out with the Tizerkane. It had been his first time riding anything, and he hadn't been dressed for it, or in any way prepared. His robes had hiked up to show threadbare slippers and bare, pale calves, and he'd known he looked preposterous. Well, today he was barefoot and wearing a dead god's underthings, but he didn't feel preposterous now. It was impossible to feel foolish when the goddess of dreams looks at you with witchlight in her eyes.

"Come back to me," Sarai told him, anxious. He had assured her he would be safe, and was able to keep himself so if need be, but she couldn't help worrying. "Promise me."

"I promise. Do you think anything could keep me away?" A glint came into Lazlo's eye. "Who would not *not* kiss me if I didn't have you?"

Sarai recalled her important job of protecting his lip from kissing. Well, she'd failed spectacularly at *that* last night. In fact, in the low light and the wonder of it all, she'd forgotten all about it, and there'd been no wincing or taste of blood to remind her. "I don't care to speculate," she said, and eyed the lip in question, which was looking much better. The swelling was all but gone, and what had been a livid gash was just a small scab now. It had healed fast, she thought.

"You don't have to speculate," Lazlo said. "I only want you. Even if you *are* a biting ghost."

Sarai wrinkled her nose at him. "I'll bite you right now," she threatened.

He leaned down and let her. Her teeth were light on his lip, and so was the tip of her tongue. "You call that a bite?" he murmured against her mouth.

"It's a bite that dreams of being a kiss," she murmured back.

"Let's teach it later."

Sarai felt warm all over, and amazed by this new life that was theirs, and all the nights ahead to share in their enchanted glade. "I like that idea," she said, and Lazlo straightened up. Sarai stroked the side of Rasalas's neck as though it were a living thing, and then Lazlo was away, and she went to the balustrade and watched him fly, thinking how, of all the things she'd conjured in years of yearning for a different life, it had never occurred to her to wish for a man who'd love her enough to come back to her even when she was a biting ghost.

* * *

Over at the sinkhole, Thyon spotted the shape in the sky and paused in his hauling to point up and say, "Look."

The pace of the donkey cart would not do, so they ran, all of them—Ruza, Tzara, Calixte, himself—through the deserted streets toward the city center, watching as creature and rider disappeared behind the roofline. Thyon ran because the others did, but he felt like an impostor. They had reason to run: Calixte out of eagerness to see her friend, and Ruza and Tzara either for that reason or else to do their part in defending the city *against* him. Thyon honestly didn't know which, and he didn't think they did, either. In any case, when they reached the garrison, they all went straight through the gate without turning to look back, and Thyon slowed, and came to a stop outside. He wasn't Tizerkane. He couldn't go in there. Calixte wasn't, either, but she was different. She was *liked*.

The things she'd said before flashed through his mind as he stood alone outside the gate. It all boiled down to what kind of outsider one strove to be, and he felt it keenly: He was the wrong kind.

He would go around the garrison wall. It only took up a couple of city blocks. He didn't know where Strange had landed, but if he walked the perimeter, he supposed he'd find out. And if he'd landed inside, well, it wasn't as though Thyon had anything to say to him. Why had he even come? He might have stayed behind, climbed down into the sinkhole, and gone into the library on his own.

To walk stupidly amongst ancient texts that he could not decipher.

"Nero!" A shout.

Thyon turned. It was Ruza, his head poking out through the gates. "What are you doing?" he called, annoyed. "Come on." As though it were a given that he should follow.

Thyon ran his fingers over the bandages on his palms, swallowed past the unaccountable lump in his throat, and did just that.

* * *

When he'd flown up from the city, Lazlo had been holding Sarai's body, too distressed to appreciate that he was flying, and too grief-stricken for fear. Not to mention that flying *up* is an altogether different proposition than flying *down*. Going over the balustrade felt like plunging off a cliff, and there was a heart-stopping moment when he feared it was a mistake, and Rasalas would drop like a stone. But he didn't. He soared. *They* soared, riding the magnetic fields like a raptor on an updraft.

They spiraled downward, descending toward the Tizerkane garrison in the center of the city. The last time Lazlo had been there, Ruza and Tzara and some of the others had joked about blowing the godspawn into "blue stew." Their hate, as Suheyla had tried to warn him, was like a disease. Would they hate *him* now, too?

Flying lower, he spotted figures on the ground: running flat out, as though to man posts. He heard shouts. His wariness increased and he proceeded slowly, holding his breath as he came level with the watchtowers. Silhouettes moved within them. He couldn't make out faces. He luffed Rasalas's wings, feeling the weight of eyes as they settled onto the street—softly, with none of the jarring or cracking of paving stones that had been Skathis's way. He dismounted and walked slowly forward, thinking that he would pose less of a threat away from the creature. Then he waited.

After a few moments that rang with raised voices he couldn't quite make out, the guardhouse door opened and Eril-Fane emerged, followed closely by Azareen. Both looked regal and weary, and, he thought, older than when he'd seen them last. Still, he had to remind himself, they weren't so old. When Eril-Fane became the Godslayer, he had been but Lazlo's age: twenty. Fifteen years had passed since then, putting him at thirty-five, and Azareen a little younger. They could still have a life ahead of them, after all this was over. Perhaps even a family.

Lazlo stood where he was and let them approach.

"Are you all right?" Eril-Fane asked.

The question caught him off guard. Of all the things he'd braced himself for, simple concern had not crossed his mind. "Actually, yes," he said, though they were bound to think it strange until he had a chance to explain. After all, the last time they'd seen him, he'd been clutching Sarai's corpse to his chest, and they had no way of knowing that she survived, in her way. "And you?"

Eril-Fane admitted, "I've been better. I hoped you'd come. Tell me now, Lazlo. Are we in danger?"

"No," Lazlo answered, and was profoundly grateful that it was true. If it weren't for Ruby and Sparrow drugging Minya, he would have landed here saddled with the decision of who to save and who to sacrifice.

From Azareen issued a sound of disbelief. "So everything's just fine now? Is that what you're telling us?"

He shook his head. "I'm telling you that you're not in danger. That doesn't mean everything's fine." He saw her wariness, and couldn't blame her for it. As succinctly as he could, he apprised them of the situation:

That Sarai was dead, but not gone. That her soul was bound by an ageless little girl, the same one who held all the ghosts in thrall, and who had attacked their silk sleigh. That the girl alone of the godspawn possessed a will for vengeance, and that she was drugged now, unconscious, buying them time to come up with a plan.

"Kill her," said Azareen. "There's your plan."

"Azareen," Eril-Fane reproached.

"You know I'm right," she said, then told Lazlo, "She wants revenge, and you want to protect us? Go back up there and kill her."

"*Azareen*," repeated Eril-Fane. "That cannot be the only answer."

"Sometimes it is. As it was for Isagol, Skathis, and the rest. Sometimes killing *is* the only answer."

Harsh as it was, Lazlo supposed it must be true, that some people were beyond all hope of redemption, and would only cause grief and suffering as long as they were allowed to live. "I hope this is not one of those times," he said. Reasons ran rampant in his mind. *She is a survivor. She is what you made her. She is my sister.* But he only said, "She holds Sarai's soul in the world. If she dies, Sarai will be lost."

This quelled Azareen's insistence. She clamped her mouth shut and remembered the way Eril-Fane had fallen to his knees and wept at the sight of his dead daughter. If it truly came down to a choice between godspawn and humans, well, then she would do what needed to be done. But she knew that if it came to that, it would spell an end to any hope, however remote, of her husband reclaiming his right to live and be happy.

"Her name is Minya," Lazlo told them, hoping to make her real to them. "She was the oldest in the nursery when... Well. She saved four babies." His eyes flickered to Eril-Fane. It all led back to the Carnage, and it felt like blame to say so. "She... she heard everything."

"Don't try to spare me," said Eril-Fane, grim. "I know what I did. And now she wants revenge. Who can blame her?"

"*I* can." said Azareen. "We've endured enough. Sacrificed enough!"

A new voice answered, "That's seldom our decision to make." It was Suheyla. When she'd witnessed Lazlo's descent, she'd been headed for the garrison already, with a stack of her big discs of flatbread, wrapped in a cloth and still hot, balanced on her head. Now she regarded him from under her burden. This was her first sight of him blue, and it jarred her less than she'd feared it would, per- haps because she'd braced herself. Or maybe it was just that his face was still his face, his eyes still his eyes—guileless, earnest, and full of hope. "Look at you," she said, lowering her bread to the ground. "Who'd have thought?" And she held out her hand to him.

He took it, and she laid her other—her tapered wrist where once a hand had been—atop it and gave a squeeze. It reminded him of the sacrifices the people of Weep had made, and also of their resilience. "I was as surprised as anyone," he said. "I'm sorry to have left without saying good-bye."

"Sometimes these things are beyond our control. Now, what's this about my granddaughter's soul?"

Granddaughter. There was claiming in that word, and Lazlo expe- rienced a keen pang of hope on Sarai's behalf. He knew what it would mean to her to be claimed as family. He answered Suheyla. He couldn't see, as others could, the way he looked when he spoke of Sarai, or know the effect it had on them—as though the idea of her was translated through his love and wonder, and all their associa- tions with "godspawn" were called into question.

"She's been going into Minya's dreams," he said. "She thinks she's trapped, somehow, by the past. We hope that she can help her to finally be free of . . . of what happened that day."

It struck Azareen and Suheyla perhaps more even than the two men: that the little girl was a counterpoint to Eril-Fane, both of them trapped by the same horrific day, both of them saviors, and both broken. Azareen swallowed hard, and was prey to an echo of yesterday's omen: the white bird and its shadow, and the sense that fate was hunting, and had already picked out its quarry.

No. It couldn't have him.

"So take the citadel away," she blurted, her voice thrumming at the border of passion and desperation. "If you can't kill her, at least do that, and let us be free, too."

A silence followed her words as the others took them in. Eril-Fane spoke first. "We need to bring our people home," he told Lazlo, who saw shame in his face as though it pained him to ask them to leave, as indeed it did. But his first duty had to be to his people, and his city.

Lazlo nodded. This was, after all, why he'd come here: to help Weep solve this very problem, little suspecting, at the time, that he was the only one who could. With Minya unconscious, there was no real impediment. "That's fair," he said, and, at the prospect of pulling up anchor and moving the whole citadel, felt both apprehension and excitement. Move it *where*?

The answer that came to him was . . . *anywhere*.

Apprehension fell away. Lazlo let the realization fill him: that he was in possession of a magical metal palace he could shape with his mind—a magical *flying* metal palace he could shape with his mind—and for the first time in his life, he had a kind of family, and together they had . . . the world, the whole world, and *time*. That was crucial. They had time.

"I'll ask the others," he said.

"*You're* the one who can move it," Azareen insisted. "It's your choice."

Lazlo shook his head. "Just because the power is mine, it doesn't follow that all the choices are." But he saw that Azareen's harshness was stemming not from hate of the godspawn, but worry. Her stern, lovely features were pinched with it, and her hands were clasping and unclasping, unable to be still. "But I think they'll agree," he told her. "Sarai already pleaded with Minya to consider it."

There wasn't much more to say. Lazlo would return to the citadel

270

and talk to the others, then come back and relay their decision. He was concerned about the anchors, and whether there might be damage to surrounding structures when he lifted them up. At least the city was empty. There would be no risk of injuries, but Eril-Fane said he would send soldiers to make sure the areas were clear.

"We could use supplies for a journey," Lazlo said. "There's not much to eat up there." He gestured to his clothes. "Or to wear."

"We can do that," said Eril-Fane.

Azareen almost felt relief—to be so nearly free of the citadel and godspawn. At least, she sensed what it might feel like, but she wasn't ready to trust it, not until the sky was clear, and maybe not even then. Did she remember how to feel relief? If anything, she was holding her breath, waiting for the words she already knew that Eril-Fane would speak.

"Do you think...Can I meet her?" he asked, hesitant. "Can I come up with you?"

Lazlo already knew how Sarai yearned for her father to want to know her, so he nodded, and didn't try to speak for fear that emotion would overcome him.

"And I as well," said Suheyla.

Azareen wanted to scream. Didn't they feel it, Fate's bowstring drawing taut? She tried to dissuade them. "Just let them leave," she pleaded. "Don't go back up there."

But the Godslayer's burden of guilt and shame would not permit him to evict the survivors of his own bloodbath as though they were a nuisance, without at least going himself to face them—face *her*, his daughter—and take responsibility, and give her a place to put all the blame she had to have been carrying all this time. He owed her that at least. He could stand there and accept the weight of her blame, and hope it left her lightened.

He passed temporary command to a captain named Brishan, and gave orders to his quartermaster to begin drawing up lists to provision the citadel.

The four of them could have fit astride Rasalas if it came to it, but such inelegance was unnecessary. The creature was the beast of the north anchor. There were three more anchors and a beast for each, and Lazlo reached out into the scheme of energies, feeling for them and waking them as he had awakened Rasalas. It was easier now. He didn't even need to be near them, or see them. He had the feeling that his power was growing all the time. He reached and they responded, each quickening, and, like Rasalas, transforming at the touch of his mind into *his* creatures, so that what Skathis had made hideous became beautiful.

By the time they landed beside Rasalas, they were no longer the grotesques that had glowered over the city.

Thyon, coming out through the guardhouse with Ruza, Tzara, and Calixte, saw them, and thought they looked like they had flown straight out of the illustrations in *Miracles for Breakfast*, the fairy-tale book that, once upon a time, Strange had brought him in good faith, and he had kept, in bad. There was a winged horse, a dragon, and a gryphon, all exquisite.

A stir went through the Tizerkane, but their fear couldn't properly kindle. These were not the beasts of their nightmares.

They mounted: Azareen astride the horse, and Suheyla behind her son on the gryphon, leaving the dragon riderless.

Inside of a second, Thyon's mind flashed before him an alternate history of his own life, in which he thanked the boy who brought him a fairy-tale book at dawn, instead of scorning him and pushing him down stairs. And later, instead of threatening him and stealing his books, and trying to steal his dream, he might have introduced

272

him to the Godslayer himself, and recommended him for the delegation. If he had done these things, all of which, he had no doubt, Strange would have done in his place, then might *he* be mounting that metal dragon now, and flying up to the citadel with them?

His brain presented this entire fantasy in roughly the time it took Strange to swing his leg across his creature's back. As the party took flight, Thyon, earthbound, felt every choice he'd made, every action he'd taken, as a weight he carried with him. He wondered: Was it weight he could shed or throw off, or was it forever a part of him, as much as his bones and his hearts?

❧ 32 ❧

ALL THE JAGGED EDGES

Sarai knew her father well. Hundreds of times she'd perched moths on his brow, watched him sleep, and plagued him with nightmares. She'd traveled the pathways of his mind, and shuddered at the horrors there. She'd even seen him in the dreams of others—as a boy, a young husband, a hero. But she had never met him.

When she saw not one flying shape but *four* rising up from Weep, she knew who it must be, and backed away from the railing, a seethe of emotions filling her: fear, hope, shame, longing, each entangled in the roots of the others. She had hated him once. Minya had made sure of it. But the more time she spent spinning nightmares to torment him, the more she'd understood that the worst nightmare she could hope to conjure would pale beside the ones that already lived inside him. It wasn't fear that ate him alive. Eril-Fane was brave; he could cope with fear. But guilt and shame were corrosive, and the great Godslayer was a husk.

Sarai had stopped hating him a long time ago, and ceased to plague him, too, though Minya had railed and ranted, called her a traitor and worse. But Sarai knew what she knew—what *only* she knew—and the greatest feat of strength she had ever witnessed was the one he performed every day: continuing to live for the sake of others, when it would be so much easier to stop.

Did she hope he would love her, be a father to her? No.

Yes.

But no. She knew what could only be known by sojourning in his mind: what Isagol had done to him—her mother, the beautiful, terrible goddess of despair. She had made him love her, and ruined love.

So Sarai smashed down the hopes that were trying to well up in her, even as she looked down at herself and transformed her slip into the respectable Weep costume that she'd worn in her dream. It would be enough if he managed to hide his abhorrence. That was what she told herself as he came.

* * *

Eril-Fane, on the gryphon with his mother riding behind him, was caught up in a memory of another ascent to the citadel. He hadn't been astride a creature that time, but caught in the claws of one, plucked right off the street where he'd been walking with his bride. And though it was Skathis who'd taken him, all the horror of the memory was bound up in another. His horror belonged to *her*. The god of beasts had procured him as a plaything for his lover: Isagol, who was as queen to his fell king. How many years the pair had played their games, Eril-Fane had no way of knowing. Two hundred at least; that was how long they'd been here in this sky. Where before? They were immortal, were they not? They might have been ruining lives since time began, for all he knew.

How the citadel had loomed as they flew up toward it, so bright, so impossibly huge, and he had been . . . *surprised*. That was the overwhelming feeling, as Rasalas—the old, hideous version—dropped him into the garden like a piece of windfall fruit. It had all happened so fast. Eril-Fane had lived in fear of Azareen being taken, but *he* was the one on his knees in the garden of the gods.

And framed in an archway of the arcade was Isagol, waiting as though she had said to Skathis, G*o and bring me back someone to play with.*

Eril-Fane had seen her before, from a distance. He knew her red-brown hair and the band of black she painted across her eyes. He had witnessed the languid way she moved, as though she were bored and would always be bored, and despised the world because of it. His hatred of her was as old as himself, and as pure as his love for his wife. But as he knelt there, reeling with surprise, still not comprehending that his life as he knew it was over, he felt something else begin to stir in him.

It felt like . . . fascination.

That was how it began. Isagol sauntered toward him. Her hips moved in a way that was entirely unlike Azareen's hips. The one, he found himself thinking, was like print: neat, economical, nothing to spare. The other was script: flowing and graceful, wasteful, hypnotic. One woman was a secret warrior, the other an evil goddess, and though Azareen wielded a hreshtek as though she'd been born to hold one, there was no doubt who was deadlier.

Isagol walked a circle around him, looking him over with interest. "Well done," she said to Skathis.

"He's in love," the god of beasts told her. "I thought you'd like that."

Her eyes brightened. "You're too good to me."

"I know."

Skathis went inside, leaving them alone. Isagol was undefended. She came near enough to touch Eril-Fane and ran her fingers through his hair—softly at first—then she clasped it in a fist and jerked his head up to make him look at her. And...Thakra help him...Eril-Fane gazed at her, when he could have picked her up and heaved her right over the balustrade.

He remembered wanting to, but wanting...other things, too, and feeling sick with it, poisoned, turned inside out, exposed, as though she were rooting out darkness in him: desire and disfaith he'd never imagined himself capable of.

Because he wasn't. It wasn't him. He didn't want her. And yet, he did.

This is what he was to learn: It didn't matter if the feelings were his, or if she put them in him. Either way, they were real, and they would rule over him for the next three years, and all the years that came after.

She made him want her, and she made him love her. But, though she easily could have, she never took away his natural feelings. Isagol liked her pets dangerous. She was hard to thrill, and it excited her to keep them at war with themselves, ever walking a knife-edge between adoration and animus. That first day, she didn't prevent him from hurling her over the balustrade. She simply made him desire her more than he desired her death, so that later—*after*—he would lie tangled in the silken sheets of her enormous bed, and believe in his bones that he had chosen this, that he had chosen *her*—over Azareen and fidelity, over justice and all that was good—that he chose her every moment he didn't throttle her in her sleep, or gut her with the carving knife while serving her at table. She was an executioner by increments, a master of subtlety and tempter of fate, ever seeing how close she could slice the difference between hate and love.

Until one day she miscalculated and lost the game and her life.

And Eril-Fane had "won," but it was a bitter victory. She had infested him, and infected him, and what he'd done in the aftermath could never be shriven.

Now he returned to the citadel, to meet the ghost of the daughter he had failed to murder on the day he turned savior and butcher.

Suheyla could feel her son shaking, and she wished she could eat his memories as Letha had eaten hers. She also had made this trip before—forty years earlier, though it all was a blank. She didn't remember the approach, the loom of the citadel, the way it shone. It might have been her first time, but it wasn't. She had lived up here a year, and returned home changed: minus a hand she didn't remember losing, and also a baby she didn't remember birthing—or conceiving or carrying, either. Aside from the signs of it on her body, it was as though it had never happened.

Some ten generations of the women of Weep had endured the same loss, or set of losses: time and memory, and all that the time and memory had held, including *babies*, so many babies. Mostly, Suheyla thought it a blessing not to have to remember. But other times she felt robbed of her pain, and thought she'd rather know everything. There was a sense among the women of Weep that they struggled with all their lives: that they were only partial people, the table scraps of the gods. That some part of them had been left behind in the citadel, or killed or devoured or snuffed out.

For Azareen it was different. She was in the citadel when it was liberated. It was her capture by Skathis that at last had stoked the rage that Eril-Fane needed. It was the sound of his wife's screams that tipped the balance and freed him at last to murder the goddess he both loved and loathed. And once he'd begun, he was unstoppable. He slew them all. He slaughtered them, and so Letha ate no more memories. The women freed from the sinister arm remembered everything that had happened to them, and not only that. Many had godspawn growing inside them when they went back home.

Azareen was the opposite of Suheyla: She'd lost neither time nor memory. But that didn't mean she was whole. No one was whole in the aftermath of the brutal occupation and its bloody end. Not in the city, not in the citadel. They had all lost far too much.

Lazlo had a sense of the colliding emotions on both sides of this meeting, but he knew that his understanding could barely scratch the surface.

He had flown on ahead, talked to Sarai and the others, gotten their agreement to bring the visitors. Now they were here. They dismounted. The garden seemed like a magical menagerie, with the gryphon, winged horse, and dragon joining Rasalas. Everyone on both sides was pale and wary. Lazlo introduced them, hoping to act as a bridge between them. He wondered if it was possible that all their jagged edges might fit together like puzzle pieces.

Perhaps it was wishful thinking, but wasn't that the best kind?

He found himself talking too much, drawing the introductions out, because everyone was so silent.

Eril-Fane had meant to speak first. He had words all lined up in his head, but the sight of Sarai sent them scattering. In color and figure she was so like her mother. At first it was all he could see, and he tasted bile in the back of his throat. But her features, so similar to Isagol's, were wholly recast by what was in her hearts: compassion, mercy, love. These changed everything. He had been braced for her rightful anger and blame, but in her face he saw only her hesitant *hope*.

There was a signal beacon on the Cusp and another atop the garrison in Weep. When one flared alight, the other was lit in immediate response. That was what it was like in Eril-Fane's chest when he saw Sarai's hope. His own flared in answer. It hurt. It swelled inside him. It was the same species of hope as hers: fragile, and sullied by shame and fear.

Their shames were different, but their fear was the same: of seeing rejection in the other's eyes.

Instead, each saw hope, a mirror of their own, and brightened like new-polished glavestones that had been muted under dust. Eril-Fane groped for words, but only one came to him:

"Daughter," he said.

The word filled a space in Sarai's chest that had always been empty. She wondered if he had a space like that, too. "Father," she answered, and he did have a space, but it wasn't empty. It had long been filled with small bones and self-loathing. Now the word dissolved them and took their place, and it was so much lighter than what had been there before that Eril-Fane felt as though he could stand up straight for the first time in years.

"I'm so sorry," he said. The words scraped up from some pit within him, and shreds of his soul seemed to cling to them like flesh to the barbs of a scourge.

"I know," said Sarai. "I'm sorry, too."

He winced and shook his head. He couldn't bear for her to apologize to him. "You have nothing to be sorry about."

"That's not true. I've haunted you. I've given you nightmares."

"I deserved nightmares. I don't expect forgiveness, Thakra knows. I just want you to know how sorry I am. I don't..." He looked down at his big, scarred hands. "I don't know how I could ever do such a thing."

But Sarai understood: A person could be driven mad by hate. It was a force as destructive as any Mesarthim gift, and harder to end than a god. The gods had been dead for fifteen years, after all, but their hate had lingered, and ruled in their stead.

And yet...these three were standing here and Sarai saw no hate in them. What made it possible? Lazlo?

He was at her side, and Sarai felt that as long as he was there, she could do anything: See the world, make a home, help Minya. *Help Minya*, so that she could stand here, too, with hope in the place of her hate. Why not? Right now, with her father in front of her and Lazlo beside her, Sarai felt as though anything was possible. "Can we leave the past behind us?" she asked.

Could they? The question was everything.

"That's an excellent place for the past," said Suheyla. "If you *don't* leave it there, it clutters everything up and you just keep tripping over it." Holding her granddaughter's gaze, she smiled, and Sarai smiled back.

And the last link in Eril-Fane's mind between Isagol and Sarai was broken. Yes, Sarai looked a lot like her mother. But Isagol's smiles had been taunting twists that never reached her eyes. Sarai's was radiance and sweetness, and there was something in it....He himself saw only light, but Suheyla and Azareen saw an echo of *him*, of the way *he* used to smile before Isagol broke him.

Suheyla reached for Azareen's hand, and they clung to each other and to the memory, and to the hope that they would yet see that smile resurrected on his face.

There was so much emotion rushing under the skin of the moment—not like blood, but spirit, lighter and clearer, Lazlo thought. He was elated. Sarai was overcome. Sparrow and Feral were moved, though they held themselves back, shy and awkward. Ruby was inside with Minya, and didn't even know what was going on. (And when she found out that they had visitors and hadn't even come to get her, she wouldn't be wrathful for all eternity, but *half* at the very most.)

As for Minya, she was lost in a lull fog, unaware that the enemy had come, and that her family was smiling at them in the garden, forming another "us" without her—an unthinkable "us" that spat on everything she'd done to keep them alive.

At least, that was how she'd see it, if she were to wake up.

❧ 33 ❧

THE UNMOURNED

It was Feral who broke the ice, asking about the bundle Suheyla carried, from which emanated a glorious warm fragrance that could only be bread—not saltless, oilless kimril loaf that tasted of purgatory, but real bread. Suheyla peeled back the cloth right then and there and watched with satisfaction as the young people reached for it with trembling hands and nearly wept for pleasure at the taste of it—except for Sarai, that is, who had to be content with the fragrance.

"I'll save some for Ruby," said Feral with a pang of guilt that this tremendous occasion was passing in her absence.

Suheyla complimented the garden. "It takes my breath away," she said, surveying its wild lushness.

"It wasn't like this before," said Eril-Fane, trying to match it to his memories, and failing. It had been formal back then, clipped and snipped within an inch of its life, no leaf or shoot daring to sprout out of place.

"It's all Sparrow's doing," Sarai told them proudly. "And it's not only beautiful. It's also all our food. We couldn't have survived without her gift."

Feral's jaw clenched with the effort it took him not to chime in and say, *Or mine.*

"Or Feral's," Sarai added, and that was so much better than having to say it himself. "We call Sparrow Orchid Witch," she told them. "She can make things grow. And Feral's Cloud Thief. He can summon clouds from anywhere in the world. Any kind, snow or rain or just big, fluffy ones that look like you should be able to walk on them, but you can't." She grimaced a little. "We tried."

"You tried to walk on clouds," said Azareen.

"Of course," said Feral, as though it were a given. "We piled pillows under them first."

"Magical gardens and walking on clouds," said Suheyla, trying to reconcile their abilities with the ones that had terrorized Weep. She bent to examine a flower that looked like a ruffle of lace an empress might wear at her throat. "What's this? I've never seen it before."

"It's one of my own," said Sparrow, blushing. "I call it 'blood in the snow.' Look." And she parted the pure white petals to show brilliant crimson stamens that did indeed look like droplets of blood on fresh snow.

With that, the two were in a world of their own, going flower bed to flower bed, while the others faced the reason for this visit, and what was to come next: moving the citadel, leaving Weep. "I'm sorry to ask you to go away." Eril-Fane swallowed. "None of the blame for any of this is yours. You shouldn't have to be the ones to—"

"It's all right," Sarai said. "We're ready to leave. We couldn't before, and now we can."

"Where will you go?"

Sarai, Lazlo, and Feral all looked at one another. They had no idea. "Sparrow would like to walk in a forest," Sarai said, starting small. "And I'd like to swim in the sea." She shared a secret look with Lazlo. Last night, at one point in their long, delirious dream, they had done just that, in a warm sea glazed with moonlight. They'd found a floating bottle with a message inside it, and they'd swum with knives between their teeth to slash a leviathan's harness and free it from its enslavement.

Maybe they would do it for real. Why not? And what else might they find to set free, if they were to go looking?

The thought made her fingertips tingle and chills run up her arms.

By chance her gaze lit on Azareen's face, and she had an answer to her question that sent a jolt right down her spine. They didn't have to look very far if they wanted to set slaves free. Azareen was staring through the arcade into the gallery, where Minya's ghost army was frozen in its ranks. There were plenty of slaves right here.

Sarai told Azareen, "I'll do everything I can to free them. I swear."

"And if you can't?"

Sarai didn't know how to answer that. If she couldn't, it would mean that Minya was beyond all reach of reason or healing, and if that was true, what then?

Lazlo put his hand to the small of her back and said, "She will. But she needs time, and she'll have it."

He was kind but firm, and Sarai knew he would protect her— and all of them, Minya too, in the life ahead with its unguessable horizons.

Sparrow offered tea. "It's not real tea, just herbs," she said, apologetic.

"We'll make sure you have real tea for your travels," said Suheyla, and a pang of sadness caught her by surprise when she thought about them leaving. All her life she'd wished the citadel away, and now it was to go, and she was *sorry*? Oh, not sorry to have the sky free, the shadow gone, a new era for her city, but to lose the chance of knowing these children, who were strong and bright and shy and hungry, who had no home but this and no people but one another. She could see such longing in them, all bound up in hesitancy, as though they yearned for connection but didn't believe they deserved it, and it squeezed her hearts and also made her ashamed that she had never even mourned them when she believed them all dead.

Godspawn. Who had first come up with the word?

Suheyla didn't know, but she knew this: She had birthed one herself, and so had nearly every woman she knew. And all those lost babies...all unmourned. Because they had no memory of them, the babies had never felt *real*. It was easier to pretend they'd never existed—until the Liberation, anyway, when Azareen and others had come home with their bellies round with the terrible proof of it all.

No one ever mentioned *those* babies, either, though they had certainly been real, and had been born in the world only to be shown right out of it, all under a pall of silence.

An unexpected grief blossomed in Suheyla's breast, so strong that for a moment she almost couldn't breathe. These four young people with their shy smiles and azure skin made all the others real, too, and not as monsters or even gods, but as orphan boys and girls.

"Are you all right?" asked Sarai, seeing her...her grandmother... bend over and struggle for breath. Then Lazlo was on Suheyla's other side, taking her elbow to help support her. There was no chair nearby but he made one. It grew right out of the floor like a metal flower on a stem. He helped her to sit and they all gathered around her.

"I'll get her some water," said Feral, running for the kitchen.

"What is it? Are you unwell?" asked Eril-Fane, crouching before her. He looked so worried.

"I'm fine," she said. "Don't fret over me."

"Can you breathe?" he asked. "Is it your hearts?"

"I suppose it is my hearts, but not like that. I'm fine. *I'm fine.*" She grew stern to make them believe her. "It's grief, not a heart attack. And I think all of us know by now that grief won't kill us."

They fussed over her anyway. Feral returned with water. It was sweeter than the water in Weep and she wondered, as she drank it, where in the world it came from, this rainwater procured by a cloud-stealing boy. And she wondered, too, where in the world they'd end up, these cast-off children claimed by no one.

"We should get you home," said Azareen, though Suheyla was only an excuse. She was eager to be gone from here. Her mind kept turning indoors, to the sinister arm with its row of little rooms, and the sound of crying babies and weeping women at all hours.

But Suheyla shook her head. "Not just yet. I want to ask..."

Maybe it was better not knowing, but she couldn't stand it any longer. This could be her last chance to find out. Could she live with wondering all the rest of her days? She wouldn't be able to pretend anymore that those babies—*her* baby—had been neither *real* nor *people*. "Do you know what they did with them all?" she asked, looking from face to face. "What they did with all the babies?"

There was a silence. Sarai, for her part, was seeing the row of cradles and the row of cribs, Kiska with her one green eye, and Minya trying to protect her while Korako waited in the doorway.

"No," she said. "We don't."

"We only know that Korako took them away once their gifts manifested," added Feral.

"Took them *where*?" Suheyla asked, afraid to hear the answer.

"We don't know," said Sarai. "We wondered whether they could have taken them all out of Weep? Like Lazlo?"

"I don't see how," mused Suheyla. "The gods never left the city. Oh, Skathis might have flown downriver to track runaways, or to Fort Misrach to execute faranji who'd been fool enough to come across the desert. But besides that, they didn't *go* anywhere."

"They didn't take them out of the citadel," said Eril-Fane.

"We certainly would have noticed," Suheyla agreed.

"No," said Eril-Fane. "I mean: They didn't take them out of the citadel."

They all turned to him, unable at first to understand the distinction between what his mother was saying and what he was. They were in agreement, weren't they? But Sarai saw that he was disturbed, his eyes not quite meeting hers, and she realized: Suheyla was speculating. He wasn't. He was telling them.

"What do you know?" she asked at once.

"Only that," he said. "After you were born, I . . . Sometimes I went by the nursery, to see if I could see you. Isagol didn't like it. She didn't see why I should care." Emotions moved over his face, and Sarai felt them all in her own chest, the same as he had felt her hope in his. "She made me stop," he said. "But before that, I saw Korako. Several times. Walking, with a child. Different children, I mean. I don't know what she did with them. But I know they went in together, and . . . she came out alone."

"Went in *where*?" Sarai asked, breathless. They were all riveted on him.

"There's a room," he said. "I never went in it, but I saw it once from the end of the corridor. It's big. It's…" With his hands, he formed the shape of a sphere. "Circular. That's where Korako took the children."

He was describing the heart of the citadel.

❧ 34 ❧

BACON DESTINY

Ruby woke, and wondered what had woken her. She lolled for a second or two...and then sat bolt upright in bed—in *Minya's* bed—remembering where she was, and why. She spun, braced for the sight of the little girl awake and maniacal or, worse, simply gone, and then slumped with relief. Minya was still laid out on the floor, eyes closed, face peaceful in sleep as it never was in waking.

How furious the others would be if they knew Ruby had fallen asleep on watch.

But it was *fine*. Minya was drugged. It was obvious that the potion in the green glass bottle was working. It was ridiculous that they had to *watch her sleep*. That was probably a sport in purgatory, Ruby thought: sleep-watching. Well, she was bad at it. It wasn't her fault. She wasn't skilled at being bored like the others were. If they expected her to stay awake on watch, then someone would have to keep her company.

"That defeats the whole purpose of taking turns," Sparrow had said when Ruby pleaded with her to stay.

"Stay with me, and I'll stay with you," she'd tried bargaining.

"No, you won't," Sparrow had replied. "You'll skip off free the instant your turn is over."

"Well, can you blame me?"

"No. And that's why *I'm* skipping off free now." And she had, and so had Feral, claiming he had to refill the tub in the rain room, and so Ruby had taken a nap, more out of spite than fatigue. But now she was awake, and as her flash of panic receded, she heard voices out in the corridor.

And . . . were those footsteps?

You never heard footsteps in the citadel, because they all went barefoot all the time. But Ruby heard them now and came instantly alive. She was off the bed and sprinting down the stairs from Minya's bedroom, through the domed antechamber to the door. Lazlo had left it open when he brought the doors back to life, since they were all coming and going so often, and it was a good thing, or else Ruby wouldn't have heard anything, or woken up, or poked her head out into the corridor to the incredible sight of *people* crossing the passage up ahead. Fully human, fully alive, boot-wearing *people.*

Ruby ducked back inside, breathing fast. What were *people* doing in the citadel? She peeked out again. They were headed into the passage that led to the heart of the citadel, and she registered what she hadn't before: that Lazlo, Sarai, Sparrow, and Feral were walking with them. Calmly.

No one was holding anyone hostage, as far as she could tell. And . . . was that the scent of *bread*?

Well. If they thought she was going to stay here and watch Minya sleep at a time like this, they were sorely mistaken. Indignantly, she followed them.

* * *

Every soul left in Weep was watching the citadel. After so many years living in dread of the sight of it, it was hard to make themselves look at it now. But their own had gone up there and none would be easy until their return, so they watched.

Into this curious waiting, Soulzeren and Ozwin returned. They'd been sent for by Azareen, and had made the trip back from Enet-Sarra only to learn that she and Eril-Fane had flown with Lazlo up to the citadel.

"I suppose that means they don't need our services after all," remarked Ozwin.

They were the husband-and-wife botanist and mechanist who'd conceived the silk sleigh, a clever flying machine lifted by the gas given off by decaying ulola flowers. They were part of the Godslayer's delegation, and had vacated the city the other morning along with nearly everyone else.

"Well, I can't say I'm sorry to be back," said Soulzeren.

It wasn't that they'd minded the rugged conditions at Enet-Sarra. They hailed from the Thanagost badlands and weren't put off by a little camping. It was their fellow faranji they'd minded. Their sourness and bickering had poisoned the very air. Soulzeren thought the others might have borne the danger and inconvenience with more fortitude if they'd still believed the Godslayer's "great reward" could be theirs at the end of it. But they were men of facts and numbers, and with Weep's problem no longer seeming likely to be resolved by mundane means, they were embittered by their sudden irrelevance.

The word *unnatural* had been tossed about like a hot potato, and sweet, earnest Lazlo Strange had been trumped up into an infernal mastermind who'd had them all fooled.

"You reckon it's safe to stay?" asked Ozwin, rubbing his balding head. Their escort hadn't been quite clear on the situation in the city, but nobody seemed panicked, and that boded well.

"Some'll be safer if we do. I'm less likely to commit murder here," replied Soulzeren.

"Well then, that settles it. Murder's an awful bother. Bodies to deal with, paperwork and that."

Soulzeren raised an eyebrow. "Paperwork for murder?"

"There's paperwork for everything. Shall we reclaim our old room, my lady?"

And so they ambled over to the Merchants' Guildhall, where they were greeted by the astonishing sight of Thyon Nero unhitching a donkey from a cart. He looked decidedly disheveled, his usually pristine clothes wrinkled and dusty, and his famous golden hair uncombed. "Oh," he said, surprised to see them, and smiled not at all unpleasantly. "You're back."

For a moment they could only stare. He seemed a different man from the one they'd traveled the Elmuthaleth with, who would certainly never have touched a donkey, or worn a dirty shirt, or smiled like he meant it. His smiles had been pickled things, as though they'd been preserved in vinegar on some earlier occasion, to be pulled out to act as garnish to his artfully plated expressions. This smile was crooked and loose and seemed born of laughter. He wasn't alone. The young Tizerkane, Ruza, was with him, holding a heavy black frying pan, a long strip of bacon lolling from his mouth like a dog's tongue. This was strange, too. Not the bacon tongue—that was Ruza to a T. But the warrior was Lazlo's friend, and there had never been any warmth between Thyon Nero and either of them.

Well, thought Soulzeren, *disaster makes strange bedfellows.*

"Care for some bacon?" Thyon asked.

"I'll never say no to bacon," replied Ozwin.

The young men were outside so they could keep an eye on the citadel. After witnessing the departure of the flying metal creatures, they'd drawn straws for who had to go back for the donkey. Thyon had lost, and he'd been halfway back to the sinkhole before it occurred to him that he should be incensed. No doubt Ruza had cheated with the straws (he had, of course), and besides, Thyon should have been exempt from such tasks. He didn't *fetch donkeys*. But his outrage had refused to kindle. He didn't want to be exempt. He wanted to go off muttering and fetch the damn donkey, and come back and be teased about it over a meal of scraps with friends.

Friends? A pair of warriors and a thief? Even now a voice within him explained that they were lowborn, incompatible with his station, and ridiculous besides. But now that voice sounded haughty and condescending, and he wanted to put it in a jar and toss it in a river, then sit and eat bacon with his ridiculous, lowborn friends.

Calixte and Tzara emerged from the guildhall with a tray piled high with odds and ends. Calixte squealed to see her fellow faranji returned, and threw her arms around them both, only to immediately draw back, put her hands on her hips, and regard them sternly.

"I can't believe you left," she said. "We *good* faranji stayed here and performed selfless works, in total disregard for our own safety."

"Selfless works like making sure the cheese gets to fulfill its destiny," put in Tzara.

Calixte said, "Don't mock. In my country it's a crime to let cheese go to waste. It's the real reason I was in prison—"

"Did you just call me a good faranji?" asked Thyon, cutting her off.

"*No,*" scoffed Calixte. "As if."

"You did. I heard you." Thyon turned to Ruza. "You heard her, too."

"I heard cheese destiny," Ruza said, though it was hard to make out because he still had his bacon tongue, and had to talk with his teeth together to keep it from falling out of his mouth.

"*I* heard," said Tzara. "He's winning you over. Admit it."

"Only because he found bacon," said Calixte, grabbing a slice out of the skillet. Holding it up, she said, very seriously, "Bacon has a destiny, too."

They'd pulled a table out of the dining room, and they fetched extra chairs for Soulzeren and Ozwin. "So how are things downriver?"

They apprised each other of the situations in both places.

"You saw Lazlo?" Soulzeren asked. "Is he all right?"

"Well, we didn't get to talk to him," Calixte said with a scowl. "He flew off. He called up the rest of the metal creatures, you know. Just like that. That's how they all got up there."

"You should have seen them," Thyon said. "It was surreal." As an afterthought, he added, "Though I can't believe none of them rode the dragon."

"I know!" said Ruza. "What was Azareen's thinking, choosing *a winged horse* when she could have *a dragon?*"

"I don't think she was really focused on which creature was best," said Tzara.

"You shouldn't have to focus on it," said Ruza. "It's instinctive. Dragons are always best."

They talked, all eyes straying upward to the citadel, wondering what was going on up there, until all the cheese and bacon, the nuts and overripe apricots had fulfilled their destinies and only crumbs remained.

"So," said Soulzeren, pushing back from the table to light her pipe. "What are these selfless works the *good* faranji have been engaged in, with such disregard to their own safety?"

"Not much," said Calixte, offhand, stretching lazily. "Just restoring the lost knowledge of an ancient civilization."

Thyon stood up, dusting crumbs off his trousers. "Come have a look," he said.

* * *

"What *is* this place?" asked Lazlo, who had not yet seen the heart of the citadel. It was vast and mathematically perfect: a flawless inverse sphere.

"We used to play in here," said Sarai. "Until we outgrew the opening. We don't know what it was for. It's . . . odd."

"How do you mean?"

"You'll see."

They crossed the antechamber, and as soon as Lazlo stepped into the sphere—onto the walkway that led around its circumference—he did see. Or rather, he felt and heard. It was difficult to describe. A muteness seemed to reach out to envelop him, as though a great void had opened up and the sound of his breathing was siphoned away and sucked into it. As for the metal's energies, they were wildly complex here, like music composed by some mad virtuoso.

Eril-Fane stepped out beside him, with his mother holding his arm. They looked around, not knowing what they'd expected to find, and all of them, whether this was their first sight of the chamber or not, were alike unable to fathom what might have been done with children here that they had gone in but never come out.

"Maybe they sacrificed them," said Feral. "No, listen. It is the *heart* of the citadel. Maybe it needed blood or spirit to function or something. Maybe the metal absorbed the children and that's what made it magical."

"That's absurd," said Sarai.

"Is it?" he queried, feeling that he was onto something.

"It is," Lazlo agreed with Sarai. "The metal doesn't feed on children, I'm not sorry to say."

"Well then, *what?*" Feral asked, disgruntled. It wasn't so much that he *wanted* it to feed on children, as that he wouldn't mind being *right*.

"I don't know," Lazlo said. He thought of Calixte's theory game that they'd played as they crossed the Elmuthaleth. He'd won by accident, with a theory he'd intended as outlandish. Could anything seem outlandish now, in this world of seraphim and magic? He took the chamber's measure, from the pair of enormous metal wasps perched on the curve of the walls, to the floating orb at its center, and began to follow the walkway.

He was holding Sarai's hand. She came with him. The others followed, including Ruby, who had joined them wordlessly, only daring Feral with her eyes to object, and goggling when she realized it was the Godslayer in their midst.

Lazlo approached one of the wasps. The orchard at the abbey had been full of wasps in summer. As a boy, he'd been stung all the time. Even at normal size they were wicked things. Enormous like this, they were nightmarish. Rasalas and the beasts of the anchors were big enough to hold several people astride, but these were on a different scale: All seven of them—eight, including Ruby—could easily fit inside its thorax.

It was just a stray thought, but it teased a thread out of the complex stave of energies that surrounded Lazlo and snagged his attention. Fit *inside* it? Sensing a door in the thorax, he opened it.

Sarai murmured, craning her neck to see inside. The others looked, too. "There are seats," she said. "And . . . cages."

Cages. Small ones, just the right size for...

...children.

Gooseflesh rose on her arms. Why were there *cages* in the belly of a wasp in the heart of the angel hovering over Weep?

"It's a ship," Lazlo said, looking from one wasp to the other. "Both of them. They're flying ships."

"With cages," said Eril-Fane.

"For children," finished Suheyla.

The chamber swallowed their breathing and shrank their words, which only increased their disquiet. In a dread-scuffed whisper, Sarai asked, "To take them *where?*"

❦ 35 ❦

WHATEVER THIS FATE WAS

Soulzeren and Ozwin had been duly impressed by the good work of book-rescuing, and had squeezed past the crates to go up to their room and rest. The other four remained outside to watch for the return of the metal creatures and their riders. Calixte was rebraiding the single stripe of hair that ran the meridian of Tzara's shaved head, while Thyon and Ruza looked over the Thakranaxet.

It was open on the courtyard table. The empty tray and bacon pan had been pushed aside, crumbs brushed away, and a clean linen napkin laid out beneath the tome. It wasn't archival treatment, but it was better than nothing. Thyon had made Ruza go and wash his hands. "It's your holy book," he'd pointed out. "Do you want to get greasy fingerprints all over it?"

"I'll get greasy fingerprints all over *you*," the warrior had muttered, going to do as he was told. Thyon, flushing, had pretended not to hear.

Now, hands clean—and brown and square and scarred—Ruza was reading the book. It was a thing of beauty, scribed hundreds of years ago by masters, and illuminated with golden designs. It lay open to a curious diagram that took up a whole spread. It was a row of tall, vertical discs, a half inch or so wide in the middle, and tapering to points at the top and bottom, each labeled in gorgeous script. When Ruza leafed to the next page, then the next, they saw it was more than the one spread. It went on and on.

Whatever it was, Ruza was enthralled by it, focused and serious in a way that made him seem both younger and older. That didn't make sense, Thyon chided himself. Regardless, it was true: younger because of his earnestness, and older because of his gravity. Thyon wouldn't have thought he had the capacity for either. He watched as his brown swordsman's hands gently turned the fragile pages. When he looked up there was awe in his eyes.

"What is it?" Thyon asked.

Ruza ignored him. "Tzara," he said. "Have a look at this."

Stung, Thyon sat back. Tzara was looking feline and sleepy as Calixte braided her hair. "What?" she asked lazily.

Ruza angled the Thakranaxet toward her, pointed at the first disc in the diagram, and read, " 'Meliz.' "

Tzara's eyes opened a little wider. Calixte, her fingers holding small sections of braid, looked as blank as Thyon felt. The word meant nothing to either of them. Ruza flipped again through all the pages of the diagram, dozens and dozens of those thin ovals all pressed together. He pointed to the last and read, " 'Zeru.' "

That word very much meant something: the world. Zeru was *the world*.

Tzara didn't look sleepy anymore. She sat up cat-fast, and all the little sections of hair tugged free from Calixte's fingers to spill in wisps over her smooth brown scalp. The two warriors spoke together, rapid-fire, in their own language, and Thyon felt as though he'd been shoved out a door. Something in his chest that had begun to uncoil seized up again, and the tightness spread. He felt his face tighten, too, and only realized then that it had relaxed and he'd hardly noticed. He re-collected himself and schooled his emotions, casting off his curiosity about the book and its diagrams. He glanced at Calixte. Her brows had knit together. She was deep in concentration, following along with whatever they were saying.

The more fool him, to think he was part of this group. He pushed back from the table to stand, but before he could, Ruza's hand closed on his. He still wasn't looking at him, but he had caught his hand so he couldn't walk away. Thyon stared at his fingers enclosed in Ruza's as though they belonged to some stranger. He hardly even registered the feeling. It was too alien. No one had ever held his hand.

Not that Ruza was *holding his hand*. He was only touching it. It was nothing. When he let go, though, and drew his hand away, Thyon felt its absence keenly. He coiled his own into a fist, and he might still have left, turmoil bubbling up through the tightness in his chest, but Ruza started talking—in Common Tongue, which could only be meant for him—and he forgot all about walking away as he was reeled into the book's mystery.

"You know the story of the seraphim?" asked Ruza.

"More or less," Thyon answered.

"Probably less," said Ruza.

"Probably," agreed Thyon, who knew no more than what Strange had told by firelight in the desert. "What of it?"

"There were twelve of them," said Ruza, either not noticing, or choosing to ignore the snap in the alchemist's voice. "Chosen of all the best and brightest of their race to voyage outward from their world and 'stitch all the worlds of the Continuum together with their light.'"

Poetry, thought Thyon, dismissive. "So they came from the stars," he said.

"No," said Ruza. "Not the stars. They came from *the sky*."

Thyon thought he was just being pedantic. "How is that different?"

"Well, I'll tell you how. The sky is right there." He pointed up at it. "Whereas the stars, you may be aware, are very far away. You've heard of astronomy?"

Thyon's eyes turned to slits. "No," he intoned, unamused. "What is this 'astronomy' of which you speak?"

"Anyway, stars are far. Space is big. And you could keep going out there forever and ever and you'd *never* get to another world."

Thyon's brow creased. He had accepted, in some way, that seraphim had been real, but when it came to the particulars, it all sounded like myth. "Then how are the seraphim supposed to have gotten here?"

Tzara took over the explaining. "The worlds lie together like the pages of a book," she said, brushing her fingers over the Thakranaxet's gold-edged pages. "Layered. All right? Only, imagine each page is infinite, stretching in all directions forever. If you were somehow to travel through space, you'd be going along the endless plane of a single page, do you see? You would never come to another page."

"All right," said Thyon. "So to get to another world, you...what? Turn the page?"

"Wrong," said Ruza with relish. "You *pierce* it. At least, the seraphim did."

You pierce it.

A tingling began to spread over Thyon's scalp. He'd had the feeling before—the first time he transmuted lead into gold, and when he stood on the Cusp and saw the floating citadel, and when Strange's

302

alkahest, which shouldn't have worked, *did*, and cut a shard of mes-arthium off the north anchor, unfurling implications that he had yet to trace. This was big. This was very big. "You mean they cut *through*," he said as once again his mind pushed at the limits of understanding to encompass the concept of worlds layered like pages, and angels slicing through them.

"Right through the sky," said Ruza. "The twelve were called the Faerers. Six went one way, and six the other, cutting doors from world to world. Thakra was the commander of the Six that came this way." He laid his hand on the book. "*This* is her testament." Lifting his hand, he pointed to the first disc of the diagram. "Meliz," he said again. His eyes were bright. "That's the seraph home world. It's where they began." He read off the next several: "'Eretz. Earth. Kyzoi. Lir.'" They all sounded mythological to Thyon. Ruza traced his fingertip over all the rest, turning the pages and tracing the worlds until he came to the last, and pronounced, "'Zeru.'"

Which was not so much *the* world, if the book was to be believed, as *this* world. One of many.

"It's a map, faranji," said Ruza, in case Thyon had missed the point.

A thrill sparked through him. He could feel the blood moving in his brain. A map. Worlds. Cuts in the sky.

A realization sliced through his thrill. His blood stilled. His head quieted. Last night he'd wondered at the coincidence of seraphim and Mesarthim both coming *here*, thousands of years apart—right here and nowhere else on Zeru. Now he understood: It wasn't a coin-cidence. If indeed there were worlds, and seraphim had cut door-ways, what was to stop . . . *anyone* from using them?

He tipped back his head, looked up at the citadel, and asked, "What if there's a cut? Right. Up. There."

* * *

Why flying ships? Why cages? Why *here?*

Lazlo surveyed the chamber with new eyes, and his gaze was drawn straight to the floating orb. He paced along the walkway, fixed on it. It was some forty feet away, and the same distance above the floor. If he wanted to get a closer look...

Mesarthium rearranged itself, and the length of walkway upon which they all stood disengaged from the wall to swing outward and form a bridge to the orb. He crossed it. The others followed. There was no railing. He made one. The span grew ahead of him, and broadened, so that at the end they could all stand abreast. Though it had seemed small, dwarfed by the chamber, once they reached it, it no longer did. It was twenty feet in diameter, its surface egg-smooth, unadorned.

"There's a door," said Lazlo, sensing it.

"Maybe we should leave it alone," said Azareen.

Sarai was thinking of Minya, who would have been the next child taken. And if Eril-Fane hadn't risen up and killed the gods, eventually all of them would have met this fate, whatever this fate was. "Open it," she said. She couldn't stand not knowing.

"Yes," added Suheyla, who was thinking of another child—boy or girl, she didn't know. A phantom child born a long time ago. Her hand brushing unconsciously over her belly, she said, "Open it."

So Lazlo did. A hair-fine line appeared on its surface like a single line of longitude on a globe. It split and melted apart, opening the orb. It was hollow, and it was empty.

A confusion of disappointment and relief washed over them all. They'd been braced for answers, and expecting them to be wrenching, but here was... "Nothing," said Sarai.

"Nothing," echoed Lazlo.

"Wait." Suheyla was squinting, leaning forward and looking up, her brow creased with confusion. "What is that?"

It was over their heads. Their feet were level with the bottom of the orb. In the middle, some ten feet up, was a kind of *warp*. It took them a moment to catch sight of it. They all shared the same impulse to blink, as though it were only a disturbance in their vision. It reminded Sarai of the anomaly in Minya's dream—a place where something was hidden.

It looked like a wrinkle, or a seam in the air, extending the width of the orb. They all leaned forward, squinting up at it.

"What is it?" asked Sparrow.

Lazlo raised the walkway to bring them up even with it. Then he reached out to it, and the hairs on the backs of his fingers stirred. "There's a breeze," he said.

"A breeze?" repeated Feral. "How can there be? From where?"

Lazlo stretched his hand closer.

"Don't," said Sarai.

But he did, and they all gasped as his hand...*vanished*, right off the end of his wrist. He yanked his arm back and his hand reappeared, whole and unharmed. They all stared at it, then at one another, trying to grasp what they'd just seen.

Lazlo was transfixed. There had been no pain, just the breeze, and a feeling like cobwebs brushing over his skin. He reached out again, only this time, instead of simply thrusting his hand forward, he felt along the gossamer edge of the seam, inserting his fingers so they winked out of sight, and then he grasped the invisible edge and lifted it.

An impossible aperture opened in the air. They all saw through it, and what was there was not the curved inner surface of the orb, or the heart of the citadel, and it was not Weep or the Uzumark canyon, or anywhere else in all of Zeru. You didn't have to have seen the whole world to know that *this wasn't in it.*

They couldn't process it, this landscape. It was an ocean, but it bore little resemblance to the sea Lazlo had crossed with Eril-Fane and Azareen. That had been gray-green and mild, with glassy swells and a shimmer like foil. This was *red.*

It lay far below them. They were peering through a slash in the sky at a rampant crimson sea. It was brighter than fresh blood, livid pink where it churned and frothed. And rising out of it, as far as the eye could see, were huge white . . . *things.* They looked like stalks, like the stems of vast pale flowers, or else like pigmentless hairs seen magnified. They appeared to grow out of the wild red sea, each one as great in breadth as the whole of the citadel, their tops lost from sight in a brew of dark mist that concealed the sky.

In their shock they all stood gaping, unable to grasp what they were seeing through this small window that Lazlo held open with one hand. If, after the sight of Weep's floating metal angel, he had believed himself gone beyond shock, he'd been wrong. This was a whole new level of shock.

As for Sarai, Sparrow, Feral, Ruby, they had no context. Their minds felt like doors blown open in a storm.

Overwhelmed as they were, the details seeped in slowly: the way the stalks swayed when great waves smashed against them, sending up spray like detonations. Or the shapes in the water: great, gliding shadows beneath the red surface that made leviathans look dainty. And finally: the place in the middle distance where one of the stalks appeared to have been cut, forming a plateau out of reach of the sea spray.

Atop it were shapes, hard to make out but too regular to be natural.

"Are those...buildings?" asked Sarai, the hairs rising on her neck.

This snapped them out of their dumb shock. They had been poised on the very verge of *thakrar*—that point on the spectrum of awe where wonder becomes dread, or dread wonder—and the acknowledgment of something man-made—or at least something *made*—sent them spinning hard to dread.

"Close it," snapped Azareen. "We have no idea what's—"

—*out there*, she was going to say, but she never got the chance. A shriek blasted through the gap and a shape appeared, hurtling straight at them. It was a vast white eagle.

Wraith!

The bird hung an instant before them, obscuring the landscape beyond. Another shriek ripped from its throat, and it dove for the portal. Lazlo let go of its edge. "Get back!" he cried out to the others. The air collapsed shut, but it was no more protection than a curtain across a doorway, and Wraith tore right through.

They had to duck, and felt phantom feathers drub them as the eagle sailed over their heads. Lazlo's railing kept them from pitching off the walkway, which he was moving, rapidly retracting. And the orb, he was closing it, its edges melting toward each other, ready to fuse.

But it was too late.

Wraith was not alone. It dragged a rush of wind behind it, and another voice came with it, twining round the bird's shriek to make a savage harmony. The warp in the air belled in and gaped open, disclosing limbs, figures, weapons.

Onslaught.

❦ 36 ❦

NOTHING SPECIAL

Once upon a time, Nova had been half a name. *Koraandnova* was musical, complete. *Nova* by itself was a brittle, sharp-edged fragment. Every time she heard it, she broke in half all over again.

"Nova! Girl. Work faster."

The Slaughter had come round again. Kora had been gone for a year. Nova had heard nothing from her in all that time. She was sure she must have written. She suspected her father or Skoyë of intercepting her letters.

Gaff in one hand, knife in the other, she hacked at the carcass before her.

This is not my life.

But I am stuck in it forever.

Minus Kora and the dream, it wasn't a life at all. In the days after Nova awoke to find herself left behind, the grief had been like a winter storm—the killing kind that blinds you and freezes you where you stand. Every thought was a stab, every memory a slash, until numbness finally descended. Walking through the village, besieged by stares and whispers, she'd felt dead already, and even less than a corpse. She'd felt like a carcass when the cyrs are done, nothing left over but bones.

"I always knew you were nothing special," Skoyë had said right after, her eyes brighter than Nova had ever seen them. "All your lives, the pair of you lording around here like princesses waiting to be fetched for the ball, and look at you now. You're no princess." She'd clucked her tongue. "You're pathetic."

Lorded around? Their whole lives, Kora and Nova had *worked*. They'd done more than their share. Skoyë had made sure of that. She had nothing to complain of; nobody did. It was never idleness that had set the sisters apart. It wasn't even airs. It was their simple belief that they were worthy of *more*. Hope was luster, and they had shone with it like twin pearls in an oyster.

But only one of them was a pearl, as it turned out. The other was naught but a bit of bone polished up by the crashing surf.

Suddenly, Skoyë appeared at Nova's shoulder. She surveyed her work, and barked, "Is this all you've done all morning?"

Nova blinked. She hadn't been properly present. She lost focus these days, and forgot what she was doing. Now she saw what Skoyë saw. The uul's hide was crosshatched with ineffectual cuts. She'd just been...chopping at it. "I'm sorry," she whispered.

"You're sorry is right. You're *paltry*. What Shergesh wants you for, I'll never know, but I'll not be sorry to be rid of you."

Nova stiffened at the mention of the village elder. At the mention of her almost-husband. She said, her voice shaking, "I think we all know what he wants me for."

Skoyë's hand flashed out, palm flat, and connected with Nova's cheek at just the right angle for a perfect, practiced *crack*. Skoyë knew how to slap, and Kora wasn't here anymore to catch her wrist in the air. The sting was fire. Nova's hand flew to her face. Heat glowed off it like a kettle.

"You'll show respect," hissed Skoyë. "I've tried to teach you, Thakra only knows. If you haven't learned it yet, I can't slap it into you now."

Still holding her cheek, Nova straightened and said, "Maybe it's your methods that are faulty."

"My methods are what you deserve. You think Shergesh will stand your backtalk?" Skoyë gestured to the unbutchered uul. "Do you imagine he'll abide your shirking? He'll do worse than slap, I can tell you that." The prospect seemed to please her.

How people love to see a dream shatter, thought Nova from far away. To see the dreamer hobbled and lamed, foundering in the shards of their broken hopes. *This is what you get for believing that you could have more. You're no better than us.*

You're nothing special.

Nova hadn't bothered begging her stepmother for mercy in the matter of her marriage. She knew that was hopeless. She'd pleaded with her father, though. He'd said she should be honored to marry the village elder. He'd said, "I have to give you to someone."

"*Sell* me, you mean."

Zyak didn't slap. That remark had earned Nova a backhand. At least it wasn't a fist—though even a fist would be kinder than what he'd said next. "He would have paid more for Kora."

Nova had laughed in his face. "Is that what he told you? The old fool could never tell us apart! He was only haggling, and you fell for it."

Zyak had been furious, because it was true, but it was Nova, not Shergesh, who'd caught the ice of his displeasure, as she had a year ago when the Mesarthim took Kora without compensating

310

him. Somehow, Zyak was sure—though Nova had never told what had happened in the wasp ship—it was all her fault. Every time he looked at her, she was reminded what his gift had been. He'd turned things to ice, though not very well. It was funny. He didn't even need his gift to freeze her to her core.

Anyway, it was done. Shergesh had paid in full—not in sheep or hides or dried fish, but actual imperial coin. Nova knew where Zyak kept them. Last week, in the night, when everyone was sleeping, she'd gotten them out and held them: five bronze coins engraved with the emperor's face. How strange to hold her value on the palm of her own hand.

Men have decided between them that this is what my body and labor are worth for life.

The only reason she wasn't married already was that Skoyë had bargained to keep her through the Slaughter, and get one last season's worth of work out of her. Not that she was getting much. "If this is the best you can do," she said now, leaning close with her fishy breath, and prodding at Nova with her gaff, "I'll hand you over to him now. Let *him* beat the work out of you, or get his money's worth how he pleases."

She turned to go. Nova was shaking. She stared out to sea. Sharks thrashed in the shallows, mad with bloodreek, all that meat just out of their reach. If she waded out and kept walking, how long would it take? How much would it hurt? Would the frigid water numb her before they began to feed? Could she drown first? Did it even matter? At most it would take a few minutes. Surely shark teeth were a cleaner pain than what was devouring her now.

And what then? What came next? Was there anything after death, or only nothingness forever? It was a mystery. As the saying went, the ones who know can't tell us, and the ones who tell us don't know.

A little flare burst in Nova's heart. A curious lightness overcame her. She saw herself do it, one step, then another into the killing water. She felt the cold around her ankles, then her calves. She thought it was real until Skoyë's voice rang out. "Thakra help me, are you *really* still standing there? Did they do something to your brain inside that skyship?"

Nova blinked. She was still on the beach. She was almost sorry. Dully, she turned to face her stepmother. Other women had paused to listen. One shook her head in sympathy—for Skoyë, not Nova. "I don't know how you stand her," said another.

"I *don't* stand her," said Skoyë. "I never have."

"Look at her," said someone else. "It's no wonder they didn't take her."

"She thought she'd be so strong," scoffed Skoyë, "and they spat her out like gristle."

They thought her gift was weak, like all of theirs. They thought she was like them.

Nova was nothing like them. "You're wrong," she said, and there was a snarl in her voice. "They might have spat me out, but not because I'm weak. They left me behind because I'm too strong. Do you hear me?" She looked around. "They left me because *they were afraid of me.* And you should be, too."

Brows furrowed. Laughter mocked. No one feared her. She sounded mad. Skoyë shook her head in disgust. "You're becoming a tragedy, girl. You thought you were something and you're not. Time to get over it, like everybody else."

Nova looked around at the gloating, gore-smeared women, and pulled a smile out of some deep place inside her. It was the smile of a girl backed up to the world's edge, ready to spread her arms like wings and fly or fall. "I *am* something," she said with a fervor dredged up from those same depths. "And one day you will know it."

The words felt like a vow, and she wanted to make them true. There would always be the sea, cold and sure and full of teeth. It was there for her if she needed it. But not today.

❧ 37 ❧

THE PUNISHMENT IS DEATH

After the Slaughter, while the cyrs picked the uul bones and the year's crop of flies died in winter's first frost, Nova married Shergesh—or was married *to* him; the ceremony did not require her consent. That morning, beforehand, she went down to the beach. In bride's garb, amid the skeletons and the swirling contemptuous carrion birds, she stood and considered the sea.

The sharks had left the shallows. She could probably drown before they got her. If she breathed water in, it would be over quite fast, with hardly any pain at all.

Such thoughts were only playthings, though. She wasn't going to do it, but it helped. It still helped every day to remember that she could.

She went back up the switchback path, and walked alone to her own wedding. No one worried that she wouldn't turn up. After all, where could she go? For the whole of the ceremony, which had not space in it for her to utter so much as a single word, she stared at the old man who'd bought her for five coins. She stared without expression, hardly blinking, never smiling, and spoke to him with her mind, as though it were a conversation.

There are things you can't own, old man, not for five coins or five thousand.

And:

I am not what you think. I'm a pirate. What do you say to that? Did you know I stole power from the Mesarthim smith?

He feared me.

I saw it.

He struck me.

I remember.

I hate him.

I hate you.

I'm not afraid of him.

And I am not afraid of you.

If she said it enough, would it become true?

I'm not afraid of you, I'm not afraid.

I. Am not. Afraid.

Shergesh didn't care for the weight of her stare. Later, he made sure it was dark, so he couldn't see if her eyes were open. They *were* open, the whole time, and he felt their weight as she felt his, crushing her flat in their sleeping furs, his rancid breath on her face.

Weeks passed. Days shortened, which, perversely, meant nights lengthened. Nova still went, while she could, to play her game with the sea. This, too, became a conversation. With Kora by her side, she'd always had someone to talk to. Now that she had no one, she talked to everything, but only inside her head.

Good morning, sea, still here?

She imagined its voice, seductive. It knew her by her old name only, and she didn't correct its mistake. *Koraandnova*, it called her,

315

beckoning, and she closed her eyes and smiled. *Are you coming to me today?*

No, thank you. I think I'll stay ashore. You see, I'm expecting my sister.

It's too late, said the sea, but Nova didn't listen. She knew—she knew, *she knew*—that Kora would not desert her. So each day she turned her back on the sea, and mounted the path that would take her back up to the village and the labor and the old-man husband that were what passed for a life. And every day, morning came later and dimmer, until the sun clung sluggish to the horizon, barely peering up at all before subsiding. Deepwinter's Eve dawned—the day when Kora and Nova had always climbed the ridge trail to bid the sun farewell for an entire month.

This year Nova went alone. The trail was treacherous with ice, and sunless but not dark. Cold starlight lit her path. She stopped at the ridge, toes inches from the edge, looked up, and chose a star. She chose it of the thousands and, as was now her way, she talked to it.

Is she coming? she asked it. *You should know. I bet you can see everything from there. Will you give her a message for me? I don't know how much longer I'll last. Tell her that. Tell her the sea knows our name. Tell her I'm waiting. Tell her I'm dying. Tell her I love her.*

The rim of the sun appeared. It had never seemed so flimsy: That rind of light was all that stood between her and a month of darkness. She knew better than to look right at it—it was slim, but it was *the sun*—but she couldn't help herself. She looked. She must have looked too long. A white aura bloomed in her vision. She blinked but couldn't look away. Something about it . . .

The sun vanished but not the white aura. It must have burned into her eyes. It was dead center and growing. She blinked again. It was getting bigger. She squinted. It had a shape.

And then she saw what it was—if she dared to trust her sun-struck, wondering eyes.

She would ever after believe the star had passed her message to Kora. Because the shape gliding toward her was the huge white eagle that had effused from her sister's chest. How was it here? Was Kora here, too?

Nova was filled with lightning—the brilliant flare, the thunder's peal. She opened her arms to the bird. She wept. Her tears froze on her lashes. Kora had come to save her.

But where was she?

There was only the bird. There had been no vessels in the harbor for weeks, and wouldn't be now for months. The ice was closing. Winter was upon them, and the sea around Rieva became a treacherous wilderness of tide-borne ice shelves crashing together, buckling, heaving open into narrow straits only to smash shut again and splinter any ships caught in between. No one could approach. No one could escape. Kora couldn't be nearby. There was only the bird, but the bird *was* Kora. Wasn't that what the Servant had said?

It's not an 'it.' It's you, Korako. That eagle is you, as much as your flesh and blood is you.

Its wingbeats stirred a wind. Huge as it was, it seemed weightless, coming to hover in front of Nova. Its eyes pierced her and she wondered if her sister was really looking at her through them. She tried to smile and be brave. "Kora," she said. "Can you hear me? Can you see me?" Her voice sounded strange to her own ears, and she realized only then that it had been weeks since she'd said anything out loud. Shergesh preferred her silence, and whom else did she have to talk to? All her conversations happened only in her head.

"I miss you," she choked out. "I can't . . ." She started to say what she'd told the star. *I can't bear it. I'm dying. Save me.*

But the words wouldn't come. They filled her with shame. The bird made no sound but Nova felt Kora's presence, and she wanted to be strong for her. She summoned a smile. "It's Deepwinter's Eve. I don't suppose you have that in Aqa. Well, let me tell you," she said, and tried to hide her desperation under a thin veil of chatter. "The Slaughter was a fine time this year. I'll bet you're sorry you missed out...."

The bird was fading. Nova blinked. It was luminous in the starlight, but it was dimming like a dying lamp. Nova wondered with a lurch of her heart: Was it really here at all? What if she was only imagining it, some thread of sanity snapped? But then it clicked its beak and shifted in the air, its great taloned raptor foot thrusting a bundle at her. It was small. She clutched it to her chest with her mittened hands and gasped as the bird vanished before her.

"Don't leave me," she whispered, but it was already gone.

She thrust the bundle down the front of her coat; she couldn't open it with her mittens on, and didn't dare take them off in this cold. She went back down the ridge trail to her husband's house. No one paid her any heed. She crept in quietly and built up the fire before removing her outer layers. Shergesh was snoring. She hated the sound, but hated it less than his querulous voice snapping orders at her unceasing.

With shaking hands, still numb from the cold, she opened the eagle's bundle. A part of her mind still thought she'd imagined it, bird and bundle and all. Maybe even now it was all hallucination, however real it seemed in the firelight of the house.

It was a length of cloth finer than anything she'd touched— slippery as water, the light gliding over it, dancing like the aurora. It was patterned with tiny flowers in a hundred different colors. She thought she'd weep, it was so lovely. But that was just the wrapping. She unwound it.

There was a letter. It said:

My sister, half of my own self. I am not free to come for you, as our mother could not come for us. It is not as we imagined here. The empire is failing.

Nova blinked. The words were senseless. The Mesaret Empire was everything, and always had been. It could not fail. What did that even mean? The letter did not say. It went on: *I send you this with deep misgiving. I don't know what else to do. I know you know this, Novali: The punishment is death.*

For what it's worth, I heard the Mesarthim talking. They said that when you stole their gifts, you made them stronger—the way a lighthouse lens amplifies light. Nova, my heart. You are stronger than Rieva. You are stronger than the sea. Find me.

Find me. I am not free.

Nova's heart stuttered, then it raced. *I am not free.* Twice Kora had written those words. All this time, Nova had imagined her sister training, growing strong, living the life they'd dreamed of. It had been so real in their minds. How foolish it seemed now. It hadn't even occurred to her that they'd invented it whole cloth. She'd been so deep in her own self-pity, she'd never even considered...What was Aqa really like? What was Kora's life, if it was not the one they'd imagined?

And the empire...*failing*?

Nova would have been less stunned to see the sky shatter like a sheet of ice.

There was an object in the bundle. She saw it and stopped breathing. She knew better than to touch it. Through the wall, she heard Shergesh's snores falter into the snorts that heralded his waking. Her hands were shaking so badly she almost dropped the thing several times trying to wrap it back up. She shoved the bundle into

319

the back of a cupboard, but the letter, it was still in her hand. She heard Shergesh's sitting-up grunt, then *thump-thump* as he swung his feet out of bed, and she panicked and threw the letter in the fire.

No no no no no. She tried to grab it out. It was Kora's writing, and she didn't want to lose it as they had lost their mother's. Too late. It crisped and curled, and then Shergesh was in the doorway, scratching himself and wanting things, as was his way.

Nova didn't dare take the bundle back out till the next night's snores settled into rhythm. She crept out of bed and unwrapped the floral cloth with trembling hands.

The punishment is death.

It was a nothing less than a godsmetal diadem, as fine and perfect as the ring made by a raindrop fallen on still water. She couldn't fathom how Kora had gotten ahold of such a treasure. Every gram of godsmetal mined in all of Mesaret was accounted for in multiple ledgers and guarded by imperial soldiers. Only Servants sanctioned by the crown were granted the use of it, under strictest oaths and oversight. People killed for it, fought wars for it, wasted fortunes mining for it.

And what was Nova even supposed to do with it?

If she touched it, her skin would turn blue and give her away, and what good was her gift to her, anyway? *Pirate.* Skathis had spat out the word like a bite of rotten meat, as though there were nothing more contemptible in the world. She hadn't understood it then, but she'd had a lot of time to think, and now she thought she did. Her power was to *steal* power, but there was none on Rieva worth stealing. On her own, she was helpless, godsmetal or not, trapped on an island at the bottom of the world.

But Kora knew all that, and still she'd sent it, with the message: *Find me. I am not free.*

Which could only mean that Kora was even more trapped than she was.

A seismic shift occurred in that moment. Nova had been waiting for her sister to save her. But what if *she* had to save her sister?

Purpose possessed her, and a strange calm descended. She wrapped up the diadem. She hid it well. And while Shergesh snored and the sea iced over for the long winter dark, Nova began to plan.

38

THE SEA STARED BACK

The waiting was the worst part. The plan was madness, and there was no way to know if it would even *work*. Nova couldn't very well *test* it. For all she knew, she would be caught and executed. Still, there was nothing to do but try to act normal, day in, day out, *waiting*. Always, she carried on her silent conversations.

With the star:

Tell Kora I'm coming.

With the sea:

Haven't you frozen yet? Could you hurry, dear? I'd be obliged. You see, I've somewhere to be.

With her husband:

You don't know what I am, old man, but you will. I promise you that.

And her father:

I'm going to use you, and ruin you, and then I'm going to laugh. I hope you enjoyed your five bronze coins.

And they couldn't read her thoughts, but nor could they hold her gaze, and always looked away first. Well, except the sea. The sea stared back, and even as it slowly iced over, it was warmer, Nova thought, than her husband or her father.

At last, the time came. The sea froze. The only escape from Rieva was across the ice to Targay, a larger island with a harbor where ice-breakers docked even in winter. Nova had considered striking out alone, but the ice was treacherous. It was never still. It buckled and cracked, broke apart, smashed together, with force enough to behead breaching uuls. To make it all that way, she needed more than luck. She needed someone who could freeze water and make a solid path.

Someone like her father.

His gift, of course, was dormant. It was also weak. But Nova kept coming back to that one line from Kora's letter—how the Mesarthim had said she had made their gifts *stronger*. She wondered: Could it be true? That day in the wasp ship was such chaos in her recollection. But once the notion gripped her, she could not let it go. It really was her only chance. Of course, Zyak would hardly agree to help her escape.

That was where Shergesh came in.

Nova crept out of bed. Heart pounding, she took the diadem from its hiding place, peeled back the beautiful cloth, and gazed in awe at the godsmetal. If she was going to do this mad thing, she would have to touch it, let it work on her. *The punishment is death*, as Kora had reminded her, though she needed no reminding. If she touched the diadem, she would become blue, and there could be no going back.

Her hands shook as she let the cloth fall and grasped the circlet in both hands. The metal was cool and smooth. She watched her skin flush gray, then blue, as the hum moved over her and into her, awakening what was inside her. She recognized it now, and drew it forth. And then she went and knelt beside her sleeping husband.

Everyone knew what Shergesh's gift had been. He bragged of it all the time, and liked to say what he would use it for if it were at his disposal. On their wedding night, when Nova had balked at taking off her clothes, he'd told her, "If I had my power, you'd do what I tell you." He'd wiped the back of his hand across his mouth and leered. "But that would take the fun out of *making* you do it."

Which he had then proceeded to do.

Mind control. That was his power—too weak for the empire's use, but, Nova hoped, not for hers. If she could amplify it, then she could use it—to control not only him but her father, too. Careful not to wake the shriveled old tyrant, she touched the diadem to his wrist. He stirred while the hum moved through him, but he was a deep sleeper and did not wake. When it was all done, and he was as blue as she was, she gave him a hard shove and said, "Wake up, old man. It's time you found out what you married."

Wake up he did, and he blinked at her in the firelight as though he must be dreaming. She didn't give him time to realize he wasn't. She snatched his gift. It was easy, bless Thakra. It was right there for the taking. And as soon as she had it, she turned it back on him. "Get up and get dressed for a journey."

Still blinking, confused, Shergesh rose from the furs.

And did exactly as she bid.

And that was how Novali Nyoka-vasa came to cross the frozen sea with a sledge, a team of dogs, and the men who had bought and sold her.

It took a month. Targay was not near, and the way was anything but easy. When they ran out of food, they had to fish, and that took time. Over and over they came to broken ice, and each time Nova looked into the black water, she felt its soft persuasion all the way down to her bones.

It's too far, it said. *It's too late.*

324

Every day it got harder and harder to tune it out. She had to pour all her power—and Zyak's—into mending the ice, to forge a way onward. The single diadem between them, they had to take it in turns to hold it against their skin, so their power could not ebb away, and all that they did—every single thing—was the work of Nova's will, using the power she stole from them to keep them in line.

There was no room for mercy, and they deserved none. She felt no pity, and no triumph, either. She was too weary for triumph, and aware at every moment how quickly it could all go wrong. She could only sleep in snatched moments, when they were both sleeping, too, and in her fatigue she felt like she was floating, unable to settle in her skin. Shergesh was not strong, and had to ride in the sledge. Nova feared he'd die before they reached their destination, and she only cared because if he did, she would lose her control over her father. It took a great deal of her focus to keep her grip on his mind. Whenever she slackened her hold, she could feel him trying to resist her, even occasionally gaining a moment or two of freedom. Once, she nodded off, only to jerk awake and see him charging toward her, his silence at odds with the viciousness of his face. "Stop!" she commanded, and he jerked to a halt. She was afraid to sleep after that.

Every day, she'd find her star in the sky, and ask it to pass a message to Kora.

I'm coming, she always said, and always she hoped that the white bird would appear, as it had on Deepwinter's Eve. But it never did. In fact, she made it to Targay, and from there all the way to Aqa, but she never saw the bird again. She reached the imperial city to find it fallen into chaos—the emperor dead, his godsmetal stolen, and all hell broken loose.

And Kora? She was already gone.

❦ 39 ❦

TREACHEROUS WHISPER

The seraphim of long ago had made the portals because they could.

The endeavor was wrapped in words of glory, and there *was* greatness in it: The discovery of the Continuum that was the great *All*, an infinite number of universes lying pressed together like pages? The ability to pierce through them, and voyage from world to world? Who, with such a power, would not use it?

The Faerers were called the lightbearers, and glory was their mission. Six went in one direction, six the other, and they wrote the greatness of their race into each world they discovered. They were magnificent. It was only natural they should be worshipped. Religions sprang up in their wake. So did mass graves. Saviors to some, they were destroyers to others. In the world of Zeru they slaughtered one race to liberate another, and the name of their leader, Thakra, came to signify the dualism of beauty and terror.

Angels were not for the faint of heart.

The two Sixes put hundreds of worlds between them, flying ever outward from Meliz. And then one of them cut a door too far. It opened into darkness, and the darkness was alive.

This came to be known by survivors as the Cataclysm, though survivors were tragically few. The Faerers fled back whence they'd come, and the great beasts of darkness pursued, pouring after them through the cuts they'd made from sky to sky to sky. All the way back to Meliz they came, and every world the Faerers had opened, they devoured. Even Meliz was lost, Meliz eternal, the garden of the Continuum. Those seraphim who escaped into the neighbor world Eretz managed to hold the portal closed, and they held it to this day, pouring their strength into shoring up their sky to keep the darkness at bay.

A bold young queen in that distant world was even now training a legion of angels and chimaera to battle the darkness and hopefully destroy it. But that's another story.

As for the other Six, led by Thakra—who knows? Perhaps they died long ago, or perhaps they're still going, far, far out in the infinity of the great *All*. That's another story, too.

This is the story of the portals between Zeru and Mesaret, and how they were used after the angels had moved on, and by whom, and at what cost.

Mesaret was the world with the extraordinary blue metal that made its people like gods. Through the cuts in the sky their empire spread. With their skyships and soldier-wizards, they were invincible. For a time.

All empires fail. They overreach, spread too thin, collect one enemy too many. They're gnawed at from within by corruption, greed, betrayal. The Mesaret Empire was no exception. There was fighting on all fronts when a young smith called Skathis looked into the swirl of chaos and saw . . . opportunity.

He slew the emperor, but he did not take his place. He had other aspirations. He wished be a *god*. So he took the emperor's godsmetal, and then he left the world with his ship and a small, handpicked crew that included his spy, Korako, whether she wanted to go or not.

Nova reached Aqa just too late. She missed them by *a week*. And she might as well have wished to fly to the moon as follow them through the portal. It simply wasn't possible. Nevertheless, she did it. Not that year or the next, but she did it. Skathis had a mesarthium skyship to navigate portals and realms. She had nothing but her wits and her diadem, and still she found ways to follow. Sometimes it took her *years* to get from one world to the next. The trail grew old and faint, but always she kept on going.

There comes a certain point with a hope or a dream, when you either give it up or give up everything else. And if you choose the dream, if you keep on going, then you can never quit, because it's all you are. Nova had made that choice a long time ago. She was so far down this path that to turn around would be to face a howling, dark tunnel with nothing at its end, not even ice or uuls. There was no going back. There was nothing else. There was only Kora, and the words that haunted Nova:

Find me. I am not free.

It had taken her more than *two hundred years* to track Skathis's skyship to the edge of the shattered empire. She had lived many lives in that time, finding her way—*making* her way—through world after war-ravaged world. It was something, to have survived so much and come so far. The sea, she thought, would not know her now. She scarcely knew herself. No one still lived—in any world—who remembered Koraandnova, save Kora herself, her other half, so long ago severed from her.

She had been just *Nova* for centuries now, but the broken edges of that sundered name had not grown smooth with time. If anything they had gotten sharper. Touch them and you'd bleed. Through it all, whatever life she was living, whatever way she was surviving, she never stopped searching for her sister.

There was a treacherous whisper that lived inside her—the sea's voice, which she couldn't leave behind. Thakra knows she'd tried. Whenever she felt it stirring, its words starting to form in her mind, she'd bite the inside of her cheek or lip, hard enough to draw blood. The blood was a tithe she paid to keep it silent, or else it was a prayer that she would prove the whisper wrong.

Too late.

Those were the words she couldn't kill. That was the fear she quelled with her blood—that she would always and forever be *too late*.

But now, at long last, she had found the white bird—or it had found her, as it had once before. And as she followed it through the portal, she knew: It could only be leading her to Kora.

❦ 40 ❦

ONSLAUGHT

Sarai was numb with the shock of the red-sea vista as Wraith burst through the portal. The warp stretched to disgorge the eagle, its massive wings spread wide, and snapped back into place only to open again as figures poured in behind it: one...two...*four* black-clad marauders, one in the lead, three fanning out behind.

Wraith's shriek was twinned with a scream, and even muted by the chamber, it was bloodcurdling. It was no natural scream. Sarai, Lazlo, and the others were *racked* by it. It invaded them, body and mind. It came from a woman, the one in the lead. She was fair-haired and slight. She was *blue*, clad in tight black garb that made her seem dipped in oil. At her brow, like a crown, she wore a circlet of mesarthium. Her eyes were mad, and her mouth was open to pour forth this soul-scouring scream.

Sarai had never heard a wilder sound. There were wolves in it, and war cries, carrion birds and storm winds, and she'd never have believed it came from a person if she weren't seeing it with her own eyes. It struck terror in her, in all of them, rendering them stunned and helpless.

It was magic. It was an assault. It drilled into their minds and cut them off from their instincts, muting their natural reactions.

Lazlo faltered, stricken. He was in the act of pulling back the walkway and closing the orb, but everything halted. Where he might have sent forth a surge of mesarthium to engulf the intruders, he did not. Even the defensive instincts of Eril-Fane and Azareen, razor-honed by years of training, were overpowered. They didn't draw their hreshteks, which should have been second nature, but shrank from the sound, hands flying up to flatten against their ears.

* * *

Nova breached the portal screaming Werran's scream. He was one of her cohort, and this was his gift: a scream to sow panic in the minds of all who heard it. There was no better way to stun one's foe in the opening assault. Nova liked to lead with it, and buy herself a moment to assess her opponent at leisure. Usually, she let Werran use his gift himself, but she had a mighty need to scream as she followed Kora's bird into this unknown world, so she took it over and let it loose, and relished the way it ravaged her throat.

At last she had come to the moment she'd been chasing for more than two centuries, since the night she unwrapped the diadem and vowed to free her sister.

She'd lost count of the number of worlds there were between this one and her own. And she hadn't kept track of the men she'd killed since Zyak and Shergesh. But she knew the years, and the months, and the days since the white bird came to Rieva. It had been so long, but now she was here. She was going to save her sister, and she was so much more than ready.

She scanned the room, still pouring out the scream, her heart pounding fit to burst. Five Servants and three humans, she counted. Her eyes flicked over them fast, then over them again even faster. Kora's bird flew in circles, its cry twining with her scream. Nova's heart beat harder. She bit off the scream. She'd thought the bird would lead her to her sister. The need to see her was a violent fire within her.

But Kora wasn't here.

Too late, came the treacherous whisper. She bit her cheek, and her mouth filled with the metal tang of blood.

* * *

Humans and godspawn cowered, paralyzed by the scream, and when it cut off—when the woman bit it off and bared her teeth at them in an animal snarl—they were left reeling in silence, each of them feeling *stranded*, as though the scream were a wave that had hurled them onto a beach and left them alone and gasping, the bits and pieces of who they were strewn all around them.

The invaders fanned out before them in the air. They were flying, or floating, impervious to gravity. Besides the leader, there were two men and a woman, all blue, and all clad in the same oily black—a uniform that fit like skin, with boots that looked built to crush bones underfoot and somehow stood on air. Sheathed short swords hung at their sides, and they were grim-faced with menace, all wielding rods of some gray metal with two short prongs at the end. Lightning leapt between the prongs, emitting an ominous crackle.

The sight brought Lazlo back to himself. In the wake of the

scream, instinct returned—not in a surge but slowly, as though scattered bits of his mind were trying to reassemble themselves. His first thought was to put Sarai behind him. For her part, she could only stare. She felt as though she were back in Minya's nightmare, because this woman with her fair hair and pale brows...she *knew* her. She'd seen her in the nursery doorway.

Korako, she thought.

So did Eril-Fane, though he knew it was impossible. He remembered his knife plunging into her heart, the life leaving her eyes. But her eyes glittered now, alive with brutal intensity. He drew his hreshtek. Azareen did, too.

Lazlo, hearing the twin sounds of blades unsheathing, gave his sluggish head a shake and reached for his power. It was too late to close the orb and keep the intruders out. They were *in*, but that didn't mean he couldn't stop them. Already, he had learned: Nothing could stop mesarthium. He opened himself to the energies that were alive all around him. Gritting his teeth, he willed his metal to strike, and up from the floor of the chamber, a geyser of mesarthium erupted. It was a shining blue jet of liquid metal, propelled with volcanic force. It surged up at the woman. It would annihilate her on impact. But Lazlo didn't have annihilation in him. He willed the geyser to hollow and open, making a molten tube that would, instead, surround and contain her.

Or, it *should* have. But just as it reached her, it froze. Gaping open like a mouth around her feet and ready to swallow her, the whole explosive jet of metal...stopped.

With a sickening helplessness, Lazlo felt his mesarthium awareness *peel away* from him. The sensation of claiming—the metal claiming him, and he it—evaporated, and the energies, too, as though the air had emptied of its staves of silent music. It was akin to sudden blindness or deafness, the loss of this new sense. He sought his power, desperate, and . . . nothing.

The others looked to him and back at the intruder, their eyes wide, confused. Why had he stopped? "Lazlo . . . ?" asked Sarai, a quaver in her voice.

"My power," he gasped. "It's gone."

"What?"

The walkway had come to rest hanging out into the chamber like a half-finished bridge. Sarai and Lazlo and the others were all clustered together at its end. They had shrunk back at the first screech of onslaught, only to be paralyzed by the unnatural scream. Now they all snapped out of stillness.

Ruby kindled into Bonfire. Her eyes filled up with flame. Her hair writhed and glowed like rivulets of lava, and sparks hissed in her closed fists. She'd never attacked anybody before. Minya had told her she was a weapon, but she'd never felt like one until now. But before she could do anything, she felt it snatched away. *It:* her fire, her spark.

It was *taken,* and no sooner did she register its loss than the attacker's eyes turned red and leapt alight. Her flaxen hair smoked, aglow like a bed of coals. Ruby saw. She felt gutted and guttered, as though the woman had reached inside her and stolen what made her *her.* "You," she choked, outraged. "That's *mine.* Give it back!"

At the same time, Feral, with a gulp, closed his eyes and ripped a thunderhead from a sky half a world away. The air above the attackers darkened. The rain was instantaneous—a gyre of stinging, half-frozen pellets, each one a tiny ice blade. The dense cloud strobed and crackled, lit from within by unborn lightning. The roar of the thunder flattened out under the chamber's muting properties, but it still reverberated in their bones. For years, Minya had tried to make Feral do this very thing: summon storms as weapons, aim and strike with lightning—but he'd always been afraid, so he'd always failed. Now he felt his power as though it were *boiling* in him and pouring out like steam, as though he were a conduit for the sky's full might, the untamable power of nature itself. For the first time in his life, Feral felt like a god.

And then the feeling vanished like vapor.

The invader, wet-sleek, with icy rain rolling down her face and her fair hair slick to her skull, lifted her arms from her sides and made a show of her stolen powers.

In her open hands, fireballs flared, hissing and dancing under the pelting rain. And they weren't just balls. They were blooms. They were *flowers* sculpted of fire. They began as buds and opened, unfurling petals of living orange flame, blue at the center and paling to white at the ruffled fringes of their petals.

Ruby's breath caught. She'd never made anything half so beautiful, and envy infused her outrage.

Sparrow made no move with her gift. Minya had always scorned her for her uselessness in a fight, and she had never minded, but now she did. She felt small and helpless as the thunderhead roiled and crackled overhead, glowing with its bounty of lightning. Then it split open and three bolts shot out, white and fast, right at the walkway. They had to hurl themselves down, and only the railing Lazlo had made kept them from falling off. The smell of ozone settled around them, clean and sharp, and they huddled there, all watching, awestruck and afraid, as the frozen mesarthium geyser turned molten once more. It didn't erupt or engulf the woman—at least, not as Lazlo had intended. Instead, it flowed with slow grace up her legs, over her torso, and out along her arms, shaping itself into plates of armor. They were nothing like the heavy bronze plates the Tizerkane wore, held in place with buckles and thick leather straps. These were as smooth as poured water, and so fine they were virtually weightless. They added no bulk, and they moved with her body, and still they were stronger than anything in this world. They wove themselves into the black fabric of her costume, and shone mirror-bright: on her shins, up her thighs, in an elegant fanfold over her knees. A breast-plate formed, worked in a pattern of an eagle with its wings spread. She still held the fire flowers in her open palms, even as the metal flowed out and wrapped her arms in pauldrons and vambraces more elegant than any ever wrought with anvil and hammer.

She floated in the air before them, eyes glowing red, flames blooming in her hands, wearing mesarthium armor and wielding lightning like spears, and the godspawn and humans were humbled and appalled.

"Who are you?" asked Feral, his voice shaking.

"What do you want?" Sarai demanded, afraid of the answer.

"How is she doing that?" asked Ruby, overwrought. "I want my fire back!"

With a sudden motion, the woman dashed the fire flowers toward the floor far below, where they sizzled into sparks and died. An impatient jerk of her arm, and the thunderhead vanished, too, taking the rain and the lightning with it. There was still a muted patter of drips sluicing off the invaders' soaked forms, but the air cleared, and the thunder faded. Ruby and Feral both groped for their gifts, hoping they had them back, but they didn't. The invader still held their powers, and Lazlo's, too—as he was reminded when she raised her arm, fingers flexed, and summoned a ball of mesarthium down from the ceiling. It flew to her hand faster than falling, meeting her palm with a *smack*. She clasped it and spun it around her fingers, weightless as a magic trick. The flames died out of her eyes. They were brown and livid and fixed on Lazlo. She spoke to him in a language they couldn't understand. It was harsh to their ears as rusted hinges and crows.

* * *

"Do you remember me?" was what Nova asked.

She perceived her foe through the haze of her hatred, and if he didn't look quite as she remembered, it had been more than two hundred years. Who else could he be? Those were his gray eyes, and this was his ship, and the world he had chosen.

Skathis, after all this time. She felt his power surge through her, as it had long ago. She said, "You feared me once, but not enough to kill me, and I have crushed your throat in a godsmetal collar in a thousand glad murderous dreams. You called me a pirate when I was no such thing. Now, though. *You have no idea.*"

She threw the ball, just as he had thrown one to her, and to Kora. She whispered, "Catch."

* * *

Lazlo did. It was reflex. But as soon as it touched his hand, there was nothing left to catch. It splashed over his arm and rolled up it, blue metal shining in motion. As he recoiled, arm outheld, the metal sluiced up his shoulder, coalescing as it moved into a sinuous streak. It elongated and shaped itself into a serpent, and wound itself around his neck. This was all inside a second, and before he quite knew what was happening, it opened its mouth and gulped down its own tail.

Lazlo grabbed it. It writhed under his hands, and he felt it alive in the same way that Rasalas was alive, or the songbird he'd detached

337

from the wall—no longer dumb metal but a creature, animated by a will.

But it was not *his* will, and as he grasped the writhing-alive metal snake in his hands, it cinched tight, devouring itself, and his neck was caught in its noose.

Sarai seized it and tried to pry its jaws off its tail, but she couldn't shift it. It constricted, and her fingers were captured between the collar and Lazlo's throat. She had to turn them incorporeal—make her ghostflesh like air—to pull free. But she couldn't do the same for Lazlo. She couldn't turn *him* incorporeal, and she saw the panic in his eyes as the snake tightened, cutting off his air. His mouth opened in a ragged gasp, and Sarai whirled to face his attacker. "Let him go!" she cried.

What she saw in the eyes of the Korako apparition was a mania veering between victory and rage. It was a killing mania, make no mistake. She had stormed in here to do harm, and she was *savage*.

Everything had happened so fast. Just a moment ago they'd been staring through the slit in the air at the impossible landscape. Now they were invaded, their magic stolen. Eril-Fane and Azareen stood helpless at the edge of the bridge, the enemies out of reach of their blades. Ruby and Feral were stripped of their magic, and Minya wasn't even here. The absurdity struck Sarai like a blow. Minya, their protector—*always* their protector, since before they could even remember, Minya who had saved them and spent her life building an army to *keep on* saving them—was lying on her floor in a gray, drugged slumber, defenseless and also useless, and it was all their fault.

And now Lazlo was choking, and if he died, Minya wasn't here to catch his soul. With a sob of rage, Sarai launched herself at the enemy.

She leapt. She flew. She *attacked*.

And if the enemy was savage, she was better, because she was not constrained by being alive, with all its *fixity*. When *her* lips skinned back from her teeth in a snarl, she was more vicious than this foe could ever hope to look, because her mouth widened to become a *maw* straight out of her nightmare arsenal. Her teeth grew long and sharp, like the spines of some venomous sea-thing. Her eyes went blood-red from the whites to the irises—solid, shining, ghastly red—and her hooked fingers became talons to rival Wraith's. She locked eyes with Nova as she hurtled toward her, and she saw the way the woman's gaze narrowed, intent but unworried as she snatched Sarai's gift just as she'd snatched away the others'.

Sarai felt it, but barely. Her fear and fury muted everything. Her godspawn gift was stolen? So what. It wasn't her gift that let her fly and grow fangs. This was just the upside of being dead. When she didn't falter, much less fall, Nova's face went slack with surprise. Sarai experienced her own dark satisfaction.

And then she was on her.

❦ 41 ❦

ONLY EVERYTHING

Nova thought the girl's gift must be flight, because she was flying, and with no gravity boots such as she herself wore. Then she thought she must be a shape-shifter, because her face changed. It went from pretty to horrible in an instant, her mouth splaying impossibly wide, teeth bristling out like needles. Could she have *two* gifts? Nova had never heard of such a thing, and when she reached out with her mind to seize them, she felt only one. She couldn't even tell what it was. Sometimes it was obvious, but this was obscure, no gift she'd ever encountered. Regardless, she ripped it away.

The girl ought to have plummeted. Those terrible teeth should have shrunk and vanished, to say nothing of the claws. But none of that happened. She didn't fall. She didn't change back. She hit Nova full force and they went sprawling—back into the open half shell of the orb, beneath the gash of the portal. They smashed into the metal. Nova's shoulders bore the brunt, but her head was not spared. Her vision blurred, and a ringing filled her ears. The girl's voice fought through it. She was screaming something at her, but Nova couldn't understand her language. The girl was gripping her shoulders, her weight pressing down. Her talons *skree*'d over the godsmetal plates Nova had just armored herself with. If she hadn't, those claws would be sunk in her flesh.

Nova's wrath exploded. Was the girl *stupid*? Did she think she could best her, and with all this metal just waiting to be quickened? She felt its energy all around. It seemed to vibrate with an urgency to *become*. But become what?

More strangling serpent collars? A thousand biting spiders shining like evil gemstones? No sooner did Nova think it than they *were*. As the two women grappled in the hollow of the orb, its curve gave birth to an arachnid *swarm*. The smooth surface dappled with sudden texture. Then the texture disengaged, grew legs, and crawled free. Hundreds of spiders surged up. Nova was on her back, pinned down. The spiders climbed over her shoulders onto the girl's hands, then swarmed up her arms into her dark red hair. She let go then. Nova shoved her off, right into the swarming mass. They skittered over her and in seconds she was cloaked in living metal—a thousand spiders, *eight thousand legs*, and how many teeth between them? Just before the girl was submerged by seething, multitudinous spiders, Nova saw her eyes—her shining, full-red eyes—flare wide with horror. She felt a distant stab of the same horror for what her mind had birthed with a mere skim of her will. But it was smothered by triumph.

She'd dreamed of the day she'd steal Skathis's gift. It had taken the place of her earliest dream—the one she'd shared with Kora, in which Servants came to Rieva and chose them. She had dreamed that dream for sixteen years, and this one for more than two centuries.

In it, she didn't kill him, but stole his gift, and stole *him*, too. She would set Kora free, and they would seize this ship and keep Skathis in a cage too small for him to stand up in. She imagined it as a birdcage hanging in a corner, and they'd torment him relentlessly. They would be his hell, and they would use his gift to sail the skies of all the worlds and be untouchable.

Did this girl think she could beat her? Did she think she could keep her from Kora? No one would *ever* do that again. The girl was swallowed by the spiders. A clamor of voices screamed and pleaded, but it all sounded distant and alien. And in the next second, the impossible:

The girl turned to smoke. She was drowning in spiders, only her hands visible, clawing them away. Then she was floating up as they all fell *through* her to scrabble over the orb's curve whence they'd been born a second ago while she rose, weightless, made up of wisps, and came together again, whole and flesh and fury.

Nova gaped. She'd taken her gift. It was in her possession. She could feel the weight of it, along with the others—the drain of them all on her power. So how in the name of Thakra had she done *that*?

The spiders forgotten, the orb resorbed them. The girl surged forward, through the air. Nova unleashed a wave of godsmetal to knock her back, but when it broke over her, she turned to smoke again. She couldn't pass through the solid metal, but melted into wisps that streamed free of its path and came together again on the other side of it, still coming for Nova.

She reached her, and seized her once more by the shoulders. Werran and Rook, the two men of Nova's cohort, thrust their lightning prods at the girl, the charge flashing between the prongs, emitting its deadly crackle. But the rods passed right through her and came close to jolting Nova instead.

Struggling to get free, Nova kicked out with one of her heavy boots, but her foot went through her, too. She could feel the girl's realness in the grip on her shoulder, and yet her foot passed through her like vapor.

"*What are you?*" Nova snarled.

The girl was speaking, fast and urgent. Her language was mellifluous, and though Nova understood not a word, she could hear the pleading plainly. Her eyes weren't red now, but clear-sky blue. Her teeth weren't a horror. They were even and white. She was young. She was weeping. Then she pointed back toward the bridge, where the smith was on his knees choking.

She wanted her to save him? In what world would a girl beg for that monster's life? "You're pleading for *Skathis*?" she spat, her lip curled.

The name registered. The girl might not understand her language, but she knew that name. She recoiled from it.

A voice spoke inside Nova's head. It wasn't the treacherous whisper. It was her telepath, the third of her cohort, speaking directly to her mind. Her voice was clear and calm. She said, *Nova. That's not Skathis.*

As soon as Nova heard it, she knew it was true. She'd been blinded by vengeance and the mad rush of finally breaching the portal that had kept her out all these years. She looked at the smith now, his face dark, his eyes desperate, and she saw similarities, but differences, too. "Then who is it?" she snarled, unable to comprehend what it meant: a different smith here in Skathis's ship?

I don't know, but, whoever he is, you're killing him. Is that what you wish?

If it *was* what she wished, they wouldn't object—her loyal cohort, her crew. She'd killed to free them. She'd killed to take what they needed to survive. She'd killed for safety, and honor, and spite. She always had her reasons, some of them better than others, and they knew what this moment meant to her.

Only *everything.*

Only Kora. Only the missing half of her very soul.

Where was she? And if that wasn't Skathis, who was it? What had happened here? Why had the portal been closed for so long?

Nova eased up on the serpent collar. Its tail slipped out of its mouth and it came open. The smith flung it away and took a choking breath. The girl let go of Nova and flew to him. She caught him and held him while he sucked in air, his purpled face returning to Mesarthim blue. He was holding his throat, his eyes red and streaming. The two human warriors stood guard on either side of him. They were tense, still wielding their blades. The older woman was clutching the railing. The other three Mesarthim were clustered round the smith. Nova had assumed they were Skathis's crew, but she saw now how young they all were—barely more than children, perhaps the same age as she'd been when she was sold to an old man for five coins.

It felt as though cinders were burning a hole in her. Who were they, and where was Kora?

Where was Kora?

WHERE WAS KORA?

The smoke-girl, shape-shifter, whose magic defied theft, looked up and asked a question. Nova asked one right back. In her head, the question thundered, but it came out small and plaintive, because it took every ounce of her anger to quell the treacherous whisper that was telling her, always telling her, *Too late.*

* * *

"Who are you?" Sarai implored. "What do you want?"

Nova asked, *"Where's my sister?"*

They couldn't understand each other. Their languages clashed like alien armies, one harsh, one fluid, both raw with the same awful, bloody suspense. They stared at each other in mistrust and confusion. Across worlds and through portals cut long ago by angels, their lives collided right here. Both came to this place seeking something.

Sarai and the others were trying to discover what they were, *why* they were, and what had happened to the ones who came before them.

And Nova, she just wanted her sister.

Sarai and Lazlo had joked about meeting strangers at crossroads to swap answers to mysteries. Now here they were. This was a crossroads of sorts. Two groups faced each other. They were strangers, and they held each other's answers. But this was no laughing matter, and these weren't the kind of truths you could trade and walk away from.

They were explosive, and they couldn't all survive them.

Of all of them gathered here—five godspawn, three humans, four Mesarthim invaders—only Eril-Fane understood. For three years, he had been Isagol's pet. He still had nightmares in her language. To hear its harsh sounds picked scabs off old wounds that were only just beginning to heal. But worse by far than the sounds were the words.

My sister, said the intruder.

She wasn't Korako. She was looking for Korako. And who knew better than he that she was never going to find her? His hands were slick with sweat, and in that moment it felt like the blood of old murders that would never wash off.

Wraith chose that moment, circling overhead, to let out one of its haunting wails that sounded like a woman lamenting her fate.

And, of all of them, only Eril-Fane knew that, too. Not just what Wraith was. Nova knew that: her sister's astral self, projected into the world. And not just that Korako was dead, because all the godspawn and humans knew that. But only the Godslayer knew both and understood that the ghostly white eagle was the last shred of the dead goddess's soul, cast adrift when the knife pierced her heart. If the bird had been in her when she died, then surely it would have ended with her. But it hadn't been. It had been on wing, and it remained, left behind like an echo that refuses to fade, or a shadow outlasting its caster.

All would come out. Eril-Fane's throat was tight, his fists tighter, and his hearts felt huge with a sudden, immense, uncomplicated love—for his city, his people, his mother, his wife, and for these beautiful blue children who had survived all on their own. Ever since Isagol, any feeling of love had triggered other feelings—unspeakable, crippling ones that filled him with shame and revulsion. It was like stroking the pelt of a magnificent animal—soft, sun-warmed, a marvel of creation—to find it crawling with maggots, its glassy eyes rolling as it was devoured from beneath. She had done that to him.

But as he stood there in the heart of the citadel, witness to this collision of stories in which he himself played such a part, he felt no shame and no revulsion, just love—simple, pure, untainted love.

And a terrible clear-eyed certainty that his reckoning had finally come.

💫 42 💫

"Dead" Was the Wrong Answer

Sarai had been so fixed on the pale-haired, wild-eyed Korako apparition that she'd hardly looked at the three who came behind her. Then one of them spoke up—the second woman, and she spoke in *their* language, the language of Weep. Her voice faltered, and her accent was strange, but the words were plain enough.

"Who are you? Where is Skathis? Where is Korako?"

Sarai looked at her, and whatever thoughts those questions stirred in her, she forgot them as soon as their eyes met. Recognition sparked in her, sharp as a shock. Like all four marauders, the second woman was armed and black-clad, her expression severe. Her blue face was plain, her hair brown, and one of her eyes was brown, too. But the other . . . The other was *green*.

Sarai felt light-headed. She was overpowered by a sudden certainty that she was still trapped and wandering inside Minya's dreams. "*Kiska?*" she asked, unbelieving.

The woman blanched with surprise. All the severity fell away, and she looked even more like the little girl from the nursery. "How do you know me?" she demanded.

Ruby audibly sucked in a breath. Feral and Sparrow stared. They didn't know her face, the way Sarai did from the dream, but they certainly knew her name. Minya had kept the names of the lost alive, all those she could remember. She'd made sure the others remembered them, too. They had a litany of them, in reverse order: *Kiska Werran Rook Topaz Samoon Willow,* and on.

"Your eye," replied Sarai, dazed. Then something clicked into place in her mind, and her gaze flashed to the two men.

During the scream, she'd been too distraught to put it together, but now it clicked. The boy taken away before Kiska, his gift had been a war cry to flay minds and wreak havoc. *"Werran?"* she asked, her eyes darting between the two men. One looked sharply at the other, whose face showed the same surprise as Kiska's. The hard varnish of his ferocity was softened by confusion. He seemed to be about Lazlo's age. In fact, he looked a little like Lazlo. They could almost be brothers.

Or, they could *really* be brothers. Because it was clear from their reactions: These invaders in their oil-black garb with their lightning prods—these strangers—were the last godspawn taken from the nursery. They were *kindred.*

Sarai's hand flew to her mouth. A thrum of wonder filled her, along with an unexpectedly sweet surge of *gladness,* in spite of all the fury and fear from the violence of a moment ago. Perhaps it was all a misunderstanding! She dropped her hand from her mouth to her hearts, and looked at the second man. He was young, too, sharp-featured, with dark hair and dark eyes and a shadow of beard growth. Repeating the litany in her head, she said, "I don't suppose you're Rook."

She saw from his rapid blinking and hard swallow that he was. "You're alive," Sarai breathed. All her life this mystery had hung over them, but she had hardly dared hope that she might learn the truth from the lips of the missing children themselves. Could it be so neat? The last three taken, all returned together?

"But who are you?" asked Rook.

"We're like you," she told him. "We were born in the nursery, too. We're . . . we're the last."

"The last," repeated Kiska, taking in the five of them. Her brow furrowed. She was thinking of the last thing she saw as Less Ellen dragged her to Korako. She was thinking of Minya, and the rest— the toddlers they'd swung in their makeshift hammock. "But there were so many more."

The fate of those others hung heavy over them all, and so did the fate of the rest, all those who came before. "There were," Sarai said, their loss a part of her forever. "But what happened to you? Where did they take you? Are all the others alive, too?"

Kiska turned to Nova, whose ferocity had softened not a whit. Her pale brows were pinched together, her eyes slitted and flinty. They spoke, quick and harsh. Sarai couldn't tell how much of the harshness was anger and how much was just the language. Kiska gestured toward them while she talked, explaining who they were.

Nova's voice grew harsher still, and Kiska, flustered, nodded once, and turned back to face Sarai and the others. Sarai saw her compose herself and put her severity back in place like a mask. A chill went down her spine. Whatever kinship there was between them, she was setting it aside in favor of her allegiance to this woman. "Answer me," said Kiska. "Where is Skathis? Where is Korako?"

If her voice had been less cold, they might have told her, but no one did. The way Nova was looking at them, it felt like a knife to their throats. What answer did she hope for? A new wave of fear washed over them all, and none of them spoke. At least, not out loud. But their minds answered the question in chorus: *dead they're dead they're dead they're dead*. The words were echoing in Sarai's thoughts when she saw Kiska stiffen.

She remembered then what her gift was.

Kiska was a telepath, and it was clear from the look in her eyes—the dismay, the sorrow, the fear—that "dead" was the *wrong* answer.

* * *

Nova saw Kiska's look, too, and she knew it could only mean one thing. The treacherous whisper broke loose from inside her.

too late too late too late too late

Nova had peered into a volcano once, in some world whose name she'd forgotten. She'd seen magma, hot and bright, churning in its core, and that was how she felt—her gorge, like magma, rising, her rage ready to erupt. She didn't wait for Kiska to spit out the words, stammering and sorrowful. She seized her gift.

She was already holding four gifts, and each one was a drain on her power. Kiska's made five, as many as she'd ever held at once, and she felt the strain, but didn't hesitate. With Kiska's telepathy, she threw herself at the strangers' minds and plunged right into them.

It was like flying into a tornado. She'd used Kiska's gift before, but not often enough to get used to it—the whirl of thoughts and feelings. Fear, anguish, confusion, uncertainty assailed her eightfold and she almost recoiled. She heard the same words that Kiska had heard, but she didn't know what they meant. Words were meaningless, but there weren't just words. She could *see* their memories, too, a messy, mad tumult of them, like reflections in boiling water. There was so much chaos, so many images, but the one she wanted—or rather, the one she *didn't* want, the last thing she *ever* wanted—was there among them. She saw, and she could not unsee, and she could not undo.

too late

She saw the life leave Kora's eyes.

too late

She felt the knife as though it entered her own heart.

too late

Nova saw her sister die in the killer's own memory.

forever and always too late

She let go of Kiska's power. Kiska felt its return like a punch, and staggered with the blowback of Nova's feelings. She wasn't ready, and the raw emotion was crushing.

Nova was shaking all over. Her eyes had become pools of fire. The air was thickening around her with a cloud so dark it looked as though it had been pulled from a night sky with night still clinging to it. And as she shook, the room shook, too. The walkway heaved and juddered. Those on it had to grasp the rail.

"You killed my sister!" Nova wailed. She wasn't using Werran's scream, but her own voice was nearly as wild.

Eril-Fane heard and understood. He might almost have been waiting for this. That didn't mean he wanted it. If he hadn't always been sure, now he was: He wanted to live. That didn't mean he believed he deserved to, but he wanted to, so very much. He even thought that he might be free, finally, of Isagol's curse, because as he faced his reckoning, there was no more shadow to his love, no maggots feasting at its soft underside, but only love so pure it burned.

Whatever happened to him, though, he would protect all the others as he had failed to before. Azareen, the children. He had another chance to do that, at least. "Get out of here, all of you," he told them. "Go!"

Little Sparrow was beside him. He gave her a nudge back up the walkway toward the door. She grabbed Ruby's hand and tugged her along, both of them clinging to the railing as the walkway shuddered underfoot. Lazlo was still on his knees, Sarai crouched beside him. Eril-Fane took his daughter's arm, pulled her upright, and urged her, "Go," as he pulled Lazlo up, too. He was a commander. His voice brooked no dissent. Feral wrapped a protective arm around Suheyla and braced her between himself and the railing as they made their way back toward the door. Azareen did not leave Eril-Fane's side.

He said to the goddess, in her language—how he hated the feel of it in his mouth!—"They are innocent. Please. Let them go."

Azareen didn't understand the language, but she understood his fixed footing well enough. He wasn't retreating. Why wasn't he retreating? "Come on." She pulled at him but couldn't budge him. His eyes were riveted on the goddess.

Nova was beyond thinking. The whisper had become a roar. *TOO LATE. TOO LATE.* Grief, formless and rampant, was sucking at her and pounding at her till she could hardly feel her own edges. She was entangled in dark mist with her eyes on fire, spilling out wrath, pain, and power. And all of it, right or wrong, was directed at her sister's killer.

Azareen saw the burning gaze, and she felt her husband's stillness. She looked back and forth between the two. Her eyes were open very wide, rings of white showing full around her irises, like someone who's just bolted upright from a nightmare to find the nightmare real all around her. She'd known something was coming. Since she saw the bird's shadow fall over Eril-Fane, she'd known and been power-less to stop it. Wasn't there anything she might have done? Fought harder, raged harder, *made him listen?* She shook her head, still trying to deny it. She shook her head and shook it as though she couldn't stop, would *never* stop defending him or defying fate or waiting for him to come back to her.

Nova raised a hand. The energy of the mesarthium surrounded her. She conducted it like music. The wasp ships were on the wall. Their stingers were as long as spears and as sharp as needles. At the lightest touch of her mind, they disengaged and hung poised in the air.

Eril-Fane and Azareen saw at the same moment. At least, they saw one of them. And as it shot like an arrow, Azareen raised her sword and stepped in front of her husband.

A deep horror filled him. He roared, "Azareen, *NO!*"

The stinger was a blur.

Azareen's hreshtek blurred to meet it.

There was a sound, too small and sweet, almost like a bell's chime, as she knocked the stinger away. It careened, spinning, off course, hit the wall, and fell to the floor.

Eril-Fane's roar of protest died. He said, with an edge of desperation, "Azareen, go with the others. *Please.*"

She shook her head, grim, and adjusted her grip on her sword.

He remembered the first time he'd handed her a hreshtek, in the training cave when they were just children. He remembered her look of wonder, and the first awkward clash of their blades, and he remembered the first desperate touch of their lips, and he remembered her screams in the sinister wing, and he remembered her hollow-eyed after it was all over and the gods were dead and she needed her husband but he couldn't even hold her because his soul was *filthy.* But she had never forsaken him, and he knew she never would. She would share his fate, whatever it was.

And she did. She shared it exactly.

The second wasp was on the wall behind them. They never saw the stinger coming.

If Azareen hadn't stepped in front of him to deflect the first, she would still have been at his side, clear of the path of the second stinger when it hit between his shoulder blades and cut right between his hearts to burst out of his chest, slicing through his armor with an eruption of blood that painted her red in the instant before it cut through her, too—as though they were as insubstantial as Wraith, as ethereal as Sarai. But they were neither smoke nor phantom. They were flesh and blood and bronze, and the stinger ripped through them. It was moving with so much raw power it didn't slow, but shot across the chamber to strike the far wall with a faint, bright *tink!* before rebounding to cartwheel backward in slow motion, spraying blood as it spun.

The two warriors dropped their swords. The blades hit the walkway and clattered off to fall to the floor down below. Azareen was close to the edge, and the force of the blow drove her back, so she teetered at the edge and almost went over. But Eril-Fane caught her and reeled her to his chest, even as he lost the strength to stand and fell to his knees, taking her with him.

Blood was flowing from the holes in their armor, pumping out in spurts and mingling between them, catching and pooling where they pressed together. Azareen thrust her hands against Eril-Fane's chest to try to keep his blood inside him, as though she didn't notice her own was escaping. But her hands were inexplicably weak, and she couldn't even get to his wound to apply proper pressure. His armor was in the way. The hole in the bronze was so small. Metal jutted out, sharp, where it had been pierced. She sliced her palm on it. His blood pushed out through her fingers, slicking down her wrists, all the way down her arms. Her own blood was mostly hidden, sluicing down inside her armor, her back and belly slick with it. It was so hot and there was so much and it was emptying them like spigots. His eyes were vague and her vision was swimming but she saw him clearly when he fixed on her and rasped, "Azareen. I wish..."

He pitched forward, as though he were falling asleep. She caught him, but couldn't hold him upright. Her arms were numb, and he was so heavy. She collapsed to the side, and he slumped down over her. "What?" she asked, desperate, with her shallowing breath. "My love," she pleaded as his eyes went dull. *"What do you wish?"*

But the time for wishing had passed.

Eril-Fane died first, Azareen just after.

43

VIOLENT RADIANCE

Sarai saw it all. She'd reached the doorway and spun to look back, surprised to see her father and Azareen still at the end of the walkway. Had she thought they were following? She hadn't thought at all. She'd just panicked and done as he'd ordered.

Now she screamed. Lazlo couldn't. His strangled throat could only croak. Suheyla couldn't, either. She couldn't even breathe. Feral was all that was keeping her upright. Ruby and Sparrow were sobbing. The unnatural quiet of the heart of the citadel echoed with gasps that were part scream, part sob.

Nova heard none of it. Something had come undone in her mind. She had hung on so long by a single filament of purpose, and the moment she saw Kora's death, it snapped. The whisper broke free. It filled her head, her body, her soul, like the black water of the sea under ice, many worlds from here. Everything was roaring. Everything was slow. Kora's killer died. Nova felt her own blood pulsing in time to his arterial spurts, and even in the roaring slow motion of her shock, she thought he died far too quickly.

What now? Was there an after? Would time keep traipsing forward, indifferent? Nova wasn't ready for *after*. There was no "next," not for her. She had failed. This was all there was, only *this*, forever.

There was one last gift in her cohort that she hadn't yet commandeered: Rook's. She snatched it from him now and threw out her arms in a spell-casting motion.

As Sarai started back up the walkway, a faint iridescence, all but invisible, appeared in the air like a bubble around her father and Azareen.

"Sarai, no," said Lazlo. He gripped her hand, wanting to stop her, but she turned to smoke and slipped out of his grasp. She couldn't fathom what she had just witnessed. It couldn't be real. She was still trapped in Minya's dream. That had to be it.

If it was a nightmare, she could change it. She could *fix* it. She reached them and came up against the faint, shimmering sphere that enclosed them. It looked fragile as a soap bubble, but when Sarai went to push through it, she found she couldn't even get near it. A field of stillness seemed to surround it. There was no sensation of a physical barrier. She couldn't feel anything. Simply, the air redirected her movement, her will, like a slow running dream, so that no matter how hard she tried, she just couldn't get close to the two fallen Tizerkane. She cried out in frustration.

Their blood was flowing. It oozed out from under their breastplates, spreading over the walkway and dripping off the sides. "Father," said Sarai, for only the second time in her life. He was slumped over Azareen. Their eyes were open and unseeing and *dead*.

A sob choked up Sarai's throat. "No no no," she said. She felt hands on her back. Lazlo had followed her. He came to her side, his arms wrapping around her. She clung to him. Together they stared at the bodies, and over them at the invader.

At the murderer.

Today Sarai had finally met her father. He had spoken the word *daughter* and filled an empty place inside her, and now it was empty again. He was dead at her feet. He was *dead*.

. . . wasn't he?

Eril-Fane *moved*. Sarai was staring across his body at Nova when a movement caught her eye. She looked down and beheld the incredible sight of her father sitting up. He had slumped. Now he straightened. Sarai caught a glimpse of Azareen's eyes that a moment before had been lifeless, and they were *not lifeless*, not anymore. They were haunted, bleary, fierce, imploring, and unmistakably alive. She sat up, too.

There was a moment when it was possible to hope.

Eril-Fane and Azareen were alive. It could not be denied. But some part of Sarai froze and waited, feeling nothing, holding off relief, because the dead don't come back to life. Who knew that better than she? But more than that, it was the way the two were moving. It didn't make sense. They had subsided to the floor. To pick themselves up, they ought to have had to push up with their arms. But they didn't. They rose up like they were on strings, and . . . and *their blood*.

The blood that had pooled around them and was running in rivulets off the walkway, it was flowing back *up* them, back *into* their armor.

Their blood was pulsing back into their bodies.

Sarai and Lazlo didn't understand what they was seeing, not when it seemed as though Eril-Fane pushed Azareen backward to teeter at the edge of the walkway, or when she regained her balance, or when their swords, which they had dropped, flew back up from the floor far below to clatter against the walkway and then...jump back into their hands?

From the corner of their eyes, they saw a bloody blue streak. It was the stinger, flying back at them. Sarai gasped when it reentered Azareen's back and burst out through her chest before cutting again through Eril-Fane. His blood that had painted her...it peeled away from her and was sucked back inside him, and the stinger exited between his shoulder blades and shot backward, bloodless now, to the wasp whence it had first come.

"...*what?*" breathed Sarai, speechless.

Her father was only a few feet in front of her. She clearly saw that there was no hole now in his bronze backplate. It was unpierced, as though nothing had happened.

"...*how?*" asked Lazlo.

They understood that they were witnessing magic. The bubble, the field of energy. The invader possessed this gift, the extraordinary ability to *turn back time*. And she had used it to *unkill* her victims. They understood, but they didn't trust it.

And they were right not to.

Time snapped back and it all played out again, precisely as it had before. The stinger, the blood, the dropped swords. Azareen teetered at the edge. Eril-Fane caught her and pulled her to him. He said, "Azareen. I wish..." They collapsed to their knees.

"What? My love," Azareen pleaded. "What do you wish?"

He hadn't answered before, and he didn't now. Again, as before, they died.

Then it all reversed and happened *again*.

Eril-Fane died with his wish unspoken on his lips, its irony bitter on his tongue. *I wish we could start all over again.* That was what he'd wanted to say to his wife. He meant start a new life—together. Instead it was death they would share. Again.

And again.

And again.

* * *

Nova couldn't stop. There was nothing after this. So she just *kept on killing him.*

* * *

Rook's gift was to close off a loop in space and time—a small space, a short time—so that events trapped inside happened over and over until he opened it again. Or, until Nova did, as the case may be. With her hands, in that spell-casting gesture, she had sketched the bubble around her sister's killer. Everything inside it was trapped in the loop. It stretched from the moment the stinger disengaged from the wasp to when it fell, bloody, to the floor of the chamber—around five seconds, all told. It was meant for him, but it caught Azareen, too, because she'd gotten in the way. And so over and over they played out their deaths, aware every second of what was happening, but powerless to break the cycle. Each time the stinger cut through them, the pain burned through them anew. And each time their vision dimmed and life ebbed, the other's anguished face was the last thing they saw.

The first time Rook ever used his gift, he'd been five years old, in the nursery. One of the toddlers had vomited right in Great Ellen's lap. He'd thought it was funny, and wanted to see it again. When it happened again, he'd had no idea it was his doing. Then it happened *again*, and kept happening, all while Great Ellen grew red with rage, and the toddler's eyes streamed frantic tears. It quickly stopped being funny.

And then it *really* wasn't funny, because Korako came and took Rook away.

She'd brought him *here*, to this very room, as she brought Werran and Kiska after him, and hundreds before him, thousands. It was surreal for the three of them to be back in this hangar and see the wasp ships on the wall. They couldn't see the cages within, but they would never forget them, or all that had come after. And they could never betray Nova, who had saved them.

She looked so much like Korako that the first time they saw her, they had thought she *was* her. But Korako had put them in cages. Nova had gotten them out. She'd killed the men who kept the keys, and anyone else who came looking for them, until finally they were left alone.

"Where did they take you?" Sarai had asked. "Are all the others alive, too?"

What was, to her, a mystery was Kiska, Rook, and Werran's life. And yet even *they* couldn't answer the second question. The others, all those taken before—were they alive? Maybe. Probably. Some of them, anyway.

As to the first question, they were taken to the island in the wild red sea, and transferred from the cages in the wasp ships to larger cages there. When Rook was brought, he the first of the three, all the cages were empty, and he was all alone—except for the guards with their lightning prods, that is, which they employed liberally to discourage him from even thinking about using his gift. Those were the worst days of his life by far: five years old, alone in a cage in a row of empty cages. There were signs that other children had been kept there. He'd wondered at Topaz, taken before him, and Samoon and Willow before her, but he hadn't understood until much later: There had been an auction just before he came.

The others had already been sold.

And there it was, the truth at the dark heart of it all. Two hundred years of tyranny, and it all came down to *this*: Skathis, so-called god of beasts, was breeding magical children to sell as slaves across dozens of worlds. In the wake of the empire's collapse, wars had broken out all over as factions fought for dominance like pit dogs all turned loose at once. Who wouldn't pay a king's ransom for a girl who could stir up the sea just by looking, and drown the whole enemy navy in an hour? Who wouldn't bid on a child who could pass through walls and murder foes in their sleep, or marshal scourges of insects, read minds, shake the earth, persuade, teleport, control wind?

Skathis amassed a fortune, all while living as a god and siring bastards to sell as slaves to the highest bidder. Several times a year he held an auction. Buyers came from worlds away, paid princely sums, and took home children to fight their wars for them. Rook was the first of what would have been the new lot, to be sold at the next auction. Werran came soon after, then Kiska, then...no one. No more godspawn came after Kiska. Because the portal never opened again.

Nova arrived soon after, and she set the three of them free. She was too late to free her sister, but she had never given up the belief that she would. Now Rook saw that it was all that had been holding her together. He exchanged a grim glance with Werran and Kiska, troubled by the ruthless death loop. They'd come here hot with the wrath of their youth, ready to look into the eyes of the monsters who'd bred them and sold them like litters of puppies, but the monsters were gone, dead already, and Nova was killing humans. She was killing them over and over.

They didn't know what to do.

Sarai tried to interfere with the loop. Lazlo wanted to help, but she made him stay back. "They can't hurt me," she said. "I'm already dead. You're not." She didn't add that Minya wasn't there to catch his soul if he died. "I can't lose you, too."

She edged forward, watching the stinger's trajectory, thinking that if she timed it right she could push her father and Azareen clear so the stinger passed by them, breaking the cycle while they were alive. But she couldn't get to them. She tried turning herself insubstantial, but it didn't help. There might as well have been an invisible wall. "Stop it!" she screamed at Nova.

Nova did not stop. Eril-Fane and Azareen kept on dying. The scene took on a numbing sameness, as though they weren't people but automata locked in a clockwork drama. Sarai couldn't bear it. She rose into the air, as she had before. She would *make* her stop. She had flown at her before as a nightmare, with teeth and claws and bloodred eyes. This time she took a different form. It wasn't one she knew well. She'd only seen her in dreams. In an instant, Sarai was no longer Sarai. Her cinnamon hair and blue eyes were gone, and her sunset lashes, her sprinkling of freckles, her full lower lip with the crease in the middle. In her place was another blue woman—with brown eyes and fair hair and pale brows, wearing a mesarthium collar.

Sarai became Korako as she'd looked in the nursery doorway, and she flew right up to Nova and screamed in her face. "Is this who you want? Is this who you're looking for?"

What did she expect? A snarl, more spiders, a heavy booted kick? She got none of that, but something far worse.

Nova's eyes had been burning with Ruby's fire, but the flames cleared in an instant and they were revealed: soft and brown and lambent with sudden *joy*. The wrathful goddess was transfigured. The change left Sarai breathless.

"*Kora?*" Nova asked, her voice quavering but bright with an eagerness that was childlike in its pure, naked vulnerability.

Sarai's own rage died like a smothered fire. Her remorse was instantaneous. This woman might be her enemy, and she might even now be tormenting people Sarai loved, but this was a cruelty she wouldn't wish on anyone—to be taunted with phantoms of the beloved dead, and given hope where there was none. She hadn't meant it. She wanted to take it back.

Nova reached out with trembling hands and laid her palms to Sarai's face—Sarai's face that was shaped into her dead sister's face. Her touch was unspeakably tender, and her smile unbearably sweet. She practically glowed with relief—as though she'd thought her reason for living lost, and been granted a last-second reprieve.

Sarai drew back and returned at once to her own form. "I'm sorry," she said quickly. "I'm not . . ."

Her words trailed away.

Again, Nova was transfigured, but not by hope this time. Sarai felt as though she were seeing into a bottomless well of anguish. She had the feeling of falling headlong into it, and she hardly knew if it was Nova's anguish or her own. For that instant, at least, they seemed one and the same, as though all anguish exists in the same deep well, no matter what loss or misfortune leads us to it. We might be at odds, hate each other, and desire each other's destruction, but in our despair, we are lost in the same darkness, breathing the same air as we choke on our grief.

If the anguish had been black before the false hope, what Nova felt after was indescribable. With a wail she flew at Sarai and wrapped her hands around her neck. Sarai became mist. Nova couldn't grab her. She couldn't strangle or strike her. She didn't know what Sarai was, but she was beyond trying to figure it out. All she wanted in that moment was to hurt her, and there was more than one way to do that.

Her mind lashed out like a whip and seized Kiska's power. Telepathy was a gift of great subtlety. It could infiltrate minds and sift memories, hear thoughts, feel emotions, plant ideas. Nova had no use for subtlety now. She turned it around and used it to pour all her pain into Sarai.

From the very first, back on Rieva, Nova's power had been like a lighthouse lens, amplifying the intensity of whatever gift she wielded. It had only grown since then. Now it was more like her name: *nova*, a star that steals energy from nearby stars and explodes into violent radiance.

Her pain exploded at Sarai. Like a blast, it blew her backward, out through the door to hit the wall of the passage and slide down to the floor.

Sarai had died and cremated her own body. She had known crippling nightmares and the misery of a people oppressed by bad gods. But she had never felt despair like this before. She felt flayed open, skinned and hacked apart and left for the flies and carrion birds, like the husks of dead creatures on a desolate beach at the bottom of a faraway world.

She buckled under its weight. A voice inside her told her to fight, but it was so faint, and she felt so heavy—*so alone*—and she knew she was lost. They all were. Her own feelings—any hope and courage that were in her—were washed away by the torrent of despair. Nothing and no one could save them now.

"What have you done?"

The voice barely registered. It was outside the misery. It couldn't possibly matter. Nothing mattered anymore.

"WHAT. HAVE. YOU. DONE?"

The voice was icing sugar and iron. Sarai blinked, shock searing a path through the haze of despair. She managed to turn her head.

And there stood Minya with her army behind her.

44

A PIRATE'S SMILE

Ghosts flooded into the heart of the citadel.

Nova and her cohort didn't know what they were. They were floating. They cascaded off the edge of the walkway, a rippling river of men and women buoyed on the air without boots like their own to countervail gravity. Most were old, their hair white, gray, or sparse, faces lined. But there were younger men and women, too, and even some children among them. They weren't wearing anything resembling armor, but they were formed up in ranks and moving with precision. They wielded knives and meat mallets. Some hefted big iron hooks. Others carried nothing, but had claws and fangs, and there seemed no end to their numbers. In they flowed, dauntless, expressionless. Inexplicable.

They were human. Their skin was brown, not blue. So what magic was making them *float*? There was no time to wonder. They attacked.

Nova met them with her stolen powers. Fireballs bloomed in her fists. She hurled them. They hit the leading edge of the oncoming assault and exploded in bursts of white flame. The soldiers—if that's what they were—ought to have been engulfed in fire, but they weren't. Sparks rained down, harmless. The flames died away, and the soldiers came on, unfazed.

Rook, Werran, and Kiska held their lightning prods before them, and they drew their short swords from their scabbards, but they had little faith in their weapons. These foes were not natural. Could they even be hurt?

Nova unleashed godsmetal next. She peeled strips from the curve of the walls, shaped them into scythe blades, and sent them spinning so fast they blurred. The soldiers ought to have been maimed, dozens at a swipe, but they didn't even bleed. Their flesh re-formed with every strike and they just kept on coming. They engaged.

There was a ringing of metal on metal as Rook and Werran parried the first blows.

Nova let go of Kiska's telepathy, and the torrent of despair dissipated. Sarai rose shakily to her feet in the passage. Ghosts were still pouring past her. Minya was standing stock-still. Her face was terrible, both bleak with hurt and dark with disgust. Her eyes were slits, her nostrils flared. She was flushed violet and breathing fast. Her little body was shaking with rage.

Sarai had never been so glad to see her. "We're under attack," she told her in a rush. "The orb. It's a doorway. They were waiting."

"You drugged me," seethed Minya through gritted teeth while her ghosts clashed in the air with an enemy she had not yet laid eyes on.

She had woken up alone on the floor, with a bad taste in her mouth and a worse one in her mind. In that first moment, she'd thought—*what else would she think?*—that the Godslayer must have attacked and won. Her mind had screamed and all she could think was that she'd failed again to protect her people—that she'd gotten the fight she wanted, and, unthinkably, lost, and lost them.

That had been a very bad moment. The next was...complicated, because she saw the green glass bottle, and the truth struck her backhanded. Her people were alive, and had betrayed her. It stole her breath. They'd drugged her and left her defenseless. They'd taken the Godslayer's side, and left her on the floor like dropped laundry. She'd picked up the bottle and hurled it at the wall, where it smashed into a million pieces. Then she'd turned on her heel and marched out of the bedroom, down her stairs, and out into the passage.

Her army was just as she'd left it, formed up in ranks in the gallery. The Ellens rushed to meet her and tried to placate her. "Now, let's not assume the worst, my love," Great Ellen had said in a warning tone. "They may have had their reasons."

"Where are they?" demanded Minya, ready to *spit* on their reasons.

But the Ellens didn't know where they were. They, too, were just waking up, and were as confused as she was. "Something's not right," said Less Ellen.

As soon as she'd voiced it, Minya knew it was true. The whole citadel was thrumming with a dark, unwelcome energy. "There's somebody here," she said.

She was furious at her family for what they'd done to her. But they were *hers*, and this was her home, and gods help anyone who interfered with either.

Now Sarai, stricken, said, "I'm sorry."

"*Shut up*," Minya spat. "I'll deal with you later."

And she followed her ghosts into battle.

Ruby, Sparrow, Feral, and Suheyla were still in the entrance to the chamber. Eril-Fane had wanted them to flee, but they'd been too stunned by his and Azareen's dying—and *dying* and *dying* and *dying*—and stood rooted by their horror. When Minya stalked past them, they were overwhelmed by relief at the sight of her.

Who'd ever have thought they'd be so glad to see Minya?

Lazlo stood halfway up the walkway. When Sarai had been hurled back, he'd spun to follow, but halted as the army came flooding in. He flashed hot and cold at the sight of them bearing down, remembering the last time, in the silk sleigh, when he had barely escaped with his life. They weren't coming for him this time, though. They parted around him and overwhelmed the invaders.

In the heart of the citadel, the battle raged. Nova held five gifts in her keeping: Lazlo's, Ruby's, Feral's, and Sarai's—though she still didn't know what Sarai's *was*—and Rook's. She lashed out with godsmetal, disarming soldiers only to see them turn monstrous and attack with their teeth instead. Rook, Werran, and Kiska were fighting with their lightning prods and short swords, but their thrusts went right through these foes, and fear was showing on their faces. Kiska was bleeding from a wound to her arm. Werran grappled with a little girl who'd gotten through his guard when he was too appalled to strike her. This was Bahar, nine years old, who'd drowned in the Uzumark and was always sopping wet. Rook saw her bite Werran, her teeth clamping down on his wrist, and he tried to drag her off, but she melted under his hands, somehow keeping her teeth in Werran's flesh. She ground down, savage. Werran gave a cry and Bahar wrested away his prod with unchildlike strength and turned it on Rook, sending a jolt of lightning through him that blacked his vision to null and sent him flying back into the open orb, his eyes rolling back in his head.

He didn't get up.

Nova knew fear such as she hadn't felt in many years. They were so outnumbered, and this enemy made no sense. They weren't flesh, or even magic. They swarmed at her with their blank faces and preternatural strength, and she deflected them with godsmetal, throwing up shields to protect herself and her cohort. She was on the defensive, losing ground. How could they be stopped? Werran's war cry, she thought, but she was stretched too thin, holding five gifts already, to seize it and use it on her own.

"Werran!" she barked. *"Now!"*

He dragged in breath, ready to comply.

But the breath rushed back out in a hard exhale. Werran didn't scream. He stared. Because the ranks of attackers had melted apart to reveal a figure in the doorway. She was neither floating nor wielding a weapon. She stood with her arms at her sides, head lowered, peering at them from the tops of her eyes with exquisite, unblinking animus. She was a child. She was so small, her wrists as thin as gnawed bird bones. Her hair was short and choppy, her garment in tatters, hanging loose off one shoulder to show a clavicle as frail as the shaft of a feather. Everything about the sight of her was improbable: her size, her stillness, her black-eyed wrath. But none of that was what stopped Werran's breath. He faltered because he *knew* her. So did Kiska. Rook, unconscious, would have known her, too. She was not forgettable, not even a little, and she had not changed in fifteen years.

"...*Minya?*" asked Kiska, her voice breaking.

Minya's brows knit together, then fell smooth as her face blanked with shocked recognition. Her ghosts paused, all as one, including Sarai. Lazlo had just reached her. He saw her expression freeze.

Nova saw, too. All the soldiers stopped moving at precisely the same moment, and, in a flash, she understood. Just like that, the army's orchestrated movements made sense. This enemy she couldn't hurt, these smoke soldiers she couldn't stop, they belonged to this fierce little creature. They were doing her bidding. This was her magic.

And suddenly, this unstoppable foe wasn't unstoppable anymore. With a pirate's smile of vicious delight, Nova reached out and stole Minya's gift.

45

IF STABBING WERE A DANCE

There was no way Nova could have known.

Nothing could have prepared her. She was a pirate, her gift rarer than rare, her magnitude off the charts. She'd ripped power from elementals, shape-shifters, war witches. She'd fought duels and battles and never been bested. But seizing this gift, she found out at once, was like taking hold of a mountain, and with a sharp little tug, pulling it down on her own head.

It was *impossible*, the weight of it. A wave of blackness rolled across her vision, threatening to churn her under. She fought it with every fiber of her being, knowing that if she lost consciousness now, she would never regain it.

With an effort of will that burst stars across her vision, she fought her way free of the dark. Staggering, she stared at the little girl in the doorway and couldn't fathom how she could hold such power. It was so much heavier than any gift she'd ever taken. She could feel it burning through her as though she were a candlewick. How was it possible for such a tiny thing to bear such magic and not be consumed?

* * *

If Nova was stunned by the weight of Minya's power, Minya was stunned by its loss.

She had gathered her souls one by one over years. The weight had built up gradually, and she'd built up a tolerance with it. She didn't know what she carried until it lifted. She didn't know that she was crushed until she wasn't. She couldn't remember what it had been like before, when she was just a girl, and not an anchor for ghosts. She wasn't like the others, using her magic only as needed—to light a fire, catch a cloud, send out moths, or grow the garden. She was using it *all the time*. If she let up, her ghosts would evanesce. There was no drawer she could put them in to give herself a rest, no hook she could tie their tethers to, to keep them in the world. It was just her, and the fist she imagined in her mind, with all those fine gossamers clutched in it.

Even in her rare snatched moments of sleep, she held on to them. She'd grown up under the burden of them—or rather, she'd *not* grown up. Minya used up every ounce of her energy in this colossal, incessant expenditure of power. She spent too much. She spent *everything*, and had nothing left over to grow on.

She *was* a candlewick, and her power was a fire burning her up every moment. But she was a candlewick that, by sheer cussedness, refused to be consumed.

Nova felt as though a mountain fell on her. Minya felt the same weight *lift*. The strain evaporated. As lungs fill with air, her body filled with life. She was as light as a dust mote, as buoyant as a butterfly. And it wasn't just the weight of the souls, but the incessant drag of their *hate-fear-despair*. All that clamor and misery *cut off*, and the quiet of its absence was as soft as velvet, and as deep and rich as the night sky.

She felt reborn. For a brief, amazed moment, she felt something like peace.

Then the panic set in. She was powerless. Her army was her might. Without it she was naught but bird bones and rage.

Minya and Nova faced each other across the heart of the citadel—the one stripped of magic, the other overwhelmed. The ghosts, for the moment, were still, as Nova grappled to bear up under the threatening tide of darkness. She had no choice but to let go of the other gifts she was holding, though she knew that once she did they would be turned against her. She released Rook's first, but not until after she severed the time loop and set Eril-Fane and Azareen free.

She didn't have to. She could have left it to keep on going and going, and would have, but she saw that Rook was regaining consciousness, and she knew that if she didn't break the loop, he would.

The thing about Rook's time loops: They didn't have to be opened in the same place as they'd been closed. That was the true beauty of his magic. It was for more than repeating an event over and over, or glutting a grieving goddess on vengeance. It was for reaching back in the flow of time—ten seconds at the most, but ten seconds could be *everything*—and saying: *No. I don't want that to happen.* And fixing it so it didn't.

Nova had made the loop *after* the stinger sliced through the two bodies. But she could, if she chose, break it open *before*. Rook would, if it were up to him.

Eril-Fane and Azareen could have lived.

But Nova had no mercy. Even under the crushing avalanche of Minya's magic, she held out for a second, then another, until the stinger cut its path, and blood painted its pattern, and the damage was done. Only then did she slash the loop so the bubble vanished and the capsule of trapped time spilled back into the flow, Eril-Fane's and Azareen's lives spilling with it.

As soon as it was done, she let Rook's gift go, and felt a scintilla of relief.

The others all saw what happened. No matter how terrible the loop, as long as the warriors kept coming back to life, there had been some hope, and now it was lost. This time when they slumped over, it was final. They didn't rise. Their blood flowed only outward, and there was just so much of it. Suheyla let out a cry and sagged against Feral, weeping. Lazlo stood with Sarai, who was frozen along with the rest of the ghosts. It was Sparrow who pelted down the walkway, heedless of danger, to try to press on the wounds as the warriors bled out.

Nova let go of Ruby's and Feral's gifts next, and they felt their return like missing pieces slammed back in place, and immediately called on them. Ruby kindled fireballs, and Feral clawed a thunderhead out of a far-off sky. Sarai's gift returned, too, but it was useless as a weapon, even if she hadn't been frozen with all the ghosts.

Nova struggled to wield Minya's power. It was so big it was like trying to ride a wild creature that wanted to swallow her whole. She knew she couldn't keep it, or it would annihilate her. And she couldn't let it go, or the little girl would. The solution was simple. She'd done it countless times before, starting back at the beginning, with Zyak and Shergesh.

She managed to turn some of the ghosts toward Minya. She made them raise up their knives.

Minya's eyes grew wide, and in a startled split second she got an inkling of the powerlessness she had inflicted on others. If stabbing were a dance, it would look like this: a score of blades flashing in flawless unison. They had her surrounded. She stood there, stunned, as they arced toward her.

Lazlo didn't think. He just moved. He grabbed her from behind and turned away, holding her like a doll against him. His linen shirt stretched taut across his shoulders as he curled over her to shield her with his body.

To shield her with his own body.

Sarai, unable to move, watched the blades stammer to a halt mere inches from his back.

Nova almost didn't manage to stop them. The effort used up the last of her strength the way a gasp uses up breath. She felt the rumble of thunder, saw the flash of a fireball, and knew time was up. She had to end this. *Now.*

* * *

Down in Weep, Thyon and Ruza, Calixte and Tzara were still out in the courtyard watching the citadel. They weren't poring over the Thakranaxet, or eating bacon, or even bickering. They were leaning back in their chairs, staring fixedly up at the great seraph overhead. They didn't know what was going on up there, but they knew one thing: Eril-Fane, Azareen, and Suheyla had been gone too long. And with their minds full of worlds, slashed skies, and angels' maps, they wouldn't be easy until they returned.

So they were all looking up, and all of them saw the seraph move. It was just a twitch of its fingers first, then its whole massive arm suddenly bent at the elbow, reached in, and tore open its own chest.

❧ 46 ❧

LIKE A MAN TEARING OUT HIS OWN
BEATING HEART

Nova wasn't delicate. She wasn't careful. The godsmetal thrummed all around her, alive. Earlier, the lightest skim of her will had been enough to shape it. But she was beyond all lightness now.

She wrenched open the citadel's chest and it reached inside itself like a man tearing out his own beating heart. But it wasn't a heart it tore out. It was people—humans, corpses, godspawn, ghosts. The huge metal hand reached in, and the metal walls and walkway turned liquid and caught them, conspiring to drag them into its cupped palm.

Nova couldn't hold out any longer. She released Minya's gift. The relief was tremendous.

There was a myth, back on Rieva, about Lesya Dawnbringer who held up the sky. Every day she lifted it over her head, and only at dusk could she let it fall. But at Deepsummer, the sun didn't set for a month, and she had to hold it for all that time.

When Nova let Minya's power go, she thought her relief had to be like Lesya's, when night finally came and she could shrug off the sky.

She had to get rid of the girl and ghosts fast, before they could retaliate. She made the seraph's hand close over them in a fist and ripped them out into the sky.

Sarai thought it would drop them. She was sliding over smooth metal, first one way, then the other. She tumbled in a tangle of limbs. Metal was above and below her. She heard Ruby cry out. Someone caught her hand for a brief moment and tried to hold on to it. Was it Lazlo? She couldn't tell. They were dragged apart, fingers straining. Their motion through the air was dizzying.

Then the hand opened. It tipped. She slid. She scrabbled for purchase. It was just like her fall, and in her panic she forgot she was a ghost now and could float. But what did that matter if Minya fell? If she died, so would Sarai. If the others all died, she wouldn't *want* to live. She saw Minya slipping over the edge, and tried to catch her hand. She missed.

Minya went over.

Sarai went numb. This couldn't be happening.

Feral was next. Arms flailing, face shocked, he vanished over the side. There was nothing to hold on to. The hand had turned sideways, and was fully vertical now. The others fell, too, every one of them. For a moment, Sarai was alone on the hand. She clung out of fear, her memory of her last fall pounding in her mind. Then she let go and fell, too.

Before, it had seemed an eternity of falling before she hit and broke and died. This was no eternity. Almost at once, the ground rushed up, hard. She rolled, every joint jarring, before coming to rest with limbs splayed out, her vision blurred and spinning.

From inside the fist it had been impossible to see. The seraph had descended, knelt on the cushion of its magnetic fields, and reached down into the city. It hadn't dropped them out of the sky, but rolled them like dice into the amphitheater in the center of Weep. It wasn't gentle, but it wasn't death—Sarai hoped.

She looked around at her scattered loved ones. She saw Eril-Fane's and Azareen's bodies splayed out. Sparrow was between them, bleeding from a gash on her brow. Feral was crawling to Suheyla, who wasn't moving, and Ruby was staring around wide-eyed at the empty market tents, and the tiered walls of the amphitheater surrounding them. Minya was on her hands and knees, shaking. Her head hung down. Sarai couldn't see her face. Her ghosts were all around her.

But where was Lazlo?

Sarai whipped around, eyes darting, frantic, desperate for the sight of him. She turned a full circle, then another, trying to keep panic at bay. But she couldn't. Panic took hold with claws.

Lazlo wasn't here.

The enemy—the magic thief, the murderer—had kept him.

PART IV

* * *

torvagataï (tor·vah·guh·tai) *noun*

When an extraordinary feat is accomplished, after time has already run out.

Archaic; from the tragedy of Torval, the hero who performed three impossible tasks to win the hand of his love, Sahansa, only to return to find her kingdom annihilated and every last man, woman, and child slain.

🌿 47 🌿

A Secret with a Secret

I would have chosen you, if they had let me choose.

Kora and Nova had memorized their mother's letters—which they had cause to be glad of after Skoyë burned them—and that was the part that meant the most. *I would have chosen you.* They'd needed to believe they'd been loved. They hadn't really wondered about the "they" and the "let," or who had made Nyoka's choice for her—or, indeed, whether she was ever free to make a choice again.

After what happened in the wasp ship, they wondered.

"What are you going to do with us?" Kora had asked Skathis after her sister's gift exploded into chaos. She'd been cradling Nova's inert form, more afraid than she'd ever been in her life. She'd thought surely the smith would kill them. The most she could have hoped was that he'd leave them behind—that their dream would die, but they would not. Even then, as she crouched in her torn smallclothes on the cold metal floor with her unconscious sister in her arms, it hadn't occurred to Kora that they could be separated.

"You are no longer an *us*," Skathis told her before melting open the floor under Nova so she fell—right out of Kora's arms and out of the ship to land hard on the ground below. "No!" Kora had screamed, but the floor closed as quickly as it had opened, and Skathis told her, with icy satisfaction, "You're mine now. Your only 'us' is with *me*."

Kora didn't understand then what that meant, but she would. She would come to understand it the way a bird understands its cage, or a slave her shackle. Those words would define the rest of her life, every moment of it for more than two hundred years.

You're mine now. Your only "us" is with me.

Together with Nova, she had built a vision of the future, in which they would be soldier-wizards, never again at the mercy of men like their father. They'd had such dreams of what it would be like, imagining the academy Nyoka had described for training the gifted like themselves. It was full of powerful Mesarthim youth from all over the world—the best and the brightest. They would serve the empire together with honor, see worlds and fight battles, win treasure and know glory.

They had dreamed it all in such detail.

In fact, their dreams were stunningly close to the truth. The academy was just how their mother had described it, but Kora never saw it.

Skathis might have been recruiting for the imperial service, but he never delivered her into it. When they reached the capital, he had words with Solvay, Antal, and Ren, and, whatever he said to them, they went pale, and did not interfere when he kept Kora for himself. He made her spy for him. He was not a patient teacher. He directed her where to send her eagle, what and whom to look and listen for. Some nights he left after.

But not all.

She was confined to his quarters in the wasp ship. She thought he must have had rooms in the city, because he'd leave and sometimes be gone for days, and she would play a game of asking herself if she'd rather he came back or not, because if he didn't, she would die trapped here, and if he did, well. He always did, and there were times when she'd rather have wasted away and died alone.

He told her that if she ever defied him or tried to escape, failed to do his bidding, or sent unsanctioned messages out with her eagle, he would fly straight to her miserable island and make her pirate sister sorry she'd ever been born.

Kora didn't doubt him. There was a look in his eyes as though he hoped she'd make him do it, so she was careful never to anger him, and this became her life. She was a secret, a slave, and a spy. She saw no one but him, at least not with her own eyes. Through her eagle, she explored Aqa, and came to know the city and its players: the emperor and his advisors, and, most of all, the other smiths. At first, none of it made any sense to her—their talk, which Skathis made her relay to him word for word, or the layers of meaning underlying it, but she wasn't stupid. If her mind had been empty of understanding of the world—*worlds*—it began to fill in, layer by layer. There was subterfuge and scheming, and there was so much *ending*.

Reports coming back through the portals told of uprisings, and of mercenary armies, too long unpaid, turning on the emperor. They told of governors murdered, and worlds allying to throw off the empire's yoke, as revolutions ignited like a chain of firecrackers. All this instability was like blood in the water, and Skathis wasn't the only smith who swam in it. Kora came to know the others as she spied on them, and they reminded her of the beaked sharks that thrashed in the shallows during the Slaughter back home.

She thought of Nova and her chest felt hollow, as though someone had shoved an oyster blade between her ribs, cracked them open, and slurped out her heart. Determined to keep her sister safe, she did everything Skathis told her. She sent out her eagle, and her sight and senses with it. It could pass through stone, brick, even steel, but not mesarthium. They learned that early on. But all godsmetal ships, and even the emperor's floating metal palace, had small openings for ventilation, and she could pass through those, no matter how small. The eagle could fade almost to nothing, so that it was no more than a glimmer, and it could hear, see, and even steal—tokens and paperwork, maps, messages bearing the royal seal.

It could even steal a godsmetal diadem right off the brow of a dead Servant, and it did. Or, rather, *Kora* did. Her bird wasn't an *it*, but a projection of herself. *She* stole the diadem, after Skathis, acting on her information, ambushed a rival smith, slew him and his whole cohort, and assumed possession of his battleship.

Kora hid the diadem. The crime—stealing godsmetal—was so extraordinary. Once upon a time, the mere thought would have sent her into a panic. But it paled to insignificance next to espionage, treason, and murder. But what to do with it, once she had it?

Her sister had always been a force of nature, even before her gift manifested. If anyone could save Kora, it was her, and she was surely the only person in the world who cared to. Kora fantasized about it: Nova arriving like an avenging goddess and strangling Skathis with his own precious metal.

Kora still wore the collar he'd put on her. He never did take it off. Only another smith could get her free of it—another smith, that is, or Nova.

The more she thought about it, the more she built up her sister as an unstoppable avenging force. But how could she get the diadem to her? How long would it take her eagle to fly there and back? Days? She didn't have days. Skathis could come anytime. If he found her eagle away, he wouldn't rest until he knew where she'd sent it.

388

And so the diadem stayed hidden, until the day that Kora discovered her eagle could...pierce space.

That was what it felt like: cutting through the fabric of space so that distance lost all meaning. There were Servants who could do it. They called it teleportation. They could will themselves from one side of the world to the other, and vanish and appear there instantaneously. If Kora had had training at the academy, they would no doubt have teased out this aspect of her ability, but as it was, she was left to discover it alone and under duress, when she sent out her eagle on her own.

This was forbidden. She was to use her gift only at Skathis's command, but she began to defy him. So she would go out through the air shafts and fly, where no one could see her, and the air and boundless space of the sky kept her sane when the metal walls felt more like coffin than cage, and even her body felt like a prison.

It was a kind of escape. She could pour herself out, leave all her helplessness and weakness behind. And one night, after Skathis left her, she let her soul drift farther up into the crystal-cold ether than she had ever dared before. She was remembering what Antal of the white hair had said: how the first astral had claimed he could voyage through the stars. And that's when Skathis returned, unexpected. Kora panicked, and the next instant the bird was back, effusing into her chest. She was so shocked she hardly knew what had happened, except that she hadn't been caught. She'd been miles away and snapped back in an instant.

She tested it later, when she regained her nerve. It was real: Her eagle could travel any distance in a blink, melting through the air as though space were just another wall.

She kept it secret. She was a secret with a secret. Finally, she dared to take the diadem to Nova with the message: *Find me. I am not free.*

But Nova never found her. And Kora was never free.

She had thought that Skathis would make himself emperor, but he didn't. He said, "I'd rather be a god," and he killed the other smiths one by one, and finally the emperor, too, and he took their metal as the empire collapsed, and he took his ship—now the biggest that had ever been, shaped, in irony, like an angel—and flew it through portal after portal, world after world, until he found the one that suited him.

Zeru existed just beyond the edge of the empire's farthest expansion, and, as such, its people did not know of Mesarthim. There, Skathis and his crew could play gods to their hearts' content, and that was just what they did, crushing a beautiful and ancient civilization into a slave people, stealing their children, their memories, their freedom, and forcing Kora—now Korako—to play a part. She was no longer confined to the wasp ship. Skathis had other means of controlling her, and not just her collar, but Isagol, his lover. His *willing* lover, that is, alone of the many who bore that...distinction. Isagol was different. She was his accomplice in cruelty, his counterpart in depravity. They goaded each other to new lows, punished each other, grew bored and came up with new games to play. If ever Kora showed any defiance, Isagol reached inside her and deposited small gifts of emotion, such as terror or her specialty, despair.

The worst, though, was lust. She could make Kora go mad with it, and every time she did, and Kora was caught in a sick pantomime of desire—and its abominable fulfillment—it left a rotten place, like a bruise on fruit, somewhere on her soul.

Letha did her part, too. She had a way of rooting out one's most cherished memories. They called to her, somehow, as the scent of blood calls to beasts. She threatened to devour every memory of Nova. "I'll make you forget you ever had a sister."

And anyway, there was no escape. Skathis sealed the portal with a godsmetal orb. Kora was trapped in this world called Zeru, one of six monstrous "gods," and forced to spy as ever, though she only told Skathis what she wished him to know, and was consistently negligent, over the years, in the matter of the warriors training in the river caverns underground.

The irony would not be lost on her when one of those very warriors put a knife through her heart. But that was much, much later, and she couldn't blame him for it.

At first, Skathis had no purpose in Zeru beyond godhood and debauchery, but that changed. Later, he would claim it was all by design, but that was a lie. He was a rapist for fun before he began to turn a profit.

It was the children—the ones born to the first of the unfortunate human women in the citadel's sinister arm. That "gods" should claim concubines was to be expected. That children would result was only natural.

That the children should be special, now, *that* was a surprise.

Over centuries of empire, plenty of half-breeds had been born in dozens of different worlds. Some had no gift at all, no apparent receptivity to the magic in their blood. At best, they might test for a weak gift, though under imperial law half-breeds had been forbidden to serve.

But every blue bastard born to a human mother in Zeru tested at a magnitude as high or higher than his or her Mesarthim parent. And considering that Skathis's crew were all of exceptional magnitude, this was something extraordinary. Kora thought maybe it was because of the mysterious, clear fluid, spirit, that flowed alongside their blood. As far as she could tell, it was the only anomaly that set these humans apart from others who fit in that broad taxonomy.

Whatever the reason, if Skathis had still been recruiting for the empire, he could not have found a better source of soldier-wizards for the ranks. But there was no more empire. In its place there were worlds at war—with one another, within themselves, too many wars to count, and more starting every day. And where there's war, one thing's certain: There are kings or generals or potentates willing to pay for weapons.

So Skathis sold his bastards off and set about making more. Vanth and Ikirok were pleased to aid in the effort. Over the years, Isagol and Letha both took human lovers and birthed babies themselves, though they were far less efficient bastard-makers than their male counterparts, and that was fine. There were women enough in the city for that.

Skathis had an outpost built on a broken-off tezerl stalk growing out of the red sea just the other side of the portal, and he held auctions there. Buyers came from as far off as Mesaret itself, and Skathis, the god of beasts, began to amass a fortune. He sold shape-shifters and elementals, seers, healers, soporifs, every kind of warrior. There were gifts that had no application in war, but he put every child on the block—almost every child—and the leftovers were bought at a discount by traders, to be sold off down the line, wherever they might be wanted.

One gift never made it to the block. Smiths could be identified as babies. They had only to touch godsmetal and their little fingers would leave marks in its surface. These babies he slew.

And so years passed, and Kora was given the task of testing the children and taking them to the wasp ship and locking them up in the little cages. And every time she did, she died a little more, and she might have chosen to die in body as well as spirit were it not for one thing. She dreamed that her sister was still looking for her. She

392

had only to imagine Nova arriving too late, coming to save her only to find that she'd taken her own life, and she wouldn't be able to do it. She stayed alive.

And one day a baby boy in the nursery manifested smith ability. Kora snatched him. She *stole* him, and sent him, in her eagle's grip, through pierced space to a place far away where Skathis wouldn't find him.

She hadn't planned it. It was luck. But once she had the baby, it all began to take shape in her mind: her mutiny. The boy would grow up, not knowing what he was, and one day she would bring him back, and he would set her free. She daydreamed of murdering Skathis. If his hobby was breeding slave children, hers was dreaming up his death.

She planned to wait until the baby grew into his power. Then she would bring him back—to fight the gods and kill them, and open the portal and fly her through it. She had it all planned out.

But it wasn't to be.

Because Eril-Fane killed her with the rest of the gods, and the little boy was cast adrift without a single soul knowing what he was. And all that survived of Kora was a shred of her soul in the form of an eagle, which went on as it always had, circling, watching, and waiting for the day when it could finally escape, and go home— wherever that was now.

Because home was and had always been Nova, and Kora died believing her sister would come.

48

They Beheld Abominations

The citadel of the Mesarthim had come alive in the sky. It had ripped its chest open and reached inside, grabbed a handful of people, then knelt—a giant, wings flaring, dwarfing the city—leaned down, and tossed them like litter.

Lazlo was not among them.

When the hand had thrust into the chamber, and the metal, flowing, had swept everyone into it, he had tried to follow. He'd seen Sarai and reached for her, but the metal hadn't let him. *Nova* hadn't let him. She still held his power, and she kept him here. He was sunk to his knees in the walkway, trapped. He struggled but couldn't pull free. He could only watch as the hand drew away, taking everyone he cared about with it.

"*Sarai!*" he screamed till his throat went raw.

Now they were gone and he was still here. He watched in horror as Nova set about doing what he himself had planned to do, but with none of the care he would have taken. She pulled up the anchors one by one. The seraph maneuvered to set a foot on each in turn—east anchor, south, then west. Metal adhered to metal, and she ripped them up, heedless of the buildings around them, which swayed and toppled, sending up billows of dust as the citadel resorbed the mesarthium and grew larger.

Nova turned last to the melted north anchor, and Lazlo tried to stop her.

"Leave that one," he pleaded. With his gift gone, he could no longer sense the metal holding the fractured bedrock together, but he remembered. He had done it, and he knew what would happen if she ripped it out. "The ground will collapse," he said, looking in desperation to Kiska, Rook, and Werran, as though they might care, or intercede. "The river will flood. The city could fall. *Please.* Just leave it."

But Nova did not.

Like a beautiful nightmare, the seraph crouched over Weep. It plunged its massive fingers into the sinkhole, gouging down into the rock to find and suck up every dram and rivulet of mesarthium. The ground began to tremble and crack. The sinkhole grew. Its sides collapsed. Huge chunks of stone calved away, and the foaming churn of the Uzumark broke free. Rows of buildings were sucked underground, including the ancient library so recently unearthed. The roar was distant. Plumes of spray and dust fountained up, filling the air with haze.

From above, to Lazlo's horrified eyes, it looked like a toy city falling to pieces. "No!" he choked as the devastation spread, block after block collapsing into ruin as the river chewed its way out of the ground like some hell-banished creature seeking the light.

How far would the destruction reach? How much of the city would crumble? Was the amphitheater safe? Were Sarai and the others?

Lazlo wasn't to know. The citadel righted itself in the air and he could see only sky through the hole in its hull. Weep's fate—and Sarai's—was hidden from him. "Let me go!" he begged his captors. "Leave me here!"

Nova didn't even look at him. She didn't look at anyone. Her eyes had gone out of focus. A veil of exhaustion had fallen over her. Ashen-faced and heavy-lidded, she undertook her grandest feat of piracy yet. Skathis's ship was the largest concentration of godsmetal that there had ever been. It was the most powerful vessel in the Continuum. There wasn't a force in any world that could touch it in battle. And now it was hers.

With a deep breath, she began the task of moving it through the portal to the world on the other side.

* * *

The earth shook under Sarai. A dull roar sounded from all directions. What was happening? Was the city coming down? She couldn't see over the walls of the amphitheater, but only up at the sky, where the seraph was moving like a creature of mercury, rippling in the sun.

She saw its right hand attenuate, fingers stretching, thinning. It was a moment before she understood what it was doing. It was feeding itself through the gash in the sky. It was *leaving the world*. It was leaving them behind. It was going fast, pulsing like blood through a tube. In a matter of seconds it had vanished to the wrist, just like Lazlo's when he thrust his hand through the warp. Sarai realized that her terrace, where she had paced every night, must now be above the ghastly red sea. Soon all the rest would follow, and Lazlo with it.

Lazlo.

She couldn't catch her breath. It was all too much. Her father was dead. Azareen too. Her home was stolen, and Lazlo was taken. The rest of them had been jettisoned here. She could hardly process this basic fact: She was in Weep.

A thought hit her like a sobering slap. Everything else went quiet, all other fears blurring to background. She was in Weep, yes. But more to the point, *Minya* was.

Minya was in Weep.

This was just what the little girl had wanted, what she'd threatened Sarai's soul for, what they'd all tried so hard to prevent. Minya was in Weep with her army. Sarai turned slowly to face her. She had been on her hands and knees, her head hanging down. Not now. She'd gotten to her feet. Her stance was wide. Her hands were fists. She was still shaking, almost shuddering, her thin little chest heaving under her ragged shift. Her ghosts were fanning out to form a protective ring around the strewn godspawn and humans. They were just closing the circle when the Tizerkane warriors came pouring into the amphitheater and had them surrounded in seconds.

There were scores of them. Their movements were fluid and seemed too quiet for such imposing figures as they. Their armor was bronze, their helms tusked. They carried swords and spears. The spectral-mounted towered over the rest, and the creatures' branching antlers shone in the late-day sun.

There were men and women, both young and not. Their faces were hard, their color high. They were hiding their terror as best they could, but Sarai knew their fear as well as her own. She had nurtured it with nightmares, never letting it fade. Their hate they didn't even try to hide. It was etched into every line of their faces. They breathed through bared teeth. Their eyes were slits. The way they looked at the godspawn, it was brutally clear: It wasn't young people they saw, survivors, half human, afraid. They beheld abominations.

No. It was worse than that. They beheld abominations with blood on their hands.

Sarai saw the scene as they would see it. Ghosts and godspawn would have been bad enough, even without the corpses. But there were Eril-Fane and Azareen, laid out so still, limbs askew, and Sparrow—sweet Sparrow who would never hurt anyone—was kneeling between them, ashen-pale, eyes closed, her arms red to her elbows as though she were wearing blood gloves.

Gentle Sparrow looked like a ghoul who fed on the hearts of heroes.

Shock ripped through the warriors. At a barked command, they raised their spears. A hundred arms cocked back as one. There was such power in the motion—the collective strength of a people who had borne so much and would risk no more, forgive nothing, and show no mercy. Their hate, already blazing, burned hotter.

A movement from above drew Sarai's eye upward to the tiered heights of the amphitheater. Archers had taken up positions, and were sighting down their arrows straight at them.

Dread lanced through her. It looked as though Minya was getting her fight.

But could anyone survive it?

❦ 49 ❦

GOOD LITTLE GIRLS DON'T KILL. THEY DIE.

Minya was reeling. She was not herself. To have felt that lightness—the weight of souls lifted—even for a minute, had stunned her. And the *hate-fear-despair*. She hadn't known how pernicious it was until it ceased.

For a moment she'd known lightness and silence, and then it all slammed back—the souls and their despair, crushing her once more, all the heavier now that she knew. She was staggering, aware for the first time of the toll she paid every second for her magic.

It was so much. And there was more. There was just *so much*, all spinning and crashing around in her head:

She was aching at the betrayal of waking up on the floor, discarded by her own people.

She was aghast at the invasion, and gutted, gasping with disbelief, to find herself defeated, cast out, dispossessed.

When Minya won at quell, she upended the game board and sent the pieces flying, so the loser had to crawl around on hands and knees to gather them up. Now, down on the ground for the first time in her life, her bare feet not on metal but stone—she felt keenly: *She* was the loser. Nova had upended the board, and *she* was one of the scattered pieces.

But who would gather her up?

She had a flash memory of Lazlo grabbing her and holding her against him to shield her from her own ghosts' knives, and it joined the crashing, spinning whirl in her head. He'd saved her. He'd risked himself. He'd *held* her. No one had touched Minya on purpose for a long, long time, let alone held her, and even now, after the fact and in the midst of all this, the feeling of arms and strength and safety overwhelmed her.

Of course, she told herself, he'd done it for Sarai's sake, not hers. Who would ever save her for her own sake?

And anyway, Lazlo wasn't here now. It was up to her to save them. It always had been. But how? The air pulsed with tension. You could *feel* the drawn bowstrings, the flex of scarred knuckles, the warriors' hissed breath, and their sharp desire to let go, to let fly.

To *kill.*

Minya felt it all. The humans' hate spoke and hers answered.

When a hundred sets of eyes pin you in place, and all of them see the same thing, how can you not *be that thing*? The Tizerkane looked at children and saw monsters, and Minya's darkest self rose to the challenge. It was her oldest, truest reflex:

Have an enemy, be an enemy.

The Tizerkane captain barked out a command. "Lay down your weapons. *Now!*"

The ghosts were gripping kitchen knives, cleavers. They were paltry weapons against spears, swords, and bows, but Minya knew her army's strength, and it wasn't in their steel. "Lay down *yours!*"

she hollered back, and her high bell voice was absurd after the low, rough depths of his. "And I might let you live."

A rough murmur rumbled through the Tizerkane troops.

"Minya," Sarai said, frantic. "Don't. *Please.*"

Minya turned to her sharply. "Don't *what?* Keep us alive? You want me to be a *good little girl* like you, Sarai? Let me tell you something. If I was a good little girl, we'd have died in the nursery with all the rest!"

Sarai swallowed hard. Now that she'd been in Minya's dreams, those words had a meaning they wouldn't have before. She didn't know if she was right about the Ellens, but if she was, it was true what Minya said. Good little girls don't stab their nurses and drag toddlers over their corpses in order to save their lives. Good little girls don't kill. They *die.*

And Minya was not a good little girl.

"I know what you did for us," said Sarai. "And I'm grateful—"

"Spare me your gratitude. This is all your fault!"

"Now, pet," said Great Ellen, coming between them. "You know that's not fair. We're caught up in something older than ourselves and bigger than our world. How could it be all Sarai's fault?"

"Because she chose *them* and left me on the floor," said Minya, her anger only thinly covering her hurt. "And now look where we are."

Sarai did look, and she did wonder: *Was* it her fault? Maybe. But what happened now depended on Minya. "We're stranded and we're surrounded," she said. "We can't hide or retreat. Our only hope is to *not fight.* You must see that."

"Let me guess. You want to beg."

"Not beg, just talk."

"You think they'll listen to *us?*" Minya scoffed.

"I said, lay down your weapons!" the captain commanded, though he had to know that the ghosts themselves were the weapons, with

401

or without their knives. One might excuse him, though, for not knowing how to demand the surrender of a magical child with an undead army. Eril-Fane had chosen wisely when he put Brishan in charge. Any other commander would already have attacked. Even he wouldn't wait much longer. His voice grew harsh. "On the ground! I won't tell you again."

And they came to it: fight or surrender. Minya felt herself torn at by two possible outcomes, as though she were lashed to creatures straining in opposite directions, but she couldn't see what they were.

Fight, and what then? Sarai was right: They were stranded. It wasn't supposed to be like this. She had planned to sweep down on Rasalas, wreak her vengeance, and fly home to safety.

But her vengeance was stolen—Eril-Fane was dead—and so was home and safety. Overhead, so high and hopelessly out of reach, the citadel was *disappearing*.

The seraph was up to its shoulder now, one whole arm eaten away. That was what it looked like to her: as though the sky were *eating* the angel. Minya hadn't seen what the others had—the portal, and the world beyond it, or Lazlo's hand vanishing when he reached through the warp. She didn't know what was happening. Confusion pounded in her temples. She couldn't catch her breath. She felt light-headed, *frail*, as though her power, now that she understood its heft, had become too much for her to bear.

A slither of fear writhed through her. It left a cold trail. Could she win this fight? She'd lost once today already. If she lost again, there would be no pieces to pick up off the floor. This would be the last game she ever played.

Surrender, though? Put their fate in the hands of humans? Impossible. Minya had seen what humans did to godspawn. Surrender was simply not an option.

Sarai saw all of this play over her face. "*Minya*," she pleaded, her throat tight with mounting fear. "They'll kill us."

A ripple went through the ring of ghosts. Sarai braced for the worst, and was stunned when they dropped their knives without fanfare. Steel clattered and skittered over cobbles. She was dumbfounded. For an instant she almost believed they were surrendering.

Then their quicksilver substance transformed. *Wings* unfurled from their shoulders and flared open. They were wings of fire, each feather a flame. The ghosts took on the forms of seraphim, and out of magic and air, in their hands, spears appeared, and the same smile shaped all their lips. It was tight and grim. It was Minya's smile echoed across all their faces.

"They'll kill us no matter what we do," the little girl said. "And I'm going to take them with us."

🌿 50 🌿

More to the Story

Violence erupted in the amphitheater of Weep.

The Tizerkane hurled their spears. Fire-winged ghosts surged up to block them.

Any hope Sarai had of survival dissolved under the first clash of metal on metal. She looked up at the sky. The citadel was half gone. Her hearts cried out for Lazlo. She imagined she could hear his hearts crying out for her. It was all so unfair. They'd never had a chance—any of them. Their lives had come to them tangled in hate. They'd tried to untangle them and failed. And now?

The ghosts deflected the hurled spears with their own, and none made it through to the godspawn. The Tizerkane roared and attacked with their swords, and, up above, the archers loosed arrows. Sarai heard the twang of bowstrings from all sides, and felt a whisper of air by her cheek. Arrows are swifter than spears, and much smaller. The ghosts couldn't possibly block them all and the archers had the advantageous position. Sarai, gasping, looked around to see if anyone was hit. She saw Ruby and Feral looking wide-eyed and frantic, Suheyla between them, beginning to stir. Minya stood stock-still and furious, flanked by the Ellens. And Sparrow—

The instant Sarai's eyes lit on her, Sparrow jerked. She was on her knees between Eril-Fane and Azareen, and an arrow slammed into her back and threw her forward.

"*No!*" screamed Sarai, and rushed toward her. Where was she hit? She couldn't tell. *Please. Not her hearts, not anything vital*, she prayed as more arrows flew.

Sparrow was slumped across Azareen. Sarai reached her as she struggled to push herself up. "Stay down!" she told her, trying to shield her with her self.

"No," said Sparrow, pushing up with a cry of pain. The arrow had hit high, off-center, burrowing under her right shoulder blade. There was a lot of blood. It was vivid carmine. Against it her skin looked sickly pale. Sarai didn't think the wound was mortal—at least, not if it could be tended, and if it wasn't followed by another, and another.

If this battle didn't end in all their deaths.

An inner ring of ghosts rose like seraphim into the air, their fire wings outspread and overlapping. Minya used them to shield the godspawn. While they still couldn't block all the arrows, they could keep the archers from taking aim. But Sparrow was still right in the center of the circle, where there was least protection.

"Over here," said Sarai, putting an arm around her and urging her—gently—away from the bodies, to where Ruby, Feral, and Suheyla were huddled under cover of wings.

But Sparrow resisted. Again, she said, "*No.*"

In frustration, Sarai looked at her, prepared to be less gentle, if that's what it took to get her to cover. "Sparrow, it's not safe…" she began, and trailed off, but she saw her clearly and ran out of words. She had thought Sparrow was pale. But Sparrow wasn't pale. She was *gray*.

Sarai knew what that meant, but before she could make sense of it, a voice surged above the chaos.

"*HOLD YOUR FIRE!*" it boomed.

It was deep and rich. Sarai heard it, and knew it, and couldn't believe it for the obvious reason that it was impossible.

It was Eril-Fane's voice. But Eril-Fane was dead. He'd been pierced through the hearts. His body was right...

...*here?*

Sarai turned to where Eril-Fane's body was sprawled out on Sparrow's other side. Only it wasn't sprawled out anymore. It was—*he* was getting to his feet.

But *how?* The stinger had cut clean through his body. Sarai was no expert on wounds, but even she knew that one was mortal, and she'd seen how it ended the first time, before the time loop began. Their eyes had been lifeless. There had been no mistaking it. And yet her father was picking himself up off the ground. She stared, disbelieving, wanting it to be true, but unable to trust it. Was it the same magic as up in the citadel that had brought him back only to kill him again?

But that didn't make sense. The citadel was almost gone. Their enemies were far away.

And then the sickening realization struck her: Eril-Fane had an enemy right here. Of course. This was Minya's doing. It had to be. She'd captured his soul. He wasn't alive at all. This was just his ghost, under Minya's control.

But... if that was true, then where was his body?

Sarai felt dizzy. All the possibilities of life, death, and magic spun in her head. If Eril-Fane was a ghost, there would be two of him, as there had been two Sarais in the garden: ghost and corpse, side by side. But there was no corpse. There was only *him*—weak, in pain, covered in blood, but *alive*, and rising shakily to his feet.

"I said, *HOLD YOUR FIRE!*" he boomed again, and the rain of arrows stuttered to a stop. "Tizerkane, stand down!" he commanded. "These children are under my protection!"

A stark silence fell. Even the ghosts fell still as Minya stared at her foe, hate and confusion at war in her expression. All eyes were on the Godslayer.

All but Sparrow's. Hers were closed. Her breathing was shallow. The arrow jutted from her shoulder, and blood drizzled, brilliant, from her wound. All these things told a story—of a girl caught in crossfire—but there was more to the story, and Sarai was just seeing it.

Up in the citadel, when the time loop broke open, it was Sparrow who had pelted down the walkway to the warriors. When the hand reached in and grabbed them, when it dropped them here on the ground, she'd stayed with them, and now she was bent over Azareen. Her hand was thrust under the warrior's breastplate. Sarai could see her fingers through the hole the wasp stinger had punched through the bronze.

Sparrow's hand was on Azareen's wound. That was the story.

Eril-Fane was alive. That was the story.

Sparrow's eyes were closed in deep concentration, and her skin was gray, and *that was the story*. She was gray, but as Sarai looked on, this ceased to be true. Sparrow's color was fugitive, changing fast enough to watch. The gray hue took on a new richness as the last hint of blue left her flesh, giving way to beautiful, silken, chestnut brown. Except for the blood, the arrow, and her clothes—a slip from the closet of the goddess of secrets—she could have been a girl of Weep. Sparrow looked *human*.

"*Oh*," breathed Sarai, trying to understand.

Sparrow—Orchid Witch—could make things grow, and not just

flowers and kimril. But could she really have done *this*, regrown what was sundered inside Eril-Fane?

What other explanation? And she was trying to heal Azareen, too. But... if all the blue was gone from Sparrow's skin, did she have any magic left to do it?

Sparrow was still bent over her, eyes closed, but if Azareen wasn't healed already, she wasn't going to be.

Sarai swallowed hard. By now everyone was watching. Eril-Fane had no sooner risen and stopped the battle than he dropped back to his knees beside his wife. His face was strained, his jaw clenched. He focused on Azareen with an almost savage intensity. He gathered up her hand and curled it in both his own. "Live," he whispered to her. "Azareen, *live*." A choked sob escaped from his throat, and he added, like a prayer: "Thakra, *please*."

Azareen opened her eyes.

For a moment, the pair gazed at each other with all the hope and wonder of their younger selves, as though their lost lifetime—these past eighteen years—hadn't happened, and all was before them. When Azareen spoke, it was to ask, her voice faint, the question that death had repeatedly interrupted. She'd thought she'd never get to hear her husband's answer, or know what he'd wanted to tell her at the end. "My love," she whispered. *"What do you wish?"*

But she would have to keep waiting for the answer.

Sparrow collapsed. Eril-Fane caught her, noticing the arrow and blood for the first time. "Medics!" he hollered, and barked out several names.

Outside the protective circle of ghosts, the Tizerkane who belonged to the names were caught between obedience and a wall of souls with wings and spears.

"Stop!"

The shriek came from Minya. It was shrill. In one fluid motion, a score of ghosts turned to the center of the circle and trained their spears on Eril-Fane. When Minya looked at him, she saw slaughter. He *was* the Carnage, and now he had Sparrow. "Get your hands off her, *child-killer!*" she snarled.

"Minya!" Sarai turned to her, heartbeats spiking. Would she undo Sparrow's miracle, and kill what she had saved? Was Minya so far gone, so broken that she would throw away this last chance to set aside their hate and *live?*

But everything Sarai might have said died at the sight of Minya, and so did all that might have been. For her, anyway.

Because Minya was gray, too.

✿ 51 ✿

Happy Evanescence

Lazlo roared his voice to a rasp, but Nova seemed not to even hear
him. An unsettling, serene vagueness had come over her like a
trance—as though she were elsewhere, and her body was just holding her place in the world.

Lazlo was still trapped, his legs held fast in the metal, as the citadel poured itself through the portal, and any hope of saving Sarai
grew more and more remote.

When he'd begged Nova to leave the last anchor, he'd been
thinking of Weep—its bedrock and buildings, its river raging underground. It was only after she ignored him, and all the mesarthium
was sucked from the cracks, that the other implication struck him.
In that instant, when he realized what it meant and what would
happen, he had felt like he was back in the street, bereft at the sight
of Sarai's broken body arched over the gate. He had vowed never to
fail her again. "Do you think anything could keep me away?" he'd
asked her just that morning.

Now something—someone—*was* keeping him away, and he was

losing his mind. Nova wouldn't listen, and didn't understand him any-way. He'd tried appealing to the others. "They have no mesarthium. They'll fade. *Do you understand what that means?*"

Rook, Kiska, and Werran were uneasy with the way things had gone. Lazlo could tell by their tight expressions and the quick, dark glances they were giving Nova and one another, but they were clearly afraid to defy her. "At least leave them some metal," he pleaded. He saw that they wore medallions at their throats, as Nova wore her diadem. They all wore mesarthium against their skin. "Like that," he said, pointing at Werran's medallion. "Just enough to keep them from fading."

Werran lost patience, his conflicted guilt making him snap. "Being human isn't a fate worse than death. They'll learn to live with it."

Learn to live with it. Hysteria welled up in Lazlo. "You think I'm losing my mind because *they'll become human?*" His scream-ravaged voice thundered, feverish and rough. Never in his life had he raged like this. He looked like a man possessed. "Listen to me! That little girl you grew up with? Don't you know what her gift is? She catches souls. She keeps them from evanescing. If she fades, yes, she'll become human. Maybe she'll *learn to live with it.*" He shoved his fin-gers into his hair and clutched his skull, digging in, trying to dull the roar of despair. "But Sarai won't. She won't live with it, because *she's not alive.* You've got to help me! If Minya loses her power, *Sarai will evanesce.*"

* * *

Minya didn't understand what was happening. She stared at Sparrow, whom Eril-Fane had passed into Ruby's arms. She was unconscious, and no medics had been bold enough to breach the barrier of ghosts. "*What did you do to her?*" she demanded. She wasn't referring to the arrow or the blood, but Sparrow's color—as though humanity were a disease and Eril-Fane and Azareen had infected her with it.

"They didn't do anything," Sarai told her. Azareen was sitting up now, too, with help from Suheyla. Like Eril-Fane, she looked weak and drawn, but she was alive. "Sparrow did it herself," Sarai said. "She healed them, and it used up all her magic."

Minya had never looked so scornful. "Don't be stupid. Our magic can't get *used up*."

"It can," Sarai said, cold with the terrible truth of it, and what it meant for her. "It does. If we're not in contact with mesarthium."

"It's the source of our power," Feral explained. "We never knew until we put you on your bed and you started to turn gray. We thought you were dying, but Lazlo knew what to do. He put you on the floor."

He kept talking, but Sarai stopped hearing. At the sound of Lazlo's name, she nearly doubled over. It felt like being punched, and unable to draw breath, because she understood right then and there that she would never see him again.

By the hue of Minya's skin, Sarai knew she didn't have much longer.

She recalled Lazlo's surprise at Minya's fading so quickly. The rest of them slept in their beds every night—or in Sarai's case every day. They were out of contact with the metal for hours at a time and showed no sign of fading. But then, they weren't using their gifts in their sleep; Minya was. She had no respite from hers. All those ghosts, she had to be bleeding power every second, but it had never mattered before, because she was always in contact with the metal. The citadel had constantly been feeding her power. And now it wasn't.

412

Sarai threw back her head and looked up at the sky, just in time to see the last glint of the seraph vanish from sight. It was gone from Zeru. In desperation, she turned to her father. "Is there any mesarthium in the city?"

"The anchors..." he said, uncertain. He'd been unconscious when the citadel reclaimed them.

Sarai shook her head. "They took them. They're gone. Was there any somewhere else, even a little bit?" There was urgency and fear in her voice.

"What is it? What's wrong?" Eril-Fane asked.

But Feral understood, and so did Ruby. Tears sprang to her eyes. Her hand flew to cover her mouth. "*Oh*. Oh no. Sarai."

The Ellens understood, too. Stricken, they both looked at Minya. Her brows knit together with ferocity, confusion, and something like dread. She looked down at her hands, which were the color of ash, then sharply back up.

Sarai couldn't have said how she expected her to react. Minya had threatened her with this very fate, and been willing to see it through. She'd called Sarai a traitor, used her as a puppet, held her soul as a bargaining chip. It wouldn't altogether have surprised her if Minya shrugged and bid her happy evanescence, as coolly as saying happy birthday.

But she didn't. The ghosts with their spears trained on Eril-Fane closed in, tightening around him, their weapons raised. "There must be mesarthium somewhere," Minya said. *"Get it!"*

Eril-Fane shook his head, helpless. "There was only ever the anchors."

"You're lying!" she accused, and the ghosts thrust their spears right up against his throat. His life pulsed there, and the lightest thrust could end it.

"No!" gasped Sarai. Azareen and Suheyla cried out in horror. "There isn't any more," Azareen insisted. "I swear it. We would give it to you if there was!"

"My darling, my viper," said Great Ellen to Minya, with rueful, velvet tenderness. "You're only hastening it, sweet girl. Don't you see? The more you use your gift, the faster you'll use it up."

Minya froze as the truth of this struck her. Everything was rushing—like wind in her ears, though there was no wind; like racing toward a cliff, though there was no cliff. Suddenly, as though an axis tilted, she experienced her tethers in a new way. Always before, she had been conscious of the emotions pulsing *up* them, the *hate-fear-despair* never not assailing her. Now, though, she felt what went out of her and *down* them: her own strength, her gift, ebbing away by the second—a reservoir that would not refill. She could feel herself emptying. She'd come to think of her ghosts as her strength, the thing that could protect her, and with which she could protect her family. Now that presumption was dead.

She looked at her hands and they were gray. And she looked at Sarai, then around at her ghosts, and what she did next stunned them all.

She let go.

She had always imagined her gift as a fist clenching a tangle of threads. Now she opened it. The threads slipped free. A tremendous weight lifted as she released every soul she'd collected since the Carnage, save three. Sarai's tether was like a filament of spidersilk, fine and fragile and shining like starlight. Minya clutched it, tight but gentle, as though she could keep it, hold it.

The Ellens' tethers were different. When all the rest fell away, they remained. They were the first souls she'd ever caught, and she'd done it gasping in the bloody aftermath of the Carnage, when all the screaming and dying was over and she was alive and alone with the four babies she'd saved.

The Ellens' tethers weren't fine and fragile. They were tough as leather, and they didn't rest in her keeping like gossamers that could slip away. They sank into her very self, like taproots. They were part of her, and the Ellens stayed right beside her as the rest of the ghosts—the whole encircling ring of them—simply melted away.

Their faces flushed with freedom. Sarai saw little Bahar among them, and Guldan, the old tattoo artist who had done the most exquisite eliliths. Kem the footman was there, fading. And she saw Ari-Eil, her father's young cousin and hence her own, and felt a pang of remorse for his evanescence, all the more so when it seemed that a flicker of rue crossed his face, as though he wasn't ready to go. But then he was gone, they all were, and it was as though a great sigh breathed itself out of the amphitheater, sweeping like a sweet wind past all the Tizerkane, to ebb away in a skyward tide that drew all loose souls with it.

In the aftermath, it was utterly quiet. Minya knew, once more, the silence and lightness she'd felt when Nova took her gift. The crushing weight lifted, and the thrum of hate ceased, but she didn't feel relief. She felt pure terror.

There was no more barrier between godspawn and Tizerkane. They could all see one another clearly. Minya was overwhelmed by their numbers, their size, their *hate*. It was the look she knew so well, the one that said: *abomination*.

She had never felt so exposed, so vulnerable.

At least...not for fifteen years.

Her hearts started to stutter just like they had in the nursery when a stranger appeared in the doorway with a knife, and in the blink of an eye she was right back there, powerless and surrounded by adults who wished her dead. Terror hammered at her. Panic tore at her. Flashes of that day besieged her.

The Ellens, standing on either side of her, both reached out to try to soothe her, but she shrank from them, seeing a strobe vision of faces that were theirs but not theirs, and that scared her worse than anything else. She closed her eyes but the faces followed her into the dark. They were triumphant and vicious, and it was the Carnage all over again, only now it was worse because she didn't have a knife, and there was nowhere to hide, and the Ellens would stop her from saving the others. Just like they'd tried to before.

The mind is good at hiding things, but it can't erase. It can only conceal, and concealed things are not gone.

Minya's memory had a trick spot in it, like a drawer with a secret compartment—or a floating orb with a portal inside it, leading to a whole nightmare world. Now it all blew open, and the truth spilled out like blood.

DREAD WAS A PALE-HAIRED GODDESS

Once upon a time, there was a little girl who thought she understood what dread was.

Dread, she thought, was a pale-haired goddess who came to take you away. Away *where*? No one knew, but if it were nice, surely she'd smile when she came for you.

Korako didn't smile. Nor was she cruel. She was barely there. Her voice was low and her touch was light. Her eyebrows looked white but weren't. She was the goddess of secrets, and on the day that Minya learned what *real* dread was, she was keeping a secret of her own.

Her gift had come. It took the form of an awareness of something passing within reach. She didn't know *what*, but by the third or fourth time she felt it, she knew she could grab it, keep it. She just *knew*, but she didn't do it. She ignored it as best she could. To be seen with a faraway, puzzled expression was as sure a sign of gift manifestation as doing actual magic. The goddess's spies would go and tell—*Minya's been seen thinking!* Then Korako would come with her low voice and light touch, and it wouldn't matter that she wasn't cruel. You might even imagine she was sorry, but that didn't matter, either. It wouldn't stop her from taking you.

Kiska had been gone for three weeks. They couldn't play the dizzy game now. None of the others were strong enough to hold the other side of the hammock. Korako's spies were watchful. Minya felt their eyes on her all the time. She would be next. She was overdue. When she felt the awareness, she pushed it down deep inside herself.

"You'll outgrow your cot before long," Great Ellen observed that morning. Minya woke to find the nurse had been watching her sleep. That wasn't good. Sometimes godspawn on the cusp of their gift slipped up in their sleep and gave themselves away.

It was true, what Great Ellen said. Minya's toes were starting to hang out over the end of her little metal bed. "I'll curl up," she said. "I don't need to sleep all stretched out."

"This isn't your home," said the nurse.

Less Ellen chimed in. "Don't think you can trick us. We've seen it all."

Minya took the words as a challenge. She was good at games. She *would* trick them. She would not give in to her gift, no matter what it was.

But she did, and only hours later. She still won the game, though, because the Ellens were dead, and when Minya learned what it was she could do, it was *them* she learned it on.

It all started with strange noises in the corridor: shouts and running feet. And then a man appeared in the doorway, out of breath, with a knife in his hand. He was small and trim, with a pointed beard. He was human, brown-skinned like the Ellens. He skidded to a stop in front of the door, his face all lit up with triumph.

"They're dead!" he shouted, glorying. "All dead, every one. The monsters are slain and we are free!"

Monsters? Minya wondered with a jolt of fear. *What monsters?*

The Ellens peppered him with questions, and when Minya grasped what monsters were dead, she was not in the least bit sad. Dread, after all, was a pale-haired goddess, and she didn't have to fear her anymore. When the Ellens whooped for joy and shouted, "Thakra be praised! We're free!" she actually thought, for a sweet, thrilling moment, that *she* might be free with them, and all the rest of the godspawn, too.

The shouting alarmed the babies. Some began to cry. And the Ellens turned and looked at them, and Minya knew then that whatever cause for joy they had, it spelled nothing good for her and hers.

"There's still the little monsters to deal with," Great Ellen said to the man.

And the three of them surveyed the rows of cribs and cots with such *revulsion.*

"I'll bring Eril-Fane," said the man with the pointed beard. "I reckon he deserves to do the honors."

The honors.

"Don't take too long," Less Ellen told him. She wore an eye patch. The eye she'd had there had been lazy. Isagol hadn't cared for it, and so had plucked it out with her fingers. "I can't stand to stay here for one more minute."

"Here," said the man, handing over the knife. "Take this in case you need it."

He looked right at Minya when he said it, and then he was gone and the Ellens were giddy, laughing and saying, "We're getting out of here, at last."

A little boy named Evran, four years old, went up to them, infected by their laughter, and asked, bright and eager, "Where are we going?"

The laughter evaporated. "*We're* going home," Great Ellen said, and Minya understood that she and the other children were going nowhere.

Ever.

The man who had killed the gods was coming to kill them, too.

She grabbed up Evran and darted for the door. It wasn't a plan. It was panic. Less Ellen grabbed her by the wrist and yanked her right off her feet. Minya kicked out at her, and let go of Evran. Less Ellen dropped the knife. Minya got to it first. The little boy scrambled back to hide behind a cot.

All the rest was a blur.

The knife lay on the ground. The red was spreading—a glistening pool on the shining blue floor. The Ellens were lying still, their eyes open and staring, and...and they were standing there, too, right beside their own bodies. Their ghosts were staring at Minya, aghast. She was the only one who could see them, and she didn't want to look. None of it felt real—not the bodies, the ghosts, the spreading pool of red or the slickness on her hands. Her fingers moved, smearing it over her palms. And it wasn't sweat. It had never been sweat. It was *red*, red and wet, and when she grabbed Sarai and Feral, she got it on them, too. They were stricken, too shocked to cry, emitting hiccuping gasps as though they'd forgotten how to breathe. Their little hands kept slipping out of her grip. They were pulling away. They didn't want to go with her.

Because of what they had seen her do.

Do you want to die, too? Do you?

They probably thought she was going to kill them next. She

dragged them over their slain nurses and out into the corridor. She didn't know her way around the citadel; she had hardly ever been out of the nursery. It was luck that brought her to the almost-shut door, too narrow for adults to squeeze through. If she'd gone any other way, they would have been caught and killed. She pushed the little ones through the narrow opening and went back for more.

But she was too late. The Godslayer was already there. All she could do was listen, frozen in place, as the screams were cut off one by one.

❧ 53 ❧

A CREATURE RIDDLED WITH EMPTY SPACES

"Minya, it's all right. Minya!" Sarai crouched at her side. She saw the sheer, naked panic in the little girl's eyes.

"They were all I could carry," Minya told her, shaking.

"I know. You did so well. It's over now," Sarai told her. "I promise. It's all over."

But Minya saw the Ellens' ghosts and recoiled. She couldn't unsee their leering faces, and she couldn't unknow the truth. She'd killed them once, and she'd *kept* them. She'd needed them. She could never have cared for four babies on her own!

The rest had been unconscious. It was the first time she ever used her gift. She didn't even know what it was, and she did it in a haze of trauma. She was six years old *and everyone was dead*. She took hold of the nurses' souls and made them into what she needed them to be: someone to love and look after them all—like mothers, as best she could imagine, never having been privileged to know one. And her mind had smeared a blur around it, and the Ellens' tethers had grown into her, concrescent with her own soul, like the rhizomes of Sparrow's orchids all tangling together.

She couldn't just release them. She had to uproot them.

And she did.

She *ripped* them out of her, and for a brief moment, before the tide of unmaking took hold of them, the Ellens were themselves again. For fifteen years they'd been shoved down deep into the recesses of their own souls while a stronger will guided them, *became* them. They'd been there, underneath, all along, trapped, and now they surfaced.

Sarai saw them become the women from the dream, eyes like eel flesh, puckered mouths, and menace. Just for an instant, just enough to know. Then the air took them up and pulled them apart, and the Ellens were no more.

* * *

When Minya let go of her army, a tremendous weight lifted. That was not what happened when she let go of the Ellens.

She hadn't known she was crushed until she wasn't, and she didn't know she was fragmented until she became whole. Fifteen years ago, she'd desperately needed someone to care for four babies, and she'd *created* those someones. She'd *been* them, and the whole time, she'd hidden it from herself, because . . . *she'd* needed someone, too.

And so the parts of her that nurtured and sang and loved went out of her to animate them, and *she* was what was left: fear and rage and vengeance.

When the Ellens evanesced, her fragments came back to her. It wasn't weight, exactly. It was more like . . . fullness. She had been a creature riddled with empty spaces, a ventriloquist, a puppet master, a little girl in pieces.

Now she was just a person.

Eril-Fane beckoned the medics to approach. They did, wide eyes darting from one godspawn to the next, giving Minya a wide berth, and hesitating in front of Sparrow. Ruby held her sister in her arms and glared at the warriors. Feral planted himself beside her and helped her glare. It was a detente. Suheyla went over to mediate.

Eril-Fane told them, "You are all under my protection. I swear it."

Minya looked to Sarai. The Godslayer was the last person in the world whose vow she could believe. But Sarai nodded. "You're safe," she said. "You'll all be safe now."

And Minya heard what was hiding in her words. *You*, not *we*, because of course Sarai was not safe. By releasing her army, Minya might have slowed her fading, but she couldn't stop it. Just by holding Sarai, she was using her gift. She would use it up, and Sarai would evanesce. The question was: How long did she have?

Minya looked at her hands, and it was even worse than she'd feared. The gray was already shading into the warmer, richer realm of brown. Her breath left her in a rush. She looked up and met Sarai's eyes, and saw fierce, sad courage in them.

"What can we do?" Minya asked her.

Sarai shook her head. She was fighting back tears. She, too, saw the brown creeping into Minya's color, but there was a far worse tell that was hers alone. She could already feel the cold of the unmaking seeping through the ether to claim her. It wouldn't be long now. "Listen to me, Minya. Whatever you do, promise me you'll find Lazlo. You have to save him from her."

Minya's eyes and nostrils flared. Anger chased away all her meek, unwelcome fear, and she relished it. Standing up as tall as she could, which wasn't very, she said, with all her old ungraciousness, "Save him *yourself*." And then she turned on her heel, stalked up to Eril-Fane, whom all her life she'd dreamed of killing, and *spoke to him*. Her teeth were gritted the whole time, but nevertheless, she spoke. She said, "I seem to recall you have some flying machines around here."

❧ 54 ❧

MERRY HELL INDEED

Lazlo had stopped struggling. His long hair hung in his face. His legs were bruised and aching from trying to pull them free of the metal, but he'd finally given up. How much time had passed? An hour? He didn't know. Was it more than the length of time it had taken Minya to fade before? If it wasn't, it was close. Sarai might already be gone.

A void opened up inside him.

All last night, in the glade he had made for her, in the sunken bed he'd crafted for the goddess of dreams, they had lapped in and out of sleep like waves gliding over soft white sand. And in both states—awake, asleep—they were together. "I want to try something," Sarai had said, bashful, her teeth teasing her luscious lower lip. Her mist dress had been evaporating off her like dawn fog wicked away by the sun.

"So do I," he'd replied, his voice seeming to surface from somewhere deep inside him.

"You tell me yours," she'd coaxed, half sultry, half silly, "and I'll tell you mine."

"You first," he'd said, and she'd told him her idea: that since she, being...*differently alive*—as they had taken to calling her ghost state ("dead" not feeling even remotely accurate)—couldn't experience new sensation, he would share his. That is to say: While they were awake, it was his responsibility to discover pleasure for them both, and then, while they were asleep, to impart it to her through the generous medium of dreams.

"That sounds like a lot of work," he'd said, acting weary, and she'd batted at him, and he'd caught her hand, and captured her waist in the crook of his arm, and fallen sideways, carrying her with him onto the bed sunk down between hummocks of mesarthium moss and leaning trees with leaves shaped like stars.

It turned out that her idea extravagantly encompassed his own, and quite a few other things, too.

They hadn't made love. They'd come to it in the course of things, more than once, both awake and in dreams, and each time they'd paused and held this tremendous thing between them—this certainty, this promise. That was what it had felt like: something that was theirs to come to in sweet time. And maybe waiting had been a way of laying claim to the future, and all the nights and mornings yet to come.

Now it felt as though they'd challenged fate to a duel and lost. There would be no more nights and no more mornings, not for Sarai, or with her. All the fight went out of Lazlo, and all the joy and wonder and witchlight. He slumped and lay back on the walkway where he was still trapped by his own magic that had been stolen and turned against him.

The metal beneath him was sticky with the blood of Eril-Fane and Azareen, and this grief burned cold in his gut beside the other.

He thought back to the day the Tizerkane came to the Great Library of Zosma. Eril-Fane had stood before the scholars in the Royal

Theater and told them that his people had passed through a long, dark time and come out of it alive and strong. But now he was dead, and Azareen, too. Weep's long, dark time had tracked them down.

Or Nova had, anyway.

She had remained, all this while, in her vague state, exhausted but intent on transferring the citadel out of Zeru. There had been a bizarre, protracted moment when the chamber had to warp out of shape to pass through the portal. The sphere had folded in on itself and narrowed to a tube before slowly reclaiming its shape on the other side. That was the only way Lazlo knew they were through to the other world.

Wraith circled, relentless, never far from Nova. Kiska, Rook, and Werran waited at the threshold, keeping a wary eye on their leader, and a conflicted one on Lazlo.

Kiska came over, hesitant, a while after he'd given up pleading and struggling. She wanted to ask him...many things. She couldn't get Minya's face out of her mind—the version from years ago, as she'd looked defying Korako, and the version from this day, when she'd looked just the same defying Nova. Exactly, impossibly the same. But Lazlo's eyes looked like burned-out holes, and all she could bring herself to ask him was: "...are you all right?"

He stared at her, unable to process the question. *All right?* Was he...*all right?* Dead-eyed, and recalling that she was a telepath, he gestured to his head and said, "Why don't you come in and see."

Kiska declined the invitation.

* * *

"What in merry hell is going on out there?" asked Calixte.

She might have meant it rhetorically, not expecting Thyon to know, but his mind was working on the puzzle and would not let go until he had an answer. Sky portals, melting armies, gray children, plenty of blood. Merry hell indeed.

The two of them were crouching in the first tier of the amphitheater. Arrows had, until a moment ago, been whizzing over their heads. They had witnessed everything, and understood…*not* everything.

When it had all started to go mad—the citadel coming alive—Thyon had considered, with admirable calm, that he might die. The whole city could topple. It had felt likely for a few minutes there. Or else the citadel might outright *step* on him. An image had popped into his mind of an elaborately carved headstone engraved with the words STEPPED ON BY AN ANGEL IN THE PRIME OF HIS LIFE. A hysterical laugh had escaped from his throat, drawing a glare from Calixte, who couldn't imagine what was funny.

He hadn't tried to explain.

Back in Zosma, months ago, he'd boasted to Strange, "Stories will be told about me." It gave him chills of shame to remember his pompous airs, and he couldn't help thinking that being stepped on by an angel made a fitting ending to *that* story. But he was glad he wasn't dead.

And he was glad that Ruza and Tzara weren't, either, and no one else, that he could see—if you didn't count all those apparitions who had melted into the air. What had they been? Illusions? If so, how had their weapons rung out like that, clashing against the Tizerkane spears?

The sound alone had left him trembling, even up here. Ruza and Tzara had been in the thick of it, fighting that mystifying army, and Thyon had flinched with every blow that shuddered through his friend.

Friends, plural, he corrected himself. He hadn't just watched Ruza, of course. As he bargained under his breath with imaginary deities, he'd made an excellent offer for Tzara's safety, too. He wondered if he would have to pay up, now that the fighting was over and his friends were alive. Or maybe the debt would fall to Calixte. She had threatened rather than bargained, much louder than he, and with far more profanity.

"Isn't that Lazlo's girl?" she asked now. Since the mystical army had mystically vanished, they had a clear view of what and who the citadel had dropped here—and what and who had been the target of all the spears and arrows. It was rather egregious overkill, if you asked Thyon.

He saw:

—Eril-Fane and Azareen, both looking weak in blood-smeared armor
—Eril-Fane's mother
—A thin little creature of a girl who wasn't blue but gray
—Two young women and a young man, of whom two were blue, and one apparently human, with an arrow sticking out of her shoulder
—Strange's girl, maybe. Thyon hadn't gotten a good look at her the other day, but she'd had this same whip of red-brown hair.

"I thought she was dead," he said.

"Maybe she is," said Calixte. "This is Weep. You can't expect things to make sense here."

Thyon didn't agree. "I expect they make perfect sense," he said. "Just under a different set of rules." It was a matter of learning the rules, like learning a new language. He felt doubly in the dark then, locked out of both rules and language, as a heated discussion broke out below, the little gray girl's high voice vying with Eril-Fane's deep one.

He wondered at her being gray. Having already deduced that the skin coloration was a reaction to touching mesarthium, and having seen Strange undergo the process, he supposed that she was midtransformation, either becoming blue, or the opposite. Which? Since she wasn't touching mesarthium, he thought it must be the latter.

When he heard her *say* "mesarthium," unmistakable in the flow of other words, he asked Calixte if she could understand what they were talking about.

She scrunched up her nose. "She's talking really fast," she said, and he gave her a half-lidded look.

"And this is your marvelous fluency."

"Shut up, Nero. It's harder to understand someone else's conversation than when somebody's speaking right to you. But I think she's asking...well, *demanding*, she's really bossy...that he let her have a silk sleigh?"

Thyon's eyebrows went up. He hadn't been expecting that. The citadel was gone, which was less mysterious than it would have been had he not already concluded that there was a portal in the sky above Weep. But *why* had it gone, and why had it left these refugees behind, and where in merry hell, to use Calixte's words, was Strange? This morning he'd brought his guests up to the citadel astride marvelous metal beasts. Why, then, had they been dumped unceremoniously and the worse for wear?

Something was really wrong, he thought. "Let's go closer," he said, and they did.

* * *

Sarai looked on, speechless at the sight of Minya talking to Eril-Fane. All right, talking *at* him, and very rudely, but it was a far cry from trying to kill him. And if she was rude, he was all courtesy, listening without interruption, intent and responsive, immediately sending a Tizerkane running to the guildhall to fetch Soulzeren and Ozwin.

And he would have led them to the silk sleighs, and let them take one up into the sky, and maybe Soulzeren would have agreed to pilot it and maybe she wouldn't, and maybe they would have found the portal up there in the fast-falling dark, and flown into the other world, and found the citadel and pulled up beside it and moored there so that Minya could lay her palms to the metal and turn blue again and not lose hold of Sarai. And then, while they were there, they could have rescued Lazlo and won back their home and lived happily ever after, just like in a storybook.

But it wasn't going to happen.

There wasn't time. Sarai knew it. The cold was in her. She could already feel herself leeching away.

Eril-Fane tried to lead them out of the amphitheater, and Minya was ready to follow, but Sarai shook her head. "Minya," she said, and Minya looked at her and knew.

Sarai was softening around the edges, her outline blurring the way Wraith's did right before it vanished. Minya saw and knew, but she refused to accept it. She put her own hands behind her back so she wouldn't have to see their color.

Everyone else could see her, though. She already looked human, if a little ill perhaps, a lingering ashy cast to her newly brown skin.

"We have to get to the citadel!" she insisted. "I just have to touch it. We just have to get alongside it and *touch* it."

Sarai knelt in front of her. "It means so much that you still want to save me," she said, her eyes filling up with tears.

432

Minya's eyes filled, too. She swiped at them with an angry hand, then wished she hadn't, because she couldn't help but see how human it looked. It couldn't be *her* hand. Her hands were blue. She was blue. She was godspawn, not some useless human whelp who couldn't keep her people safe.

Minya now held but a single tether—Sarai's delicate starlight gossamer. Once upon a time, she'd held Sarai's little toddler hand in a crushing grip. She'd saved her then, but there was no way to grip the gossamer tight enough to keep it. It was dissolving.

"We just need to go," she said, still in denial.

"We're out of time," Sarai whispered. The world seemed to swoop around her, as though she were a top at the end of her spin, wobbling toward collapse. She swallowed hard and tried to find her center of gravity, her strength. She looked around at all the people she loved— all of them right here, except Lazlo. "I love you," she told them.

Minya felt the tether melting away. In a panic, she reached out to grasp Sarai's hand. But she couldn't. It was only a shadow in the air.

* * *

The girl was transparent. It was the same thing that had happened to the army, and Thyon didn't think she was an illusion. Everyone was so distraught it was as though she were *dying*.

"I thought she was dead," he'd said to Calixte.

"Maybe she is. This is Weep," she'd replied, and he'd mused that he just didn't understand the rules. So what *were* they? *What was she?* What was happening? The little girl wasn't even gray now. The more human she looked, the more the other girl vanished.

They'd wanted to fly to the citadel. The little girl had distinctly said "mesarthium."

It was the source of their power, and Thyon knew well enough that there was no spare mesarthium in Weep, not even shavings or ingots. In the course of his own work, he'd had to walk to the anchor to test each batch of alkahest.

And the anchors were gone.

Understanding, like an electric shock, seared through his whole body, and he was in motion, stumbling forward, his hands numb with a flood of adrenaline, so that he could hardly feel his fingers as he groped in his pocket for the thing he had put there and all but forgotten. He grasped it, and tried to pull it out. It snagged on the edge of his pocket and he was tugging away like an idiot—like a raccoon that won't just open its fist—and he took a deep breath and tried again, pushing the thing down to unsnag it first. And then he had it and he was holding it out. The little girl flinched as though it were a knife.

Strange had flinched the exact same way when Thyon showed it to him. Quickly, he shifted his grip, so that instead of wielding it, knifelike, it lay across his palms like an offering.

"Will this help?" he asked, breathless. "Is it … is it enough?"

It was the shard of mesarthium he'd cut from the north anchor using donated "spirit of librarian." It was sharp and uneven and inelegant, and it had Lazlo's fingerprints in it.

And yes.

Yes. It was enough.

🌿 55 🌿

PEACE AND PASTRIES

Not long ago, Suheyla had prepared a welcome meal for a young far-anji who was to be a guest in her home. It had been *such* a pleasure to have a young person to cook for again, and Lazlo had deepened every delight with his astonished appreciation of the bounty she set before him. Anyone coming out of the Elmuthaleth would be sick to death of journey food, but it was more than that: He was an orphan, and had never been cared for properly, or eaten food made specially for him. For the short time he'd been in her home, Suheyla had relished making up at least a small part of that lack.

Now she found herself with *five* orphans to feed—five orphans kept alive for years on "purgatory soup" and kimril loaf with carefully rationed salt—and she was in her element.

So, indeed, were they.

When Suheyla produced a platter of pastries glistening with honey and nuts, Ruby actually swooned at her feet. She fell to the floor and lay on her back, her arms outstretched, pleading theatrically for reassurance that it wasn't all a dream.

Feral, with a polite "May I?" plucked a pastry off the platter, knelt beside her, and held it just shy of her mouth. "Not unless we're in the same dream," he said. Brow furrowing, he looked to Sarai. "We're *not*, are we?"

Sarai shook her head, smiling, and it was a sweet smile but incomplete. There was much to be relieved about—being saved at the absolute last second from evanescence, Minya having stopped trying to murder everyone (at least for now), and everybody being miraculously *alive*—but until they could rescue Lazlo, she would be incomplete, and so would her smile.

Ruby raised her head up off the ground to take a bite of the pastry. Feral, predictably, pulled it away and crammed the whole thing in his mouth. There followed a ravening outrage and a loud *rip* as Feral's shirt gave way to clawing, and Ruby was on her feet again, pushing wild dark coils of hair out of her face to stand, demure and passingly penitent, in front of Suheyla. "I'm sorry," she said, and explained, "It's hard to be calm. We ran out of sugar ten years ago."

"You poor things," Suheyla commiserated, proffering the platter, and Ruby took a pastry and took a bite and was lost to bliss, eyes closed, cheeks flushed, unable to speak or even chew for a long dreamy minute. She just let the flavor permeate her being.

It was the most rewarding reaction to her baking that Suheyla had ever had.

She would have liked to take these children home and pamper them properly, but they were at the Merchants' Guildhall instead, for a number of reasons: It was nearer to the amphitheater; the silk sleighs were in one of its pavilions; and Suheyla's house had fallen into the river along with a broad swath of the city, and was...gone.

"Oh," she'd said, bringing her hand to her mouth, when Eril-Fane returned from assessing the extent of the destruction and broke the news. "Well, it's a good thing no one was home," she'd declared, and set about seeing Sparrow installed in a bed at the guildhall instead.

That was still early in the night, not long after Thyon Nero surprised them by saving Sarai. He seemed to have surprised himself as much as anybody, and when Minya seized the shard from him and clenched it hard in both her hands, and Sarai's silhouette shaded back to opacity and she shuddered and wept with relief, he started to shake, besieged by the enormity of life and death, made real to him for the very first time.

There is a humility that comes with this understanding, and it was a good look for him, knocking the hauteur away and leaving a pleasing vulnerability in its place—as though the world needed Thyon Nero to be any better-looking.

Ruza had remarked, inanely, the other day that Thyon was like a new linen napkin you'd be afraid to wipe your mouth on. Well, when he went over to him and led him to a place where he could sit down and remember how to breathe, Ruza found the alchemist much altered—more... *lived in*, somehow. Less untouchable.

But he still kept his mouth to himself.

The amphitheater had emptied. Sparrow had regained consciousness, and she'd regained *blueness* as well. The Tizerkane medics had removed the arrow, stanched the bleeding, and cleaned out her wound, but beyond that, she had undertaken her healing herself—once Minya could be prevailed upon to share the shard of mesarthium, that is.

"Since when can you *heal?*" Ruby had asked with a scowl.

Sparrow was taken aback by her sister's accusatory tone. "Well, if I'd known you'd be so *happy* about it," she'd said, sarcastic, "I'd have told you right away."

"I *am* happy about it," Ruby had said unhappily. Then: "*I'd* have told *you*."

Sparrow softened. "I'd have told you, too, goose. I was just figuring it out."

First it had been the flowers. She'd reattached the plucked blossoms to their stems and they'd lived and kept on blooming. After that, she'd tried it on Lazlo's lip. They'd been interrupted almost right away, but she could tell the bite had begun to mend. When it came to Eril-Fane and Azareen, she'd just rushed over, put her hands on them, and hoped for the best. Mending two mortal wounds at the same time had been quite the learning curve, but it didn't require skill so much as a steady lavishing of magic. "It's not exactly that I can *heal*," she told Ruby, sitting in bed with hardly a mark on her skin to show where the arrow had been. "I mean, I couldn't help someone who was sick. It's part of being able to make things grow. It works on bodies, too."

A devilish light came into Ruby's eyes. She put her hands on her breasts. "Does that mean you can make *these* bigger?"

"*No.*"

It was morning now. They hadn't slept—Soulzeren had been teaching them how to fly the silk sleighs—and Ruby had not given up on the notion. "You know I'll give you no peace," she said with equanimity. "You might as well just do it and save yourself a lot of pestering."

"Ruby. I am not touching your breasts."

"*What?*" This was from Feral, who had overheard.

Sparrow appealed to him. "Would you please tell her that her breasts are perfect as they are?"

He sputtered, going violet. Ruby also appealed to him. "But they could be *more* perfect, couldn't they?"

Poor Feral didn't know the right answer. He sensed danger in all directions. "Um."

The girls weren't listening to him anyway. "Something can't be *more* perfect," Sparrow scoffed. "It's literally impossible."

Ruby made her favorite disgusted gargling sound in the back of her throat and drawled, "Don't start with the *literally* or I will *literally* die of boredom," before, with a lightning movement, grabbing Sparrow's hand.

"If you force me to touch your breasts, I swear to Thakra I'll make them *smaller*."

Ruby let go. "Fine. But the next time you need bathwater heated, don't come to me."

"Oh, is that how it is? In that case, I expect you'll stop eating the food from our garden."

Ruby rolled her eyes. "We don't even *have* our garden, and anyway, if I never see another kimril or plum in my entire life it will be too soon."

Sparrow couldn't disagree with that. They made peace and ate pastries—and fruits that weren't plums, and vegetables that weren't kimril, and to top it all off, *sausage*, which they had never had before and which made for excellent proof that food could have flavor, in case there was any lingering doubt after the pastries, which there really wasn't. No one actually swooned, but some eyes might have been moist with gratitude. Suheyla made sure they didn't eat too much. "Your systems won't know what to do with it," she warned. And the tea was real tea, not crushed herbs, and there was a bowl full of sugar with a miniature spoon that Ruby loved beyond all reason, and held between her fingertips as though it were a doll's spoon, her face lit with wonder while she scooped tiny spoonfuls into her cup, and then, bypassing her tea altogether, directly into her mouth.

They were to have clothes as well. Suheyla took them through the back door of a shuttered shop, and they put on blouses and embroidered belts, and leather cuffs to cinch their sleeves. The girls eyed skirts but chose trousers, considering their plans for the day. Feral got his first pair of trousers that weren't gods' underclothes, and a shirt and cuffs, too. They declined the offer of shoes, all being accustomed to bare feet, not to mention mindful that being barefoot at home was what kept them magical.

And they had every intention of being home again soon, walking on their own metal floors and sleeping in their own beds.

Minya didn't go to the shop or try on blouses or trousers. Suheyla picked out a few things that might fit her, but she left them untouched on a chair. She did eat, and perhaps she enjoyed it, but if she did, she didn't show it.

She'd been very quiet since the amphitheater. Sarai didn't know what she was feeling, and Minya wasn't likely to tell her, but she stayed close to her—not that she really had a choice—and she found that she didn't mind. That was a change from the last few years, as Minya had grown more and more difficult, increasingly dark-minded.

It all made so much sense now, and Sarai was ashamed she hadn't seen it before. All these years, all those souls. Who might Minya be if she hadn't borne that burden? Who would she become, now that it was gone?

Sarai had seen the Ellens' faces at the end, and she knew she'd been right: They'd been puppets. All that was warm and motherly, funny and thoughtful and wise in them had been Minya all along. Knowing it, though, didn't mean she didn't feel the nurses' loss keenly. Ruby and Sparrow and Feral did, too, and Sarai thought even Minya did. The ghost women had been a huge part of their lives. So they were a lie? They weren't *real*? Knowing it and feeling it were two very different things, and Sarai kept catching herself wishing for a hug from Great Ellen or a hummed tune from Less Ellen and trying to internalize that it had all been Minya.

It didn't help that Minya showed no sign of those traits now. Would she ever? Were they in her?

Only time would tell.

They didn't linger in Weep. Sarai had wanted to leave at once, but she'd had to admit that finding the portal by daylight would be difficult enough. By night, likely impossible. Now, healed, fed, and clothed, they assembled in the pavilion where the silk sleighs rested. Sarai was a bit anxious about flying them themselves, but she wouldn't have felt right bringing the pilots into danger, even if they'd volunteered, which they hadn't. She thought Soulzeren looked wistful, and might have liked the adventure, while Ozwin was the practical one of the duo, in charge of keeping them alive. And they all accepted that there was no certainty of that, but they chose not to dwell on it.

If they were lucky, the citadel hadn't gone far. The silk sleighs might have been a marvel in Zeru, but they wouldn't do for protracted pursuit of a mesarthium ship through an unknown world or worlds. Their only hope was to catch up to it before it got away.

"And then what?"

Eril-Fane voiced the question, but they were all thinking it. If—when—they caught up to the citadel, what then? The invader, who they all now knew was Korako's sister, had beaten them badly. What would be different this time?

"We'll surprise them," said Sarai, though that hardly constituted a plan. How could they plan when they didn't know what they'd find, or even if they'd find anything at all? They could go through the portal and be greeted by the nightmare landscape, the white stalks

441

growing out of the tempestuous red sea, but no citadel, and no idea which way to go.

"This enemy steals magic," said Eril-Fane. "You can't rely on your abilities. It wouldn't hurt to have warriors with you."

Azareen, by his side, went cold, but she was unsurprised. She knew by now that Eril-Fane would never be free of the past, never able to turn and face forward. She didn't look at him, but stood rigid, braced to hear him offer himself up to die again for his sins.

"But not us," he said, and she felt the warm weight of his hand on her back, and turned in shock to look up at him. "Our duty is here," he said. "I hope you understand."

"Of course I do," said Sarai, who would not have let him come in any case. This wasn't his fight. She hoped his fight was over, and anyway, it was best not to tempt Minya's forbearance any further. Sarai knew better than to imagine she'd forgiven him. This could be just a game of quell in which she found herself outnumbered in enemy territory. Who was to say she wouldn't yet seek her vengeance when she regained her advantage?

Azareen was blinking back tears. Sarai, moved, pretended not to notice. "We don't need warriors," she assured them.

"Can we come anyway?" someone asked.

Sarai turned to see two Tizerkane standing back, awkward and hesitant. She knew them, of course. She knew everyone in Weep. They were Ruza and Tzara. Lazlo's friends.

"*You* want to come?" she asked, caught off guard. Lazlo had told her, despairing, how deep their hatred of godspawn ran.

"If you'll have us," said Ruza, looking uncomfortable. "If it were me gone missing, he'd come looking. Not that I'm special, I mean. He'd come looking for anyone." He turned to the golden godson and wrinkled his nose with unconvincing distaste. "Even *you*."

442

"I know he would," said Thyon, who understood now, as he hadn't before, what it was to help someone for no other reason than that they needed it. "Can I come, too?" he asked, afraid that the girl—the ghost—would reject him and that they would leave him behind.

And Sarai did hesitate. She had not forgotten what it was like inside his dreams—how airless and tight they were, like coffins. And she remembered him at Lazlo's window, too, arguing, right before she died. His manner had been so guarded, so scathing and cold.

He seemed different now. Not to mention, he had saved her. "If you wish," she said.

Calixte appealed to come, too, and was welcomed, and that made nine: five godspawn and four humans. Two silk sleighs and one cut in the sky. That was the math of their rescue operation, and there wasn't a moment to lose.

56

Pirates of the Devourer

In every world, the seraphim had cut two portals: a front door and a back door, so to speak—a way *in* from the previous world, and a way *out* to the next. When navigating the Continuum, there were two directions: not north and south, right and left, up and down, but *al*-Meliz and *ez*-Meliz. *Toward* Meliz, and *away from* Meliz. The seraph home world, where the Faerers' journey had begun, was the only compass point that mattered.

The cut in the sky over Weep was Zeru's ez-Meliz portal. The world on the other side was called Var Elient, and it was not all red sea and mist. But the red sea, called Arev Bael, went on for many weeks' journey, and had eaten more ships than it had ever let pass. The seraph Thakra, in an age long gone, had dubbed it the Devourer, and balked—or so the story went—at destroying the monsters that swam in it.

Var Elient was a world whose point of pride was that its monsters were too monstrous for even gods to destroy.

And maybe they were, or maybe the Faerers had just been too tired after destroying Zeru's beasts.

Only the foolhardy and desperate ever sailed the Devourer now that there were airships. There had been, for a long time, a high portal tax and a thriving transport business in flying outworlders to the island that wasn't really an island, but a cut tezerl stalk—one of the vast white stalks that grew out of the sea. They used to come to buy magical children. It wasn't a secret. No one in Var Elient could afford them themselves, but they had relied on the tax and the transport revenue. And then it all came to an end.

They blamed Nova, as well they might, since she was the one who crashed a stolen kite skiff on the island, slew the guards, and took over, killing on sight anyone who came after, and collecting their airships like it was a portal harbor.

But it wasn't really her fault. The portal, which was Var Elient's al-Meliz door, had closed before she got there, and stayed closed. Skathis's auctions were over.

She had found three children in cages and freed them, but she had only freed them so far. She might have taken them somewhere else—*anywhere* else—so they could have some other life. But she chose to stay, and what could they do? She made the choice for them all, so that she could be near the portal when it reopened, as she never doubted it would.

And that is how Kiska, Werran, and Rook became pirates of the Devourer—"pirates" in the nonmagical sense—and grew up boarding and seizing airships over the roiling red sea. Perhaps Nova had bowed to fate, and determined to embody the word that defined her.

They were loyal to her in the blind way of saved children, but as they came home from Zeru in the godsmetal warship, they were not quite as blind as they had been before.

"That was *Minya*," Kiska said under her breath as Nova guided the seraph down to their island, to moor it as though it were just another ship they'd seized for their fleet. "We just stole this ship from *Minya*."

Werran shook his head. He might have believed it was her for a moment, but it was deniable after the fact. "How could it be? She'd be our age." He was holding one arm gingerly against him, his wrist a mess from his ghost bite. "Whoever that was, was just a little girl."

"Maybe she was Minya's daughter," said Rook. The math would have had her giving birth at fourteen or fifteen, which was uncomfortable, but not impossible.

"Don't be stupid. You both know it was her."

"So what if it was?" asked Werran with a belligerence born of discomfiture. "What are we supposed to do about it now?"

"Go back?" suggested Kiska, hugging her arms around herself and pacing. She'd shut off her gravity boots and they clicked against the metal floor with each step. "Make sure they're all right?" The words *all right* nearly stuck in her throat. She darted an uneasy glance in Lazlo's direction. He was lying deathly still with the crook of his arm flung across his face, concealing it. If what he had been saying— *screaming*—was true, then they were not all right.

"We can't go back," said Rook.

"Why not?" Kiska stopped pacing. "We have plenty of ships."

"That's hardly the point," he said, shooting a look toward Nova. There was a pounding in the base of his skull, and his joints ached and his fingers were numb from the lightning blast that had thrown him. It reminded him of being five years old, in a cage, with guards teaching him what to be afraid of. Nova had freed him from that.

They all watched her and fell silent. She hadn't said a word during the entire transition between worlds, and they hadn't bothered her, for the ostensible reason that she had to concentrate to pilot the immense ship through the narrow gap. But that wasn't the only reason. They didn't like to admit it, even to themselves, but they were worried.

There was something unknowable and untouchable about Nova. They'd lived with her for most of their lives, but not for most of *hers*. They were twenty, twenty-one. She was...well, they didn't know, but she was old. Her life reached deep into a past they couldn't imagine. What they knew of her was like...like rain on the lid of a cistern. They couldn't even *see* the dark water below, much less guess what it held. And sometimes her eyes were faraway, and sometimes they were murderous. She could be funny, and she could cut throats, and she could sink into silence for days. But whatever else she was, she was, above all, single-minded.

Nova had a purpose, or she'd *had* a purpose: to find her sister. So what would she do now?

The ship—citadel, seraph—came to a stop, and Nova moved for the first time in many minutes. She'd been floating out in the center of the room, the white bird gliding its endless circles around her, but now she turned and came toward where they were waiting in the door. Lazlo still lay on the walkway, and Kiska was glad to see Nova free him.

For all of half a second.

She released his legs from the metal, and he felt it, and flung his arm off his face to come upright, but even as he rose, two masses of godsmetal, each as big as his head, detached from the walkway and flew up to meld themselves around his upper arms and shoulders and lift him into the air so that he was suspended, feet dangling. "Let me go!" he said, hoarse from all his futile screaming. Nova went around him and he tried to grab at her but couldn't reach, and she didn't seem to notice or hear him holler. She just floated him along behind her.

Kiska, Rook, and Werran were three abreast in the doorway. They'd have to step aside to let her pass, but for the moment none of them moved. They looked from Lazlo's grief-ravaged face to Nova's, which was very weary, and...blankly benign. The wrongness of it held them all rooted as she slowed to a stop before them, waiting for them to step out of her way.

Why wasn't *she* grieving?

Though they'd been fearing the form her grief would take, this clear lack of it was jarring. Not to mention seeing her cavalierly take control of a young man who was, well, one of them. They didn't know him, but what did that matter? He was innocent, not to mention that he bore more than a passing resemblance to Werran and was probably his brother. Nova *freed* slaves; she didn't *take* them. And of course it was even worse than that, if what Lazlo said was true: By taking this ship and leaving the others behind—who were also their kin and kindred—they had doomed at least one of them.

"Nova," said Kiska in an uncertain tone. "What are you going to do with him?"

"*Do?*" Nova regarded Lazlo. "Well, I suppose that depends on him. I always planned to keep Skathis in a birdcage."

That didn't answer the question. They would have *helped* her keep Skathis in a birdcage. "But he's not Skathis," Kiska pointed out.

"No, but he is a Mesarthim smith, and that is a very rare treasure."

"Treasure?" repeated Rook. In the course of their piracy, they had looted many a treasure, but they had never stolen *people*. Having been rescued from the certainty of slavery themselves, the very thought was anathema to them. "But you can't just *keep* him," he blurted, as though nothing were more obvious.

"I have to," said Nova. "I need him if I'm going to find Kora."

Rook's mouth opened and then closed again. There was a

moment of stunned silence, which Nova took advantage of to move past them, pushing between Rook and Kiska, who stood as though their boots were magnetized to the floor, even as Lazlo was pulled past, struggling, the bird following in their wake.

In a low voice, Werran asked Kiska, "You're sure Korako's dead?" After all, he and Rook hadn't heard the mind chorus of *dead she's dead she's dead*, or seen the memory of the knife going into her heart the way Kiska had.

"Very sure," she replied, chilled to her core.

"Then what was that about?" asked Werran. They all felt as though some fundamental truth had been yanked out from under them, leaving them in free fall.

"She's lost it," said Rook. "Did you see her eyes? That's madness."

"It's grief," said Kiska. "It's shock."

"It's kidnapping," said Werran. "It's slavery."

"I know," she said, and they followed Nova down the passage.

There was a surreal familiarity to the route. They came to the crossing of passages, and they all stopped in their tracks, hit by the same memory at the same moment. They had all three followed Korako this way. The nursery was to the left. Kiska had the strangest feeling that if she went that way, she would find it all exactly as it had been on that long-ago day when Minya had screamed and tried to stop Korako from taking her away.

It shamed her that she had said and done nothing on Minya's behalf when Nova took *her* away. "This isn't right," she said.

They went through a door into a large room with a dining table at its center. The far wall was an arcade of archways open to a garden. The metal was almost entirely covered in a profusion of flowers and vines. There was a large chair at the head of the table. Nova pulled it back and sat, her arms on the armrests as though she were trying on some new role. She was already pirate queen of the Devourer. Now she was captain of an avenging angel that no force in the Continuum could stop.

Lazlo was still suspended in the air, and he was still struggling. Seeing Nova in Minya's chair, he thought, was almost too neat: one foe sliding into another's place. The game board was even sitting there, but all the pieces had fallen off and scattered across the floor, and in Lazlo's state of extremis, that seemed to say everything. When this game was over, would anyone be left standing?

"I won't help you," he told her, and there was venom in his own voice.

She turned to him, but her face was tired, incurious. He knew she didn't understand him, but he spoke anyway, because threats and promises were all he had. "Whatever you plan to do, whatever you mean to use me for, you'll fail." There was a new darkness in him, as though a root of his soul had tapped down into a hidden pool of poison and drunk, tainting him with vengeance, and a will to do violence that he had never known before.

She had kept him from keeping his promise to Sarai, and it felt as though, in so doing, Nova had remade him into a shadow version of himself. "You'll slip up," he said, "and I'll be ready, and I'll take back my power and make you pay."

In response, with a flick of her wrist, she sent up a spray of mesarthium from the floor, and met it with a spray from above. The two fused in the middle and formed, in an instant, a cage all the way around him. It shoved at his legs, and pushed down his head as it shrank, closing him in. It was so small. He couldn't even sit up in it, and his legs, already bruised from his earlier attempts to free them, were torqued back against his body. He let out a roar of pain.

"Stop!" cried Kiska, taking a few frantic steps toward them. "Nova, he's not our enemy. He's like us."

The gaze Nova turned to her stopped her in her tracks. It was dark with suspicion, as though she were just now seeing them for who they truly were. "My enemies are your enemies," she said.

"He's not—" Kiska started, but Nova cut her off.

"You're not going to stop me from finding her. No one's ever going to stop me again."

It was more than Kiska could bear. She said, in distress, her voice rich with empathy, "Nova, Kora's *dead*."

The word *dead* possessed the air. For an instant Kiska beheld the same bottomless anguish that Sarai had seen in Nova's eyes, and then it was gone, and there was only wrath.

And the wrath exploded.

🌿 57 🌿

Awe, Elation, Horror

"I wish we had the dragon," said Ruza, clutching the safety rail of the silk sleigh, and not sounding *quite* as unflappable as one might hope one's warrior escort to sound.

"I'd even take the winged horse," said Thyon, likewise clinging. Both were remembering the mesarthium beasts Lazlo had quickened to fly Eril-Fane, Azareen, and Suheyla up to the citadel. They seemed a much sturdier method of transport just now than this contraption of silk and gas rocked by every breeze.

The city was very far below, this aerial perspective supremely new. Weep's domes and byways made patterns that could not have been guessed at from below, and the devastation of the ripped-up anchors was clear to see. It would have been fascinating if it weren't so terrifying.

In one sleigh, the negligible weight of Sarai, Minya, and Sparrow—a ghost, a stick-child, and an underfed sixteen-year-old—was offset by Thyon and Ruza. In the other, Feral and Ruby shared with Calixte and Tzara. Sarai and Feral were the primary pilots, though Ruby and

Sparrow could each step in if needed. They'd practiced in the pavilion, learning how to operate the outflow valves and, when it came time to descend, release the ulola gas and slowly deflate the pontoons.

The trouble would come in getting back again—if the worst happened and they failed to achieve their aim of reclaiming both Lazlo and their home. (Well, they were all mindful that this was not the very worst that could happen, but they did not speak those other scenarios aloud.) Once the ulola gas was released, which it would have to be for them to descend, the craft would be unable to re-ascend. It was an imperfect device.

They had one advantage that humans would not, and that advantage was Sparrow. Ozwin had given her some ulola seedlings to take with them. If it came to it, she could cultivate them as only she could—with unnatural speed—and essentially grow more gas for a return journey. It was a last resort, but not one Sarai wished to consider, because if it came to that, it would mean Lazlo was lost, and she could not bear the possibility.

With the citadel gone from Weep's sky, it was not easy to guess precisely where the floating orb had been, and the warp had been hard enough to spot when they knew just where it was. That, combined with their novice flight skills, made for a fraught several hours of flying in circles.

"On the upside," said Sarai, trying to contain her growing frustration, "I'm really learning how to maneuver this thing."

It was Ruby who finally spotted it—the quirk in the fabric of the air—and as they circled over to it, the godspawn found their anxiety somewhat alleviated by their anticipation of the humans'—and Minya's—reactions to what they were about to see. Even under dire circumstances, there is a unique pleasure in introducing the bizarre and inconceivable to others.

Ruby did the honors. As Feral brought the craft near, she reached out to the vague, dreamy line in the air and, as Lazlo had, grasped its edges and tugged it open.

The ensuing silence was the sound of two warriors, an alchemist, an acrobat, and Minya forgetting how to breathe. It was short-lived. Calixte shattered it with an exclamation. The words were in her language and thus unintelligible, but they were clearly profane, and captured the mood perfectly: awe, elation, horror.

They saw into the other world.

To their immense relief, the citadel was visible in the middle distance. It had been twisted into a nightmare version of itself. In Weep, the seraph had stood upright, arms outstretched in a pose of supplication. Here, it was hunched and contorted, as though it were cowering under the low gray sky, afraid to stand upright lest the mist enshroud it. Its wings, which had been elegant, were ragged, and the ridges of its spine stood out sharply on its gaunt, warped back. Its arms were wrapped around itself, as though it were cold or afraid, and its face, which had, before, been placid, was a rictus of rage, eyes tight shut, mouth open in a scream.

"That bodes well," said Feral, deadpan.

"What's she done to it?" demanded Ruby.

They all felt the same protective anger—as though the citadel were alive, and the stranger who'd stolen it had harmed or frightened it.

"I'm just glad it's here," Sarai breathed, swallowing her fear. "Let's go get it back."

They flew toward it. In Weep, it had been full daylight, but here it seemed a gloaming time, maybe dusk, maybe dawn. Or maybe there wasn't night or day here, but only perpetual half-light. Sarai couldn't shake the feeling of having slipped not through a cut in the sky, but into a stranger's dream—or nightmare, more like.

There was the sea with its lurid blood color, its violent froth and roar. Silhouettes of great beasts moved dark beneath its surface, vying and clashing in savage attacks that seemed to make the water roil redder. The massive bristling white stalks were awful for their sheer improbability, and the ceiling of mist seemed as much a barrier as the sea, too dense, too dark to navigate.

The silk sleighs were quiet, making only a low, steady *shhhhh* as air streamed from the propulsion bladders on their undersides. The warriors held their swords at the ready. Thyon drew his dueling blade and felt like an impostor. Ruby conjured palmfuls of fire, and glanced more than once out of the corner of her eye to see if the humans were impressed—the golden one, especially. She couldn't get enough of the sight of him, which had not gone unnoticed by Feral.

Minya held the mesarthium shard; they had passed it around, taking turns holding it to keep their magic fresh, but she was never easy until it was back in her possession. She stood in the prow of the sleigh, small and straight, and looked into the face of the seraph as they approached it.

She felt a strange kinship for it. The rage in that frozen scream spoke to something deep within her. As she had lived inside the citadel, so, too, had she lived inside her rage. Every thought she had and every feeling had been filtered through it. But now it was as though she had taken a step backward and could see it there like a red haze. And she saw the fear at the heart of it, too, like a thorn deep in a festering wound. Everything looked clearer now. She was even able to understand that what she saw on that immense metal face was a reflection of the woman who had altered it, whether consciously or not.

Which meant that the flutter of kinship Minya was feeling was for her.

Where was she, though, the real woman? They approached the

citadel with caution, coming up from behind, over the wing to the left shoulder. Their options for entry were limited by the seraph's huddled pose. With its arms clutched around itself, the doors in the wrists were cut off. And even if they'd been able to get in that way, the corridors would have become vertical shafts, too smooth to try to climb. There was only the garden and its arcade.

They were afraid to approach directly, lest there be guards on watch. They would have to ease around from the back and try to get a look in without giving themselves away. Sarai was afraid the sleigh wouldn't be able to reverse quickly enough if someone was there. With its bright red pontoons, even a glimpse of it would draw any remotely vigilant eye. Still, they would have proceeded, had Calixte not proposed another solution.

"Let me off," she said. "There." She pointed to the seraph's shoulder. "Let me climb around and scout it out first. I'll be much less conspicuous."

"*Climb?*" The godspawn were astonished. "It can't be climbed," said Feral with authority and the lightest whiff of disdain.

"Maybe not by *you*," replied Calixte in kind. "We all have our strengths, and that's mine. That and assassination." She winked over her shoulder at Thyon, who had never given any credence to that claim, but was now rather wishing it were true. He wouldn't mind if Calixte were to slip away for a few minutes and quietly solve their problem.

Sarai knew who Calixte was, both from her dream explorations and Lazlo's descriptions. She knew all about the tower and the emerald, and even her practice climbing the anchor in Weep. Still, she looked at the place Calixte indicated, and the thought of her climbing overboard onto sheer mesarthium was terrifying, especially since she knew all too well what it was like to slip over that surface and not find a handhold. But Calixte insisted. "Furthermore," she added, "I can finally win my bet with Ebliz Tod."

Her fellow delegate and countryman had wagered that she couldn't climb the anchor. Well, the anchors were no more, but the citadel itself seemed a suitable substitution, especially considering the risk of sliding off into a red sea filled with monsters. "And anyway," she concluded decisively. "This *is* why I'm here." She paused and sketched a quick glance around. "Well. Not *here* here. But in Weep, at least. Eril-Fane brought me along in case I might come in handy. I haven't yet, so let me."

And so it was decided. Sarai looked to Tzara in case the warrior might object or at least look alarmed, but she only embraced Calixte and kissed her and stood back to watch with fierce pride as Calixte did what she had, after all, come halfway round the world to do: climb.

Feral, somewhat chastened, maneuvered the sleigh closer to a spot on the wing that Calixte indicated, near the shoulder blade. She climbed over the railing, her slight weight not tipping it at all, and...stepped off. None of them were expecting it. Their breath caught in a unified gasp. Sarai rushed to lean over the railing and look down, sure she would see the young human reeling down the metal, scrabbling desperately for a handhold.

But she wasn't. She was scaling it as easily as an ordinary person might walk across a street.

For a moment they just watched in awed silence. Then Ruby asked simply, "...how?"

"She's part spider," Thyon said, remembering she'd told him that.

"Come again?" said Ruby.

Tzara smiled, her eyes never straying from Calixte. "It's quite scandalous. Her great-grandmother apparently fell in love with an arachnid."

"Well, that makes *us* seem positively normal," said Sparrow as they all watched Calixte make her way up the curvature of the angel's shoulder and lower herself over the other side, vanishing from their view. They stayed out of sight, and could only stare fixedly at the last place they'd seen her, waiting for her to reappear and either motion them nearer or . . . perhaps not reappear at all.

But she did, after five minutes that felt like an eternity. Her head popped up, followed by a beckoning arm, and they all let out their breath as one. How easily, Sarai mused, they'd all fallen into rhythm. Adjusting her valves, she set the silk sleigh to scud gently forward, and followed, full of trepidation, as Calixte led them over the edge and all the way down into the garden. *Their* garden. Their home. Their plum trees and kimril patch.

At first it was a surprise to see it crowded with metal creatures, but then Sarai remembered—this wasn't Nova's doing, but Lazlo's. He had brought their guests up on the beasts of the anchors, and here they were with Rasalas.

Her hearts were pounding as she made her descent, expelling enough ulola gas to bring the silk sleigh down to rest on the very same patch of anadne flowers where her body had been immolated. She was conscious as she did so that they would be unable to re-ascend, and could not now reach the portal to make the return journey home. They were committed.

"Aren't they here?" she asked Calixte in a whisper, looking all around, furtive.

"Ye-e-es," Calixte said, the word unfolding like an accordion. "They're here." And, with a hushing gesture, she led them to the arches of the arcade.

Sarai, following warily, caught a glimpse of movement from within and flattened herself against a pillar, gesturing to the others to halt or hide.

"It's all right," said Calixte, then reconsidered her words. "Well, no, it's really not. But anyway, you'd better look."

Sarai peered around the pillar, and the whole ungodly scene was revealed.

 58

A DYING WISH

The gallery wasn't empty. As Calixte had said, they were here, all of them: Nova, Werran, Rook, Kiska. And Lazlo.

Lazlo.

He was in a cage far too small for his long frame, his head bent and his legs shoved into an agonizing crouch. Sarai longed to run to him, to wrench the cage open, but there was no chance of that. The mesarthium cage would yield only to Lazlo's gift—whoever possessed it—and anyway, she wouldn't be able to get to him.

A faint iridescent bubble enclosed him, like the one that had held Eril-Fane and Azareen as they endured their deaths over and over. Kiska and Rook were trapped inside it, too, and this was the movement Sarai had glimpsed. Lazlo, in his cage, was still. It was Kiska and Rook who were in motion—the same motion, the same few seconds repeated, so that Sarai and the others were witness to the moment of their mutiny.

It could only be that.

Kiska was in profile. Sarai saw her hand clench into a fist as she lowered her chin. There was intense focus in her one visible eye—the green one—and then it was gone as her head snapped back and she was thrown off her feet to collide with Rook, who caught her with one arm, the other reaching out in the same spell-casting gesture Nova had made earlier, as though he had tried—and clearly failed—to create a loop of his own.

His target was still right where she must have been then: at the head of the table.

"She's in my chair," Minya whispered with stiff displeasure.

And she was. She was asleep in it, slumped forward over the table with her head cradled in one arm and the other hanging limp, as though she had finally succumbed to an exhaustion so profound she could do nothing but sink down where she was and lay down her head.

After neutralizing the threat of her own people who had turned against her.

Werran too. He wasn't caught in the time loop. He was just outside it, the worse for wear, because *he* was caught in a serpent's mouth.

The beast was mesarthium, like Rasalas and the others in the garden, but it was inchoate, half formed out of the metal of the floor, from which it appeared to emerge, like a breaching sea creature, to capture its prey in massive jaws. Werran's feet hung out one side of the beast's mouth, his head and shoulders from the other. One arm was free and had fallen still, as limp as Nova's, and blood-encrusted from an earlier wound. When he caught sight of them in the arch, he renewed struggling, though feebly.

Sarai remembered what his gift was—that terrible, soul-scouring scream—and tensed, but he made no sound.

461

He couldn't, of course. She saw that that was the point. The serpent's mouth was crushing his chest. He could barely breathe, let alone draw enough air to scream.

"They must have tried to help Lazlo," Sarai whispered, and she was so glad. She'd hated believing they'd been betrayed by their own kind.

"They'd better," Minya said, grim. "To take the side of Korako's blood over their own? I would be very disappointed."

Sarai experienced a flutter of sympathy for the three of them, to be torn between loyalties to Nova and Minya, two terrifying forces of nature. The scenario in the gallery suggested they'd chosen sides.

It also suggested that they'd been effortlessly thwarted, and didn't stand a chance against Nova.

Did *anyone*?

She was asleep, or more like passed out, which could be counted a distinct advantage on the part of those crouched in the archway, but for one thing: Wraith.

The bird was perched on the back of Nova's chair, huge and white and very much awake, watching them with its gleaming dark eyes.

Eril-Fane had told them the truth about Wraith, and it was so strange to think that all these years, the ghostly white bird had been...what, exactly? Not Korako, but some shred of her, some echo? Did the bird even have a consciousness, or was it just acting out a set of old patterns, old hopes, without comprehension?

Sarai wondered if the bird was naught but a dying wish, flying endless spirals, just waiting and watching for an avenue to open that would allow it to fulfill its purpose. Had it been, all this time, just trying to get to Nova? Would it act to protect her?

She had to assume it would. "What do we do?" she breathed.

"Kill her," Minya said, but she didn't say it with relish the way she might have before, and Sarai saw that her hands were fists, her fingers moving over the slickness of blood on her hands.

Sarai had to admit that was the obvious answer. And yet, through no love loss for the woman who had wreaked such havoc, nearly cost Sarai her own soul, and trapped Lazlo like that, it still felt wrong. She hoped that killing would always feel wrong. "I don't think Wraith will let us near her," she ventured.

"We don't have to be near her," said Minya, gesturing to Tzara, who held a bow at the ready. "Are you good with that?"

Tzara's affronted look said that yes, she was.

"Would she die instantaneously?" asked Feral. "Because if she takes even a few seconds, we could all end up in snakes' mouths like him." He gestured to Werran, and they all noticed that he seemed to be gesturing to them.

His free arm, which had been hanging limp and bloody, was now making a frantic beckoning gesture. Sarai, exchanging a quick look with the others, said, "I'll go. You all stay here."

With a look at Wraith, she took her first tentative step. Immediately the bird deepened its protective hunch over Nova, its wings fanning out at its sides. Sarai froze.

She gave up walking, and simply floated, venturing very slowly into the room. When Wraith just watched her, she continued, slow and steady. It was so hard to see Lazlo frozen in that agonizing pose. She wanted to pop the shimmering time loop like a soap bubble and pull the cage apart with her hands. What a power was Nova's, to be able to do that and more.

Wraith followed her with its eyes, but made no further move as Sarai, with ghosts' grace, approached Werran.

Up close, she could hear the wheeze of quick, shallow breaths as he struggled to draw enough air into his compressed lungs to keep himself alive. There was desperation in his eyes as though he was fighting a losing battle. Sarai's hands fluttered uselessly toward him with the urge to help him, but there was nothing she could do. He was wedged deep in the broad metal mouth, the serpent's fangs curved and interlocked around him. The serpent, at least, was inanimate, no more than a statue. Sarai didn't think she could have stood it if it was watching her with its slit-pupil eyes.

Werran was trying to say something to her, but he couldn't do much more than shape sounds with his lips. He had so little breath to work with he could barely whisper. Sarai leaned close and made out the words "*. . . don't . . . kill her . . .*"

She was chastened. Planning to kill somebody was what Minya did, and she hated the feel of it in her mind. "I don't want to," she whispered back, defensive. "But if she wakes up, we're all finished. If she were dead, Lazlo would get his gift back and free you from this thing."

With urgent impatience, he shook his head. "*. . . loop . . .*" It took him a few wheezes to be able to form the next whispered words. "*. . . only . . . she . . . can break . . .*"

It took a moment for Sarai to understand what he was telling her. "Are you saying that if she dies, they'll be trapped like that? But . . . their gifts will go back to them. Rook . . ."

But Werran was shaking his head. "*. . . loop . . .*" was all he could say.

Sarai turned to watch the loop play out another iteration. Kiska's fist clenched. Her head lowered. She was thrown backward. Rook caught her, raised his arm. He was trying to use his magic and failing. And as long as he was caught in the loop, he would keep on failing, just like Eril-Fane and Azareen had kept on dying. These were the seconds that were preserved. And all the while, Lazlo was motionless, powerless, cramped in his cage. Would he stay that way forever? Or would he die slowly of dehydration, starvation, while Sarai was just steps away, unable to reach him? Either thought was unbearable.

"What can we do?" she asked, helpless.

Werran's desperate eyes told her that he could suggest no plan. All he managed in his airless whisper was, ". . . *help*."

🔥 59 🔥

A Game that *Kill* Could Not Win

Help.

Werran might have been trying to plead "Help me," or even "Help *us*," and run out of breath, but it was the single word that rang in Sarai's head.

Help. Help. Help.

It seemed to take up position opposite *kill*, as though they were facing queens on a quell board. This was a game that *kill* could not win—or, if it did, it would be an unbearable win that destroyed the very meaning of winning. If they killed Nova, they were sentencing Lazlo, Kiska, and Rook to either eternity in the loop or to dying in it, while Werran would suffocate in the serpent's jaws. The rest of them would be alive, trapped in this terrible sky instead of Weep's, and here they would stay until Sparrow could grow enough ulola flowers to refill the silk sleighs' pontoons with lifting gas, and then what? Go back to Weep? Make some sort of life? Leave the seraph here, leave Lazlo here, alive or dead in that shimmering bubble for strangers to find some day in the future?

It was, all of it, unthinkable. There had to be another way.

Sarai went back to the others, still clustered in the archway. She told them what she'd learned and let it sink in. In their stricken silence, she felt her own desolation deepen. Perhaps she'd hoped that someone else would see a way out that she wasn't seeing.

Calixte ventured, "Maybe she won't kill us when she wakes up?"

But Calixte hadn't been in the citadel to see Nova in action, and judging by the scene in the gallery, she had not become more tolerant since then. Besides, "maybe she won't kill us" is very thin ice to skate on. There had to be something they could do.

Help. Help. Help.

Werran's word was still ringing in Sarai's mind. *Help.* All her life, Sarai had been a prisoner and a secret, and she had wondered what her fate would be. Would the humans find her and kill her, or would she remain a secret prisoner forever? Then Eril-Fane and his delegation had returned to Weep and changed everything. It had become a certainty: The humans would discover the godspawn, and they would kill them—unless Minya and her army killed the humans instead. It was only a question of who would die, and who would get to clean up the blood and keep living.

And then Sarai had met Lazlo—in his mind, in his dreams—and once again, everything changed. This dreamer-librarian from a far-off land had taught her to hope for a different life—one without any killing at all. In his mind, ugly things were made beautiful, and that went for the future, too.

But now he was trapped, and Sarai realized she'd been relying on him to make it all come true. His gift—power over mesarthium—had meant their liberation and their strength, but it wouldn't help them now.

What *would* help them? Who would save them?

A panicked thrum was building in her blood—illusory blood, illusory thrum, but still real, as *she* was still real—and Sarai scanned the hopeless scene again: the monstrous half-formed serpent crushing a man to slow death in its jaws; the shimmering bubble too pretty for a prison; the huge white bird guarding the sleeping goddess.

Nova looked so small and exhausted, slumped over and limp, and Sarai couldn't help but remember the terrible anguish she'd seen in her eyes, and worse: her brief, brilliant joy, when, for an instant, she believed she'd found her sister.

She heard herself say, "Maybe I can do something."

Everyone looked at her. Minya spoke first. "What can *you* do?" she asked, and some of her old scorn clung to her words, but not much, thought Sarai. Not like before.

"She's asleep," said Sarai. "I...I could go into her dreams."

"And do what?" Minya queried.

"I don't know. Help her?"

"*Help* her?" Minya stared. They all did. "Help *her?*" she repeated, her shift in emphasis eloquent. "After what she's done?"

Sarai was at a loss. "That's *grief*," she said of the scene in the gallery. She knew that Lazlo would have understood. "You don't have to feel sorry for her, but killing her won't solve our problems, and maybe the only way we're going to get through this is if we can *help* her."

Minya was studying Sarai, contemplative. "You can't save everyone, Sarai. You know that, don't you?"

Sarai wondered if Minya remembered her coming into her dreams, unwrapping the babies, making an escape door, trying to help her and failing. "I know," she said. "But we can *try*. And... maybe that's how we save ourselves."

Minya took in these words. Sarai could *see* it—that she took them in and turned them over, considering them. The change was so tremendous it almost stopped her breath. She was so used to Minya *not* taking things in, but only spinning them round, sharpening them into weapons and flinging them right back. She was already tensed for it, so when Minya's consideration seemed to *absorb* her words, and the expected recoil didn't come, she felt . . . lightened? As though it might really be possible.

"All right," said Minya.

All right, said Minya. Sarai struggled to keep her astonishment from showing. Minya was *never* agreeable. It was part of her makeup. Sarai hoped that the miracle of her acquiescence might be the start of a chain of miracles that could see them through this, back to the strange and wonderful future Lazlo had taught her to believe in.

It occurred to her that those miracles—and that future—rested entirely on *her*. With a deep breath, she turned toward Nova and Wraith.

* * *

"I'm not going to hurt her," Sarai breathed, slowly approaching the chair, though she didn't know if the bird understood. She held its gaze the whole time. Its black eyes were intense, unblinking, but it didn't object as Sarai drew near. Uneasily, she came to stand beside Nova, near enough to touch her. Where, though? She was still wearing that oil-black garb with the plates of mesarthium she'd rendered into armor. Sarai was reminded of trying to find a place for her moths to land on sleeping humans, though that had been so much easier than this. Back then, if a dreamer woke, she herself wasn't looming over them.

Sarai wondered if she would have been able to torment the people of Weep with nightmares if she'd had to stand right beside them, touching them, feeling their pulse spike under her hand. It was so much more intimate this way.

Tentatively, mindful of Wraith, she reached out for the little triangle of blue skin where Nova's fair hair slipped over her neck, revealing it. Sarai's hand hovered just above it as she kept eye contact with the bird, trying to assure it with her gaze that she meant no harm. It could have been her imagination, but it seemed the bird understood.

So she placed her fingertips very softly against Nova's skin and was drawn into her dream.

60

THIN ICE

Sarai found herself in a place that was not the citadel or the red-sea world or Weep or anywhere else she knew. It was killingly cold, and as far as she could see in every direction, there were only sheets of white ice. It wasn't peaceful, as she had, in the past, imagined snowy landscapes in dreams. This was the sea, and it was frozen, all its latent violence still boiling beneath the surface. A skin of ice lay over it, but not quietly. It moaned and shrieked, shifting under Sarai's feet. When a crack opened up, lightning fast and jagged as teeth in a monster's jaws, she had to leap aside or be sucked down into the fathomless black water.

Fear slammed into her, and she had to remind herself that it wasn't real, and that she had power here, and was at nobody's mercy.

It took conscious effort to *unfeel* the cold. She'd never experienced anything like it, not in Weep, where there was no real winter. Feral's stolen snowstorms didn't even hint at this penetrating *ache*. Sarai could have willed it warm. She could have changed it to some other landscape altogether, but it was important to learn why she was here—or, rather, why Nova was.

Sarai searched for her. She turned a circle, gazing around at the sweep of vast empty white, and perceived a set of figures on the horizon.

They were three, too distant to make out. She started toward them, thinking Nova must be one of them, but before she'd gone more than a few feet, something caught her eye under the surface of the ice.

A face.

She recoiled from it, then forced herself to look, because in that split-second glimpse, she'd seen who it was.

It was Eril-Fane. He was dead and staring, trapped beneath the ice.

What was he doing in this dream? This world had nothing to do with him. Just beyond him, Sarai saw another face and braced herself. It was Azareen. Her eyes were open and staring and filmed with ice crystals. Her dying scream had frozen as bubbles welling out of her mouth.

It was terrible to see them like this, and Sarai clung to the knowledge that there was no truth to it. The two of them were very much alive and together in Weep. She went on, and almost right away encountered another dead face—a stranger this time. Then another. A trail of them lay under the ice all the way to the figures in the distance, like a path of awful stepping-stones. She stopped looking, stopped counting, and grew numb to them as she went past, rushing to get to the trio of figures as though that would be an end to it.

She reached them. They were garbed heavily in skins and furs, their faces—blue, all three—recessed into fur-lined hoods. The smallest of them was Nova. She looked afraid, determined,

472

exhausted, grim. With her were two men: one old, and one of middle years. There was a sledge and dogs as well, and they were near the end of a long journey, their destination visible as smudges of chimney smoke on the horizon.

At least, it was Nova's destination. The men would be going no farther. As Sarai watched, Nova spoke to them, her voice flat and her words final, issuing a command they were powerless to refuse. With a start, she realized that she could understand the command, the sense if not the precise words, the dream feeding her meaning on some level below language. It was very simple.

Go into the sea.

With terror in their eyes, the men stepped off the edge of a shelf of ice and sank like stones into the frigid black water. Just like that, they were gone.

Sarai felt sick, as though it were really happening. And she understood that it *had* really happened, just like this, and that these were the first men Nova had ever killed. These were the first, and Eril-Fane and Azareen the most recent. And that whole trail of faces, those were all the ones in between. Sarai turned to look back the way she'd come, and their sheer quantity numbed her. How many lives had Nova taken, how many souls loosed to their evanescence? After so many, would she even hesitate to add to her terrible tally?

Turning back, Sarai saw with a jolt that Nova was looking at her.

In the rush of her decision to try this, it hadn't occurred to her to wonder whether Nova would be able to see her. Minya was only the second who ever had, after Lazlo. Did this mean that Mesarthim could and humans couldn't? Or was it one more way Sarai's gift had changed since her death? It didn't matter now. All that mattered was Nova's dark-eyed suspicion, pinning her in place.

"What are *you* doing here?" she asked, and Sarai saw that she recognized her. Hostility flickered in her gaze.

"I followed the path," she said, indicating the faces under the ice. The two men who'd just died were there now, too. The rift in the ice had refrozen, and their faces were pressed right up against it, as though they'd tried to get free. She wondered if Nova would understand her, as she understood Nova.

She seemed to. "From where?" she wanted to know, squinting out over the ice. She sounded very young. Her face was fuller, her eyes wider, not yet shaped by centuries of horizons.

"From...the end," said Sarai.

"That's not the end," said Nova. "You don't get to the end until you die."

Sarai tried to process these words. Did she mean that you weren't done killing until you were dead, that the life you left behind you was a path of corpses? She didn't ask. Instead, she ventured, with a gesture at the two nearest faces, "But this is the beginning, isn't it." This was where Nova had become a killer, and there was no evidence of remorse in her. "What did they do, these two?"

Nova looked down at them with no more emotion than if they really were stepping-stones. She pointed to one. "He sold me." The other. "He bought me." She didn't say the words *father* and *husband*, but the knowledge was imparted to Sarai through the medium of the dream.

Nova's father had sold her to an old man when she was younger than Sarai was now. "I'm sorry," said Sarai, her gut knotting with sympathetic misery.

While she watched, Nova pushed back her hood and took off her diadem. Her skin drained immediately of blue—and not to warm brown, like Sparrow's had, but a paler shade of skin than Sarai had ever seen—a kind of milky ivory that, combined with her fair hair, made her look washed out, like a bit of sun-bleached bone. Even her lips were pale. The only thing that really stood out were her brown eyes, shining like wet river stones.

"Not as sorry as they were," said Nova with a nod to the ice. "I couldn't let them live." She held up the diadem. "I can't be blue when I get to Targay. I have to fade, but they'd have killed me as soon as my power was gone."

"Your own father?" asked Sarai, and she was thinking of Eril-Fane, and her own very recent worries of what he'd do when he discovered her.

Nova shrugged. She sounded far away when she said, "No one loves anyone here. They all just scrape against each other, like rocks in a bag."

Gently, Sarai said, "But you loved Kora."

Loved. The instant Sarai spoke the word in past tense, the ice beneath her feet gave a deafening crack and opened up like another set of devouring jaws beneath her. She had to leap into the air and stay there. It took far more than the usual effort to believe she could float and not be sucked down. The aura of the dream was like a weight pulling at her feet, and when she chanced a look below, she saw all the staring dead gathered together like jetsam on a tide.

Nova still stood there, impossibly, her feet curled over the very edge of the ice that Sarai could see was as thin as paper. She was staring at Sarai. Her pupils had dilated, and there was menace and madness in them. "I *love* Kora," she corrected, harsh. "And I'm going to find her, and if you try to stop me, you'll end up with the rest of them." She gestured to the dead.

A chill went up Sarai's spine that had nothing to do with the ice. This might have been a scene from Nova's youth, and this place might be her provenance, but when she spoke that threat, her eyes weren't young at all. Everything was in them: all her years of seeking and failing and believing—believing what? That she would save her sister, when there wasn't even a wisp of hope to grasp at, let alone a strand to hang on to and follow into the dark. Belief like that, that hasn't tasted any real hope in centuries, but has been fed and nurtured on darker things—loneliness, desperation—it doesn't simply subside when faced with its own end. It doesn't accept or adapt. It exists in spite of reason, and will only ever defy it.

Kora was dead.

The truth would destroy Nova. Somewhere, her mind had built a blur around it, like the one Sarai had encountered in Minya's mind. But the truth has a way of seeping out. The mind can't erase. It can only conceal, and concealed things are not gone.

It struck Sarai that Nova's belief was like this ice: It was fragile, it was thin, and it was all that was keeping her from plunging into her own black depths. A spark of panic chased the chill up Sarai's spine. All of their lives rested on this ice, and it would not hold.

Nova was a half step in any direction from madness. Sarai could feel it in every crack of the ice, and in the pull of the black water, almost as though the sea were calling out to her by name.

Urgently, she fed her own will into the dream, refreezing the ice, strengthening it, and settling it, as though by doing so she could strengthen and settle what was breaking apart inside Nova. If only she *could*. Her mother could have, but wouldn't have.

What could Sarai do? She had an arsenal of nightmares. If she wanted to *hasten* Nova's madness, she was well equipped. But she didn't want to be the Muse of Nightmares anymore. Who *did* she want to be? She remembered Lazlo telling her, before she went for the second time into Minya's dreams, "You're not trying to defeat her. Remember that. You're trying to help her defeat *her* nightmare."

But how could you defeat a nightmare that was only and simply the truth?

"I wouldn't try to stop you," she said to Nova, trying to keep her voice calm even as the ice fragmented under her. Thinking back to Minya's dream reminded her how futile it was to try to alter the pattern, when fear had carved so deep a path. She would have to try something else. She wished Lazlo were here to help her. What would he do? she wondered, and as soon as she did, the answer came to her, and the dream wavered and changed. The whole bleak ice landscape vanished, and she and Nova were standing instead in the amphitheater of Weep.

No, not Weep, and not as Sarai had seen it last, full of ghosts and warriors. This was Dreamer's Weep, a place built of stories and longing and wonder, to be found only in Lazlo's mind—and hers. Always before, he had made it for her. This time she'd gotten here on her own.

"Where are we?" demanded Nova. She wasn't wearing her cold-weather gear now, but her oil-black skin with its armored plates.

"A safe place," said Sarai. That was the answer that had come to her. That was what Lazlo would do—*had* done, time and again. The library, the riverbank, her father's house, and, above all, Dreamer's Weep with its wingsmiths and tea stalls and wonders. He had brought her somewhere safe.

"There are no safe places," scoffed Nova, and Sarai felt the ground give under her feet, and realized, with a sinking sensation, that they hadn't left the ice behind. "If you haven't learned that yet, you will."

That was the lesson of Nova's long life: that there were no safe places. Or perhaps, Sarai thought, there was one. She shifted the dream again.

Surely mesarthium floors were stronger than ice. She brought Nova home—to her own home, that is, which Nova had stolen—to the very room they were actually *in*.

In reality, Nova was asleep in Minya's chair and Sarai was lightly touching the back of her neck. In the dream, they were standing under one of the arches, looking out into the garden. There were no huge white stalks, no low gray mist. A sun was rising in the distance. What sun, what world, it didn't even matter. They couldn't see the ground from here, but only plum trees against the balustrade, and clouds like spun sugar. "Is this better?" she asked Nova.

"It's only as safe as the one who controls it," said Nova, but the metal was firm underneath their feet, and Sarai thought that was something.

"That's true," she acknowledged. Skathis had used the citadel to set himself up as a monstrous god. Lazlo would have . . .

She swallowed hard. Lazlo would have and would *still* make it a safe place, and not just for them but for others who needed it. "People," she said. "*People* are our safe places. I have one: a person who's a home and a world to me." Her eyes welled with tears. "And I can't imagine losing him, as I know you can't imagine losing Kora."

"I *won't* lose her," said Nova, defiant, and Sarai caught a flash of anguish in her eyes, and something else: She tasted blood. It was in the aura of the dream, and it carried with it an undertone like a hum that went *too late, too late*. Nova was biting down on the inside of her cheek, and Sarai began to understand, in some small way, the effort it was costing her, every second, to maintain her denial.

"Tell me about her," she urged, to keep her talking—as though it could keep her from doing anything else, like waking up or shattering into a million pieces. "What was she like?" As soon as the past tense slipped out of her mouth, she tensed and added hastily, "Before, I mean."

Nova was on the edge, but she let the slip pass. "Before" made sense to her in a profound way. Before Skathis, before blue skin, before they were torn apart. "She was *Kora*," she answered, as though everything was in the word, and, in the way of dreams, everything *was*.

Nova gave Kora to Sarai in the same way that Lazlo had given her cake and expanded the boundaries of pleasure: through this medium of joined minds that was Sarai's gift. Memories washed over her. She saw two motherless girls in a barren world who were more real to each other than reflections in a mirror. Indeed, they had no mirrors where they came from, and each imagined the other's face as her own. Sarai felt what it had meant to be half of a whole, and to trust in a voice that would never fail to answer. The memories sank into her.

She learned the stench of uuls and the sting of Skoyë's slap, and she saw the glint of a ship in the sky and understood what it meant. She saw Skathis when he was just a minor imperial officer in the home world he would later leave in anarchy and chaos. And...

She saw Wraith emerge from Kora's chest.

It startled her. Eril-Fane had said that Wraith came out of Kora, but Sarai hadn't been able to imagine it. The bird was so big it hardly seemed possible that it could come out of so slight a girl, and even less so that it could return, but it did. It poured out of her chest like a ghost, and melted back in like a soul returning to its body.

It wasn't a ghost. They'd always known that. It was more like

Sarai's own moths had been. "Korako's gift was always a mystery to us," she told Nova. "I never knew it was like mine."

Nova looked at her sharply. "You're an astral?"

"A what?" Apologetic, Sarai explained, "No one ever taught us about our gifts. We were all alone here."

"No one ever taught me, either," said Nova, and she didn't need to add that she'd been all alone, too. "Astral means 'of the stars.' It's someone who can send their soul out of their body."

Of the stars. Sarai liked that. She wanted to tell Lazlo. "Mine was moths," she said. "A hundred of them." Wrinkling up her nose, she added, "They flew out of my mouth."

Nova's eyes went wide, and Sarai had to smile. "I know it sounds terrible," she said, "but it wasn't."

"Wasn't?" asked Nova, noting the tense.

Slowly, Sarai nodded. For a moment she indulged herself in imagining a future in which she would meet new people and have to decide if and when to tell them, *By the way, I'm not exactly* alive. To Nova, she said simply, "I died, and my gift changed. I suppose I'm not an astral anymore. I'm not sure what I am now," she admitted. "Besides a ghost."

Nova looked at her as though it finally made sense, how Sarai had been able to turn into smoke, and all the rest of it. "You're a *ghost*," she said.

Sarai nodded. She kept thinking of Wraith melting in Kora's chest. She remembered the burgeoning sensation in her own every night just after sunset. *Astral*, she thought with amazement. There was a name for it, because there were more of them—more godspawn like her, and Kora had been one of them.

A wild thought took hold of her.

Abruptly, without leaving the dream, she shifted part of her awareness back to reality. With her moths, it had been seamless, shifting among the hundred of them with the mad choreography of a flock of swifts. She hadn't tried splitting her attention since she'd lost them. It made for a strange twinning: the real room and the dream room, both at the same time. Nova was still cradling her head on one arm, and Wraith was still there, perched on her chairback, watching Sarai's every move.

Sarai stared into the bird's eyes and murmured, thoughtful, "Why are you still here?"

Words came back to her from her own earlier musing: A *shred, an echo.* Both of those sounded haphazard, but could it really be chance, that the bird remained?

A *dying wish*, that was more intriguing.

A *message in a bottle*, she thought, and it lit up her mind like the moment the setting sun touches the sea. Was she mad or brilliant? There was one way to find out. Did she dare? Was it possible? She was a ghost and Wraith was a ... a left-behind piece of a soul? Who knew what arcane rules governed the likes of them. Holding the bird's gaze, Sarai put her hand to her own chest, in the same spot where she had seen it melt into Kora's, and she tapped her breast-bone in invitation.

The bird understood. It didn't hesitate. Its look sharpened and it dove. Sarai was overwhelmed by a rush of white. It felt like wind blowing into her through an open window—right into the very core of her.

From the archway, Minya, Thyon, and all the rest saw it happen. At first, they thought Wraith had lost patience with Sarai's trespass. They gasped. Ruza started forward, his hreshtek in his hand, as though he would be able to defend her. Minya convulsively tightened her grip on Sarai's tether, lest it be tugged from her grasp. Then

Wraith flew at the very center of Sarai's chest and they could do nothing but watch. Its vast wings folded back, and it vanished into her like inhaled smoke. Her back arched. Her head snapped back. Her feet weren't touching the floor. Before anyone understood what was happening, Wraith had disappeared into Sarai.

"*That can't be good,*" breathed Ruby, shocked.

Or, then again, maybe it could.

❧ 61 ❧

MESSAGE IN A BOTTLE

Just the other night, Sarai had swum in the sea with Lazlo in a dream, and found a floating bottle with a message inside. She had spotted it bobbing in a patch of phosphorescence, shaken out the rolled page, and read: *Once upon a time there was a silence that dreamed of becoming a song, and then I found you, and now everything is music.*

That was ink on parchment, preserved in glass, all of it delivered in a dream.

This was memory and emotion, preserved in . . . Well, if anywhere in the layered worlds there existed scholars of godsmetal and its gifts, perhaps they could explain, beyond merely "Magic." But "magic" will do.

When Wraith poured into Sarai, Kora appeared in the dream.

She was a phantasm, of course, but not of Sarai's making. She looked like the woman Sarai had seen in the nursery doorway—she was even wearing the mesarthium collar—but she also *didn't* look like her, because that woman had been blank-faced and stiff, and this one was anything but. There was so much in her expression, a lifetime's worth of feeling—many lifetimes' worth—concentrated into a moment. Fear was vying with courage, and courage was winning. Danger pulsed all around her. There was a feeling of having raced through a labyrinth and found only dead ends—a labyrinth with no solution. She was striving to face her last moments with grace, and there was sorrow, and regret, and there was longing, and yearning, and love.

So much love. Her eyes shone with it, and it was all for Nova.

As soon as Nova saw her, her hands flew to her mouth, one atop the other, as though to hold her sobbing in, because immediately her tears spilled over and her shoulders were shaking and her eyes were shining. "Kora?" she asked in a sweetly hesitant voice that knocked the centuries of hardship and bitterness off her, so that she seemed more like the girl who had crossed a frozen sea more than two hundred years ago. "Is it really you?"

Kora, or this phantasm of her, said, "My love, my own heart, I don't have much time."

She went to her and took her by the shoulders and just looked at her as though to fill herself up with the sight. Nova looked back at her the same way, and here, after all these years, was the face that was truer than a mirror—similar to her own, but not a copy. They weren't twins, and...

With no mirrors on Rieva, Nova never saw her own face clearly until she left. And when she did, it wasn't the *right* face. It was close, but wrong. Always, the sight of her own face had jarred her with its *almostness*, its *not-quiteness*. It had never felt as real to her as the one she grew up looking at. *Here* was her real reflection. *This* was who she was: what she saw looking back at her when her sister looked at her, and it had been the same for Kora. Apart, each had been like a cry into empty space, no walls to throw an echo back. There had been no way to *get* back, only decades of hurtling headlong in silence, no reflection, no echo, no self.

Now they drank each other in and filled each other up, and Kora's phantasm—this little piece of herself she'd managed to leave behind—spoke.

"I don't have much time," she said again, and licked her lips, and doom hung on her like a shawl. "I so desperately wanted to be here when you came. I always, *always* knew you would. I never doubted you for one second in two centuries. I could *feel* you out there, *trying*, and it broke my heart every day. From the moment I sent you the diadem and the letter, I knew you wouldn't give up on me." She let out a little choked sob. "And not a day of my life has passed that I haven't been sorry. I'm so sorry, my Novali. Can you ever forgive me? I was so selfish. I knew you could make it to Aqa and save me, and we could kill that monster"—for an instant, her pretty face contorted with savage hatred that Sarai thought could only be for Skathis—"and we could be together and do anything." Like a stanza of a poem worn soft with repetition, she whispered, "As blue as sapphires and glaciers, and as beautiful as stars." Tears streaked her face. "But he took me away."

She was holding Nova's hands now, clasping them tight. "He took me out of the world, and then I knew that what I'd asked of you was impossible. And I knew that you'd do it anyway, and that I'd ruined your life."

"*You* didn't ruin my life," said Nova, fierce. "*He* did, when he took you and left me in the dirt. And our father did. Rieva did. You *gave* me a life, with the diadem. A purpose. Do you think I could have stayed there and had that old man's babies? I'd have walked straight into the sea. Kora, it knew my name. It called to me. The only thing that kept me alive was knowing that you were out there, and you needed me."

Back in the wasp ship all those years ago, when Nova's gift had erupted and gone wild, it was Kora who'd brought her back to herself, her sister's voice like a rope thrown into a churning sea. And that was what her purpose had been like, all this time, and what Kora's phantasm was now: a rope thrown into a sea, saving Nova from drowning.

"And the only thing that kept *me* alive was knowing you would come," said Kora. "I couldn't bear the thought that you'd get all the way here and find me gone."

There was a half beat of silence, and then Nova asked, in a child's broken whisper, devastated, unbearable, "*Are* you gone?"

And Kora, sobbing, her blue face shining like wet lapis, said, "Oh my Nova. I am."

Sarai, standing back, watching, was overcome by the sisters' welling grief. She was sobbing, too.

"*No.*" The word was pulled, twisting, out of the depths of Nova's soul. Her treacherous whisper had always been right. "I was too late," she said, weeping. "I'm sorry, Kora."

"*No,*" said Kora with tigress ferocity. "What I asked of you was impossible. How could a girl from nowhere, with nothing, cross dozens of worlds all on her own?"

"It wasn't impossible," said Nova. "I did it! Which only means I could have done it *faster.*"

Kora was shaking her head. "It's not your fault. I should have gotten free and found you. I should have been stronger."

"It isn't weak to ask for help."

"It's weak not to help yourself. But I tried. Nova, I almost did it. In a few more years I'd have been free. I stole a smith baby before Skathis could kill him. I took him and hid him far away, so that when he was older I could end Skathis and not be trapped on the wrong side of a portal. I would have found you. But I ran out of time."

"I know," said Nova, teeth gritted, because she had seen Kora's death in her murderer's own memory.

"I'm running out of time right now," Kora said, and Sarai was pierced by her urgency. "Nova, listen to me. If you're here, then you'll know what became of me, and also . . . what I became." Shame clung to her words. "I know you would have been stronger. You'd have saved all those children instead of helping *sell* them. My love, I know you'll be angry, but I want you to listen to me. I wanted so much to be here for you, but that doesn't mean I deserved to live. I was part of something terrible, whether I chose it or not. They weren't wrong to kill us. Promise me: *no vengeance*. Let all the ugliness end here. I love you so much."

Kora wrapped her arms around Nova, and Sarai caught a glimpse of Nova's stricken face before she buried it in her sister's shoulder and gave in to racking sobs. And as heartbreaking as that was, it was far worse when Kora faded—the phantasm faded, its energy expended in the fulfillment of its purpose—and left Nova sobbing alone. Alone again, truly and forever.

Sarai was standing, devastated, in the dream, her arms wrapped around herself, her face slick with tears. Nova met her eyes, and Sarai felt like she was falling with her into the black place inside her. There could be no denial after this. Kora was gone and Nova knew it.

"I'm sorry," Sarai whispered.

Nova's face crumpled and she curled over herself, the pain too much to bear. She shook her head from side to side, saying, "No, no," but it wasn't denial anymore. It was devastation. Her eyes were frenzied, mad with loss. Had the ice given way? Would she drag them all down with her?

Hearts hammering with fear, Sarai made an effort to infuse the dream aura with a feeling of calm. "She loved you very much," she said. "She never doubted you. She knew you would do the impossible for her. Do you know how rare it is, to trust someone like that?"

"I already killed them," said Nova.

Sarai didn't know who she meant. All those faces under the ice. She had killed so many people.

"She said *no vengeance*," said Nova, rigid with the horror of what she had done, "but I already killed them."

Sarai understood in a rush. "Oh! No," she said. "They're alive. Sparrow saved them," and Nova's eyes closed—not squeezed shut, but softly, with unmistakable relief. "Really?" she asked, as though it were too much to hope that this small portion of her burden might lift.

"Really," Sarai told her, a little of her tension cautiously ebbing. If Nova was feeling remorse for that, then maybe her sister's words had gotten through to her. "He's my father, the one who..." She trailed off. "He also did terrible things to save the people he loved. It wasn't his fault. And it wasn't Kora's, or yours. It was the gods, like a canker at the center of everything. But they're gone. Let the ugliness die with them."

Let all the ugliness end here, Kora's phantasm had said.

"Can you?" Sarai asked. "Please?" There was a note of desperation in her voice as she thought of Lazlo, caged, and Rook, Kiska, and Werran trapped, and all the others as good as trapped, too, all of them at Nova's mercy, and all depending on her. Nova heard the note in her voice, too, and understood it—and the reason for it. Here, in the dream, she'd been lost in the past. Now, suddenly, she recollected the present, and the dream split in half and spilled them both out.

Nova lurched awake and came upright, twisting free of Sarai's light touch and turning, rising, all in one movement to face her. They were both breathing fast. The truth ached between them like a heart, but things were different in the waking world. Their communion had evaporated, that had allowed them to feel what the other was feeling, and understand each other, beyond all language barriers. Sarai couldn't tell what Nova was thinking.

She held very still, as though she were facing a wounded predator, unpredictable in its pain and its power. She was conscious that Tzara's arrow must be trained on Nova, ready to fly, and she was desperate that it *not*. She wanted to turn her head or call out, but she was afraid to take her eyes off Nova, or to alert her to the others' presence if she hadn't already noticed them. So she only turned one hand toward the arcade, palm out, and silently willed them: *Hold.*

Her gaze flickered to Lazlo in his cage, and Nova's followed. Nova winced when she beheld the tableau and had to reckon with what she'd done, then she flicked out a hand to open the loop. The iridescent bubble evaporated and Kiska and Rook were free. They stumbled, disoriented. Rook's hand was still raised, ready to draw a loop of his own, but he stopped when he saw Sarai, and blinked.

Next, the serpent's jaws opened and spilled Werran out before the creature collapsed back into the floor, leaving nothing but smooth mesarthium.

And then Lazlo.

The cage swelled as it sank, releasing him slowly as it melted away and set him down on the floor. Sarai flew to him. She caught him in her arms. His face was a rictus of pain, his limbs cramped in the position they'd held for so long. She helped him lift his head, and she set her brow against his and breathed his breath and kissed his perfect imperfect nose that stories had left their mark on, as they had left their mark in him.

"You're still here," he whispered like a prayer. His voice was ravaged. It sounded like he'd screamed until he wore his throat bloody, and Sarai realized he had believed she'd evanesced. He touched her face as though to make sure he wasn't imagining her. "Are you all right?" He looked at her and looked as though he couldn't get enough of looking, as though he'd been saving all his witchlight, and then he was crying, and she was crying, and he was smiling and he was slowly unfolding his limbs, wincing, and Sarai's hearts felt as though all her moths *and* Wraith were living inside her chest, and a sweet wind had caught them and sent them all spinning.

Rook and Kiska were helping Werran to sit up. He was drawing deep, heaving breaths into his lungs. In the archway, the others were wary, glancing back and forth between Sarai and Lazlo, Kiska, Rook, and Werran, and Nova, who stood alone. Tzara had not lowered her bow.

Nova seemed aware of no one. Sarai saw her turn, moving slowly, her gaze unfixed, and take a step toward the arcade. There were a half-dozen open archways. Minya and the others were in the center. She didn't look at them, but went around them to the right. Sarai helped Lazlo to stand, and they followed her into the garden.

Out there it was all flowers and metal creatures, their own familiar garden until you looked out past the plum trees, where the massive white stalks rose up and disappeared into the mist. There was no Wraith flying circles, and there never would be again. The bird had vanished for the last time.

Nova went to the balustrade. Sarai followed her. The others hung back.

She stood looking out, one hand on the railing. She spoke, but her words didn't filter into sense as they had in the dream. They made an impenetrable thatch of syllables. Sarai, uneasy, glanced back over her shoulder and saw Kiska take a half step forward. She caught Sarai's eye, gave a little nod, and then spoke into her mind.

It was all for nothing, she translated. *She says the sea tried to warn her. She didn't listen.*

"The sea?" Sarai queried, looking at Nova and hearing Kiska's voice in her mind.

When Nova answered, Kiska's translation came simultaneously. *It always knew.*

"How could it have known?" Sarai asked gently. She thought of the cold black water in the dream, and feared Nova was again losing her grip on reality.

But when Nova turned to face her, she looked more sane than Sarai had yet seen her. She spoke, and Kiska translated. *It knew my name*, Nova said. She was calm. *The sea always knew my name.*

And then she took a step back.

The balustrade was there. But then it wasn't. She hadn't given back Lazlo's gift yet. For a moment her eyes locked on Sarai's. All the ice was gone from them. They were brown and tired and sad. Just as Sarai realized, just as she reached, Nova leaned back.

And fell.

❧ 62 ❧

THE ONES WHO KNOW

Once upon a time, a sister made a vow she didn't know how to break, and it broke her instead.

Once upon a time, a girl did the impossible, but she did it just a little too late.

Once upon a time, a woman finally gave up, and the sea was waiting. It was the wrong sea—red as blood and just as warm—but falling felt like freedom, like letting go of trying, and on the way down she took her first full breath in centuries.

Then it was all over.

Or maybe it wasn't.

The ones who know can't tell us, and the ones who tell us don't know.

Part V

* * *

Amezrou (AH·may·zroo) *noun*

When something deeply precious, long lost and despaired of, is found and restored, against all expectation.

New; not yet in common usage.

❦ 63 ❦

It Would Be Stranger If There Weren't Dragons

Lazlo did not bring the citadel back through the portal. The last thing Weep needed was the hated metal angel pouring back into its sky. Weep would never again live in shadow.

It would also never again be *Weep*.

Kiska, Rook, and Werran remembered its real name. When Letha, goddess of oblivion, had eaten Weep's true name, her power had not reached past the sealed portal into Var Elient. And so, three godspawn born in the citadel to be sold as slaves to fight other worlds' wars restored what had been devoured.

Amezrou.

Once upon a time, a little boy in a frost-rimed orchard had roared it out like thunder, like an avalanche, like the war cry of the seraphim who had cleansed the world of demons, only to have it stolen from his mind between one slash of his apple bough sword and the next. Now it was back, and it felt, as it ever had, like calligraphy, if calligraphy were written in honey.

Though Lazlo let the citadel remain above the red sea, he and Sarai and the others went back and forth between worlds often over the next few weeks, making preparations for their journey. They had no shortage of transportation for the short trip through the portal. They returned the silk sleighs to Soulzeren, which left them with the entire fleet of vessels seized over the years by Nova and her pirate crew, as well as Lazlo's metal creatures—Rasalas and the others—and the pair of wasp ships, which were no longer wasps.

Mesarthium skyships are shaped by the mind of their captain, and Lazlo transformed these into *moths*, in homage to those that had brought Sarai into his dreams, his mind, his hearts, his life.

He transformed the citadel, too.

"You have to admit, it's magnificent," said Calixte from the small airship she had commandeered for her own and christened *Lady Spider*.

"Fine," drawled Ruza, peevish. "It's magnificent."

They had just come through the portal for the last time in the knowable future. The citadel was before them, looking quite different now that it was no longer in seraph form. They had all discussed what new shape it might take, and offered suggestions, though the ultimate decision had been Lazlo's. He needn't have consulted anyone, but, being Lazlo, he had. Anyway, he had made the only obvious choice, and no one disagreed except Ruza. "A dragon would be *more* magnificent," he said, not letting it go.

"You and your dragons," remarked Tzara. "Don't worry. I'm sure Lazlo will let you have a dragon to ride."

Thyon kept thinking he was through being surprised by statements like, "I'm sure Lazlo will let you have a dragon to ride," but no. It just didn't seem to sink in. The scope of Strange's power defied normalization. Maybe the day would come when Thyon was no longer gobsmacked by the fact that the meek junior librarian who used to walk into walls while reading was now in possession of a massive, impregnable, interdimensional skyship that he controlled with his mind. But that day was not today.

Ruza was wondering aloud how it would work—whether Lazlo alone was able to control the metal beasts, or if they could be made to obey other riders. "It wouldn't be any fun if it was like a pony at the fair just being led around by the bridle," he said.

Thyon could easily imagine Ruza as a little boy on a pony. He looked at him and saw the child he'd been, and he saw the man he was—warrior, prankster, friend—and he felt a warmth that he had never felt before for any other person. It was affection, and something that frightened him, too, that he could feel in his knees and fingertips and face. It made him unsure what to do with his hands. He noticed things like knuckles and eyelashes that he didn't notice on other people, and sometimes he had to look away and pretend to be thinking of something else.

He said, "I'm sure there are *real* dragons out there somewhere. You can hatch one from an egg and raise it to be your loyal steed."

Ruza's whole face lit up. "Do you really think so?"

"Out of hundreds of worlds?" said Thyon. "It would be stranger if there *weren't* dragons."

Hundreds of worlds. *Hundreds of worlds*, and they would see them, because they were leaving Zeru, and he, Thyon Nero, was going with them. He would never go back to Zosma, where the queen wore a necklace woven of his golden hair, and some blurry outline of a future wife awaited his return. Instead he was joining a crew of gods and pirates for a mission straight out of a myth. It wasn't even an alternate version of his life. He hadn't gone back in time and done everything differently to get to this place. It turned out that sometimes it's enough to start doing things differently *now*.

"You'll hatch one, too, of course," Ruza informed him, as though they had already found their dragon eggs and it was only a matter of divvying them up.

"Yes, I will," agreed Thyon, "and mine will be faster than yours."

Ruza was affronted. "It will *not*." For his part, he could not have imagined Thyon as a boy on a pony. For all that he was less untouchable than he had been, the golden godson still looked as though he'd been made by a god in a dreamy mood and delivered in a velvet-lined box.

"Will too," said Thyon.

Calixte, with her fingers to her temples and eyes closed, said, "I'm seeing a vision of the future in which you're both eaten like idiots trying to steal dragon eggs in some weird world."

But they hardly heard her, because a breeze had caused the *Lady Spider* to yaw just enough that Thyon's shoulder came to rest against Ruza's, and he left it there, and that took all their focus as Calixte navigated into the new skyship hangar that Lazlo had integrated into the citadel's magnificent new form.

It was an eagle, of course.

There had been no real question. Ruza's dragon arguments aside, the only other option had been leaving the citadel as a seraph, and nobody wanted that. Their feelings for seraphim in general were complex. The angels' hubris, in cutting the portals, had resulted in strife across the Continuum. And yet, if they'd never done it, there would be no godspawn and none of them would even be here to debate the shape of skyships.

As a practical matter, it would have been easiest to leave it as it was. As an emotional one, they couldn't purge off the taint of Skathis fast enough, so Lazlo had set to work transforming it.

Everything was shifted. In seraph form, it had been vertical and long. Now it was condensed, broadened. Gone were the dexter and sinister arms, replaced by the eagle's wings. The nursery was no more, and the small, barren rooms that had once held human mothers were likewise erased, much as the memory of what had happened in them had been erased. Their own large chambers, once the gods', were replaced by more modest ones, and more of them. Minya no longer claimed a whole palace she didn't need.

The gardens had quadrupled in size, in their new location between the eagle's wings, and were growing quantities of new vegetables and fruits. Sparrow glowed with purpose and pleasure. She had even brought up some ferns from the forest and planted a shady glade just for them. Feral, too, retained his purpose. Water would always be essential, and he was keen to work on developing other dimensions of his gift. Perhaps, one day, he would be more than a cloud thief, able to strike with lightning.

As for Ruby, she was feeling a little obsolete, now that nonmagical systems were in place for cooking and heating up bathwater. She did not respond with grace to Feral's suggestion that she take up a hobby.

"I know just the thing," she said, and flicked a look at Werran, who was minding his own business in one of the new deep chairs in the gallery.

As one might imagine, the introduction of *four* new young men into their circle had made Ruby rather giddy.

When they'd finally, properly had a chance to meet Kiska, Rook, and Werran, she had eschewed all the obvious questions, such as what their life had been like for the past fifteen years, and wanted only to know which god had been their parent.

When Rook revealed that he was the son of Ikirok, she'd gasped with dismay, "You're my *brother?*" before adding, insincerely, "I mean, oh, good, a brother," and turning to Werran to ask, hopefully, "What about you?"

Werran's resemblance to Lazlo was no accident. He was Skathis's son, and Lazlo greeted the news of a brother with much more enthusiasm than Ruby did.

Feral found himself disposed to like Rook, while standing up taller and casting his voice deeper whenever Werran was around. He'd have thought the golden faranji would be his primary rival— the fellow was just ridiculous—but the degree of wariness he showed around Ruby suggested otherwise. He seemed almost to take refuge behind his Tizerkane friend when she approached him with that hungry look in her eyes, and she gave up eventually and left him in peace. "He must have something against blue skin," she reasoned, piqued, and tossed her wild hair. "His loss."

As to whose, if anyone's, *gain*, that remained to be seen.

In the new configuration of bedrooms, there was no question of keying doors to touch. Lazlo, determined that no one should ever be trapped if something happened to him, reconceived all the doors to open and close, lock and unlock like normal ones—with keys or crossbars.

He also made medallions for them all to wear, like the ones Kiska, Rook, and Werran had, so that they wouldn't have to worry about losing their magic, no matter where they were.

There were discoveries to be made in the citadel, notably inside the seraph's head, where they found Skathis's treasure chamber. It was a flat-out marvel: a museum of alien currencies, with coins and gems and vials of curious dusts, whole barrels of *eyes*, from what creature they had no way of knowing, and crystals that gave off glints of amber light, and strands of pearls that floated like air bubbles. There were feathers and geodes, fabrics and maps, contraptions of arcane technology. It wasn't terrible to find themselves in possession of an enormous otherworldly fortune.

There were new rooms, too: one for games, and not just quell; a full alchemical laboratory; and a library with books of actual ink on paper. Most were donated by the people of Weep—*Amezrou*—but there was one that had come from much farther away—though even that distance seemed humble now. Thyon, returning from a supply run, had approached Lazlo, stiff and shy, and thrust a book at his chest. "This is yours," he'd said, half swallowing the word *sorry*.

Lazlo, taking the book, had discovered it to be none other than *Miracles for Breakfast*, the volume of tales he'd brought to the Chrysopoesium in what seemed quite another lifetime. His eyebrows shot up. "It's not mine," he said, flipping to the first page, where it was stamped *Property of the Great Library of Zosma*. "What would Master Hyrrokkin say if he knew the golden godson was stealing library books?"

"I didn't bring the rest of your books," Thyon said. "I'm sorry." He did a better job with the word this time. "I had no right to take them."

But Lazlo held no grudge. "Do you realize, Nero, that if you hadn't come to my window in Weep that night with your shard of mesarthium, I'd never have stopped the citadel from falling, and we would all be dead?"

"Do you know, Strange," returned Thyon, who was not about to take any credit, "that if you hadn't given me the spirit from your veins, I wouldn't have had a shard to begin with?"

"Well then," said Lazlo, wry. "It's a good thing we were always such excellent friends, working together for the good of all."

It mightn't have been true before, but perhaps it could be.

It took all their efforts to make the citadel a home that could shelter and sustain them. All trace of the gods was now gone—including their hideous clothing, left to molder down on the island, in the very cells that had once held the children they sired and sold—save this one: the ship's new form, an homage to Korako, who may have been the one to take them from the nursery but had saved them, too, in more ways than they'd realized.

The eagle had dropped the kimril tubers that saved them from starvation, and for that they'd always been grateful. (Except Ruby, who declared she'd have preferred to starve.) But now they knew that Korako had also saved Lazlo as a baby. Skathis would have murdered him, as he had all babies with his gift, but Korako had gotten to him first, and, by way of Wraith, spirited him to Zosma—a sort of hidden key with which she'd hoped to one day unlock her prison.

She hadn't lived to see her own freedom, but she had provided for theirs—back then and then again when she used her last moments of life to leave a message for her sister that said, "Let all the ugliness end."

And so it had, at least for them, and for Amezrou too.

But out in the layered worlds were blue children who'd grown up in slavery—their own brothers and sisters—and there was no question of leaving them there. They themselves had been granted deliverance, and with it came the duty to deliver others. Skathis's book, which they had begun to translate—with help from Rook, Kiska, and Werran, whom Nova had taught the gods' tongue—contained not only navigational charts but a ledger. Every godspawn birth was recorded, and every sale: dates, gender, gift, buyer, and even amount paid.

They should be able to trace them. Some trails would go cold. Some would be dead. Some might neither need nor want rescuing. But they would do their best to deserve their freedom and power, and to be the antithesis of Skathis and Isagol.

"We aren't our parents," Sarai had told Minya shortly after her own death. "We don't have to be monsters."

Minya still maintained that monsters are useful to have on hand, and Sarai had to agree—so long as they were on your side, and weren't, for example, making you *bite* a lip you wished to *lick*, or any other such grave misdeed.

Minya shrugged and declared her "boring."

Boring was not the word Sarai would use to describe licking Lazlo's lip, or anything else in her life these days—or her *after*life, if you wished to be technical. She was still bound to Minya, and still a ghost, with all the restrictions that went along with it. As Great Ellen had told her before, "It isn't life, but it has its merits."

"Such as being a slave to Minya?" she'd asked then, but she had good reason to hope it wouldn't be like that. Minya hadn't possessed her since waking up on the floor, and though she'd yet shown no outward signs of . . . *Ellenness?* . . . to hint at new wholeness, she was not her old self, either. Sarai found herself watching her, wondering what was at work in her. Were her fragments finding a way to mesh back together into a single person?

This scrutiny did not go unnoticed. "Must you look at me like that?" Minya demanded.

"Like what?"

"Like I'm a child you need to take care of."

503

Sarai didn't know what to say to that. Was Minya a child or not a child? She was both and neither. "Fine. But I haven't thanked you yet. For saving me."

"Which time?" asked Minya, ungracious. The last thing she wanted to do was talk about feelings. As she looked at Sarai, the impulse to make Great Ellen's hawk face was overwhelming, but of course her face couldn't do it. The fragments *were* back, and they felt too big for her, like extra pits shoved into a plum. Add to it the gratitude and tenderness that were coursing up Sarai's tether, and she felt like she might split apart and explode.

"Minya..." Sarai started to say, because she actually still hadn't thanked her, but she found that her mouth abruptly stopped working, and then she was turning, and her feet, through no effort of her own, were carrying her away. She couldn't even make a sound of startled protest. The conversation was over, and the clock reset on how long since her last possession.

✳ ✳ ✳

With the arrival of the *Lady Spider*, the crew of the *Astral* was all accounted for—that was the name they'd decided on: the *Astral*, as "Wraith" sounded menacing, and they all appreciated the layered meanings of star voyagers and souls sent forth, and that it honored Sarai's gift as well as Korako's.

They were eager to go, to cast off from this moorage and *begin*. It was as easy as wishing. Lazlo had only to will the eagle to fly and it did. It glided above Arev Bael—"the Devourer," which had devoured Nova—and even navigated between the tezerl stalks with an endowed intelligence that did not require his conscious guidance. They went west, toward Var Elient's ez-Meliz portal, where, in a few days' time, they would encounter people—people from another world—and make themselves and their mission known.

They were fourteen in all: nine godspawn (including one ghost) and five humans, which had necessitated a lengthening of the table in the gallery. They all convened for their first meal of the voyage, and found themselves settling into places that were beginning to feel like their own. The food was so much better now, and they were all learning how to cook, thanks to the tutelage of the fourteenth and most unexpected member of the crew: Suheyla.

"Are you *sure*?" Eril-Fane had asked his mother at least a hundred times before their final farewell.

"Quite," she had assured him, bright-eyed. "What else am I to do? My house washed away."

Eril-Fane was a patient son. "We can build you a new house," he'd pointed out. There would be quite a lot of that going on in Amezrou.

"What a bother," she'd said, "when this one's already built." She'd gestured around herself, and how could he argue? Already she'd made her mark on this place, from the rugs and cushions she'd looted shamelessly from the Merchants' Guildhall to the hooks she'd directed Lazlo to fashion over the table, for the hanging up of discs of hot bread.

Suheyla had grasped her son's hand. "I'll be back, you know, but I do have to go. Our people need you. These children need me."

It was true, and it was good to be needed, and to think that she could have a hand in shaping the men and women these powerful young people would become. They needed a grandmother, someone who knew how to do things, who could teach them how to take care of themselves—and, all-importantly, *bake cake*—and provide a seasoned perspective as they faced their unguessable trials.

That was her main reason for joining them, and it was reason enough. The other she hadn't spoken aloud, but her interest in Skathis's ledger did not go unnoticed. Lazlo, without comment, made sure to find time to read it with her, tracking down the names of babies born in a certain month forty years earlier, and trying to trace when and where they'd been sold.

Perhaps she would find her lost child, perhaps not. She would certainly find lost children—*more* lost children, that is. Make no mistake, that's what these children were, though a little less lost every day. She did what she could. They were remarkably resilient, even Minya, who had been through the most. She didn't say very much, and Suheyla didn't press her. She mothered her by stealth, in small doses, and often without direct eye contact, the way one might set a skittish cat at ease.

The girl had changed her ragged garment, at last, for one Suheyla left where she could find it, and she had a loose tooth, her first ever, which had to mean that whatever had frozen her age at six had unfrozen, and that she would not continue forever a child. That night at dinner, the tooth came out.

She was biting into bread and gave a little gasp. Her hand flew to her mouth, and out it fell, tiny as a kitten tooth. She stared at it with mingled wonder and horror. "A piece of my body just fell off," she said darkly.

Tzara choked a little on the wine she was swallowing.

"It's all right," said Kiska. "There's a better one where that came from. Just wait."

Minya knew how it worked. She'd been through it with Sarai and Feral, Ruby and Sparrow, and had, as Great Ellen, strung their baby teeth onto little necklaces she kept in a wooden box. As for what to do with her own, Suheyla said to put it under her pillow and make a wish. "That's what we do in Amezrou."

"And I suppose all the wishes come true," Minya said, sarcastic.

"Of course not, silly girl," Suheyla retorted. She had not grown up in an era of optimism, but that didn't mean they'd lived without dreams. "Wishes don't just *come true*. They're only the target you paint around what you want. You still have to hit the bull's-eye yourself."

🌿 64 🌿

A New Generation of Wishes

Sarai was still thinking about those words later, when she went with Lazlo back to their room. They were sharing one, larger than the others', but not by double. It preserved some elements of the glade Lazlo had made, notably the bed crafted especially for the goddess of dreams. The iguana was still around, occasionally prowling out from the undergrowth to beg for a treat.

"Do you remember what Suheyla said about wishes?" Sarai asked, sinking down onto the bed.

"About the bull's-eye?" Lazlo asked, following her down. His weight made a divot in the mattress that pulled her toward him. "I liked it." He nuzzled her, his breath warm on her cheek. "I must be a pretty good archer, because all my wishes have come true."

"All of them?" she asked, closing her eyes, smiling as he kissed her neck. "Then you'd better get some new ones. You can't let yourself run out of wishes."

"I could never run out of wishes." He propped himself up on his elbow and looked at her, serious. "They just might be mostly on other people's behalf, since I have all I could ever want."

So did she. Family, freedom, safety, *him*. She leaned in and kissed him. She had more than she had ever dared dream, and yet, new dreams sprout up when old ones come true, like seedlings in a forest: a new generation of wishes.

As sweet as her kiss, Lazlo could tell she had something on her mind. "What about you?" he coaxed.

"I've been thinking about my gift," she said, "and what I might do with it. And...who I might be."

He waited for her to go on.

"When I was in Minya's dreams, and Nova's, I could see, or sense, what was wrong, but I couldn't *fix* it."

"Fix *them*, you mean?"

She nodded. "I keep seeing her fall," she confessed. "I should have known she would do something like that. I'd just been *in her mind*."

"I think it was just too late for her," he said gently. "Sometimes it will be. It wasn't your fault, Sarai. But you saved the rest of us. And if you want to help people—if that's your wish—then you will."

"It is," she said, and felt it take root within her, this purpose, as though speaking it had given it the light it needed to grow. *This* was her wish: to help people whose minds were unquiet, who were trapped in their own labyrinths, or stranded on cracking ice. This was what she wanted to paint a target around, to use Suheyla's metaphor. "But I felt so...useless with Minya and Nova. I think I need to work on my archery." She tried to make a joke out of it, her worry that it would always be beyond her, that conjuring nightmares was her true calling and she would never be able to do anything else.

And Lazlo might not have been able to fill her up with certainty, but he could fill her with witchlight, and he did. The way he looked at her, she felt like some kind of miracle, as though his dreamer's eyes cast her in their glow of wonder. "Sarai," he said. "It's *stunning*, what you can do. And of course you need practice. It's *the mind*. It's the most complex and astonishing thing there is, that there's a world inside each of us that no one else can ever know or see or visit—*except you*. I just tell metal what to do. You meet people inside their minds and make them feel less alone. What's more extraordinary than that?"

She let herself start to believe it. She ran her fingers over the rough edges of Lazlo's face—the line of his jaw, the angle of his broken nose. His lips, which weren't rough at all. The bite had healed. There wasn't even a scar.

She had found herself wishing, several times during all the chaos, for her mother's gift, so she could just take away all the hate, the fear and fury. But she saw now that Isagol's gift might be useful in defusing a threat, but it couldn't *help* people, even if it was used for good. It was false. To just take away someone's hate like that, it would be stealing a part of their soul. But maybe Sarai could help them let it go on their own, guide them, show them new landscapes, make new doors, new suns. Maybe.

She couldn't yet begin to imagine the lives all the other godspawn had been living out in whatever worlds had claimed them, but she thought some of them might need that. She even thought that all her years immersed in nightmares might help her to navigate theirs, if only to lead them through and out the other side. If they wanted it. If they invited her. Maybe she could help.

She stretched like a cat and rolled her neck from side to side. "Isn't it funny that I don't have a real body but I still imagine aches as though I did? Why not just leave that part out, self?"

"You *do* have a real body," Lazlo argued. "I can feel it perfectly well," he said while conscientiously doing so.

"You know what I mean." Sarai closed her eyes as Lazlo rubbed the imagined soreness from her imagined muscles.

"If you left that part out," he said, "you'd feel less real, wouldn't you? Being alive includes aches, as well as pleasure."

"I wonder . . ." Sarai mused, dreamy, as waves of imagined pleasure rolled through her.

"What do you wonder?"

"Of all the godspawn out there, in all the worlds, with all their gifts, might there be *one* who . . . I don't know." What would even help her? Her body was gone. How could she possibly live again properly? "Someone who . . . makes new bodies for souls who need them?" She had to laugh at herself. It was a highly specific and unlikely sounding gift. "What are the chances?"

Lazlo, who had heard from Ruza at dinner all about dragon eggs and Thyon's theory, said, "Out of hundreds of worlds? It would be stranger if there *wasn't* someone like that out there."

"Well then," breathed Sarai, wanting to believe it, "I wish to find them, wherever they are, so that I can feel all the aches and all the pleasure that are the privilege of the living. In the meantime, you'll just have to keep on sharing yours."

She stretched against him, feline, and Lazlo took her in his arms, his ghost girl, goddess, muse of wonder, and assured her that he took his responsibility very seriously. And as the great metal eagle, the *Astral*, made its way through night and mist, they lost themselves in each other, the very same place they had each been found.

511

EPILOGUE

Back in Amezrou, too, as it happened, there were those who were thinking about wishes.

Eril-Fane and Azareen could scarcely believe that their sky was clear and they were alive. They were tired, still recovering from having their hearts regrown, and there was a lot to see to these days, what with organizing the clearing of rubble, and slowly, in a more orderly fashion than they'd left in, bringing their people back from Enet-Sarra.

Still, a quiet moment found them, and Azareen finally asked the question that had been on her lips since her husband died in her arms. "My love," she said, trying to read his face, as she had been trying all these years. "You said, 'I wish...' *What* do you wish?"

Eril-Fane found himself shy—the great Godslayer blushing like the boy who had given his sparring partner a bracelet for her sixteenth birthday and danced with her, his big hands trembling on her waist. For so long, he had been poisoned and poisonous, but now he felt…clean and thirsty and expansive, like a root-bound plant repotted in a new and generous garden.

"I wish…" he said, his gaze holding hers taut, his eyes wide with sweet, boyish fear. "To marry you," he finished in a whisper, and he took something out of his pocket. He hadn't forgotten his own dying wish. He'd thought of it just as much as she had over these past few weeks. You learn what you want when you think you can't have it, and Eril-Fane wanted his wife. He held a ring in his fingers. It wasn't the one he'd made her before, that she'd worn in her sleep all these years. It was new, gold and lys, with crystals making the shape of a star.

"We're already married," said Azareen, trembling, because a storm had kicked up in her mind and those were the first words to spill out.

"I want to start again," said Eril-Fane. He looked hopeful and worried, as though there was the smallest chance of her saying no. "Will you start all over again? With me?"

Azareen did not say no.

The priestess could perform the rites some other day. They consecrated their marriage themselves. Eril-Fane carried Azareen up the stairs of their little Windfall house as though she were made of silk and air. He kicked the door shut behind them, as he had eighteen years ago. *Eighteen years.* It had been longer since they'd last made love than they'd even been alive before the first time.

They took their time. They had forgotten so much. Slowly, it all came back.

Fate must have been feeling sympathetic for all the time they'd lost. They made a son that night, though it would be some weeks before they knew it, and months before they met him and named him Lazlo—and some years after that before he met his namesake, *and* his grandmother and ghost half sister, as well as a whole lot of others when the *Astral* came back and visited Amezrou on its way to begin a new journey in the opposite direction, toward Meliz, the seraph home world, and whatever—and whoever—they might find along the way.

But that's another story.

THE END
(OR IS IT?)

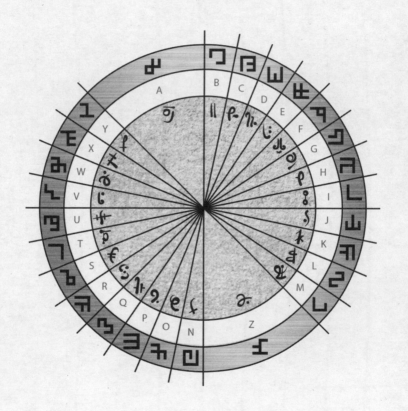

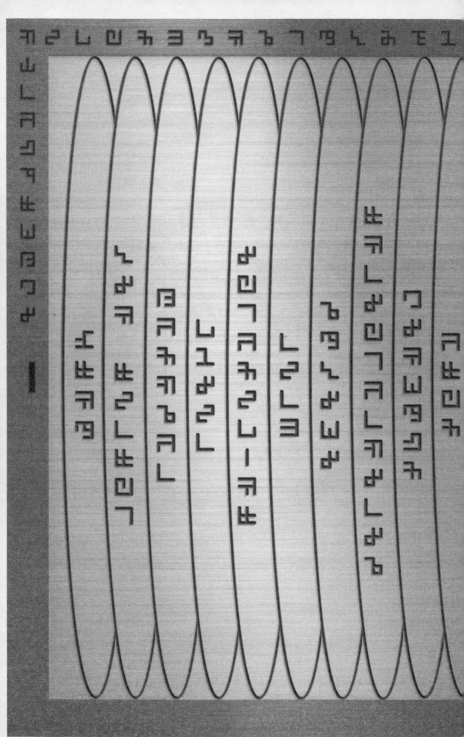

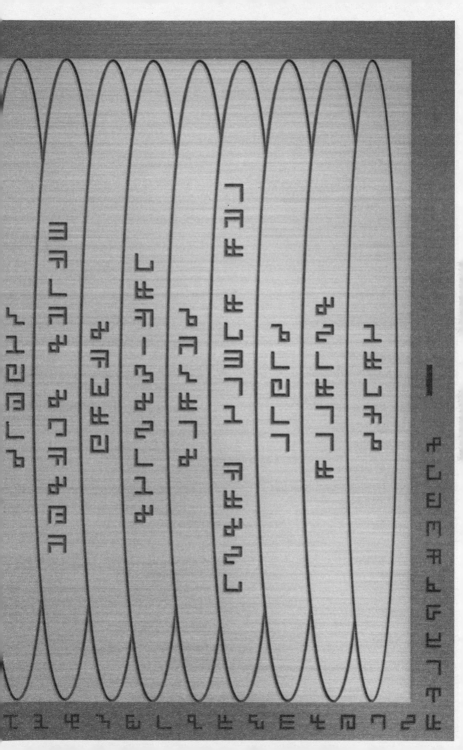

Acknowledgments

This marks eight years and six books with the fantastic family at Little, Brown Books for Young Readers! That's close to three thousand pages of gods and chimaera and moths and wars and young people searching for hope, love, and identity in this world and others. I'm so incredibly grateful to everyone who's helped turn my words into better words and then magicked them into *books*, my favorite objects in the world. Thank you!

To my editor, Alvina Ling, whose graceful insight helps me find the best possible versions of my stories and characters, and whose calm presence eases the panic—mine, anyway. I hope I don't cause *you* too much panic!

Thanks also to Nikki Garcia for multifaceted organization and support; Jessica Shoffel and Siena Koncsol (welcome!) for publicity; Victoria Stapleton and Michelle Campbell for school and library wizardry; Emilie Polster, Jennifer McClelland-Smith, Elena Yip, and the whole marketing team; Sasha Illingworth and Karina Granda for gorgeous design (including the amazing alphabets in this book!); Jen Graham for copyediting; Shawn Foster and the sales team for that all-important selling business; Jackie Engel; and the always amazing boss lady Megan Tingley for *everything*.

To Hachette Audio—Megan Fitzpatrick, Michele McGonigle, and narrator Steve West, thank you for bringing *Strange* and *Muse* so stunningly to life for the listening crowd. They sound *so good*.

I've also been blessed with an amazing *second* publishing family these eight years. Hodder & Stoughton in the UK, you guys are magic. Thank you, Kate Howard, Vero Norton, Sara Kinsella, Melissa Cox, Lily Cooper, Thorne Ryan, Rachel Khoo, Carolyn Mays, Jamie Hodder-Williams, and Ruth Tross. Big thanks also to Joanne Myler for exquisite cover design, Claudette Morris for production, and Catherine Worsley and Megan Schaffer for sales!

My eternal thanks to my tribe: readers. Thank you for giving my stories a place to live—*inside your gorgeous heads*. And a special thanks to readers who go the extra mile and give stories life outside their heads, too, by way of recommendations, fandom, art, cosplay, bookstagramming, booktubing, coming to events, and even *tattoos*. It's an inspiration to write books for you, and an immense pleasure to see many of you writing your own books and creating in so many other cool ways. We're all in this together!

To librarians, teachers, booksellers, and all other professional book supporters, literacy champions, and reader-makers, thank you for everything you do. To Angela Carstensen, Julie Benolken, Kathy Marie Burnette, Edi Campbell, Megan Fink, Jenna Friebel, Traci Glass, Scot Smith, Audrey Sumser, and Karen Ginman, aka the 2018 Printz committee, *thank you so much* for the extraordinary gift of a Printz Honor. It is a highlight of my writing life.

To my agent, Jane Putch: You are family. You're also, like, the person who attaches the ends of the tightrope from one skyscraper to the next and makes me believe I can make it across, even when I'm barely clinging on by my toes.

To Mom and Pop, you gave me a childhood of books, adventure, freedom, and unwavering love and support, and you never tried to talk me out of this uncertain path. I love you so much, and I'm so lucky to have you.

Alexandra, you're the best of all possible best friends, and a sparkling soul who makes every day, every conversation, every text exchange unique, funny, unpredictable, and *good*. I wish you ran the world.

Tone Almhjell, writing kindred spirit, I wish regularly for a teleportation booth (or maybe a teleportation *spell*, which sounds somehow less risky and terrifying than a machine, because magic *never* goes wrong...) so that we could write together and hold up sentences like strings of beads to catch the light in café windows in Oslo, Hvar, and wherever else we feel like meeting.

To Robin LaFevers, another writing kindred spirit, thanks for all your help with *the brain situation*, and being so available for advice and moral support. You're incredible.

To my cats, thanks a lot for allowing me this tiny corner of my desk for working. It's so generous of you.

And lastly, to the other sides of my triangle, you two are everything to me. Clementine, sassy ray of sunshine, clever, kind, joyous creature, always singing, never still, soon-to-be-fourth-grade force of nature. You make life bigger, funnier, *louder*, and more wonderful. Thanks for being my kid! And above all, Jim, my person, my place, thank you for building this life with me, for being my first and last sounding board for all my endeavors, both writing and otherwise, for dreaming the same crazy dreams (which makes them feel less crazy, even when they totally *are*) and keeping the house full of mangoes and flowers, and making me laugh, and being the most fun, thoughtful, romantic, supportive, wonderful partner anyone could wish for—not to mention really cute and super talented! I love you vastly and forever.